THE
DELPHI
EFFECT

ALSO BY RYSA WALKER

The CHRONOS Files

Novels

Timebound
Time's Edge
Time's Divide

Graphic Novel

Time Trial

Novellas

Time's Echo
Time's Mirror
Simon Says

Short Stories

"The Gambit" in The Time Travel Chronicles
"Whack Job" in Alt.History 102
"2092" in Dark Beyond the Stars
"Splinter," in CLONES: The Anthology

THE DELPHI EFFECT

The Delphi Trilogy
Book One

RYSA WALKER

SKYSCAPE

SKYSCAPE

Published by Skyscape, New York

www.apub.com

Amazon, the Amazon logo, and Skyscape are trademarks of Amazon.com, Inc., or its affiliates.

ISBN-13: 9781503938823
ISBN-10: 1503938824

Cover design by M. S. Corley

Printed in the United States of America

This one is for Gareth, who braved the ghosts of the Tome School.

CHAPTER ONE

"Are you Jerome Porter?"

The man arches one bushy black brow and expels a cloud of cigarette smoke in the other direction before turning back to respond. "That's me. Do I know you?"

"No. But I have a message for you." I pull my phone from my pocket and extend it toward him, trying but failing to keep my hands from shaking as I turn the screen in his direction.

"A message? From who?"

I hesitate, pushing the phone forward again. "It's a text," I say. "From your granddaughter. From Molly."

His dark face tightens, eyes narrowed to tiny slits as he glares down at me. "My granddaughter is dead."

"I know."

Porter drops the half-smoked cigarette and crushes it under his foot, his jaw clenched and angry as he disappears into the building.

❖ ❖ ❖

I sit with my back against the gray cement wall, close enough to give me a clear view of the revolving glass door but far enough away to avoid inhaling the fog of smoke that surrounds the entrance. The door spits out a new body every minute or so. About half of them huddle near the building, zipping up their jackets or wrapping scarves around their necks to ward off the chill, settling in for a short cigarette break before heading back up to their cubicles for a few more hours of work.

The afternoon is windier and colder than it was when I left the house. Colder than it has any right to be in late October. I glance longingly at the café at the end of the block. It would have been nice to watch for Porter from one of the small tables near the windows, but they were all taken. So I'm stuck here, waiting, as the wind whips hair into my eyes and assaults my already chapped lips.

Should we check the back entrance again?

I flex my feet in an attempt to get the blood flowing, hoping her answer will be yes. Anything would be better than just sitting and waiting.

There's a pause, and then I hear Molly's voice.

No. He'll be here.

I stand up anyway and chuck my half-full coffee cup into the trash. Even doctored liberally with sugar, a practice I usually scorn, it's still too burnt to drink and now much too cold to serve its secondary purpose as a hand warmer.

I think Molly is a bit too optimistic. It's entirely possible the old guy decided to give up smoking cold turkey rather than risk seeing me again.

I've been hounding him on and off for over a week. I've mixed things up a bit, depending on my work and school schedule, once approaching Porter in the morning as he left the Metro station, twice in the evening as he left work. Usually, though, I've cornered him during his late-afternoon smoke break, since that allows me to still make my usual shift at the deli if I hurry. Each time, Porter has either avoided me completely or, after calling me a few choice names, walked away.

Until yesterday, that is. The music clearly hit a nerve, just as Molly said it would, because Porter didn't even speak. He just stormed over to where I was standing, snatched the phone from my hand, and went back inside. *With* my phone.

Several times this week, I dragged Deo with me, but today he had an appointment with Kelsey. He missed the last one, so I told him he needed to go. It would have been nice to have him along, though, both for moral support and as a witness. Despite Molly's assurances that her grandfather isn't the type to resort to violence, I got an up-close-and-personal look at his expression yesterday. I've seen enough anger to know when someone is one short step from swinging his fist.

Pa won't hurt you. He's a good man. He was a cop.

He took my phone. That phone cost me two weeks' salary.

He'll give it back.

Molly's voice is confident, without even a shadow of doubt, and I feel a twinge of jealousy. Her life may have been short, but she'd had someone she could count on. Someone she believed in completely. Even the fact that he wasn't able to save her didn't shake that faith.

A delivery drone skims the downtown skyline and drops its package on a roof two blocks down. The drone is probably several yards above the building, but from down here it appears to be a precision operation with mere inches to spare. Once it whizzes away, I look back toward the entrance and see Porter standing a few feet behind the glass, watching me.

He just stands there, a heavyset black man with a moustache and close-trimmed beard sprinkled with gray. He's wearing a tweed coat over his usual suit, and the buttons gape a bit over his belly. My phone is clutched in his right hand. A pack of Marlboro Golds is in his left.

Usually, I avoid his eyes, but today I meet his stare with one of my own, jamming my hands into the pockets of the threadbare Old Navy hoodie that is, at least for the time being, my only winter coat. I don't have to be here. I could leave. I'm doing him a favor, damn it.

A few seconds later, Porter slips my phone into his pocket and pushes through the revolving door. He crosses over to me with long, purposeful strides and rams a thick finger in my face. "I want to know how you got this information, young lady. How did you know Molly? Who put you up to this . . . this *sick*, twisted—"

Tears sting my eyes, from anger or the wind. Maybe both. "Just give me my phone. I'll leave."

No. NO, please, Anna, please.

"You're not going anywhere," he says, his voice rising. "I still have a couple of friends on the force, and you're gonna answer some questions. Otherwise, I'm turning this phone over to them and—"

"Fine!" I snap back at him. "Keep the stupid phone. Do you think I *enjoy* standing here in the cold? Sucking in secondhand smoke? I told her this wouldn't work. I *told* her."

"You told who?" Porter asks, gripping my arm.

"I told *M-Molly*," I reply, teeth chattering as a gust of even colder wind whips around the corner.

Porter glances down at my clothes, and his eyes, which actually look a lot like Molly's, soften the tiniest bit. "You wanna go inside where it's warmer, Anna? I'll trade you a cup of coffee for some answers."

I pull my arm away. "How do you know my name?"

He shrugs. "Your phone is the property of Anna Elizabeth Morgan. I can put two and two together."

I move toward the café door. "No coffee. It's burnt. But I wouldn't say no to some hot chocolate."

The café is gloriously warm. Debussy's Arabesque no. 1 plays softly in the background. Six months ago, I didn't know Debussy from Devo—both are way before my time—but since Molly came on board, it's like I have a radio announcer in my head whenever I hear classical music or pretty much anything piano. A lot of it isn't really my style, but this one is nice. Arabesque kind of reminds me of a waterfall, and I find myself relaxing just a bit.

There are two open tables. One is grungy, but the cleaner option is a booth positioned against the mirrored tiles that cover the wall of the café. I grab a few napkins and wipe the crumbs from the messy table onto the floor. Molly is so close to the front right now, so intensely *present*, that I know exactly what I would see if my eyes strayed to that mirror.

The day we recorded the song for Porter on my phone, I caught a glimpse of myself in a framed picture near the piano and saw my reflection mostly through Molly's consciousness. Her brown skin superimposed over my own pale complexion, the chocolate color of her eyes nearly obscuring my own deep blue. Her black hair pulled back, a few tendrils escaping, and only a hint of my own dark-blonde curls around my shoulders. Like I'm the ghost and she's the living. Vivid, angry bruises on her neck and upper chest. A small trickle of blood on her left temple, and when I glanced down at the piano keyboard, a red gash where my left pinky should be.

Is that what Molly saw the last time she looked in a mirror? Or was it her last glimpse of her body before leaving it behind? Either way, it spooks me. No mirrors when Molly is wound up like this. And I make it a point to keep my left hand in my lap as much as possible these days. Just in case.

A few minutes later, Porter slides a cup of cocoa in front of me, a glob of whipped cream on top, and takes the other chair. He risked the coffee, despite my warning, and grimaces as he takes a sip.

"I was hoping they'd made some fresh, but I guess not," Porter says, dumping three creamers into the mug. He takes another taste, frowns, then adds two more.

Apparently satisfied with the brew, Porter leans back, pulling my phone out of his pocket as he shrugs the coat from his shoulders. He doesn't give me the phone. Just holds it there in the palm of his hand, taunting me.

"So. How come you know that song, girl? You go to school with Molly? She'd be about your age now."

"No."

"You take piano with her or somethin' like that?"

"I've never taken piano lessons," I say, stirring the whipped cream into the chocolate to cool it.

"Then who was playin' that song you recorded on the phone?"

"Me. Sort of." *My fingers, but more Molly.* Saying that would probably end the conversation however, so I push forward to the key point. "Molly said you'd recognize it."

"Of course I *recognized* it. My granddaughter wrote it for me. Well . . . that's not quite right," he amends, more to himself than to me. "I sang it to her first, so I guess I wrote it, really. But she's the one who figured it out on the piano."

He's silent for a moment, then continues. "So, let me get this straight. You're saying you didn't know Molly before . . . before she died. But yet you know all this stuff *somehow*. Did she write it down, or

6

what? I mean, I didn't see her or her mama much those last few months. If Molly left some sort of message or diary or somethin' and you found it, why not just give it to me now and save us both a lot of trouble? Are you expectin' me to offer you some sorta reward?"

"I don't want your money. I'm not even sure I want to help you anymore. I *would* like my phone back, however."

He turns the phone over in his hand but still doesn't give it to me. "I know you sent that text message to yourself—it's from your own number."

"Of *course* it's from my number," I say, rolling my eyes. "You think Molly has a phone? She's dead."

Porter glares at me and I look down again, taking a sip from the cocoa before I continue. "It was a lot to remember, and Molly wanted to be sure it was in her words. If I'd known you were going to steal my phone I'd have made her write it down on a sheet of paper."

"As you just reminded me, Molly's dead. Been dead goin' on three years. How's she gonna be writin' anything down?"

And we've now reached the part where Porter will decide I'm crazy. Mad as a hatter. Nutty as a fruitcake—pick your favorite metaphor and run with it. I've tried explaining this before. It never comes out sounding sane, even to my own ears.

"I let Molly . . . borrow me. For a little while. I don't usually do that. But Molly was persistent. She said it was important. That you could find this guy and stop him. That she could help. That other people might die too, if I didn't."

He leans forward across the table and looks directly at me, clearly hoping my eyes will dart away or I'll give some indication of a lie. I hold his stare, and after a moment he leans back in the chair again. "Yeah. Right. So, answer me this. Why now? Why not back in 2016, when there were a few half-decent leads? Why not when they found her body?"

I shrug. "It's not like she could contact you on her own, Mr. Porter. I didn't show up at the shelter until late February. That's where I picked up Molly. The one over on U Street?" He nods, either recognizing the shelter or simply meaning for me to get on with it. "And . . . it took a while for her to convince me."

That's a major understatement. I'll usually help them if it's something I can do easily, but I don't contact friends or family directly. *Ever.* They all have issues, they all have some last urgent message they want to deliver, an *I love you* or *I'm sorry* that was never said. I don't back down on this anymore, because getting involved only brings me trouble—and it's pretty clear this time is not going to be the exception to that rule.

Porter waits, but I don't have anything else to give him. Why even bother? I should just go. Does he want to know how I picked up Molly when my fingers brushed the piano keys at the shelter? Does he want to know why she can communicate with me but not with anyone else? I don't even have the answers to those questions, so good luck, buddy.

"Why am I even here?" he asks, echoing my own thoughts. "You need help, girl. Serious help. This kind of harassment ain't right, and I know you've been in the nut hou—*institutionalized*," he corrects, "on more than one occasion. I called your doctor and—"

I push away from the table, sloshing cocoa onto the black linoleum as I get to my feet. "You called my *doctor*?"

Enough. I reach over, snatch the phone from his hand, and turn toward the door. Molly protests, but I tamp her down, hard.

This isn't going to work, Molly. I'm sorry, but no.

"Wai-wai-wait a minute, girl," Porter says. "Hold on. Hold on. I called her, yeah, but she didn't tell me jack, other than that I'd better return your phone or she'd help you find a lawyer. Said the only way she'd discuss anything with me is with your consent and then only what you authorized her to discuss." He grabs my arm, not hard like before, just a gentle pressure, pulling me toward the table. "Sit back down, finish your hot chocolate. Okay?"

Please, Anna! Give him a chance. He was a detective—
nosing around is what he does. Please.

I sit down but stay on the edge of my chair, hoping to signal that this is a *very* shaky truce.

"Your doctor didn't betray your trust, okay? I just did some checkin' on my own—like I said, I still have some contacts on the police force. And you got a long paper trail, given how many years you've been in the system. You change foster homes more than most people change their underwear."

I seriously hope that isn't true, since my average is five or six months. But he's correct that fifteen years leaves a lot of paper. "So, you've found out I'm a nutcase, Mr. Porter. Also a frequent runaway, occasional truant, and borderline delinquent. Why even bother talking to me?"

Porter's mouth twists. "After talking to Dr. Kelsey, I decided I'd better return your phone."

I hold up the phone and give him a tight little smile as I stand. "Mission accomplished, then. Thanks for the cocoa."

I'm two steps away from the table, and I almost miss what he whispers. "It was the music."

When I turn back, he's sitting with his forehead cupped in folded hands, rubbing his thumbs against his temples.

"You asked me why I showed up today? It was the music. That recording. Molly—she'd always miss that one note if she hadn't played the song in a while, and she'd make this little huffing noise 'cause she was pissed that she messed it up, you know? Just like this recording. I listened to it over and over, and it's her. I know it is. So you gotta tell me where you found it."

His eyes are sad, pleading, but I can see I'm not reaching him where it counts. "I've already *told* you, Mr. Porter. But you don't believe me. Unless you want me to invent some lie that fits your take on reality, what else can I tell you?"

"I don't want no *lies* from anyone," he says. "If what you're saying is true, let me talk to her. If Molly's in your head or whatever, then let me—"

Yes, Anna. I can convince him. Please, it would just be for a moment and then—

"No." I shake my head, adamant. "No way. Absolutely not. Not here."

His sad look is gone, replaced by the earlier skepticism.

"No offense, Mr. Porter. But I don't know you. I don't know Molly that well, either." That's not really true. She's been hounding me pretty much 24/7 since February. But I don't know what Molly can hide from me. What she's not telling me. "I'm not real big on trust, okay? I only let her borrow me before because Deo was there."

I have no idea what Deo would have done if Molly had somehow kept control and tried to walk off with my body, but at least he would have known she wasn't me. And he would have *cared*. I can't say the same for Porter. He might decide having his granddaughter back, even a pale, skinny version, is better than the alternative.

"So," he says, his voice rising slightly, "you only do this on your own turf? Where you can set somethin' up in advance, somethin' to make me think it's Molly I'm talkin' to? Who's this Deo? He workin' this little scam with you, Anna? 'Cause I think you're too young to be in this all on your own."

Just hearing Porter speak Deo's name ignites a ball of fear in my stomach. "Deo's just a kid. You leave him alone. This conversation is over."

I move toward the exit. Molly's screaming at me, and she's strong enough, angry enough, that my feet feel like lead weights as I drag myself toward the door.

> You know what Craig did to me, Anna! You know. It could be you next. It could be Deo. He knows people who are in the market for boys, especially boys like Deo. If he does that to someone else, if he kills someone else, it's your fault, Anna. Your fault, 'cause you can stop it! You can—

No, Molly. I can't.

I do the only thing I can in these circumstances . . . stack up the bricks in my mental wall. It won't block her entirely, won't get rid of her, but it will quiet her down to a dull, wordless roar.

I'm out the door, and Molly's still with me, still yelling.

She comes with, whether I like it or not.

CHAPTER TWO

I'm late for my shift and Joe is going to explode—it's the second time this week. I sprinted the mile plus from Glenmont station rather than waiting for the bus, which wasn't scheduled for twenty minutes. Running has the added benefits of warming me up and keeping Molly's protests down to a low, back-of-the-mind hum. I don't know if it's the endorphins or just the physical exertion, but it's almost like having my head to myself. Almost.

Deo is leaning against the wall outside Carver's Deli, munching on a bagel, when I get there. He's a tall, thin study in deep purple today—jeans, jacket, and shirt, the last two with the collars starched to stand straight up. His boots, his backpack, and his black hair all have a faint purple sheen, and his eyes are rimmed with dark-purple liner. Even his earbuds are purple. A good chunk of his allowance goes toward dyes of various sorts—there are three laundromats in the DC area that will evict him on sight because he's ignored their rules about dye in the machines. His style is usually a bit over the top, but Deo somehow manages to make Goodwill look good.

"And . . . it didn't go well," he says, after one quick glance at my expression. Deo can read my moods better than I can. We had the misfortune of landing the same set of truly horrid foster parents about seven years ago, when Deo was eight and I was nearly eleven. We left a few months later and spent about a month on the streets together before Social Services rounded us back up and spun the Wheel of Foster Misfortune again.

"I hope you at least got your phone back?" he asks around a bite of bagel. For the past year, food of some sort has been a permanent appendage to Deo's hand. Sometimes both hands at once. At first, I teased that he was going to get fat, but then he shot upward—six full inches since last summer. Now I have to look up at *him*, not the other way around. This amuses him. I don't really care as long as he doesn't call me "Short Stuff."

I squeeze his shoulder briefly in greeting and keep moving. "We'll talk after my shift. I'm late."

"Not true," he says. "You are, in fact, extremely early. Joe had to switch your shift. Said he left a message on your phone saying he needs you to come in tomorrow, same time, instead."

"A message I didn't get because that idiot had my phone." I sigh. "Oh, well, at least I'm not late again. And yes, I got the phone back, but it's completely dead."

"Jerk." Deo pulls a second bagel out of his jacket pocket—wrapped, thankfully, or it would most likely have been dyed purple on contact. It's still warm from the oven. Jalapeño cheddar, my favorite. *Thank you, Joe.* Deo and I would both be ten pounds thinner if my job didn't include free bagels.

We head north, walking toward the group home where I've lived for the past seven months and where Deo has lived for the past five. Back in May, when one of the older kids at Bartholomew House finished high school and shifted into a transitional program, Dr. Kelsey pulled a major bureaucratic miracle and convinced the county to give Deo the open slot, arguing that Deo and I might both be more inclined to stay put and avoid trouble if we were in the same location. The people in charge of Bartholomew House are mostly okay, and they don't give Deo any grief unless one of the girls complains that he's borrowing clothes (not true) or makeup (probably true). It's better than some foster homes we've been in, worse than others, but we aren't complaining. Kelsey is right—the fact that we're together for a change means that we won't be leaving Bartholomew House until we have to.

The sun dips below the horizon as we turn onto a smaller street that winds past a few newer apartment buildings and into a subdivision of fifties-era single-family homes. I pick up the pace a bit to keep warm, and we walk for a few minutes in silence, doing proper homage to the bagels.

"So—what went wrong?" Deo asks. "Porter recognized the music, right? I mean, he looked like someone had punched him in the gut when he grabbed your phone yesterday."

I nod. "He recognized the song and believes that it's Molly playing it—recorded *before* she died, of course. Wants to know where we got it, how I knew her, or where I found it. He thinks this is a scam to get money or something."

"Well," Deo says, "that *would* be the most logical explanation. Not the correct one, but definitely more logical."

We need to go back, Anna. Please . . . give him another chance. Deo's right, he's just looking for a logical explan—

Shut up, Molly. I'm talking to Deo.

She's quieter after that, but there's still a sense of her grumbling at the back of my mind—the mental equivalent of someone banging pots around in the kitchen to let you know they're good and angry.

"I don't blame Porter for questioning what I told him. But he crossed the line. He called Kelsey to check on me."

"He did *what*? What did she tell him?"

"She told him to give me back my phone or she'd help me find a lawyer." I don't have to explain to Deo how that makes me feel. Yes, Kelsey would have been violating confidentiality if she had talked to Porter, but we've both had that happen plenty of times. Maybe even most of the time. Not everyone in the system honors the privacy rights of minors.

"Ha! Go Dr. K. So if he got zip from her—no harm, no foul, then. Right?"

"Well, no. It's the principle of the thing—and he didn't stop there. He went digging around in my records and said straight out that he could make problems for me. I'm the one trying to do *him* a favor, so he can screw off. I've had it."

"And Molly's okay with this?"

"Does Molly own this body?"

"Nooo. But you know as well as I do that she's not going to just drop this thing."

"She'll go away eventually, D. They all do." I ball up the bagel wrapper and turn around to shoot it into a trash can near the bus stop we've just passed.

And that's the *only* reason I see the van.

I tackle Deo with my right shoulder at full speed and knock him sideways. He lands facedown in the grass, about four feet from the sidewalk. I wind up mostly on top of him, except for my right leg, which connects with a large tree branch that's fallen from the oak a few yards behind us. A sharp stabbing pain runs through my calf.

The van clips the bus stop sign and rips the wastebasket from its pole. Fast-food containers and other assorted crap flies into the air, then rains down around us as the van squeals back onto the road. I squint and get a quick glimpse of the license plate.

Deo lets loose with an impressive stream of cursing as he pushes himself up to his elbows. "What was that?"

"Gray van. Dodge, maybe? Maryland tag, last three digits 27J," I say.

He brushes the dirt out of his hair as he gets to his feet. "Did you get a look at the driver?"

"Not really. A guy. Tall. I think he was bald." I grit my teeth and yank a piece of wood nearly as thick as my pinky out of my leg. It's bleeding like crazy. The jeans were too worn to offer much protection, and the branch ripped straight through.

Deo winces and pulls a couple of napkins out of his pocket. I fold them into a compress and hold it against the wound. Joe buys cheap napkins, so they don't soak up much, but they're better than nothing.

"You think he'd at least stop!" Deo fumes. "Make sure we're not hurt?"

"You'd think. Are you okay?"

"Yeah. But you're not. Freakin' jerk."

"Maybe he's an illegal or something. Still, he needs to watch where he's driving. If I hadn't turned back at just that moment . . ." I shudder and shake my head. "You think we should call the tag number in when we get home?"

"*Hell*, yeah," Deo says, then pauses as he catches my expression. "Maybe. I don't know. How much of a hassle do you think it will be?"

I shrug. "We only have a partial number," I say as he gives me a hand up. I hobble over and lean against the oak tree, pressing the napkins tight against my leg. "No witnesses, so even if they do find the driver, it all depends on who they believe. And do you really think it will be us?"

He waves his hand at the mess around us. "There'd have to be marks on the van, right? Busted trash can, bent signpost? Come on, even the MoCoPopo aren't that blind."

Given that we're in Montgomery County, it's generally been the county police that have dragged Deo back to the various foster homes he skipped out on, so I'm quite familiar with the nickname for his least favorite police force.

"I don't know, D. He collided with a trash can when a couple of dumbass kids jumped out into the street and he had to swerve to avoid hitting them. You know that's what he'll say. We could end up in trouble if we call it in. But I can't think of a downside to keeping our mouths shut."

Deo kicks a Dr Pepper can hard into the bent signpost and then sighs, picking up his backpack. "You're right. What's the point?"

❖ ❖ ❖

Dinner at Bartholomew House doesn't happen around a table. Something is on the stove, cooked and more or less hot, at six. It disappears at seven on the dot, and I've yet to see any leftovers in the fridge, so I'm not sure where it goes. If you come in after seven, you know where the bread, peanut butter, and jelly can be found, and you might be able to score some fresh fruit or cookies if Deo or one of the other bottomless pits didn't beat you to it. I'm rarely in by dinnertime when I work, but I'd rather eat at the deli anyway.

We slide in the door with about ten minutes to spare. Tonight, it's stew of some sort. Deo offers to grab a bowl for me while I limp upstairs to plug in my phone and patch the hole in my leg. When I finish, he's in the living room with most of the other eight kids who live here, eating as they watch *Celebrity Family Feud*. Not my first choice, but I know I'll be voted down, so I just squeeze in next to Deo.

I pick the chunks of meat from my stew and toss them into Deo's bowl, snagging his mushrooms—one of the few foods he doesn't like—in exchange. I'm not exactly a vegetarian, but whatever meat is featured in this concoction is gray and unappealing, and he needs the extra protein more than I do anyway. Pauline is the nicest of the four house parents, but she is by far the worst cook. She should really stick to Hamburger Helper, grilled cheese, and other stuff she can't screw up.

"You okay?" Deo asks between bites.

I shrug, tugging up the leg of my sweatpants to show him the gauze bandage. "Too big for just a Band-Aid, but Pauline said it doesn't need stitches. Shouldn't get infected—she poured about half a bottle of hydrogen peroxide on it. My jeans are shot, though."

He drops his voice a bit. "What did you tell her?"

"The truth, mostly. Fell on the sidewalk, landed on a branch."

Deo nods. We both learned long ago that the best way not to get caught lying is to tell selective truths. Leave out the stuff that might get you in trouble and tell them the rest. You don't look nearly as guilty to those in charge, and it makes it a lot easier to remember what you told them later on.

Deo scarfs down the stew in record time. He doesn't get up in search of seconds, so I'm guessing the pot is now empty.

I hand him my bowl, still about half full.

"You don't want it?"

I could definitely finish it, but I shake my head. "I just had a bagel. I'm fine. I'll grab an apple later if I get hungry."

He shrugs and eats the rest as we watch a couple of the younger kids play a *Ratchet & Clank* game on the battered PS3, before heading up to Deo's room. We don't bother with my room, because I have a roommate, Libra. (No, she's actually a Capricorn, and yes, she's tired of people asking.) She's a year younger than me, but she was here before I arrived and has staked out most of the room as her own. I'm fine with that as long she keeps her stuff off my bed. I stash my phone and anything I don't want her messing with in Deo's room. His room is a single—they can never decide who to bunk with the kid who's clearly questioning his sexual orientation—so we usually hang out and do homework there. That's also where we keep the ancient Chromebook that we pooled our cash to buy a few years back. It's buggy and there's a short in the power unit, but I'm really hoping it holds out awhile longer so that we don't have to compete for time on the two communal computers downstairs.

I curl up on the tattered plastic beanbag in the corner, planning to scan through my English lit book and pick an author for the essay that's due on Monday. But first, I've promised to help Deo review for his history test.

We're four questions in, and suddenly Molly's back.

Anna, just listen to me for a few—

Come ON, Molly! Give it a rest. I'm helping Deo and then I have a paper due. I'm at the deli both days this weekend, so I can't put it off. I'm sorry it didn't work out today, but I've wasted most of my spare time for the past two weeks on this. It's not my fault that your grandfather is a jerk.

We can't give up.

I most absolutely certainly CAN give up. Go haunt him yourself. Maybe you'll have better luck.

Ha. Funny, Anna.

I'm not trying to be funny. I'm trying to make you go away. I need to focus.

Molly slides to the back of my mind, a sensation that's hard to describe. You know the feeling when you hit the top of the Ferris wheel and then it dips down? Substitute your head for your stomach and that's what it's like. Sort of. It's not exactly fun, but I've gotten used to it.

Deo is watching me, head tilted to one side, waiting. If it was anyone else, I'd be self-conscious about looking like a space case, but it's Deo. He recorded me once, so I know exactly how I look when I'm engaged in one of these internal dialogues—and that makes me determined to avoid them in public. My eyes go blank, unfocused, like no one's home—which is ironic if you think about it, since the problem isn't that nobody's there, but rather that we've exceeded the maximum occupancy of one.

"Go away, Molly," Deo says with an amiable smile. "Anna has to tell me why we started the War of 1812."

"She's already gone. You want the abridged version or the full MacAlister?"

"Definitely the abridged. We don't have all night."

It takes a few seconds, but the info is there, filed away with the rest of the debris that accumulates when your head takes in the occasional extra boarder.

"Okay," I begin as Deo slides the computer into his lap. "Britain was at war with France and we tried to stay neutral, but then the Brits started grabbing sailors off of *our* ships to force them to fight *their* war." I continue along those lines for a few minutes, pausing every now and then for him to catch up.

When I was nine years old, a good Samaritan delivered a large box of school supplies to my elementary school—just some stuff he found when cleaning out the house after the death of his mother, a retired history professor. That's how I picked up the last No. 2 pencil that eighty-two-year-old Emily MacAlister used to work her daily *New York Times* crossword puzzle. That's also how I picked up *Emily*, who was with me for nearly two years. She didn't finish her puzzle before she died, and Emily hated leaving loose ends. Having Emily in my head was like having your grandmother follow you around 24/7—*tuck in your shirt, you've misspelled the word* especially, *pull your hair back so everyone can see your pretty eyes, dear, and are you really wearing that to school?* She was a sweet old lady, but I was glad when we finally located the unfinished puzzle and she decided it was time to move on. Even now, there are a few swear words I simply cannot say without that tiny, residual ghost inside me shuddering in disgust.

Thanks to the various people like Emily that I've hosted, I've tested out of a lot of high school subjects. I still have a few gaps that the State of Maryland wants me to fill before they'll grant me a diploma how-ever, so I'm at JFK High in the mornings, and I'm taking college classes online. That means I'll have more than two years of college completed when I graduate from JFK at the end of this year. Online is nice—it's kind of difficult to pick up psychic travelers from our computer key-board, and if I need to zone out a bit to access the memory banks, no one but Deo is here to see my goofy expression.

I used to feel a bit guilty about using information left behind by Emily and the others, but Dr. Kelsey pointed out that it's really no different than someone who is blessed with an extraordinarily good memory or any other special ability. I finally decided to simply accept the silver lining, because I don't think I could fully separate all of the bits of trivia that I know from the bits that they knew, even if I tried. Using the info to help Deo rather than making him read the book is *probably* crossing some sort of academic integrity line, but, hey—it's not like I'm sneaking him the answers in class. He still has to learn it.

I wrap up and then add, "You might also want to check the text-book. Emily graduated in 1955, so . . ."

Deo rolls his eyes. "It's *history*, Anna, not science. History books don't change."

I open my mouth to disagree, but we're talking about ninth-grade US history, so I suspect he's mostly right. He asks a few more questions, then I finally open my English lit text, looking for something that I've read before or that I might have squirreled away in my psychic version of SparkNotes. I finally settle on Langston Hughes—I like his poetry, and it will be inter-esting to talk to Deo about him. Gay, black, and communist had to have been a killer combo for someone living and working in the 1930s.

Deo still has the computer tied up, so I unplug my phone from the charger on his desk and turn it on to check for messages that came in while my phone was kidnapped. There's one message from Joe, but Deo's already told me what that's about, so I click delete. Dr. Kelsey's number is next, and I wonder whether she was calling me about Porter poking around in my business, but it's only her virtual receptionist app with a reminder of my appointment tomorrow.

The third number isn't familiar. There's a short pause, then a guy comes on. His voice is low-pitched, and it's kind of hard to hear him through the heavy traffic in the background.

"The van's a warning, Anna. Stay away from Porter if you want to keep safe."

I play it back again to make sure I understood him correctly, and then I just stare at the phone for a minute. A van that barely missed us was a *warning*? Porter was a bit of a jerk, but I really hadn't pegged him as homicidal.

"Um, Deo?" I say, tossing him the phone as he turns toward me. "I think I found the downside to keeping our mouths shut."

He listens to the message, then replays it before dialing the number. We wait but no one answers.

"Even if it's a landline, who doesn't have voice mail these days?" Deo asks.

"Pay phone?"

"Do those still exist?" He picks up the phone again and stares at the display. "Anna—your shift was supposed to start at six fifteen, right? And you got to the deli at, what, six thirty?"

"I wasn't *that* late. Six twenty-five, at the latest."

"So the incident with the van was, say, six forty?"

I nod. "Why?"

"Check the time stamp," Deo says, sliding the phone across the carpet. "The call came in at three twenty-three. How weird is that?"

CHAPTER THREE

Dr. Louise Kelsey's office is blessed with an extra-large window, and cursed with having that window located directly above the parking lot and an industrial-size dumpster, which is usually full to overflowing thanks to the Asian take-out place and the convenience store that are the other tenants of the small building. Kelsey makes the best of the situation by hanging vertical blinds across the bottom half of the window. The wheat-colored slats hide the ugly but let the sunshine in. You can see a bit of sky and the top branches of the large maple tree behind the building. It's pretty, especially in the autumn.

I did the math a few months back, and I've spent nearly a thousand hours in this room. With the exception of a horrible seven months when the system put me with a different therapist, I've been in this room for two hours pretty much every week since I was five.

This office is the one place in my life that is a constant. I'm sure the shabby-chic look is due to the vow of semipoverty that therapists take when they agree to work with wards of the state, but I like knowing this room will always be the same. The furniture is worn, comfortable, and probably older than I am—she hasn't changed the décor since my first visit, aside from a few new pillows on the couch. The same oversized mirror still covers most of the wall next to the door, making the office look larger than it really is. Aside from the occasional computer upgrade, the only major change has been her family photos—the frames are the same, but the photographs of her three grandchildren have morphed from gap-toothed grins through acne and braces and finally to caps and gowns. And she added a white-noise machine a few years back to help mask the noises of the city with the soothing sounds of a waterfall.

Kelsey is also a constant. There are a few more lines around her gray eyes, and there might be an extra pound or two around the middle of her petite frame, but her hair is still closely cropped, white with a few streaks of graphite. The same rimless eyeglasses rest atop her head, ready to be pulled down if she needs to read from a file. The same large yellow coffee mug emblazoned with a *Peanuts* cartoon reading *The Doctor is IN* holds pencils and pens beside her computer. The same red mug holds her coffee, and it's always within easy reach of her hands.

She makes excellent coffee. I requested a cup, without cream or sugar, the first time I sat across from her desk. Kelsey didn't tell me that a five-year-old shouldn't be drinking coffee or insist on diluting it until it was mostly milk, like my previous foster mother had. She simply poured it into one of the disposable cups, noting only that I should be careful, since it was hot. The next Christmas, she gave me my very own mug, dark blue to match my eyes, with my name printed on the front in white script.

I open the cabinet just above the coffeemaker, pull my mug from its usual spot on the shelf, and fill it before sitting on the couch. Usually, I'd take the chair, but today it is already occupied.

Porter has his own coffee, in one of the disposable cups, and has already finished most of it. I'm late, and they both look at me reproachfully.

"Sorry," I say. "Fridays are always busy, and the girl who was supposed to relieve me at the deli arrived late, so I missed the first bus."

It's true, but I wouldn't go so far as to say that I rushed getting here. It's taken nearly a week for Molly to convince me that this appointment is something that even approaches a good idea. There are many places I would rather be than in the same room with a man who, despite his repeated denials, I still suspect of paying someone to aim that van at me and Deo.

Dr. Kelsey also had reservations about the meeting, and she doesn't look any more pleased with the situation now that she's been alone with him for ten minutes. I couldn't care less about inconveniencing Porter, but I feel bad for keeping Kelsey waiting and give her an apologetic half smile.

Kelsey rolls her eyes slightly but smiles back, and I feel more at ease. "Okay," she says. "I'm glad you're finally here, Anna. As I've told Mr. Porter, I'm not comfortable talking about your case unless you are present."

Porter nods at her and then looks at me, his eyes wary. "And, as I've told *both* of you, I'm not convinced that your doctor will be entirely honest and open with you sittin' here."

Kelsey and I discussed this, at length, at my previous appointment, and we've already come to an arrangement. I debate whether to toy with Porter for a few minutes, to show him that I don't have to put up with his demands, but I hate to waste more of Kelsey's time.

"Fine. I'll wait in there," I say, nodding toward the door to the reception area.

I grab my backpack and coffee and go into the hallway, closing the door behind me. But instead of going into the reception area, I open a door on the left and slip quickly into a small observation room. It's dark inside, but I leave the light off so that I can see through the two-way mirror into the office.

Using the observation room was Kelsey's idea. Let's just say I have control issues. It's my life. I have a right to know what they're saying.

And it's not a lie. Neither of us actually *said* that I was going into the reception area.

Is too a lie. You know that's what he thinks.

So now I'm responsible for his assumptions?

I twist the small knob on the speaker in front of me to hear what they're saying. Then I move the chair back and tilt it against the wall, so that I can prop my feet up.

Porter is talking. ". . . already know the basics, Dr. Kelsey. She's been in psychiatric hospitals, what, four different times?"

"I believe it's five, actually," Kelsey answers. "The last hospitalization was in 2012, however. Nearly seven years ago. Anna is stable now. She attends school, works fifteen to twenty hours a week, and manages most of her affairs on her own."

"Do her normal affairs include harassing people?" he asks. "I did her a favor by not reporting this harassment to the authorities. She seems to be under the delusion not only that she's in contact with my dead granddaughter but also that I hired a hit man or something . . ."

"Well, to be fair, Mr. Porter, she has some support concerning the van. I'm not saying you had anything to do with it, but she wasn't alone—"

"Yeah, but the other person she says was there is the same kid who was taggin' along behind her last week when she was stalking me."

"*And,*" Kelsey continues, ignoring the interruption, "someone did call her and warn her to stay away from you. I'm sure she played you the message?"

Porter huffs and rearranges himself in the chair. "Yeah, I heard it. She doesn't file a report after this so-called hit-and-run attempt, and then she gets a friend of hers to leave a message on her phone. I'm supposed to buy that as some sort of evidence?"

"She also received this," Kelsey says, pushing a folded sheet of paper toward him. "Someone left it in the mailbox at Bartholomew House on Friday evening."

He unfolds the paper and reads the two short sentences—*Mind your own business. Do not contact Porter again*—and shakes his head. "Again, isn't the most likely scenario that Anna or a friend wrote this? The *only* reason I'm taking time out of my day to be here, Dr. Kelsey, is because I'd like to see the girl get some help. At best, she's desperate for attention and, at worst, she's involved in some sort of scam."

Kelsey takes a deep breath and leans back in her desk chair, her hands crossed in front of her. Her two pointer fingers make a little tent that she rests against her lower lip. She always does this when she's thinking about what to say next.

"I don't agree, Mr. Porter," she says after several seconds have passed. "Anna debated whether or not to contact you for the past few months. She finally decided that it was the right thing to do."

"Okay, let's say for the sake of argument that this wasn't an attempt to con me. My point still stands. If she's sincere, then she's lost her grip on reality. Either way, somethin's gotta be done before she hurts herself or someone else."

Dr. Kelsey takes a deep breath and walks over to the counter to refill her cup. "You want more?" she asks.

He shakes his head, looking impatient as Kelsey takes her time adding the milk and sugar.

"Mr. Porter," she begins, once back at her desk, "I've worked with Anna since she was five years old. She was in the child welfare system for about two years prior to that. Someone dropped her off in a shopping mall food court just before her third birthday. Pinned to her dress was a note with the name Anna, a date of birth, and the words, *This child is possessed*."

My chest tightens and my pulse speeds up a bit. None of this is new. I don't really remember being abandoned, but Kelsey and I have

spent hours unearthing my early childhood and staking every psychological demon we could dredge up. I've dealt with all of this before. I
just don't like Porter hearing it.

"The state never located her parents, I take it?"

Kelsey shakes her head. "Only a first name on the note—someone assigned her a middle and last name later on. Either she was born
outside the state of Maryland under a different first name or she was
born on a different day, because there's no record of anyone giving
birth to a baby named Anna on December 3, 2001. Once the search
came up empty, they put her into the foster program. She was a prime
candidate for adoption—an adorable toddler, blonde hair, blue eyes,
sharp as a whip. But a few weeks later, they get strange reports from the
first foster parents. Talking in her sleep. Not toddler talk, either. Fully
formed adult sentences, and the tone of voice was different from her
usual speech. And then it starts happening when she's awake. So Anna
was placed in a children's psychiatric ward where they observed similar
behavior. She gets an official diagnosis of dissociative identity disorder."

"I've heard of it," Porter says. "Usually called multiple personality,
isn't it?"

She nods. "At any rate, Anna was hospitalized for a few months.
And then it disappeared completely. No symptoms, no unusual behavior. A new set of foster parents was rounded up and things were going
really well. They knew about her previous problems, but everything
seemed fine, so they chalked it up to the trauma of desertion. They even
started the initial paperwork for adoption."

This part I do remember. The memories are even clearer because
of the hypnotherapy I've done with Dr. Kelsey over the years. It was
the best house I've lived in. A small fenced yard, a sandbox in the back.
A yellow pail and orange shovel with a handle in the shape of a crab.
Sesame Street every morning. I can't remember the foster parents' names,
but they had a little black Yorkie named Dorothy, who licked my hands

when she sat in my lap and shared my Goldfish crackers when I left the bowl on the floor.

"I'm guessing Anna had another relapse?" Porter asks.

Kelsey shrugs noncommittally. "If you want to call it that. They took her up to Pennsylvania to meet her prospective grandparents. She was sitting on their porch swing when, according to their report, she started speaking in a different tone and calling the foster father's dad by his first name, asking him about people he went to high school with. Asking about them by *name*."

"How's that possible?"

"The house had been in the family for several generations. The older guy's sister died when she was in her teens, back in the late sixties, while he was serving in Vietnam. She never got to tell her brother good-bye. Anna . . . picked her up . . . when she touched the swing."

"Picked *who* up?" Porter asks.

"The sister's ghost. Her psychic echo, I don't know. In Jewish mysticism, they call it an *ibbur*—when a spirit takes over a host to finish some task, something incomplete that keeps them from moving on. There are similar concepts in other faiths as well. Anna thinks that, in most cases, the spirit . . . the *consciousness* of someone who can't move on to whatever comes next, eventually returns to the last place or the last thing that made them feel happy. Or safe. For the sister, it must have been that porch swing. And she couldn't let go until she told her brother good-bye."

The brother is vivid in my memory. A chin that needed shaving, the strong smell of cigarettes and motor oil on his shirt. His sister's name was Lydia and the old guy was Paul. Lydia wasn't pushy. She just said, *I never got to say good-bye. Please, would you let me say good-bye?* I could feel how important it was to her, that it was everything in the entire world to her, so I let her take control. I was too young to think about consequences, about whether I could fight her if she decided she didn't want to leave. I was still hugging him when she went away. Everyone was crying and a bit freaked out. But Paul smiled behind the tears. And Lydia was happy. She went away happy.

Porter just snorts. "And you believed this story?"

"I didn't," Kelsey admits, with a quick apologetic glance toward the mirror. She thinks I don't know this, but I do. Even five-year-olds can tell when someone doesn't believe them. When they think you're making it up or crazy or whatever. She was always nice about it, though, and most people weren't, so I didn't really mind.

"I didn't start working with Anna," she says, "until the second hospitalization in 2007. That was a few months after the incident in Pennsylvania. The couple was still considering adoption, you see. It was just that one time—and once the sister said her good-bye, Anna was perfectly normal. But then, a double whammy. The couple finally conceived, after seven years of trying. Even still, they were planning to go ahead with the adoption, but then Anna was on the subway with the foster mother and she picked up another . . . echo, ghost, whatever. Not a very friendly one this time."

Myron. I would remember Myron even if I'd never spent a single minute in hypnotherapy. He was very strong when he was angry, and Myron was almost always angry. I've spent a lot of time trying to forget Myron and keep his voice and his face out of my dreams. Trying to forget the nightmares that followed after Myron was finally gone. Trying to seal his file shut and wall it off in the most remote corner of my mind.

All of the others I've hosted fit the label of *ibbur*. They've been needy, but not malevolent. They asked for my help. And in cases where I couldn't help, they eventually went away. Myron, on the other hand, was a *dybbuk*. He didn't ask. He simply took.

I don't want her to talk about Myron.

And she doesn't.

"Let's just say her foster parents decided that it was better not to risk the welfare of an infant with a child who was so volatile. Who might be dangerous. So Anna lands back in the hospital. I started working with her when she left the hospital and was assigned to a group home. I accepted the diagnosis of the previous doctors. *Officially*, I still accept that diagnosis."

"But unofficially?" Porter asks.

"Anna changed my mind about a year and a half after I started working with her. One of my clients died that winter. Bruno was an elderly man, homeless much of the time. He had issues with kleptomania and substance abuse. I guess the chair you're sitting in was the last place he felt safe."

Porter glances down at the chair and his eyes widen. I stifle a laugh.

"Anna knew things about my client that I simply couldn't explain away. Including where he'd hidden the very nice ballpoint pen my daughter had given me the previous Christmas. I was pretty sure he'd taken the pen from my desk, and I'd been working with him, trying to get him to trust me enough to admit it. Then they found his body in Layhill Park, not too far from the homeless shelter that took him in from time to time. Later that week, I'm talking to Bruno again— through Anna—and he tells me that he stashed his treasures, as he called them, in a plastic bag that he hid in the bushes near the bleachers at the baseball field in the park. And that's where I found my pen, along with a bunch of other stuff he'd collected, including an earring I'd lost two years earlier. Guess he found it in the carpet and decided to keep it."

"He could have told her that in your waiting room, Dr. Kelsey. Maybe she read your file. Or maybe she followed him."

"Anna was *six* at the time, Mr. Porter. Their appointments were on different days, and she was accompanied to and from her appointments by a social worker back then. Believe me, I tried to think of a rational explanation. But there wasn't one, so I finally had to accept that Anna wasn't just telling me what she believed to be true, as I'd thought. She was telling the *actual* truth. And while many of my colleagues would still disavow any claims of psychic abilities, I consider myself a realist. We have mapped the human genome, but we still understand very little about the human brain. There are some sections for which no scientist, no psychologist, can pinpoint an exact purpose. The fact that I cannot tell you why Anna has this ability and others do not, the fact that I cannot quantify it, doesn't make it any less real."

Porter is quiet for several moments. "So you don't think she really has this dissociative identity thing. But you go on treating her a few times a week anyway? Is that ethical?"

Kelsey leans forward and her eyes narrow, a faint red flush creeping up her cheeks as she stands up. It takes me a moment to realize that she's angry. I've seen her annoyed in the past, pissed off about some bit of bureaucratic insanity, but never angry.

"If you think I'm in this for money," Kelsey says between clenched teeth, "take a good look around you, Mr. Porter. Yes, I kept Anna as a patient despite the fact there's no category for her actual condition in the diagnostic manual. How would *you* like to walk around each day with one or more visitors in your head? Dead people you don't know, didn't invite, and have to struggle to evict? Dead people who leave behind their memories, whose deaths you dream about in vivid detail for weeks after they finally leave? Anna needs at least as much help dealing with the effects of her condition as anyone I have dealt with in thirty-six years of practice, so I have absolutely *no* qualms about the ethics of keeping her as a patient."

Your grandpa might want to watch his mouth, Molly. Kelsey may be little, but she's fierce. I think she could take him.

Molly sniffs derisively, no comment.

"I'm still not convinced what you're saying is true," Porter begins, "but if it is, are you the person best equipped to help her? This talent you say she has sounds like something that should be studied, verified . . ."

"If I was primarily concerned about my own self-interest, I certainly *would* have written Anna's case up in a psychiatric journal. But do you really think she could have remained anonymous? That there wouldn't have been a constant battery of tests and trials to convince skeptics like yourself? Anna would have been turned into a sideshow. She had no one to protect her interests. Personally, I didn't think throwing a six-year-old child to the wolves was *ethical*." She puts a decided emphasis on that last word as she sits back down, her eyes still locked on Porter's.

He breaks the stare by glancing to the right, pausing for a few seconds when his gaze reaches the mirror. His shoulders tighten and his mouth twitches slightly on one side. It feels almost as though he can see me. I sit forward, ready to bolt into the reception area, but then he looks back toward the desk.

Kelsey lets him sit in uncomfortable silence for a moment longer and then continues. "I *know* you expected me to say something very different this afternoon, Mr. Porter, but I'm not going to lie to you. Anna made the decision to approach you, and she didn't make it lightly. Most of the spirits she picks up plead with her to get a message to their spouse, their children, somebody—it seems that only those who have some sort of regret or quest stick around. Anna was pretty certain how you'd react, but she felt she had a moral obligation to at least try, given what Molly told her about the circumstances of her death."

"She's going to have to give me something more to go on here, Doctor. You might be convinced, but I'm sure as hell not. If Molly's in Anna's head, why wouldn't she let me talk to her?"

Kelsey shrugs one shoulder. "Anna's a smart girl. It would have been beyond foolish to let Molly surface in a downtown café, without anyone she knows as a witness. Strong emotion is a very powerful motivator, and Molly's been an exceptionally determined guest. This wouldn't be the first time that Anna's had to fight—and fight hard—to get her own mind back from a hijacker, so you can hardly blame her for wanting some control over the circumstances of your . . . conversation."

Porter nods once and then looks pointedly at the mirror, a smug smile on his face. His eyes sweep past me and settle a few feet to the left of my chair. It's a good guess—that's where I'd have been if I hadn't tilted my chair back against the wall. "Anna, you can turn off the speaker and join us in here now."

Molly's not happy with the names I'm thinking about her grandfather as I sit up and grab my backpack, but I ignore her. Even though I have nothing to be embarrassed about, that doesn't stop the blush from rising to my cheeks as I walk back to the couch.

"I was a detective for over twenty years, ladies. I've seen more than one observation mirror in my time." He swivels the chair in my direction and crosses his hands on his belly, leaning back.

Face it, Molly. Your grandfather is an insufferable jerk.

I kick my black flats under the end table and toss my backpack on top of them, then sit on the couch, legs tucked under me.

My eyes dart over to Kelsey, whose expression is sympathetic and a bit nervous. She has a pretty good idea how much it costs me to give up control. But there's no sense putting it off. I suck in my breath and wait for the slide, the slipping, slightly sick sensation that marks my demotion from driver to passenger.

You have ten minutes, Molly. Make the most of it.

I can still see the office, still hear the slight whirr of the heating system. I feel the handle of my coffee cup against my palm as Molly puts it on the end table, sloshing a few drops of warm coffee on my skin. My legs unfold, at Molly's command. I feel the carpet under my sock-clad feet, and the slight thump as my knees land in front of Porter's chair. I feel the tears begin to run down my face and the polyester fabric of Porter's pants when my cheek touches his knee, his body going rigid as he tries to pull away. I feel all of these things, but it's as though

I'm dipped in plastic and there's a barrier between my mind and the sensations.

A voice very much like my own is coming from my mouth, but the words are a jumble at first, exploding like they've been pent up under pressure. A deep breath, and then her speech becomes more coherent. "Pa, it's me. It's Molly. I'm sorry, I'm so sorry. I wanted to come back to you and Mimmy. I was scared, but Mama needed me with her. She was better when I was there. And she said Lucas would never hurt us—you know how she was about him. She loved him even after she found out what he was into. She thought he was good underneath, that she could change him. But she was *so* wrong about him, Pa."

Porter opens his mouth, but no words come out. His face is ashen, his eyes glued to my hand, which is clutching the leg of his pants.

"And now it's too late for Mama, too late for me, but maybe you can stop him."

Porter just sits there for a few seconds. Then his eyes narrow and jerk back up to meet mine. "Where did Mimmy keep her wedding rings when she scrubbed pots?"

Great, I think. *He wants to play twenty questions.* But Molly's answer is instantaneous. "In the bunny cup, the one by the sink, with all the paint chipped off."

"What song did you play for her sixty-fifth birthday and why?"

Molly pauses, then says, a bit more tentatively. "'The Little Old Lady from Pasadena.' 'Cause she grew up near Pasadena. And 'cause you say she drives too fast."

"How about the year before that?" he asks.

"Jeez, Pa! I think it was 'Copacabana.' And I played it 'cause she likes it, but if you want to know *why* she likes it, you'll have to ask Mimmy."

Porter starts to speak again and then closes his mouth. "You—your grandma . . ." He stops, swallows, then starts again. "You don't know about Mimmy, then?"

I feel a streak of pure joy run through Molly.

He knows it's me, he knows, he said "your grandma."

Then my heart stops. Molly is neglecting to breathe for some reason. I struggle to shove her aside, to suck in the air on my own, but she ignores me. A long moment later, she asks in a tiny voice, "Know what, Pa?"

He moves his hand as though he's going to touch my hair, before catching himself and putting the hand back in his lap. "She's gone, Molly. She died about a year after you and Laura. It was awful tough on her, losing the two of you like that. I thought maybe she'd snap out of it. We bought that camper, traveled around a bit, but she—her heart just gave out. Told me she was ready to be with you and your mama. Though I guess maybe that didn't work out quite the way she thought . . ."

"You're all alone now, Pa. You and Mimmy were going to travel, and—"

"I'm okay, baby. Ella stops in every day or two, and Phyllis and the kids come down now and then. An' I went back to work—not much point in retirement and just sittin' around all day. But yeah, I miss her a lot."

Molly pulls my arms tight around my body and sits there, rocking back and forth, making a soft keening sound, almost like a teakettle coming to boil. Tears stream down my face, and in that second, I know Molly is right. Porter is a believer now. He's seeing Molly, not me. Seeing *her* grief, *her* anguish. There's a look I can't quite place in his brown eyes. Pain, bewilderment, helplessness—and something else. He loved her so much. His expression scares me a bit with its intensity, but I'm also envious. And yes, the irony of being jealous of a girl who was brutally murdered has not escaped me. It's just that I can't remember anyone ever looking at *me* that way.

Molly is still rocking, digging my nails into my upper arms. It hurts.

Molly! Time's up.

But she's not responding. I try to push back to the front, but Molly's pain is so strong that I can't break through.

It's my body, damn it! Give it back!

Kelsey has been watching quietly from behind the desk. I don't know if she can see fear in my eyes or maybe she can just sense my panic, but she moves quickly and kneels next to me, her arm around my shoulders. "Anna? *Anna?* Molly, I need to speak to Anna now, okay? Molly? I'm *so* sorry about your grandmother, but I need to be sure that Anna—"

"No," Molly says, wrenching away from Kelsey, her tone flat but adamant. "I'm not done."

"We can finish this another time. You need a chance to process what your grandfather has told you, and I think Anna is a bit overwhelmed."

"I said no! Anna can wait." Molly still has control, but at least Kelsey's words have snapped her out of the emotional pit she was falling into.

"Perhaps," Kelsey says. "But I'm pretty sure that if you *make* her wait this will be the last time you speak to your grandfather. You've told him that this Lucas was the one who killed you. Surely that's enough for him to get started."

"I have to finish, Dr. Kelsey. Anna's okay."

Kelsey looks hesitant, but she backs away, sitting on the sofa rather than going back to her desk. I've never seen Kelsey sit on the sofa. She looks odd there, out of place.

Then Molly turns back to Porter. "Pa, Lucas *didn't* kill me. Not directly. I'm pretty sure he killed Mama, though. I heard it. I was in the closet, Pa. Someone shot her."

I didn't think it was possible for Porter's shoulders to slump any lower, but they do. "So she's really gone, too. Lucas said you and your mama left town without telling him. We never found her body, though, and when—" He stops and shakes his head. "When your body showed up in Delaware, it seemed to support his story. There wasn't anything to tie him to your death, but I never believed him. But . . . if Lucas didn't kill you, then who did?"

"You need to listen, okay, Pa? Lucas is bringing women—girls, really—into the country. Mostly Eastern European. He has some contacts, apparently pretty important ones, who help him get around port security. The girls think they're here to train for nanny jobs or other work, but they're selling them for—well, what they always sell girls for. When he found out what I overheard about his . . . business, I think Lucas sold *me* to someone. Lucas called him Craig, but I don't know if it's a first name or last. And I'm positive Lucas understood what happens to the girls he hands over to Craig. I saw him kill another girl who was there with me."

Something isn't right. I haven't asked many questions about the circumstances of Molly's death, both because she didn't seem to want to think about it in too much detail and because I'll know all of the details eventually anyway, whether I want to or not. But I can tell that she's hiding something. Of course, she's talking to her grandfather, who's already upset and apparently not in perfect health. Maybe she's just trying to avoid putting him through further distress.

"He kept . . . souvenirs, Pa." She reaches out my left hand and rests it against his leg, and for a second, my pinky disappears, replaced by a bloody nub, bright red against the khaki fabric of his pants. And then it's just my hand again, but I feel the faint throb of remembered pain.

"He had six, maybe seven, and that was nearly three years ago. So yeah, you need to get Lucas, but you have to find Craig, too."

Porter's shoulders are shaking as tears flow down his cheeks. One catches on the edge of his moustache and hangs there momentarily, until his lower lip trembles and the tear shakes loose, falling to the carpet. "I'm so sorry, Molly. So sorry. I'll find them, baby, I will."

"I know you will, Pa." She rests my head against his knee again.

> You'll help him, won't you, Anna? You said you'll know everything that I know after I'm gone, so I can count on you, right?

The voice in my head is calmer now, less frantic.

> *What? No, Molly. I didn't mean it earlier. I was frightened, but it's okay. I understand. I'll let you see him again, and you can tell him everything.*

It always ends a bit differently. Some of them leave slowly, and I assimilate their memories gradually as they kind of fade away. Others simply vanish without even saying good-bye. When Emily MacAlister finished the last letter of that crossword puzzle, her quest was complete and her voice in my head just disappeared. Over the next few weeks, my subconscious unpacked the Emily memories and filed them away with the others. And each night, I'd dream about her last moments—vivid at first, then fading away. Each night, I'd taste the slightly too-sweet tea she'd been drinking and struggle to come up with a seven-letter word for a glandlike growth (second letter *d*, fourth letter *n*). The dreams about her death had been boring, working on that same puzzle over and over, but at least they were peaceful. I have no illusions that Molly's will be anything other than nightmares. I don't want her to go yet. I don't want those dreams.

It's okay, Anna. I'm not sure I can really leave until I know this is over. But I don't want to talk to Pa again—I mean, I do want to, but I can't. I can't talk to him about what happened to me. I can't stand him looking like it's his fault somehow. Talking to him is just too painful and it's too . . .

She doesn't complete the thought, so I do it for her.

Too tempting?

Yes. Pa believes us now, and it wouldn't be good for him to get used to having me around again, even a pale, blue-eyed version. It wouldn't be good for any of us. And I don't like fighting against you like that.

She turns back to Porter and takes his hand, pressing it against my cheek. His eyes are squeezed shut, his head down. "Pa, you be careful, okay? Listen to your doctor and take your medicine."

A brief pause and then, "No, Molly. You can't go. You need to tell me everything, to be sure we catch—"

"Pa," she interrupts. "I can't. I need to start looking for Mama and Mimmy now, so you and Anna will have to take it from here. She will know everything I do. She'll help you. Trust her, okay?"

He just stares for a long moment, tears brimming over his lower eyelids.

"I love you forever . . . ," she says. The words are soft, rising a bit at the end, almost a question.

"And I love you forever *more*," he replies, his voice breaking in the middle.

CHAPTER FOUR

Porter seems in a hurry to leave once I am back in control. I don't blame him. I'm not angry the way I was before, but I still don't fully trust him. The wary look has returned to his eyes, which tells me the lack of trust is probably mutual. I wonder if he'll manage to convince himself that none of this really happened, that it was all some elaborate ruse, once he's back on the freeway.

He shrugs on his coat and scribbles a phone number on a piece of notepaper. "This is my cell number, Anna, if you need to reach me. I'm—uh, I have a meeting I need to get to, but we should talk soon."

I take the scrap of paper. He seems to be waiting for something. "You already *have* my number, right? You had the phone long enough."

He has the good grace to look sheepish. "Yeah, I guess I do. I'll call you. I need to get in touch with some people and see if we can get the case reopened, since we have some new information."

"How will you explain?" I ask.

"An anonymous tip, I guess. They *do* happen from time to time. I'll get them to start looking into any associates Lucas has named Craig, for starters. Eventually, I'll see if they can find anything on the trafficking issue. It could be a day or two, though. I . . . uh, well, I've already called in a lot of favors over the past few years, so it may take a little persistence to convince them."

Kelsey walks him to the door. "Mr. Porter, what about the phone call Anna received? And the note?"

He shoots me a look and his eyes narrow slightly. "I don't know anything about that, Dr. Kelsey. If it does turn out that Anna needed to make those claims in order to get me here, well . . . I would certainly understand. I'm not sure I would have come otherwise, so I'm willing to forget the matter."

I open my mouth to object, but Porter has already opened the door into the stairwell and is headed down to the exit.

"He's a real piece of work, isn't he?" Kelsey says as she returns to her desk. "Do you think he'll ever admit he was trying to scare you away?"

"I doubt it. I'm surprised the stubborn old goat even believed it was Molly." I half expect to hear a complaint about me dissing her grandfather, but Molly is quiet.

Kelsey glances at the clock, and I realize that her four o'clock appointment should be arriving any minute. I go to the sink to rinse out my cup. She follows me and gives my arm a squeeze. "So, Molly's not gone, is she?"

"No." I slide my mug back into its usual spot in the cupboard. "But she doesn't think it's a good idea to talk to Porter again. Maybe she's right. I couldn't push her back today, Kelsey. Building up my wall seems to work fine for keeping them contained when I'm in control, but it doesn't work so well when I'm the one in the backseat. I was trying to take control . . . well, maybe not a hundred percent, but pretty close. Molly wasn't going to budge until she finished talking to him."

"How did that make you feel?"

I used to tease her about stereotypical therapist questions like that, and I suspect she's thrown this one in to lighten the mood, more than anything else. I roll my eyes and feed her the textbook response. "It triggered a fight-or-flight response, Doctor Freud, with a strong sense of fear and rage because I didn't have control. You know exactly how it made me feel."

She gives me a half smile. "I do, just as *you* know that putting those emotions into words helps you cope with them. And speaking of coping, do you still have enough sleep medication in case the dreams start?"

I nod. The pills help, at least enough (usually) to keep me from waking up screaming that I can't breathe, or that there's a car coming straight toward me, or whatever sensation comes along with someone's final memories. Libra has already had to put up with my dreams when one of my tenants vacated, and that woman died in her sleep. I can only imagine what it's going to be like when Molly goes.

"I'll see you on Tuesday. And, thanks, Kelsey," I add as I head toward the door. "I couldn't have gotten through this without you."

"That's what I'm here for. Call me if you need me before then, okay?"

I close the door to the stairwell. I'm one step from the bottom when I hear the squeal of rubber on asphalt. I push open the door, and a loud crack hits my ears, followed quickly by another. A gray sedan bounces off the curb at the far end of the parking lot, turning right. The man on the passenger side sees me at the door and raises a gun to his shoulder as the driver accelerates off toward Veirs Mill. There's another cracking sound, a loud ping as the bullet hits the dumpster about twenty yards to my left, then a screech of brakes.

A second, much closer screech hits my ears as a small black car whips around the corner. The driver is young, maybe twenty, and his face seems familiar. My first thought, which makes no sense, is: *Unfair. He's even cuter than he used to be.*

The guy flings the passenger-side door open, nearly clipping my leg. "Get in, Anna. They're coming back around the block!"

"Do I know you? I think—"

"Get the hell in the car, Anna! They've shot Porter."

Get in, Anna! It's Aaron—oh my God, Pa!

I pile into the car and he heads across the lot, bouncing off the curb just a few feet away from where the gray sedan exited, turning the wrong way into a one-way alley. Thankfully, there's no traffic and we make it to the intersection, where he hangs a sharp right onto Georgia Avenue. An ambulance whizzes past in the opposite direction.

Aaron who?

But Molly is too frantic to answer.

He punches the phone button on the car's communications console and says, "Call Sam."

A few seconds later, Sam—an older man, judging from the voice—says, "Aaron? You okay?"

"Yeah, I'm fine. Porter was shot, though."

"Son of a bitch," Sam says. He doesn't sound surprised, however. Worried. Maybe a little annoyed, but almost like he expected this news.

I stare at Aaron as they talk, mentally thumbing through the scattered Molly files in my head, which are far too new to be neatly organized. He has a distinctive profile, the nose a bit long, but somehow it fits his face. Above-average height, broad shouldered, dark-reddish-brown hair. Jeans. A black windbreaker over a deep-green shirt. The color brings out the greenish flecks in his hazel eyes, which keep darting between the rearview mirror and the road ahead.

"At least he's alive," Aaron says. "Got him in the shoulder. Drive-by. Two men, gray or silver Ford . . . Focus, I think?"

"Any idea on the year?"

"Late model, 2017 or '18, I'd say. Headed north on Georgia Avenue. One white, one Latino, but I don't think either of them was Lucas. He's moved up in the world . . . guess he can contract out his dirty work on occasion. Ambulance should take Porter to Holy Cross."

"Heading there now. I'll call this in to Daniel. Son of a bitch."

"Sam? Just so you know, the girl is with me."

A pause. "You think that's wise?"

Aaron gives me a quick look out of the corner of his eye. "They shot at her, too, Sam. Something's up."

"Keep me posted."

The connection ends, and without the distraction of their conversation, Molly's pain is front and center.

"You said Porter is okay? How do you know?"

Aaron Whoever glances at me again. "I called an ambulance five minutes ago. They'll get to him in time."

It's not just his face that's familiar. His voice is familiar too, like I've heard it myself, not like something from Molly's memory. I can't pin it down, however.

I try to focus and tap into the few memories of Molly's that are available. *Quinn.* His last name is Quinn. Molly had a crush on him, which I *totally* get. He's borderline gorgeous.

And Molly trusted him. That trust is the only reason I got into the car with a complete stranger—a stranger who is driving much too fast and recklessly for my comfort—rather than doing the sensible thing and running back upstairs to Kelsey's office when I heard gunfire.

Kelsey.

"We have to go back! What if they go into the building looking for me and—"

"Your doctor is safe. They won't stick around long enough to go into the building when they hear sirens."

And how the hell do you know that?

I'm tempted to actually ask the question, but another question that hasn't fully formed in my head is nagging at me. So I decide to focus on verifying his identity first. Let's see how he feels about me knowing things *I* shouldn't know.

"You're Aaron. Aaron Quinn, right? You knew Molly. You know Porter. And apparently you know my name already, although I've no idea how."

He nods once as he exits onto 495.

The question that was hanging midbrain finally takes form. It's been maybe three minutes since I got into the car, and . . .

"Wait a second! You said you called the ambulance *five* minutes ago?"

Aaron edges the car onto the Beltway. "Yeah. I was watching the building. They were acting suspiciously, so I called 911."

"But that would mean you called the *cops*. Not an ambulance. And why were you watching the building in the first place?"

"Like you said, I knew Molly. Plus, Porter is a friend."

This time when he says Porter's name the connection in my mind is almost like an audible click. "Oh, God! It was *you* on the phone!" I reach for the door handle instinctively, even though I know it would be suicide to fling it open on a highway, with cars zipping by on both sides. "*You* left the message about the van. *You* left the note at Bartholomew House."

"What? No, I didn't leave a note. But yeah, I called you. Porter doesn't know anything about that, by the way. I wish you had listened and stayed away from him. I *think* he'll be okay. But he's not as young as he used to be, and . . ."

Molly curls up in the back of my mind, in the mental equivalent of the fetal position, crying. Which I understand, given the circumstances. She just learned that her grandmother is dead, and now she finds out Porter's been wounded, too. But her emotional meltdown is very distracting when I'm trying to think. And a little constructive input from her would be really helpful right now, since she knows this Aaron guy a lot better than I do.

"There were *two* shots," I say. "Well, three, but the last was aimed at me. Are you sure . . ."

"They hit his car with the second shot. He was lucky, though. Just a few inches closer and that bullet would've hit him, too."

I process what he's said, then return to what's really bugging me.

"You're the one who called me, but it wasn't you in the van. That guy was darker, bald—pretty sure I saw a moustache."

He shoots me an incredulous look. "Of *course* I wasn't driving the freaking van! Why would you think that?"

"Did Porter even know? Or did you hire someone to scare me away without telling him?"

"What the hell are you talking about, Anna? I didn't *hire* anyone. I didn't have anything to do with the van. I was *trying* to convince you to keep away from Porter so that neither of you would get hurt. So they'd leave you alone. But you didn't listen."

He's a good actor. If I hadn't known the time that his warning call came in, I might have believed him. I debate whether to play that trump card or keep quiet and save what I know for the police. Assuming, of course, that I make it to the police. Assuming, of course, that he's not working with whoever shot Porter. Or with this Lucas. Or Craig.

I am in so, so deep.

No. I'll keep the information about the van to myself for now. "Molly trusted you."

That causes him to flinch. He switches to the inner lane and speeds up to around seventy, glancing again at the rearview mirror before he speaks. "Molly was a friend. I just wish I'd been around three years ago. Maybe I could have . . ." He trails off, shaking his head.

Again, my intuition tells me he's being honest, that I should believe him. That's the only reason I can imagine why I do a complete one-eighty on telling him what I know about the van in the space of a minute. "You say you didn't have anything to do with the van. But you left that message three *hours* before it came anywhere near us."

He keeps his eyes fixed on the lane ahead, but his face darkens.

"So the way I see it, the most logical explanation is that *you* hired the van. Or you know who did. Unless, of course, you have some sort of crystal ball that tells the future."

He's silent for a long moment, then says, "It's not exactly a crystal ball."

I wait for him to continue, but he doesn't.

"I'm going to need a little more than *that*."

"Is the most logical explanation always the correct one, Anna?"

"Not always," I admit, thinking back to Deo's earlier comment on the same subject. In my case, the most logical explanation isn't even *usually* the correct one.

We drive in silence for a few minutes. "Can I at least know where you're taking me?"

"The first place I could think of that's safe. At least I'm pretty sure it's safe. I don't think we were followed, and you can't go back to Bartholomew House just yet."

"I need to call Deo. I was supposed to meet him after my appointment. And, oh—jeez, I didn't even think. Kelsey will know about Porter by now. She'll be worried. And maybe she has an update on his condition?"

"Porter's alive . . ."

"You can't know that. He could be dead for all you know." A fresh wail from Molly reminds me that I probably shouldn't have said that. I pull up Kelsey's number on my phone. "They could have gone upstairs and shot Kelsey, too. And for all *I* know, you could be working with them."

"Anna, please." He puts his hand on my arm, squeezing lightly, his eyes pleading. "Okay, fine, if it will make you feel better. Call them. Tell them you're safe. Tell them you're with a friend."

"But I'm not sure that either of those things is true," I say, pulling my arm away. "And Deo won't believe it for a minute."

"Why not?"

Because I don't have any friends aside from Deo, I think. But I just say, "He knows me well enough to tell when I'm lying."

"Then don't let it be a lie. I am *not* going to hurt you. I'm trying to figure out the best way to keep you safe. And I'll tell you everything, or at least as much as I can, as soon as we get there."

"Get where?" I mutter under my breath as I wait for Kelsey to pick up.

Kelsey's voice is frantic when she answers. "Oh, thank heavens, Anna! Are you okay? The police are swarming the parking lot. Mr. Porter—"

"Porter?" I ask lamely. "What happened?"

"He was *shot.* They said the shooter must have mistaken him for someone else. Probably drug related."

"Is he okay?"

"He's alive, that's all they could tell me. But where are you?"

"I . . . I'm with a friend. We had plans after my appointment, but I heard shots as we were driving away and then the sirens. I realized you might have been worried about me."

"Well, I *was* worried when the police came up a minute ago, but like I told them, I didn't hear the shots. I was in the front with my next patient, and I guess the sound machine drowned it out." She pauses. "And you're sure you're okay?"

I glance over at Aaron. Part of me is tempted to send her a coded message like they do in the movies. I could say I'll see her at our appointment on Monday (which has been her regular day off as long as I can remember, because she sees patients on Saturdays) or maybe remind her to feed the fish in her aquarium (that she got rid of two years ago).

But I don't. "I'm fine. I'll see you on Tuesday, okay?"

"Okay," she answers, a tiny hint of doubt in her voice. "Let me know if you need anything."

"I will. And could you call me if you hear anything more about Mr. Porter?"

Deo is not as easy, but I knew he wouldn't be. I end up asking him to just trust me, and I promise to call him again in half an hour. And even then, I have to tell him about Porter, and that I'm with a friend of Molly's. I even have to give him Aaron's name, which Aaron clearly doesn't like, judging from his expression.

"Okay," I tell Aaron, once I've hung up. "Just so you know, Deo will call Dr. Kelsey, the police, the FBI, the entire Avengers team, and anyone else he can think of if I don't check back in half an hour."

Aaron rolls his eyes. "You have a very possessive boyfriend."

I start to correct him, but maybe having Aaron think Deo's my overprotective boyfriend is a good thing. I could say he's at the gym, lifting weights.

I feel a tiny wave of disapproval from Molly as I settle back into my seat, the first real reaction I've felt from her in several minutes.

You shouldn't lie to Aaron. He's trying to help.

Really? Because I think the jury's still out on that one.

"Not my boyfriend," I say. "More like my brother. But yeah, he'll go crazy if he doesn't hear from me—he's halfway there already, given what I told him about Porter."

We're moving north on I-95 now, toward Baltimore. After a few minutes, Aaron eases into the lane for the Beltsville exit.

"So can you tell me where we're headed now or is it still top secret?"

"I have the key to a place that belongs to some friends. I house-sit for them on occasion, take care of the cat and so forth. They're in West Virginia for two weeks—a second honeymoon of sorts. No one outside of family would connect me to them, and only Sam and my sister know I'm back in town, so . . ."

He seems to feel this should reassure me. It doesn't. Not one little bit.

What I'm thinking must show on my face, because after a few seconds he says, "Anna, the very last thing on my mind is hurting you. In *any* way. I've seen evidence of too many girls mistreated lately. You *will* be safe with me. You said Molly trusted me. Can you try to trust me, too?"

In my experience, trust isn't something you *try*. It's either there or not, and in my case, trusting Aaron seems to be an on-again, off-again thing, depending on whether I'm relying on gut instinct, which is mostly tied to Molly's memories, or relying on my own logic, which says I should bail at the first stoplight and take off running.

For the moment however, my gut seems to be prevailing. So I just nod and shift my gaze out the window. We pass a few small shopping centers, one with a Starbucks that is screaming my name, but I don't say anything. The sun is inching down toward the horizon, as sporadic prisms of orange light break through the branches of trees that are beginning to lose their leaves in earnest.

Aaron eventually turns right into a mostly residential area, then pulls into a lot surrounded by a square of two-story brick townhomes. He stops the car under a canopy near the middle of the parking lot and comes around to my side, I guess to open the door for me. I beat him to it, though. I was out of the car almost before we were fully stopped, once again contemplating making a run for it.

Molly must feel my panic, because she surges to the front, almost like she's trying to take control. That only ramps up my fear, and she quickly pulls back.

Sorry. I . . . I just . . . Aaron's okay, Anna. I've known him forever. You can trust him.

She's pushing thoughts toward me. Nothing coherent, just a fleeting slide show of memories. A summer afternoon in someone's backyard. An older man with salt-and-pepper hair sitting across from Porter at a picnic table, drinking beer, watching a group of kids playing . . .

badminton, I think. A younger girl with the same reddish-brown hair as Aaron running around in a profusely pink bedroom with a frilly canopy bed. The sensation of jumping on the bed with that same little girl, then diving beneath a Disney Princesses comforter, giggling, when a boy around seven in what appear to be Iron Man underwear—is that Aaron?—runs past the door.

I shake my head to clear away the barrage of images and sounds, but I still get the emotions behind them. *Happy. Safe. Secure. Loved.*

Molly's been through a lot, and that's why I try to pull back my first thought, which is that the circumstances of her death suggest she *might* not have been the best judge of character. And I also try to restrain my second thought—that I really hope her judgment in this case doesn't get *me* killed as well.

I apparently don't succeed in hiding either of those feelings, but Molly doesn't take offense. She just snorts.

Aaron is not Craig. He's not Lucas. If anything, he's too polite.

So was Norman Bates.

Hmph.

And then Molly curls back up in her corner of my head.

Aaron is staring at me. I've been standing here in the middle of the parking lot during my little internal dialogue with Molly. And yes, it was probably only a couple of seconds, but I'm sure I looked like a total idiot. I wipe the side of my mouth with one hand, relieved to find it's dry. At least I wasn't a drooling idiot.

"It's . . . this one," he says awkwardly, motioning toward a unit on the end, with a neat square of grass and one rather anemic-looking tree in front. He fumbles with a ring of keys, settling on one that's neon green. Then he scoops up the small stack of community papers from the stoop and tosses them into the empty recycling bin next to the door.

Empty except for water, that is. It splashes onto his jeans and soaks his Nikes. A large wet maple leaf clings to the toe of his left shoe. I stifle a laugh as he tries, unsuccessfully, to shake it off, before finally scraping it loose against the top step.

Once the door is open, Aaron stashes his messenger bag under the small bench near the door, then sits down to pull off his wet shoes. "You can leave yours on if you want," he says, when he sees I'm following suit. "These are soaked."

I shrug and put my shoes and backpack next to his bag. "I'm fine with socks."

Aaron opens a door to the right of the kitchen, tosses his sneakers into the washer, and adjusts the thermostat. The place is much more open than many townhomes I've seen. This floor is basically one big space, with a bar dividing the kitchen from the large living room.

"You want coffee?" he asks.

"So you *are* a mind reader."

"Not exactly—but I did notice you lusting after the Starbucks we passed." Aaron has spent a good deal of time in this kitchen, because he locates the coffee in one try. He seems more relaxed too, and flashes me a quick smile as he fills the pot.

Molly sighs.

That smile hasn't changed one little bit.

"Coffee would be nice," I say as a blur of gray fur whizzes past me and starts doing figure eights around Aaron's ankles. "But maybe you could answer—"

"Yes, yes. I know, Dax. Could you give me a minute?"

I get the feeling that the comment is aimed as much at me as at the hungry cat, and I guess my questions can wait until I'm fortified with caffeine. Curling into one of the wicker tub chairs arranged around the kitchen table, I stare at the scenery outside the sliding glass door. There's a wooded ravine just beyond the deck, with a small creek winding through it. I watch for a few minutes as the creek carries leaves and assorted debris toward a metal culvert about a hundred yards away.

The deck is a possible escape route if I need it. There was a bus stop a block or so back, and I think I could drop from the deck to the ground if I had to.

Jesus Christ, Anna! Would you just relax?

I don't know if it's the force of Molly's suggestion or a delayed stress reaction to nearly being shot, but I actually do feel myself starting to relax as my eyes follow the path of the leaves floating down the creek.

The sound of a mug being placed on the table in front of me yanks me back to the present. Dax the Cat is now eating out of a bowl near the refrigerator. Aaron is in the chair opposite me, with his own cup, a large bottle of Baileys Irish Cream, and a tin of shortbread cookies, which he pushes to the center of the table.

"No milk," he says, tipping a bit of the liqueur into his cup. "Would you like some of this instead?"

"I take it black. I'm not legal yet anyway."

He laughs. "Technically, neither am I—not until June. I've yet to see anyone get plastered on Baileys, though. I think you'd barf before you even came close."

I sip the coffee, which is still a bit too hot to drink, and take one of the cookies. "So . . . how did you *really* know about the van? And to call for an ambulance in advance? Because I'm not buying the story about how you happened to be hanging around and those guys looked suspicious."

"It would be so much easier if you *would* buy that story."

I just stare at him. He holds my gaze for a moment, then looks down at his mug, shoulders slumping.

"Sometimes, I . . . *sense* things. When there's going to be trouble. People planning violence, mostly, but occasionally it's more . . . vague. A bad vibe, a feeling that someone is in danger."

"You're saying you have *spidey sense*? Can you also shoot webs out of your wrist to swing from building to building?"

He raises an eyebrow. "No, Anna. I cannot. And I really can't believe I'm taking crap from the girl who speaks to dead people."

Now it's my turn to give him a questioning look. "First, I don't *speak* to them. It's more like they . . . hitch a ride for a while when they can't move on. When they have something they need to finish. And second, how do you know about *that*?"

He shrugs. "My grandfather was a cop in Silver Spring, but he started up his own detective agency a few years back. He and Porter were partners when he was on the force. They're still close. Porter's like family. And my brother is on the police force in DC now. Porter called a few weeks back, wanting us to check up on some crazy girl—his words, not mine," he adds when he sees my expression, "who was stalking him and claiming she was in contact with Molly's ghost."

A solemn look spreads over his face. "So, is it true? Molly's hitching a ride with you now?"

I nod, running my finger around the edge of my mug. "I'm not sure for how much longer, though. She needed to talk to Porter and we finally managed to do that this afternoon, so . . . I doubt she'll stick around."

"I don't suppose I could . . . talk to her?"

Molly surges to the front for a moment, then fades back before I can respond. She wants to talk to him, but she won't ask. Probably because she knows what my answer would be.

Aaron seems to know as well, so it must be written all over my face. "It's okay. It's just . . . I wanted to tell her I'm sorry I wasn't around. Maybe I could have sensed something in time to . . ." He trails off, shaking his head.

Tell him it's not his fault. Craig's fault, Lucas's fault, maybe even a little my mom's fault. My fault for not listening to Pa and staying home with him and Mimmy. But not his fault.

"She says you shouldn't blame yourself."

He looks up, surprised. "Just like that? You heard me, so *Molly* heard me?"

"Yeah. Two for the price of one, at least for the time being."

"What will happen when she . . . leaves?"

"I won't hear her thoughts anymore. But I'll know what she knew, or at least a lot of it. I can already feel it starting. I don't know how to describe it—sort of like there's a data dump going on in the background right now. If I seem sluggish, it's probably because part of my processor is working on another task."

"So you have memories that aren't yours? How many different sets?"

"Nine that I can remember, but I think there were a few others when I was younger and . . . maybe those memories didn't get processed very well. They're muddled, in the same way my own early childhood memories are. I'd probably have a lot more sets, but I've gotten better at protecting myself. Molly caught me at a weak moment, when my defenses were down. Hard to be on alert 24/7."

"How do you keep all of those lives straight?"

"Well, accessing their memories isn't quite the same as actually living through something, at least not after a while. I mean, about half of these people were married and had kids, but I don't think of their family as *my* family, you know? I remember how they felt about being married and about being parents, but it's more like a book I've read or a movie I've seen. Just a lot more vivid at first. Facts and skills I pick up from them seem to be a bit more permanent, but even they seem to . . . I don't know . . . *atrophy* a bit over time, especially if I don't use them." I take another sip of the coffee, then add, "And yes, I know how freaky it sounds."

He raises his hands in mock surrender. "Hey, the guy with spidey sense doesn't get to say other people's superpowers are weird."

The cat seems to be in a much mellower mood with a full belly. And it clearly lacks a sense of stranger danger, because all I get is one quick investigative sniff before it crawls into my lap and curls up, purring as I stroke its fur.

"It's *so* not a superpower. I never know when I'm going to pick someone up. They aren't always nice. It can take a very long time to make them go away. And when they do go . . ." A small shudder runs through me. "Well, let's just say that I have to process the bad memories, too. How they died. All combined, it makes it tough to lead a normal life. It makes you a freak."

Aaron's eyes are sympathetic. "I get it. Really, I do, Anna. Do you have any idea how many people in the average high school are actively thinking about punching, maiming, or murdering someone at any given moment? I mean, they don't usually *act* on it—ten minutes later they might even be friends again. But I spent most of ninth grade in a state of hyperalert, nervously watching the girl who was thinking about stabbing her rival with a nail file, or the guy who was thinking about pummeling me for *staring* at the girl with the nail file. Or the pissed-off teacher who was thinking how nice the vice principal's head would look mounted on his wall. I quit school at sixteen, over major objections from my mom, and took the GED. You could not pay me to walk back into one of those asylums."

"You'll get no argument from me. Unfortunately, I have to finish up two more classes this year before they'll let me es . . . cape."

How have I managed, in the space of a few minutes, to go from glancing around for possible exit routes to petting a sleeping cat while I chat with this guy I barely know about our shared freakdom? Especially when he hasn't answered several important questions.

I yank myself back on track. "You still haven't explained why you were watching the building today. Or how you knew about the van last week. I mean, you aren't picking up danger vibes at random from all over the Metro area, are you? Did Porter ask you to keep an eye out?"

"No. Porter doesn't even know about my premonitions. My grandfather knows. In fact, he's probably where I got it from, although he gets these . . . I guess you'd call them hunches, gut feelings, whatever. My dad did, too. And Taylor—she's my younger sister—she has . . . *something* going on herself. I'm surprised Molly didn't already know that about me, because anything my sister knew, Molly knew. They were really close, so you're probably going to get a lot of strange stories coming through once your 'data dump' is complete. My mom knows. My brother—technically, my half brother—he *knows*, but doesn't admit he knows, if that makes sense? He's kind of like Porter in that respect. Doesn't exactly embrace anything he can't pin a name on. Daniel just likes to believe that I'm really, *really* observant.

"And," he continues, "that's exactly what my grandfather tells people who hire us if they ask. He thinks people will be more comfortable with the idea that I'm freakishly attentive to details than with the notion that I can freakishly sense when someone's about to go medieval."

"You're a private detective?"

"Yeah. Although in Maryland, I'm technically a detective's *assistant*—too young for a license. Plus I generally try to stay well below the radar."

"So, you're sort of like a reverse Shawn Spencer? The guy on that show from a while back who claimed to be psychic, but he's really just seeing the stuff other people *could* see, if they paid closer attention?"

"Sort of."

"Do you have a cool black sidekick who's actually smarter than you and keeps you grounded in reality?"

He smiles. "You aren't the first to make the *Psych* connection. Taylor suggested Molly for the Guster role, before . . ." He clears his throat and continues. "But, no, I fly solo on investigations and then just hand whatever I find over to Sam. I'm . . . not exactly a people person."

"And who exactly is Sam?"

"My granddad."

"Oh. So, Porter hired you and your grandfather to watch me?"

"Nooo, not quite. First off, Sam would never take Porter's money. He's too close to being family. Ever since Molly's body was found, this case has been priority one for all of us. It isn't making us any money, but it's never been put on a back burner, and it won't be until we get the bastard. Sam did agree to do some checking around for him as a favor, though. Porter may have called other people who work in the area as well—you make a lot of connections when you spend thirty years as a cop. I don't know what his other friends came up with, but Sam asked Baker—the guy who was his partner after Porter retired—to give Porter your information." My expression must convey exactly how I feel about that, because he tacks on a sheepish, "Sorry."

Part of me wants to let him off the hook, but I stomp that part down without the tiniest shred of mercy. I'm not going to pretend I don't resent strangers poking around in my records even if their intentions may have been good. Now I'm wondering how much Aaron knows about my past. For that matter, what the hell is even *in* my record?

"Anyway," he says, after a few seconds. "I've been out of the area for the past few weeks. I was up in Philly, doing some surveillance, when I got the flash about the van."

I'm totally confused now. "But you said you only pick up on these things when you're in the vicinity. So . . . how?"

"The guy who hired the van—Franco Lucas—is the one I was watching in Philadelphia. I don't know how he knew about your connection to Porter. My first guess was that they had Porter's place bugged, but I searched it really well yesterday. It's clean. The only thing I can figure is that there's someone on the inside at one of the places Porter called, someone who was watching for any mention of this case. Whoever it is must have known that you told Porter you were in contact with Molly. I didn't pick up on exact facts—places, times, and so forth, but I knew Lucas was going to use the van to try and scare you away from Porter. And he clearly wanted you to think Porter was behind it. Otherwise, why leave the note?"

I nod. "But why did you have to be so cryptic? I mean, Deo and I were positive Porter was behind the entire thing, given that the call came in *before* the van nearly hit us."

"Would you have believed me?"

"Actually, yes—I would have. Molly wouldn't have given me any choice."

He twists his mouth to the side. "I didn't know for certain that you were channeling Molly. All I had to go on was what Porter and Sam told me. Believe it or not, there are actually jerks out there who will prey on people who are grieving."

He gives me a pleading look. "You understand, right? And then yesterday morning, I'm outside the apartment where Lucas stays when he's in DC, and it's like alarms going off in my head. Sam called Porter and asked him to stop by the office. I practically begged him not to go to this meeting. Told him I had a bad vibe about it. Sam even told him the same thing, and you'd *think* he'd listen to his former partner, especially when Sam's intuition kept his ass out of trouble so many times. But he's a stubborn old cuss."

"Ha! Tell me about it. It took me nearly a month to get through to him. And, to be honest, even if I *had* believed your warning, I'm not sure I could have kept Molly away from Porter much longer. Not if he was willing to meet. I mean, I usually have control in these situations, but Molly is as obstinate as her grandfather. She was determined to give him the information he needed to stop anyone else from ending up like she did."

"And did she?"

"She got him to believe *me*. That she's in here." I tap my head. "That was the important part. Molly seems to think I can take it from there. I give him the information she knew, and hopefully he finds her killer."

We're silent for a minute, and I tip back the last of my coffee. "So, this guy you were watching. Lucas. You think he's responsible for shooting Porter today?"

"I'm sure of it."

"Why?"

"Mostly because I don't believe in coincidence." He looks away as he says it, though, and something about his expression bothers me. He's hiding something. "Also, they'll probably assume you told Porter everything you know, which is why you're both on their radar now. The good thing is, someone will be watching out for him, at least for the next forty-eight hours or so, while he's hospitalized."

The word *hours* reminds me to check the clock. "Crap! It's after five and I forgot to call Deo." I get up and head toward the living room but turn back toward Aaron to ask, "So, if Lucas hired the van and was behind the shooting, where does this other guy, Craig, fit in?"

He's about to say something, but when I reach the end of the question, his jaw literally drops. "Graham Craig? How do you know about him?"

"I don't know if it's *Graham* Craig, but someone named Craig killed Molly."

He shakes his head, unbelieving. "And you're *sure* about that?"

I raise an eyebrow. "Yeah? I think Molly would have a pretty good idea who killed her. Who is he, anyway? And how is he connected to this Lucas guy?"

"I believe Graham Craig is a business associate of his. But I don't have proof yet. And believe me, it's going to have to be rock-solid proof before I talk to anyone outside the family about my suspicions. The guy's father is Ron Craig."

I shake my head. The name isn't ringing any bells.

"Ronald T. Cregg? C-r-e-g-g? Multimillionaire? Senator from Pennsylvania? Running for president?"

Oh.

CHAPTER FIVE

Deo answers immediately. "You are *so* grounded, young lady. I hope the party was worth it."

He keeps his tone light, but I can tell from the slight edge to his voice that he was worried.

"Sorry, Deo. We've had a lot to discuss, and the time sort of slipped away. Aaron is—"

I can hear Aaron talking on his own cell in the kitchen, and I hesitate for a moment. I rarely keep secrets from Deo, but I feel awkward telling him about Aaron's premonitions when it's not something Aaron tends to advertise. So even though I know I'll end up telling him later, when it's just the two of us, I decide to stick to Aaron's cover story for now.

"Aaron's a private detective. He's been working Molly's case, and he thinks whoever hired the guy who shot Porter is . . . well, shall we say he's not too happy that Porter and I have spoken. Aaron's worried they could be targeting me, too."

There's a long silence on the other end. "So . . . he's calling in the *real* police, right?"

His voice is steady, but those words speak volumes.

Neither of us have warm and cozy feelings about the local police. We've both been in situations where out on the street was safer than back in the house. Most of the time, at least in my experience, when a kid runs away from a foster home, there's a damn good reason. That's always been the case for me and Deo, at least. But each time, we've been rounded up by the cops and taken back to the place we escaped until some other arrangement could be made.

I *know* they're doing their jobs. In many cases, they even go above and beyond. But a lot of them don't seem to understand that the system they're enforcing isn't always fair and what looks safe may be just a convenient illusion.

So for Deo to even suggest calling in the police? He's *worried*.

"Um . . . that's kind of the tricky part, D. We don't know how they found out I was in touch with Porter. Aaron says Porter contacted the detective firm that his granddad runs, which is a two-person operation. But he also called friends on the DC force. Maybe elsewhere, too. There's probably a leak, but we don't know exactly where."

"They've already started sniffing around at Kelsey's. She called me about twenty minutes ago. Said she left a message on your cell, too. I don't know if it was DC police or Montgomery County, but they asked if she knew anything about a girl who might be stalking Porter. Didn't ask for you by name, but . . ."

"Oh, that's . . . wonderful. Do you know what she told them?"

"She didn't go into detail. Just asked if I knew who you were with. What do I say if she calls back?"

"Don't worry about it. I'll call her."

"And what about curfew? Pauline might cut us some slack, but Marietta's also on duty tonight, and you know how she is."

Deo and I have both toed the line carefully for the past few months, avoiding anything that might result in getting us bounced out of Bartholomew. Missing curfew is one of the cardinal sins, although, admittedly, Marietta has a long list of those. The primary reason she works in group homes is that it gives her the opportunity to save the souls of wayward teens. She marked Deo and me for special attention when we arrived at Bartholomew House, maybe hoping her congregation could pray away his possibly-gay. I'm not sure what she thought they could do for me. It's not the first time we've been in this situation—the group home where we met was even worse in that regard—but we've learned it's better to stand our ground. Neither of us has yielded to Marietta's weekly invitations to join her for Sunday services. Her smile becomes a little more wooden each time she asks and gets another set of excuses from the two of us. I'm seriously considering telling her I've converted to Judaism, Shinto, Pastafarianism—anything to get her off my back.

But my stubbornness on that front means the chance of Marietta cutting me even an inch of slack if I show up after curfew is less than zero.

Aaron is back in the living room. He sits on the edge of the chair across from me, still holding his phone to one ear. "Can Deo leave the group home? Go for a walk or whatever?"

I frown, not sure why he's asking me that.

"I mean, does he have to get permission, or . . ."

"No. He just signs out, but he has to be back by curfew."

He turns away and starts talking into his phone again. "Okay, Taylor. Just get him to the phone. You can do that. When has Daniel ever told you no?"

I hear a girl's voice, but it's competing with Deo's voice on my phone. He's still going on about Marietta, so I don't catch what the girl is saying.

"Thanks, Tay." Aaron holds his hand over the phone. "I'm going to try and get my brother to bring Deo here."

"No. Absolutely not."

But Deo heard Aaron, too. Even through the cell phone, his yes is nearly as loud as my no.

I glare at Aaron. "Deo, you're safe there. Someone *shot* at me today. For all I know they could have followed us here. They could be in the parking lot waiting to—"

Aaron is shaking his head. "We weren't followed. And he may be safer here than at the group home."

"You think they're watching Bart House?"

"I think it's possible. Lucas clearly knows who you are, so it's not unreasonable to think he might have someone waiting for you to show up. And Deo was there when the van nearly hit you, right?"

"Yes. But he'll make sure to stay in tonight. *Right, Deo?*"

"I was going to meet Asher at the game . . ."

"You can miss the game."

Compared to me, Deo is a social butterfly. He actually goes out on weekends when he gets the chance. He cares nothing about sports or school spirit, but he's made friends with a few kids in the marching band.

Aaron shakes his head. "I don't think staying in is enough. Lucas's people are armed. What's this Marietta person going to do if they . . ."

There's no need for him to complete the thought. Aside from Kelsey, Deo is the only person I'm close to. It would be perfectly reasonable for Lucas to assume that the best way to get to me is to grab *him*.

"And how is Deo any better off if Lucas's people show up here?"

He unzips his windbreaker. A brown leather holster, complete with pistol, is strapped to his shoulder.

Okay. Aaron said he was a detective, so I guess I should have assumed he carries a weapon. But if I'd known he was armed when I was in the car, I'd probably have risked jumping out on the freeway.

"It's not much," Aaron says, "but I'm guessing it's more than they have at your group home."

I steal another look at the gun, or rather at his side, since the windbreaker is once again hiding it from view. And as much as the sight of Aaron's pistol scares me, the sound of the bullet pinging off the dumpster earlier scared me even more. The idea that we have some means of self-protection is a good deal more comforting than I'd have imagined.

Aaron holds out his hand for my phone. I give it to him, even though it pisses me off to be cornered like this with no decent options.

Molly's been pretty quiet for the past hour, but as Aaron starts asking Deo for the address, she surges to the front.

Sorry, Anna. I didn't know that you and Deo—

The hell you didn't! What did you think would happen if Lucas discovered that I had information that could be used to nail him for murder? Not to mention human trafficking. Did you really think he'd stick up his hands and go peacefully?

Hey, I said I'm sorry! But none of this makes sense, Anna. Why is Lucas worried about you? Why wouldn't he just think what Pa did? That you're scamming him . . . that you're out to make money?

I'm all set to complain further, but I stop because she's just made an excellent point. And I'm going to ask Aaron to explain that as soon as he gets off the phone—or I guess I should say phones, since he's talking to Deo on mine and still has the other person on hold.

". . . about twenty minutes away. Daniel Quinn, he'll be in a blue Camry. Tall, midtwenties, short hair, pissed-off expression. Make him show ID. And if you see any unusual vehicles circling around the neighborhood before he arrives, get the hell out of there and call this number, okay?"

He tosses my phone back. I ask Deo to grab my sleep meds and tell him again to be careful.

When I hang up, Aaron says, "Just a heads-up that you're about to be knee-deep in family soap opera. I hate asking Daniel for help. But

Sam's at the hospital, Mom's on a buying trip in Europe until next week, and . . . on the off chance that someone actually *is* watching Deo, I'm not putting Taylor in the crosshairs."

"But it's okay to put your brother in danger?" I don't mention Deo, but I'm definitely thinking it.

"Daniel can take care of himself. It's just that . . . we had a bit of a disagreement last year. I haven't really spoken to him much since. We play nice when Mom is around, but—" Aaron cuts off abruptly. The voice on the other end of his phone is deep. I only catch a few scattered words, but it's abundantly clear that the man is angry.

Aaron's jaw clenches and unclenches a few times as he waits for a moment to jump in. "I don't need you to do anything in an official capacity. Just listen. Two minutes, that's all I'm asking."

". . . reason why I . . . ?"

"Because Mom would want you to! Because it has to do with Molly. I'd ask Sam to help, but his best friend got shot today, so he's kind of preoccupied. And, listen . . . I didn't tell Tay this, because I don't want to get her hopes up or for her to go talking to Mom about it. But this isn't only about Molly. I think it's tied to Dad, too."

There's a small explosion on the other end, and the few words I pick up are NSFW. Aaron's expression hardens and his voice is flat when he responds. "If you actually think I'd stoop low enough to bring Dad into this if I didn't believe it was true, then go ahead and hang up the phone. Because I've got nothing more to say to you, man."

For about five seconds, we simply sit there. I can't hear anyone speaking on the other end, but Daniel must say something, because Aaron's shoulders relax. "Thank you. He'll meet you in front of the school near the group house . . . Weller Road Elementary."

"This isn't a solution," I tell Aaron after he hangs up. "We miss curfew and we're screwed. They'll probably split us up again. Not a big deal for me. I'll be eighteen in two months. But Deo's got three whole years left in the system."

"Sam has friends who can fix things with the people at your group home. They'll say you and Deo were witnesses to a crime. He may not have been at Dr. Kelsey's office today, but attempting to sideswipe pedestrians with a van is a crime and he witnessed that, right?"

The best-case scenario is that Marietta will hear *witness to a crime* as *hanging out with criminals*. More likely, she'll interpret it as *committed a crime*. But there's probably little point going into that, when there are plenty of other things I need to ask Aaron.

"While you were on the phone, it occurred to me—well, actually, it occurred to Molly—that we're missing a big piece of the puzzle here. We get why Lucas might not want the murder case reopened, and why he might target Porter to prevent that. But why would Lucas—or this Graham Cregg guy—believe I have information that might help Porter?"

Aaron looks a bit uncomfortable. "Porter told pretty much every cop in the DC area that a teenage con artist was claiming to be in contact with his granddaughter's spirit."

"So what? Even people who've seen proof have a tough time accepting that I actually communicate with dead people. Why wouldn't they just assume I'm crazy?"

"But what if Porter's request landed in front of someone who was already watching you? Or, maybe not you specifically, but watching for people *like* you. Like me. People with psychic gifts."

For a moment, I just stare at him. "Oh . . . I see. Professor Xavier has spies on the police force who are planning to round up all of us mutants for his institute?"

Aaron rolls his eyes. "Hear me out, okay? What do you know about your parents?"

Asking me more questions isn't exactly the same as hearing him out. I don't know if it's the question itself or the prospect of having to rehash all of that for the second time in a matter of hours. Maybe it's just the fact that this has been one bitch of a day. Either way, his question annoys me. I kind of want to reach across the coffee table and smack him.

"Wasn't all that in my file?"

"I haven't *seen* your file. All I know is what Porter told Sam. That you'd been in a bunch of different foster homes. That you were stalking him, claiming you could channel Molly. Porter didn't believe you, obviously, but Sam and I warned him he shouldn't jump to conclusions."

"Why? Because your grandfather gets hunches and you have some sort of psychic abilities, do you automatically believe everything? Someone walks in your door saying she can torch the place using her mind, do you accept it as fact? Demons, vampires, werewolves? Sounds like a good idea for a TV show. Your partner is named Sam—are you sure your name isn't Dean?"

"Funny," he says, although he doesn't really look amused. "For the record, I've never seen any of those creatures. I doubt they exist. There are, however, plenty of psychopaths capable of mimicking any monster you can dream up. I've also never met anyone with pyrokinetic powers, or any sort of telekinesis, but I'm pretty sure my dad knew some when he was in the military."

"Really?"

"Yes. The government has been researching psionic abilities for *decades*, Anna. Did you ever hear of something called MK-ULTRA, run by the CIA?"

"The name rings a bell." I do a quick scan through my files from Bruno, the homeless guy who was a patient of Kelsey's. He never met a conspiracy theory that he didn't embrace with his entire heart and soul. Aliens, mind control, the Illuminati, you name it. Bruno spent a lot of time on the computers at the public library, combing through conspiracy theory sites and posting his own strange combo versions. I keep most of his memories in their own separate compartment, because I don't trust anything that Bruno "knew" until I fact-check it. "LSD, right? Government experiments with drugs to see what other powers the mind might have?"

"Yeah," Aaron says. "It continued through the midseventies, when a Senate committee closed it down. Or rather, they made it look that way. The efforts shifted over to a military program, called the Stargate Project."

"Why did they call it *Stargate*?"

"No clue. This was way before the TV series or even the movie. Anyway, the people involved lay low over at Fort Meade for fifteen, twenty years. Then in 1995, the CIA gets involved again. They conduct an investigation and close down the entire program, claiming it never yielded practical results. Except . . . I don't buy it."

"Why not?"

"A lot of reasons. For one thing, if you were the CIA and you wanted to cover up the fact that some program was getting results, what would be the best way to do it?"

I give him an *I've-got-nothing* look.

"You'd shut down the program. Say it was a waste of taxpayer money."

"Maybe . . ." He's actually starting to *sound* a little like Bruno.

Aaron stares out the window for a few moments. "I think my dad was in it."

He spends the next few minutes giving me an abbreviated version of his family history. How his dad, Cole Quinn, joined the Army fresh out of high school, then decided to take this civilian job over at Fort Meade. Sam wasn't too keen about his son taking the job. Part of it was a hunch, but the program also had some odd rules. Participants were under very restrictive security—they spent most of their time on post and couldn't get married or start a family.

Cole Quinn took the position despite his dad's objections. Said he wasn't planning on settling down for a few years anyway, and the money was really good. A few years later, though, one of Cole's colleagues, a guy named Ayers, went postal and killed a middle-aged couple down near Fredericksburg, then turned the gun on himself. The police wrote it off as random—the house was right off the interstate and there was no apparent connection between Ayers and the couple.

Only Cole Quinn knew better. He'd covered for Ayers on more than one occasion when the guy went down to Fredericksburg to visit his girlfriend and their son. She was former military, too, and they'd decided she and the kid should live with her parents for a few years until Ayers finished up his contract. That way, they'd have a nice nest egg built up. The plan was going well until Ayers shows up waving an assault rifle, screaming that the sun is bleeding. He'd have killed his girlfriend and the little boy, too, if she hadn't escaped with her son out the back.

"Based on some things Dad told Sam," Aaron says, "we think they were doing some sort of medical experiments. That's what caused Ayers to snap. The girlfriend contacted my dad a couple of days later, scared to death."

"Did he help her?"

"He did. And eventually fell into the same trap Ayers did." Aaron laughs. "Okay . . . that came out all wrong. I'm definitely not saying my mom was a trap."

"Your *mom*? So . . . that baby was Daniel? Your half brother?"

"Yeah. My mom and Daniel moved down to Richmond. Finished up school. When my dad quit the job at Meade, he joined us in Richmond . . . because Taylor and I were along for the ride at that point. Any program that wants to keep people in their twenties from having babies had better prevent it by medical means, because they'll find a way around any sort of contract."

Which is exactly what Aaron's parents did. They waited until about six months after the contract expired, then Cole joined the rest of the family down in Richmond. Eventually, they married, and Cole Quinn adopted all three kids, even though Taylor and Aaron were biologically his. When Aaron was about five, they moved back to Maryland so his dad could attend the DC police academy, and once he joined the force, they settled into normal happy family life out in the suburbs.

"Except," Aaron says, "Dad was always a little . . . erratic. Any time Taylor or I would do or say something that was . . . you know . . . abnormal? He'd lose it. He'd always apologize, but it never failed to set him off. Anyway, a couple of months before my sixteenth birthday, Dad started spending a lot of time at the library, and he'd come home with these stacks of computer printouts. Old newspapers, mostly. There was one about a congressional hearing. Claimed he was researching a cold case, but Mom wasn't buying it. They argued, and Dad stormed out. Said too many people had been hurt and he couldn't let Cregg start it up again."

"Start what up?"

"I'm still not positive. But three days after that argument, Dad, Taylor, and I were coming back from one of her soccer games. When we passed a car parked at the entrance to our street, I got one of the clearest vibes I've ever had. Whoever was in that car wanted my dad dead."

"Did they believe you? When you told them?"

"They . . . tried? I mean, no one said I was crazy. Even Daniel. Sam and I drove around the neighborhood, looking for the car. Couldn't find it, and after a couple of days, Dad goes back to work. Can't stay home forever, just 'cause your kid has a premonition. Two days later, he's checking out a stalled vehicle. The truck driver said Dad turned away from the car, looked straight at him, and stepped into the path of his truck. There was another witness who said the same thing, so . . . clear-cut suicide. The kicker, though? Taylor found a picture of the crime scene about a year ago. The stalled car was the same one I saw in my premonition. Mom says that's all it was, that I was tapping into the fact that a similar car would be at the scene when Dad died."

His eyes are red, like he's on the verge of tears. "But that's not how it works. I don't get *visions*. I don't see things before they happen. I hear someone planning to hurt or kill somebody. Even if the person they're thinking of hurting is themselves. I heard it from Mom half a dozen times in the year after Dad died. Even heard it from Taylor once. We lost Dad in 2015, and ten months later, Molly was gone, too. It was one bitch of a year. But *I never got* a suicide vibe from my dad. He visualized hurting Cregg plenty of times but never himself."

Aaron clearly believes what he's saying. But who'd want to admit his Dad committed suicide? That's an even worse kind of abandonment.

Which I guess brings us back to the question he asked me. "So, you think you have this whole spidey sense thing because of some job your father took before you were born? And that's why you're wondering about my parents?"

"Yes and yes. Listen, there are people everywhere with little glimmers of psychic ability. They never miss the bus, because they just *know* somehow which morning it'll show up five minutes early. They instinctively swerve seconds before a collision that might otherwise have killed them. Or they sense something is wrong with somebody they love hundreds of miles away. It's not common, but those people do exist. The thing is, I know of *three*, and that's not counting you and me, who have something that goes well beyond a little glimmer. One is Taylor. The other two also had a parent who worked either at Meade or at Fort Bragg down in North Carolina, which was connected to Stargate, as well. So, yeah—when Porter showed up saying some teenage girl claimed she was in touch with Molly's ghost, it *did* occur to me and Sam that there might be a connection."

I shake my head. "If there is, I wouldn't know. Someone left me in the food court at Laurel Mall. Security noticed an unattended toddler clutching a teddy bear in one hand and an empty Orange Julius cup in the other. Kelsey tried hypnosis, which has worked pretty well on me for . . . other things. All she got was fuzzy recollections about a beach and a woman with blonde hair. All I know about myself before that was on the note pinned to my dress: name, date of birth, and the very helpful information that I was possessed."

Aaron is silent for a few seconds. "That's . . . seriously messed up."

I've related these details to maybe a dozen people over the years, usually leaving out the bit about being possessed. By the end, most people have the same look of pity on their faces that Aaron is wearing right now, and I *do* understand. I'd probably look the same way if someone told me that story.

But it still bugs me a little, because I've heard much worse.

Deo always wears long sleeves, even in the summer, because he's got burn scars on his left arm from when he was a baby. They're not from an accident. Anyone can see they're cigarette burns. And someone gave him those scars before he could even *walk*. Before he could even tell anyone who hurt him.

That's my own personal definition of *seriously messed up*.

But that's Deo's secret, and I don't share it.

"Compared to some of the stories I've heard, I got off pretty light, Aaron. Claiming I was possessed was a little uncalled for, but they had good reason for believing it. And while they abandoned me, there's no evidence I'd been mistreated or deprived. No scars. Not every kid gets off that easy."

"Well, sure. I didn't mean . . ." Aaron sighs, then waits a moment before starting over. "Listen, I've seen a few nightmare cases myself in the past few years. But not all scars on the outside, right?" He holds my gaze. "I only meant it can't have been easy for you, being bounced around to different homes so many times. Without a family."

Molly sends a wave of smugness and something else I can't quite identify.

See. I told you he was a nice guy. I mean, really. Just look at him. Aaron would never hurt anyone.

I give Molly a firm shove backward.

"It's not so bad. Deo's my family. Kelsey, too."

I do consider Kelsey family, even though I can't say for certain she feels the same way. She has to maintain a professional distance, and I know she has her own family. Her husband died in a car accident years ago, but she has kids and grandkids nearby, and she used to spend weekends with her older sister on the Chesapeake Bay before the sister passed away last spring. But for me, the test of family is whether someone is really there when you need them. Even if it means going above and beyond, and maybe breaking the rules. Kelsey has come through time and again for both me and Deo. So she's family to me, regardless of whether the reverse is true.

"Speaking of Kelsey, I need to call her. Except I have no idea what to tell her."

As I pull out my phone, Aaron walks over to the messenger bag he stashed next to my backpack when we came in from the car. "You could just say you and Deo are in protective custody. Because of what happened to Porter. It's true. Sort of."

I don't respond, but I can't help thinking this is where I usually end up—hanging out with my old buddy, Selective Truth. "Could work. Better than anything else I can come up with. What are you looking for?"

He types something on his tablet. "Something for you to check out when you're done talking to Kelsey. Might answer your questions about the Stargate Project. I need to call Sam. See if he has any more news about Porter, and check in on some work-related items. You want more coffee?"

"Sure."

When I reach Kelsey, she's not happy that I can't give her more details. She's a pretty smart cookie, and she's spent enough time poking around inside my head to know when I'm hiding something. But near the end of the conversation, she backs off, possibly realizing that it might be better if she knows less, rather than more.

"As long as you're sure the two of you will be safe. You *are* someplace safe, aren't you, Anna?"

I glance over at Aaron, who's walked back into the kitchen as he talks to Sam. Between Molly's memories and my own take, I'm able to keep my voice confident. "Yes. We'll be safe."

"You'd better be," she says. "And call me tomorrow to check in, okay? Because I'm going to be worried until I know everything's back to normal."

I hang up without even mentioning my concerns that this situation will get us bounced from Bart House. Back when Emily MacAlister was hanging out in my head, anytime I was worried about something, she'd say, *Sufficient unto the day is the evil thereof.* That's apparently Bible speak for don't go borrowing tomorrow's troubles when you've got enough on your plate as it is, and I think my plate is overflowing already.

Aaron is still in the kitchen. Molly presses forward, straining to hear what they're saying, but I guess they've already discussed Porter and have moved on to other business, so I grab the tablet from the couch next to me. It's a YouTube video of a *Nightline* episode from 1995. Ted Koppel's face is instantly familiar, since Emily watched his show every night while working on her crossword puzzles.

Koppel first talks to a guy who swears his team was instrumental in helping to find a hostage being held in the Middle East through something called remote viewing. A few scientists chat back and forth about whether the program's successes are simply due to chance, then there's a panel with three men in suits. One is a former head of the CIA, Robert Gates. The others all claim to have worked in some capacity with the Stargate Project during the previous two decades. They seem to have a fundamental difference of opinion on whether psychics were of any use as spies, but all three concur that any future investigations should be handled *outside* the government.

Aaron is sitting across from me, reading e-mails or something, when I look up.

"So," I begin, "if what you think is true, all three guys in that last segment are lying through their teeth."

He nods. "Covering their tracks."

Would you ask him about Pa? I heard him talking in the kitchen, but you were on the phone with Kelsey, and—

I feel Aaron watching me, so I push Molly away.

In a minute.

"You were talking to Molly, weren't you? Your eyes get sort of . . . unfocused."

"Yeah," I snap, embarrassed. "I've seen myself on video. It makes me look stupid, but there's not much I can do about it."

"Hey. I didn't think you looked stupid. More like you were lost in a daydream. Sorry if I interrupted."

"No, it's okay. Molly just wanted me to ask about Porter."

"He's fine. He came out of surgery about an hour ago. Sam says he's stable and alert."

"That's good news!"

"I know. Sam was with him until about ten minutes ago, and Ella will stay overnight to help out."

I wrinkle my nose instinctively when I get Molly's memory of Aunt Ella.

Help out, my ass. Push Pa around and make everybody miserable is more like it.

Aaron laughs. "Okay, if I ever had any doubt that Molly's in there somewhere, your expression just erased it. Ella isn't her favorite person."

Ella isn't anybody's favorite person, except maybe her own. If she'd kept some of her opinions to herself maybe Mama wouldn't—

Chill, okay?

I feel a little guilty as I push Molly to the back again. I'm not trying to be insensitive, but carrying on a normal conversation while an extra person's ranting inside your skull isn't easy.

I want to ask Aaron more about how he thinks this Graham Cregg fits into the picture, but something outside the window catches his eye. He goes to pull the curtain aside. The parking area looks pretty much the same as before, except it's twilight now. And there's a pale-purple Jeep parked at the curb.

"Damn it, Tay!"

He doesn't explain further, just opens the front door.

At first glance, I think the girl is younger than Deo, but when she turns toward me I see that she's about my age. She's short, five one, maybe less. The green sweater she's wearing is so long her skirt barely peeks out at the bottom. Her face is heart-shaped, framed by a dark-auburn asymmetrical pixie cut. She looks like a cross between Peter Pan and Tinker Bell.

I get a surge of emotion from Molly that's nearly as strong as when she saw her grandfather.

"What are you doing here?" Aaron asks. "I told Daniel—"

"Well, hello, Aaron!" Taylor's voice is rich with sarcasm. "It's wonderful to see you, too, big bro."

He sighs, then gives her a quick hug and a kiss on the forehead.

"That's better." She flashes him a very brief, very grim smile. "I'm here to tell you that Daniel is on his way."

"I know that. He's picking up Deo."

Taylor shakes her head. "Nope. Deo wasn't there. When Daniel didn't see him, he drove by the address you gave him and there was a police officer—Baker, actually—leading the kid out to his car."

"What!" I cross over to the doorway and start tugging on my shoes. "Why?"

She ignores my question, although I guess maybe she wouldn't have the answer.

"And how do you know all of this, Taylor?" Aaron asks.

"Followed him. And then . . . sort of passed him. He doesn't know, although I'm guessing he'll have a pretty good idea when he pulls up and sees me here."

Outside the still-open door, the very conspicuous Jeep sits at the curb. If she followed someone in that, it's hard to believe he could fail to notice.

I sling my backpack over my shoulder. "I have to go get him, Aaron. Will you take me or should I head for the bus stop?"

Taylor looks at me for the first time, her expression unreadable. "Is Molly really in your head, like Aaron says?"

"Yes."

"Then tell her I said to piss off."

Molly recoils both at the words and the venom in Taylor's voice.

"Taylor," Aaron says reproachfully. "Come on, that's not fair."

I glance back and forth between the two of them. "But . . . I thought you and Molly were best friends."

"So did I!" Taylor is directly in front of me now, and she's a little intimidating, even though I'm a good three inches taller. "But best friends *tell* you when they have a problem. They don't sneak off in the middle of the night without saying good-bye. Best friends ask for help.

They don't do something so incredibly, unbelievably stupid that they get themselves killed."

Another car has pulled up to the curb, right behind the Jeep.

I was trying to help my mother! Anna, tell her, please. I didn't know—

But I don't get a chance to relay the message, because Taylor is headed back over to Aaron, who is having a heated conversation with the guy at the door. The newcomer—Daniel, I guess—towers several inches over Aaron, making his brother look short, even though Aaron is probably close to six feet himself. I wouldn't have guessed Daniel was related to Aaron and Taylor by appearance.

Daniel has lighter hair, with deep-set brown eyes and a more muscular build. His skin has a slightly weathered look, like he's spent a lot of time in the sun. From what Aaron said, Daniel must be twenty-four or twenty-five, tops, but he seems older.

". . . occurred to you that you took a witness away from the scene of the crime?" Daniel's voice is deep, a full octave below his brother's.

"Obviously it occurred to me. But I'm more worried about keeping two kids away from the people who shot Porter. And finding out who killed Molly."

All three of them are talking at the same time now, which makes it impossible to follow what they're saying. At this point, I don't really care. Kelsey will help me get Deo out. They can't hold him. He hasn't done anything wrong.

And I know he must be terrified. Our last encounter with the police resulted in Deo being returned to a privately administered foster home run by a couple one county over, a home he'd had very good reasons for leaving. The police were just doing their jobs by returning him, and one of them also did her job by reporting Deo's claim of abuse. Kelsey pushed on that front, too. Thanks to the two of them, those creeps aren't in the foster system anymore, and Deo eventually ended up at Bart House. But he was with those people for another two weeks, and they were pissed off about the increased scrutiny. Deo had bruises to prove exactly *how* pissed off they were, so I can't blame him for not having warm fuzzy thoughts about the police.

Daniel now has Taylor by the upper arm and is steering her toward the door. "Mom has called home every night this week between six thirty and seven. That gives you maybe half an hour to get to the house and answer the phone. Because if she calls my cell to ask where you are, I can promise that I'll be mentioning you used her *work vehicle* to follow me on police business."

I wonder what sort of job their mother has that requires her to drive a Jeep that looks like it's been dipped in grape Laffy Taffy.

"She lets me use it as long as I take the sign off," Taylor says, jerking her arm away. "And you weren't actually on police business."

"Do you think she'll like the fact that you were following me? Or that I saw you pulling out after I did, and yet you beat me here by what? Five minutes? Get home or I *will* tell her."

"He's right, Tay." Aaron seems reluctant to agree with Daniel. "You shouldn't be here."

Taylor gives him an annoyed look, but her eyes really flash when she locks onto Daniel. "Are you sure you want to start threatening to tell secrets, Dan Quinn? Because I can play that game, too."

They're both focused on her right now, and I doubt there will be a more opportune moment for me to get the hell out of here.

Wait! You can't—

I ignore Molly. That's much easier to do now that my brain is occupied with worrying about Deo. My eyes fall on the Jeep, still running, but it doesn't seem like a smart idea to head to the police station in a stolen vehicle, especially one that conspicuous. The bus stop is about a block away. I'll call Kelsey from the bus and—

I don't even make it off the stoop before Daniel hooks his arm around my waist and yanks me backward. "Oh, no, you don't."

He grunts when the heel of my shoe connects with his shin, but doesn't let go until I'm inside. The last thing I see before the door closes is Taylor, stomping off to her vehicular monstrosity.

Daniel tosses me onto the couch, then sinks into the armchair, rubbing his leg. "You've got a wicked kick."

"Yeah? Touch me again, and you'll have a lawsuit on your hands in addition to the bruise."

"Damn right!" Aaron says. "And I'll back her up."

Daniel tosses Aaron an annoyed glance, then looks at me again. "I'm sorry, okay? But if what Aaron says is true, you and your friend could be in danger. When I saw Baker outside your group home, I told him I knew where you were. That I'd bring you to the station. If you cooperate, maybe they'll ignore the fact . . ."

His mouth is still moving, but I don't hear the words. There's a strange feeling of pressure just behind my forehead, and my teeth clench so tightly that my vision blurs. I close my eyes and make a conscious effort to relax my jaw. What the hell is Molly doing?

Stay back! I've got enough to deal with right now.

Hey, that wasn't me.

When I tune back in, Aaron is once again yelling at Daniel, but Daniel is staring at me. He seems puzzled.

". . . even more danger if the leak is from their office," Aaron shouts.

"Except there's *no leak!*" Daniel pulls in a deep breath, then lowers his voice and continues in a softer tone. "I know you're trying to do the right thing, Aaron. So am I. Porter was talking about this to

everybody. Baker said he got someone to post a POI—person of interest—notice on the department website last week, asking if anyone
else had been victimized by a couple of teens claiming to be in touch
with relatives of murder victims. He even posted something in one
of the police-sponsored community discussion groups day before
yesterday, asking people to call him if they had any information on
her identity."

"Why? He *knew* my identity. He had my phone!"

His brow creases, but he looks back at Aaron. "My point is that
there was nothing to leak with Porter screaming all over town. You want
to see the ads, then follow me when I take Anna to the station and I'll
print you out a copy. We're on the same side here. We just need to work
through the proper channels."

"Let's just go," I tell Aaron, pointedly ignoring Daniel.

But Aaron's still not convinced. "Porter was shot in Wheaton. The
van that nearly sideswiped them last week was over near Glenmont
station. Both in Montgomery County. If Baker's so worried about
going through the proper channels, shouldn't they be questioned by
the county police?"

Daniel is quiet for a minute. Then he says, "Montgomery County
may be saying Porter's shooting was a drug deal gone wrong. But
Baker seems to agree with you . . . He thinks it could be connected to
Molly and Laura's case. From what Porter told us, it's pretty clear that
Anna knew Molly. Since that case is a double homicide, with possible
human trafficking added on, I think we can justify bringing them in
for questioning." He turns and looks at me directly. "I'm sure Anna
won't mind—"

The pressure hits me again right at the temples. It's not painful,
just intense.

Molly says it's not her before the thought is even fully formed.

"It's up to you," Aaron tells me.

Yeah, you're damned right it is. It might not be fair to be annoyed at both of them, when Aaron has gone out of his way to take my side. But I'm tired of people trying to make decisions that should be mine to make. All I really want right now is to get Deo and get back to Bart House.

"I'll go. That's actually where I was heading when . . ." There are several names I want to call Daniel. But since I might actually need the jerk's help in getting Deo home, I bite them all back. "When your *brother* yanked me back into the house. If he wants to give me a ride, that's fine with me. Saves me the bus fare."

CHAPTER SIX

The blue-white glare of the old-style fluorescent light above us isn't helping my headache. Neither is the faint buzz the damned thing is emitting, or the annoying thought that it's probably the ballast, and it wouldn't cost much at all to fix. Not sure which former tenant left that bit of info behind. Probably Abner, but I'm too nervous to sort it out.

A uniformed policewoman walks in a few minutes after Daniel and I enter the room. Aaron followed us to the station, but he's apparently not allowed back here in the sanctum sanctorum.

The policewoman parks herself at the small table by the door. "Thought you quit, Quinn."

"I did. Just doing this as a favor to Baker."

"Cop life too tough for you?"

"Can't all be supercops like you, Lupito."

We sit there for well over an hour. The female officer isn't paying much attention to either of us, just typing on the small tablet she brought in with her. I'm pretty sure she's only here because I'm a minor and a female, and they want to cover the department against any possible claims of impropriety.

I called Kelsey on the ride over, and she wanted to come down to the police station. But I told her there really wasn't anything she could do, at least not yet. She asked if I needed an attorney. I said no, but the longer I sit here the more I'm beginning to wonder if that was true.

But calling her back to change my response isn't an option. "Coverage sucks in your interrogation cells."

Daniel shrugs. "Not an interrogation cell, Anna. We're waiting on Baker, so he can ask you some questions."

"Why can't you ask those questions?"

"It's Baker's case. And as of yesterday, I'm no longer an active officer."

"But . . . didn't you just join?"

He shrugs. "Decided I'm not cut out for civilian life. I'm just here to keep you company. Make sure you don't do anything stupid."

My expression must tell him exactly what I think of that, because he laughs and says in a lower voice, "Listen, Baker's a good guy, but you need to give it to him straight. None of this psycho mumbo jumbo you told Aaron and Porter. He's not interested in whatever petty scam you guys had going, as long as you give him information on Lucas. Just tell him you met Molly at the shelter, and you were hoping Porter would pay for the info."

"Since you know all of the answers, why don't I just leave and—" I stop suddenly, as an odd tingly sensation moves across my head. Almost like Pop Rocks are going off just below my scalp.

Whoa. Feels like taking a diet pill and a couple of Sudafed at the same time. Sort of like your skin is a low-level mosquito zapper.

The thought doesn't come from Molly. It's just another one of those stray scraps of memory left behind by a mental roommate. I know this one immediately. Arlene Bennett, paralegal, mother of two, and a hypochondriac who had an unfortunate (and fatal) tendency to mix her meds.

"You okay?" Daniel asks.

"No. I have a very weird headache."

Daniel doesn't respond. He just looks annoyed, like I'm being difficult.

"I'm terribly sorry if my headache inconveniences you."

"I'll get you some Tylenol after you talk to Baker. He should be here any minute, so relax." He gives me one last look, then slides down in his chair, legs out in front of him, and closes his eyes like he's going to nap.

"And you can't let me see Deo while we wait?"

"Deo is fine. You'll see him later."

His tone is so very patronizing that I toy with the idea of kicking his feet out from under him, so I can watch him go splat on the floor.

Do it. I'd like to see his face. Daniel always did think he was in charge.

Yeah. I can see that. But there's a cop in the corner and probably hidden cameras in the room, so no. You'll just have to rely on your imagination.

Or . . . I can rely on memory.

She sends me a mental flash of a lanky kid about Deo's age, drenched, furiously shaking partially melted snow from his head and torso.

We rigged it to fall on his head, and boy was he pissed! Taylor said he . . .

Molly doesn't finish the thought, and I can tell from her little sigh that she's shifted to thinking about what Taylor said a few hours ago, rather than what she said a few years ago.

I don't think Taylor meant what she told you, Molly. She was just angry.

Yeah. I know that. But I also know she's right.

Molly slides back. After a few minutes of listening to the fluorescent light buzz and watching Daniel Quinn take his stupid power nap, I open my phone, and since I can't access any of my usual networked games, I take out my frustration on Fruit Ninja. It's kind of liberating to pretend that the pieces flying across the screen are Daniel's head, Aaron's, Porter's. Even Molly's. Deo and I were doing just fine until I picked her up.

When the door swings open a few minutes later, I mentally run through my earlier conversation with Daniel. Didn't he say Baker was a *guy*?

The person who just entered the room has very short dark hair, but that's about the only thing about her that's even remotely masculine. A burly man follows her into the room, and I think maybe *he's* Baker, but he steps forward to take the coat the woman is shrugging off her shoulders. He folds the coat neatly across his right arm and steps back against the wall without waiting for her to remove her gloves. While I doubt coatrack is the man's only function, it does seem to be one element in his job description.

Her trim bottle-green suit looks expensive—too expensive for a cop—and more like something you'd wear to a dinner party than to work. And she's young, midtwenties at most. Below her short skirt is a pair of very long legs, and below that, a pair of matching stilettos that give me vertigo just looking at them. Deo would swipe those shoes out of her closet in a heartbeat. The uniformed policewoman slips outside, and Daniel, who must have actually dozed off, stumbles to his feet, confused. "Where's . . . What happened to Baker?"

The woman peels the glove from her right hand. "Baker will be along shortly. Dacia Badea." I'm not sure I'd have recognized the words as a name, but she steps forward to shake his hand as she speaks. Her eyes are almost level with Daniel's and her voice is smooth, pleasant, with an accent that seems Eastern European. She flashes him a glimpse of something—a badge, maybe. "You look . . . familiar. We have met?"

Daniel's face goes pale for a moment, but he recovers quickly, giving her a slightly wolfish grin. "No, ma'am. I'm certain I'd have remembered *you*. I get that a lot, though. I guess I'm kind of generic looking, aside from these green eyes."

Green? I lean forward to get a better look, because I could have sworn his eyes were brown.

The woman's forehead creases momentarily, and she rubs her hand across it. Her frown vanishes, almost as if the motion smoothed away her concern. "Yes. The other man, his eyes are dark like . . . like chocolate. And he has no beard. It was the dim light, perhaps."

I wouldn't exactly call Daniel's light scruff a beard. It's barely even a five o'clock shadow. But whatever interest the woman had in him has vanished.

"You will be so good as to wait outside," she says, and there's no question that it's an order and not a request. "This will not take long."

"I . . . I was told that Baker would be questioning her."

"After I finish. I have places to be."

Daniel nods. As he leaves the room, I feel Molly sliding forward, alert.

What is it?

There's a brief pause before Molly answers.

Nothing. She reminds me of someone, but . . .

Molly slides back quickly, and I'm glad, because the woman is staring at me now. I rise from the chair as she holds out her hand.

"I am Dacia Badea," the woman repeats. Her smile is warm, and it lights up her entire face, including her sky-blue eyes. "You must be so frightened. Why did they not put us in a room less . . ." She looks around and shudders as she shakes my hand. "Horrible? And warmer! It is so cold."

It doesn't really seem that cold to me, but I nod. She's clearly trying to put me at ease, and I might as well let her think she's succeeding, even though she isn't. For one thing, that Pop Rocks sensation is back, spreading in a narrow band across my forehead. It moves more rapidly this time, and it's more intense. And I can also feel Molly muttering in the background, like she's still trying to figure out why this woman seemed familiar.

But I push all of that aside and focus on the Badea woman. I need to figure out why she's here and what she wants.

"You must wonder why I am here and what I want."

Okay, *that's* creepy. Really, really creepy.

But . . . it's just coincidence. Right? I mean, obviously, that's what I'm wondering. It's what anybody would be wondering in my situation.

Careful, Anna.

Shh.

I don't get the sense Molly has any information beyond that whispered caution, and having an extended chat with her while this woman is watching seems unwise.

"Yes, I *was* wondering that." I return her smile, although I'm pretty sure mine isn't as convincing. "I was expecting Detective Baker. Or, I guess he's a detective . . . I don't really know."

"The police will have questions to you later. But here is the thing with bureaucracy . . ." She says the word *bee-rokratzi*, and it takes me a moment to figure it out. "Always there is a pecking order. My employers are high above District police. This can be good news for you if you are wise. He can make all of this disaster go . . ." Ms. Badea makes a little poof gesture with her hand, blowing an imaginary something off the tip of the still-gloved fingers of her left hand.

I find it odd that the *employers* she mentioned are now a single man—*he can make all of this disaster go . . . poof.* But maybe it's just a language thing.

"That's nice to know, Ms. Badea."

"Please, I am Dacia."

Molly stirs again, uneasy.

Dacia takes the seat that Daniel vacated a few moments ago and motions me to the chair on the other side of the table. "You and your friend—his name is Taddeo, right?—are not in trouble. We just want information."

My stomach tightens when she says Deo's name, but I nod. "Okay. But I don't know what I can offer."

"Anna, Anna. Such modesty!"

Her expression shifts. It's a subtle change, but in that instant, I have no doubt what's coming next. It's what I've feared since I was six, sitting in Kelsey's chair, when she explained why I could never tell other people what I can do. Why I needed to pretend. Why I needed to find a way to keep my secrets safe.

This woman *knows*.

Her smile barely flickers, but there's a hint of victory, the barest whiff of *gotcha* in her eyes, as she takes my hand again. I don't like people touching me, and I start to pull away, but her grip tightens. "We have reason to believe you are a special young lady with an . . . *unusual* talent. And we are very interested to develop gifts like yours—"

A tiny frown crosses Dacia's face. That tingle starts again, directly above my ear, moving right to left.

She's causing it. I don't know how she's doing it or exactly what she's doing, but it's definitely her.

I have a vivid memory of Kelsey kneeling in front of me, her eyes level with my own six-year-old face, trying to impress upon me the importance of what she was saying. *You can't keep all of your secrets bottled up inside or they'll hurt you. They'll scream to get out and make you miserable. But some secrets aren't for sharing outside this room. Not if you want to be safe. Not if you want your life to be your own. You need to keep your wall up when you're around strangers, Anna.*

I spent many hours in Kelsey's office, stacking up those bricks in my mind, walling off the unsafe corners. Practicing over and over until I had a way to keep my hitchhikers from taking control, and to keep me from doing and saying stupid things that would land me back in a psychiatric ward. I also learned to unstack those bricks, and let out the things that frightened me so that we could examine them. But only when I was in Kelsey's office, where it was safe. And later, sometimes with Deo.

My wall is up even before it's a conscious thought. It's just a mental exercise, something to keep me feeling as though I'm in control of the situation, even when I'm not. But years of practice have made it second nature.

The tingling sensation pauses at the center of my right eyebrow. Probing. I can almost feel Dacia jabbing at my mental bricks, trying to find a chink in the wall, a place where she can get through to whatever secrets I'm hiding.

I snatch my hand out of her grasp and focus on building another wall in front of the first one. The tingle dissipates, almost like a thread pulling out of my skin.

Her eyes narrow. "You said you would cooperate!"

I keep my face blank and focus on my imaginary wall, in case she's prepping for another go at it. "You haven't asked me any questions."

Dacia stares at me, her composure clearly shaken, and nervously glances at the guy who came in with her. She focuses on smoothing her skirt over her thighs for a couple of seconds, and I lean back in my chair, waiting. I'm beginning to suspect she wasn't actually prepared to question me. She was counting on just poking around in my head to find out what she wanted to know, but now she has to figure out what to ask.

"How did you . . . how were you introduced to . . . Molly Porter? And when?"

"I met her at the U Street shelter." That's the last bit of the full truth this woman will be getting, but I try to weave in a few half-truths to help me remember the story I'm telling. "About three years ago. I don't remember the exact date. Molly taught me how to play a song on the piano. I think she was there with her mother."

Dacia nods, and again looks at the bodyguard or whatever he is, still standing near the door with her coat over his arm. Pretty sure he's military or ex-military. He's at attention, staring straight ahead at a spot on the wall, his face blank. It's odd that his presence didn't make her at all nervous when she came in. If anything, I'd have said the opposite. So I can only assume she doesn't like him being here as a possible witness to her failure to pick my brain.

"And why did you tell Molly's grandfather you were in contact with her . . ." She frowns, like she's searching for the word. "Her phantom . . . her spirit?"

I shrug. "I explained that to him already. Molly left her diary at the shelter. I read it, but I forgot to take it with me when I left. Later, I realized he might have paid for it. I'm almost eighteen and I'd like a little bit of a financial buffer when I head out on my own. I don't make much at the deli. Anyway, it occurred to me a few months back that her granddad might pay for the information, even if I didn't have her diary. And he might pay more if he thought he could actually *talk* to her through me, you know? If he thought part of her was still around."

"And this journal . . . what did it say?"

"Nothing really. Just stuff about how she missed her grandparents, but her mom needed her more. That she was trying to convince her mom to go back home. And odds and ends that she remembered from when she was a kid."

She sniffs. "Did you really believe the man would pay you money for that?"

"I thought it was worth a try."

Dacia tips her head slightly to the side. Her elbows rest on the arms of the chair, and her hands, one gloved and one not, are folded in front of her face, except for the pointer finger that taps softly at her bottom lip. She must be trying to read my face, since she's failed to read my mind.

"You are not telling me everything, Anna. I think you are still in contact with Molly."

"You believe she's still alive? I was told they found her body."

Dacia stares at me. "You know that is not my intention . . . my *meaning*."

"Well, I hope it's what you meant, because otherwise, you're crazy. Listen, I'm not proud of what I did to Mr. Porter. That's why I asked him to meet me at my therapist's office. I wanted to apologize. He said he wasn't going to press charges, so I don't understand why Deo and I were brought in."

"You have history of this." Her voice is more strident now. "This saying you contact phantoms. Since you are a small child."

The Emily MacAlister part of me really wants to correct her—*you mean since you were a small child, don't you dear?* But I resist. She seems increasingly agitated. In fact, I can't see where any of this could be leading, except to a jail cell or psych ward.

"I'm not saying anything more to you or to anyone else until I have legal representation."

"Like I tell you before, the people I work with can make your problems go away. But also they can complicate your life. My employer, he is very busy right now, and he is not patient."

"That's a shame. I've heard patience is a virtue." I get up from the chair. "I'm going to tell the officers that I won't be saying anything else without an attorney."

As I move toward the door, she pulls me back, twisting my arm so that I have to look at her. That little *poke-poke-poke* begins at the edge of my mind again, as her eyes bore into mine. She's focusing so hard that I can see a vein twitching at her temple.

Several emotions flit across her face once she finally accepts that my wall isn't going to come tumbling down. Frustration, anger, and maybe a touch of fear. She masks them quickly and pastes on a smile, but it's not nearly as broad and confident as it was when she first entered the room. I get the feeling that smile is more to impress the guard who accompanied her than anything else.

"No problem, Anna," she says, releasing my arm. She crosses over to the guard, who's holding out her coat, and slips her arms into the sleeves. "You've given me all I need. We'll be in touch."

It pleases me to see her wobble slightly on her too-high heels as she turns to leave. But my satisfaction vanishes quickly when I realize that her guard or assistant or whatever is looking directly at me for the first time since they came in. He doesn't say anything, just gives me a long, slightly puzzled look before following Dacia into the hallway.

I slump down into a chair at the table and rest my head on my folded arms. But I don't let my walls down. I can't, at least not for a while. If I was able to feel Dacia poking at my mind back at the townhouse, when she was—or at least I assume she was—miles away, then I'm not sure when or where it will be safe to let down my guard.

Sorry, Molly.

I have no clue if she can even hear me.

A few minutes later, the door opens.

"Stay here," Daniel says. "I'll be back."

As if I actually have a choice.

The next time the door opens, Deo is with Daniel. Deo is dressed in various shades of blue today, with blue streaks in his dark hair, and he's wearing the silver-and-turquoise ear cuff I bought him last Christmas. His face doesn't reveal that he's upset, but his hair is mussed, with a few strands sticking out at odd angles from his usually impeccable quiff. If Deo hasn't bothered to find a mirror, or a window, or even a shiny doorknob to make sure his hair looks right, then he's not in a good state of mind.

"I'm sorry," I whisper as I hug him. "I didn't know this would happen."

"Not your fault. Let's just get out of here."

"I don't think we can. This Baker guy—"

"No," Daniel interrupts. "He won't be questioning you now. We've been ordered to return you to Bartholomew House."

"Ordered . . . by whom?" I ask.

"Someone way the hell above Baker's pay grade," Daniel mutters, shoving two white capsules and a paper cup into my hands.

I'm a little surprised that Daniel followed through on the promise of Tylenol. I wash the pills down with the water, then follow him into the corridor.

As we approach the front desk, I see the uniformed cop who was in the room with us, holding a Big Gulp in one hand and a sandwich in the other. She's just taken a chomp out of the sandwich when she spots us.

Beyond them, I see Aaron in the lobby. He jumps up from his seat to join us, grabbing his phone and a sheet of paper lying on the bench next to him.

"Are you okay?" he asks in a tight voice. When I nod, he turns to Daniel. "The woman who just left. Who was—"

Daniel makes a kill motion and nods toward the exit. "We'll talk outside, okay? Need to take care of something first."

Aaron looks like he wants to argue. Actually, he looks like he wants to hit someone or something.

The uniformed cop gives Aaron a flat stare. It apparently convinces him to follow Daniel's advice.

"He all right?" she asks Daniel softly, nodding toward Aaron's back as he heads out the door. "Looks like he's on somethin' to me."

Daniel laughs. "Nah. Aaron's just had a rough day. He saw Porter—" He stops, apparently rethinking what he was about to say. "He saw Porter this morning. An hour or so before he was shot. Kind of has him worked up."

She nods, takes another bite of her sandwich, then starts to wrap it up. Daniel puts a hand on her shoulder.

"Go ahead and finish your dinner, Lupito. I'll take them. Just need to get their things."

"Uh . . . no," she says around a mouthful of food. She pauses to swallow. "You heard that woman. She said for *me* to take them."

"The girl here is on an antipsychotic, which she left at my brother's place. We'll run by and pick up her meds, then I'll drop the two of them off."

I have no idea what he's talking about. So I keep quiet, even though the antipsychotic comment, when I'm standing right *here*, makes me want to kick him again.

Lupito shakes her head and talks extra slowly, as if Daniel is mentally impaired. "You don't even work here anymore."

"You know they're not being charged with anything. They could walk out the door and hail a cab if they wanted. We'll pick up her meds and I'll have them back before their curfew. I'll catch up with Baker later. Just tell him you were in the can when we left."

"Hmph. Your funeral," she says as she slips into a small office on the other side of the desk. When she returns, she has my smaller backpack and the larger bag that Deo packed when he left Bart House. "Here you go. And you owe me one."

"Thanks, Lupito." He grins, but his smile evaporates before the door even closes behind us.

Aaron is at the edge of the parking lot, still on the verge of exploding. "Who was that woman?" he asks when we reach him. "And what did you do to make her want to rip your head off?"

That question is for me, but Daniel doesn't give me a chance to answer it. "Call Sam. Tell him to meet us at the office. *Python*."

Daniel emphasizes the word, and judging from the look on Aaron's face, it means something to the two of them aside from snakes, computer programming, or British comedy. Aaron nods and then gives me an apologetic glance before darting off in the other direction—toward his car, I guess. I'd much rather ride with him, but Deo and I apparently don't get to choose our mode of transportation.

"I'm *not* on antipsychotics," I say as we follow Daniel. "The only thing I take is sleeping meds, and I don't even have them with me."

Daniel pulls a bottle out of his jacket pocket and tosses it to me.

I stop under the streetlight at the edge of the parking lot and hold it up so I can read the label. Sure enough, it's my prescription. "How did you get this?"

"He confiscated it from my bag," Deo growls. "Along with the pepper spray and the other . . . thing . . . we carry sometimes."

By which he means one of my old kneesocks filled with pennies.

"What the . . ." I stop and stare at him. "You were supposed to toss those out, D!"

I'll be the first to admit that the spray and the sock both came in handy during the weeks Deo and I were sleeping in culverts or under bridges. There was one night in particular where I don't even want to think what might have happened if I hadn't pulled that spray out of my pocket when two men sneaked up on us in the middle of the night. But Deo knows as well as I do that we're not supposed to have stuff like that at Bartholomew House. Or, technically, at *all*, given that we're both minors.

Daniel sighs. "Could we just get to my car before Baker stops us?"

We pick up the pace, and once we're walking again, Daniel tells Deo, "The medicine is a controlled substance, not prescribed for you. I was simply making sure it was returned to its owner. And Baker could have written you up for the pepper spray if you'd had it on you. Just so you know."

"Pretty sure there's no law against keeping pennies in a sock."

"Shh." I squeeze Deo's arm, as we slide into the backseat of the sedan.

Daniel walks around to the driver's seat, and Deo whispers, "Grabbed the meds from your room, along with a change of clothes. I stuffed those other things inside the lining of my bag when I first got to Bart House . . . in case we ever needed to get out of there quickly. I forgot they were even *in* the bag when I grabbed it."

"It's okay."

"What happened in there, anyway? Who was that woman?"

Daniel looks over his shoulder and catches my eye as he backs the car out of the parking space. "I'd kind of like to hear the answer to that first question myself. She had Baker turn off the cameras before she spoke to either of you."

"I'll answer his first question after you answer the second one. Who—" I stop abruptly and look over at Deo. "Wait. She talked to you, too?"

"Well, not really. She shook my hand. Asked me my name. And asked me how I knew Molly. I didn't tell her anything, though. Said I didn't even know anyone named Molly. I don't know if she believed me or not. She just watched me for a minute, then smiled and closed the door. She was weird. Nice shoes, though."

"Before or after me?"

"What? I don't—"

"Did she talk to Deo before or after me?" I yell at Daniel.

"After you. Why?"

"Damn it." I slump down in the seat and rub my face. "Did you notice anything, D? A weird feeling, kind of like a buzz across your forehead?"

Daniel's head jerks upward. I can see his eyes in the mirror. His very *brown* eyes, despite what he told the Badea woman. They seem alarmed, and I've got the strangest feeling that he knows exactly what I'm talking about. Did she try her little trick on him, too?

"Yeah," Deo says, after a few seconds' reflection. "Now that you mention it, I did. I thought it was a sugar rush. I hadn't eaten since lunch, so I grabbed a Butterfinger and a Coke from the vending machine, and I kind of wolfed them down right before she came in. So . . . what do you think it was?"

If it was Aaron driving, I'd have given Deo a direct answer. But from everything Aaron has told me, his brother is Mr. Skeptic.

"I don't know. Her name was Dacia Badea. She didn't flash her badge at me like she did at Daniel, so he'll have to fill in the bit about what agency she's with. All she said was that the people she worked for could make all of our problems go away, if I'd cooperate."

"It wasn't a badge," Daniel says. "Just a card. What exactly did you tell her?"

"Well, I left out all of the *psycho mumbo jumbo* as you called it, if that's what you're worried about. Lied to her. Told her I met Molly at the shelter before she died and that Deo and I were trying to con Porter to get some cash. But she wasn't buying it. And while I doubt you'll believe this, she was . . . doing something to my head. Trying to get information. I blocked her before she could confirm that I'm in contact with Molly . . . but I'm guessing she got that information from Deo anyway."

"How?" Deo asks. "I didn't tell her anything."

"I don't think you had to, D. If I hadn't spent so much time building up my walls with Kelsey, I wouldn't have been able to block her, either. And she must have been nearby when I was at the townhouse with Aaron. Either that, or she can do it long distance, because I had a similar sensation before she ever showed up."

They're both silent, so I ask Daniel again. "Who is she with? She *recognized* you. And if she's high up enough that she can make the police turn off the cameras in that room, why are we in the car with you, headed to your grandfather's office, rather than with Officer Lupito, headed back to Bart House? I thought you were all about following the rules."

"It's complicated."

And judging from the set of Daniel's mouth in the rearview mirror, that's all we're going to get for now.

CHAPTER SEVEN

About twenty minutes later, we pull into a small office complex near White Oak, wedged between an Exxon station and a self-storage facility. The second I step outside, my stomach growls.

Deo gives me a humorless laugh as we follow Daniel into the building. "Yeah, smells good to me, too. It's coming from the Popeyes on the other side of that gas station. When did you last eat?"

"I had a bagel after my shift, which was breakfast *and* lunch since I was running late when I left this morning. Hopefully this won't take long and then we can . . ."

He gives me a questioning look, waiting for me to finish, but the truth is, I don't have a clue how to end that sentence. Going back to Bart House doesn't seem nearly as appealing now. I keep hearing Dacia saying *we'll be in touch*, her accent almost but not quite turning the *we'll* into *ve'll*.

Daniel is already a few steps ahead, punching a code into the building's keypad.

I take advantage of his momentary distraction to pull Deo back so we're out of earshot. "Did you get the money out of my old sneakers?"

"Yeah. Three hundred sixteen bucks, and change. Plus the pennies in the sock if you can get it back from Officer Friendly."

"Hurry up!" Daniel holds the door open, clearly annoyed that we're making him wait. At first I think it's just him being his usual pissy self. But a worried frown settles onto his forehead as his eyes scan the parking lot behind us. Is he looking for Aaron? Or does he think someone followed us?

The foyer is dim, lit only by pale-yellow sconces near the doorways. We take the stairs up to the second floor. Quinn Investigative Services is the only office with any sign of life. The other two, which belong to a podiatrist and a dermatologist, are dark. Given that it's creeping up on ten o'clock, they've probably been closed for hours.

Daniel raps once on the door and then opens it to reveal a small reception area. An older man is hunched over a corner workstation, typing something on one of those touchscreen keyboards. He uses only two fingers, hunt-and-peck style. The back of his head sports a bald spot roughly the size of a soup bowl, framed by hair that's mostly salt with only a dash of pepper.

"Aaron's not here yet?" Daniel asks.

The old man doesn't say anything, just holds up a hand in Daniel's direction, indicating for us to wait until he finishes the word or sentence or whatever.

Even with my mental wall in place, I can still pick up a hint of Molly's emotions. This is Sam, who she's known forever. She's happy to see him. She *trusts* him.

Her reaction makes me relax a bit. Admittedly, it probably shouldn't, but it is what it is.

The desk is too small for Sam's large frame, and when he turns to face us, he bangs his knee against one of the metal supports. He curses under his breath as he rubs his knee. "Don't know why I let your mom talk me into this furniture. They make these things for damn midgets. And your brother will be here in a few minutes. Had to make a stop."

"Fine." Daniel huffs, then heads toward one of the two doors at the back of the suite, separated by a little kitchen alcove. "I need to make some calls anyway."

Sam gives an almost identical huff as Daniel closes the door behind him.

"You're Anna. I'm guessing this is Deo?"

Deo nods.

"You've probably guessed I'm Sam Quinn, grandfather to the rude young man who left without bothering to introduce us, although strictly speaking it doesn't appear to have been necessary. My other two grandchildren are slightly better behaved, at least *most* of the time. Seems the two of you have had a bit of excitement today." He motions to the sofa on the opposite wall, which, much like the desk, was clearly chosen for its sleek styling and not comfort.

"Yes, sir," I say. "That pretty much sums it up."

Sam gets us water from the fridge and chats amiably about a couple of sports teams that Deo and I don't follow. We both make polite noises, and Deo adds a comment about some player that must make sense because Sam nods enthusiastically and takes off on a conversational track that delves much deeper than Deo's casual acquaintance with the Baltimore Ravens.

"Have you heard anything more about Mr. Porter?" I ask. It's partly to rescue Deo, but also because I want to know, and even if Molly can't press the issue from behind my wall, I'm pretty sure she wants to know, too.

"Yeah. He was awake for the last twenty minutes or so before I left the hospital. Or rather before Ella—that's his sister—ran me off, telling me he needed his rest. He's gonna be fine. I'm guessing they'll release him tomorrow or the next day. Bullet lodged in his shoulder, but the surgery went well and he didn't lose much blood thanks to Aaron's—" He cuts off, clearing his throat.

"It's okay. Aaron told me he gets . . . premonitions about that kind of thing."

Deo gives me a surprised look, obviously wondering why I didn't tell him earlier.

But I don't have time to explain, because Sam continues, "Yeah, well, Daniel would probably say Aaron had a lucky guess, but I don't question it when he gets one of those twinges. Neither does his mom. Last time we didn't listen, my only son ended up dead a few days later."

Based on what Aaron said earlier, I think Sam is being a little hard on himself. But I just give him a sympathetic smile.

"I tried to tell Jerome he was in danger," he says, "but that man is as stubborn as a damn mule. He wants firsthand evidence, and that's kind of hard to produce with Aaron's flashes."

Sam looks at me, then says, "When Jerome came out of surgery, Ella was convinced the poor man was crazy, because he kept asking if Molly was okay. Once he was a little more coherent and he and I got a moment alone, the first thing he did was ask about you. He saw them shooting in your direction, saw you jump into a car, but didn't recognize it as Aaron's. All I can say is that you managed quite an impressive turn-around. When I spoke to Jerome yesterday, I think he was half tempted to shoot you himself, and me and Aaron telling him he should keep an open mind only made him madder. Whatever you did today seems to have made a believer out of him. He swears he was talkin' to Molly. Of course he followed that up by sayin' he must be losin' his damn mind."

"So . . . you actually let Molly out?" Deo wasn't exactly keen on the idea, even with Kelsey there.

"Yes. It wasn't easy on either of us. She didn't know her grand-mother had died and she was worried about Porter, and I think there was a little part of her that was tempted to—"

"Stay. Yeah. That's exactly what I told you. I saw your eyes that day at the piano. They weren't . . . you."

I raise my eyebrows, hoping to indicate that this conversation is one we should have later when we're alone, even though I'm well aware that a simple look may not stop him. When Deo is locked on to a topic, it's like he's worried the question or comment he's holding in is going to chew his tongue off if he doesn't let it out.

Thankfully, the front door opens and Deo's focus shifts. He sniffs the air a second before I catch the scent of fried chicken that we smelled earlier in the parking lot.

"I haven't eaten," Aaron says, nodding down at the large white bag in his hands. "And I'm guessing Daniel didn't feed you on the way over, because . . . well, because he's *Daniel* . . . so I bought extra. Do we have plates in the kitchen, Sam?"

When Aaron and Sam go off in search of utensils, Deo says, "The older brother is a pain in the ass. But this one, I could learn to like."

The chicken and biscuits are nearly gone when Daniel comes out of the back office. He snags the last drumstick and leans against the desk as he finishes it. I'm not really sure that desk could hold my weight, let alone Daniel's, and I get a quick mental picture of him on the floor, surrounded by rubble, wearing the same expression he wore in Molly's memory. It's an appealing thought, especially when I remember the way he yanked me back into the townhouse earlier this evening.

But then I remember his eyes as he scanned the parking lot a few minutes ago. He was worried, and I don't think it was simply about his own well-being.

Sam scoops the paper plates into the empty bag. "You called this meeting, Danny Boy, so let's hear what you've got to say."

Daniel's nose wrinkles slightly at the nickname. "Sure thing, *Popsy*." Sam narrows his eyes and Daniel laughs. "I didn't start it. And if Taylor can call you that, why can't I? Anyway, I headed over to pick up Deo like Aaron asked, but then I ran into Baker. He'd heard about Porter getting shot, and Porter had talked to him about the situation with Anna. I don't think that would have been enough for him to haul the two of them downtown for questioning, but the captain got a request from the trafficking task force at DHS." He glances over at me and Deo, and adds, "Homeland Security."

"Obviously," Deo mutters under his breath, pretty much echoing my thoughts.

"Why would any of this be on the DHS radar?" Aaron asks, and then makes a face like he's answered his own question. "The post Porter put on that neighborhood-watch bulletin board. The one that mentioned Lucas and Anna."

"Porter put my name in a post with a murder suspect?"

"Not exactly." Aaron pulls a sheet of paper out of his pocket. "Here. You can read it for yourself."

I unfold the paper and see screencaps from two websites. One appears to be from the Metropolitan Police site and is asking for information on a person of interest who was seen around National Place mall during the week I was trying to contact Porter at work. The second looks like a community-watch board, dated four days ago:

> *Seeking information about a juvenile female, Caucasian, late teens. May be contacting next of kin of murder victims in the DC area claiming to be in psychic contact with the deceased. Possible link to Franco Lucas, suspect in the killing of two DC residents in 2016. If you have any information, please contact J. Porter at 202-555-8763.*

I can feel Molly protesting behind the wall. It echoes in my head, like someone's banging a hammer a few doors down. I doubt she's pleased with the things I'm thinking about her beloved Pa right now, and at this point, I'm glad I can't hear her. I'm way too pissed to take her feelings into account, and I don't want to sit here with my mouth hanging open while she argues that he's really not so bad once you get to know him.

Deo is reading the page over my shoulder. "Is there a delay posting on this site?"

"I doubt it," Daniel says. "They monitor the ones connected to the department, but this one is privately run. I had to comb through half a dozen spam messages to find it. Why?"

"It's just . . ." Deo shrugs. "Porter's known Anna's name for more than a week now."

"Could be he didn't want to use it because she's a minor," Sam suggests. "Or maybe this is a rerun of an earlier posting and he forgot to—"

More banging from Molly.

Shut the hell up! I can't focus on what he's saying.

There's one more defiant whack and then silence.

Daniel is talking now. ". . . wasn't just what Porter posted. Another body turned up, this time up in New Hampshire. Young girl, probably no more than sixteen, with the same markings as the other five victims they've located."

Aaron and Sam exchange a look, then they both look back at Daniel. I get the feeling they're trying to decide how much they can say in front of me and Deo. They shouldn't worry. I'm not following half of what they're saying anyway, and judging from Deo's expression, I'm not the only one. I mean, I got the part about there being another victim, but now they've moved on to talking about police procedures at the MPD and liaisons with various government agencies. Daniel says Dacia's card was from Senator Cregg's office, but he'd also seen her at some place called Decathlon where he interviewed a while back.

And between all of this, Molly's hammer keeps whacking away every few minutes. I think she'd be pounding nonstop, if not for the fact that she wants to hear what they're saying and, if I can't hear it, neither can she.

"So does the Metro Police Department throw police procedure out the window anytime a Senate staffer walks in and asks to speak to suspects?" Aaron asks, clearly skeptical. "Or do you think it's her government contractor connections with Decathlon?"

"She waltzed in like she was there on the authority of the president—and given the media attention Cregg's campaign has been getting, that may well be the case a year from now. And Cregg is on both the Homeland Security and Senate Intelligence Committees. I couldn't get much out of the front desk, but they did say Cregg's request was backed up by one from the CIA. The NCS to be precise."

I'm starting to feel like I'm swimming in a bowl of alphabet soup. "Okay, CIA I get. What's the other one?"

"NCS. National Clandestine Service. A sub-unit of the CIA," Aaron says. "They've been around in some form since the agency was created, but they got a name change to NCS after September 11. They deal with HUMINT . . . sorry, human intelligence collection. Espionage, interrogation, that sort of thing."

"So . . ." Deo pauses for a minute, like he's trying to piece something together, then points to Sam and Aaron. "You two are private investigators, right? I googled you when Anna called me earlier, and your website says you mostly help get evidence for people with cheating spouses. How come you know so much about the CIA?"

"Kind of a hobby," Sam says, brushing the question aside before turning back to Daniel. "But why is the CIA all of a sudden interested in Lucas? FBI, yeah. But the CIA doesn't have anything to do with law enforcement, even things that cross state borders like Molly's . . ." He trails off, glancing over at Deo and me, probably wondering how much we know.

"I don't think they're interested in Lucas. Did she ask you anything about him, Anna?"

I think back through the conversation. "No. She didn't mention him at all. She mentioned Molly, but only in connection to my contacting Porter."

"Tell them what you told me on the drive over," Daniel says.

I give them an overview of the conversation, including the strange sensation. "As crazy as it sounds, she was trying to scan me. To pull something from my mind. And I think she actually *did* do that, right at the beginning, because she repeated what I'd been thinking almost verbatim."

Aaron frowns. "So if she got inside your head, she knows about Molly."

"She didn't get very far. I've spent hundreds of hours learning to block off that side of my mind. Usually, it's to keep . . ."

I pause and glance down at my lap. Talking about these things in front of other people is alien to my very nature. Today alone, I've doubled the number of people who know my secrets.

When I look up, Aaron catches my expression and gives me a sympathetic smile. "It's okay. This is a safe zone. You already know that I believe you. Sam has talked to Porter and to me, so he's not going to give you any flak. Daniel might think you're full of crap, but he thinks I am too, so—"

"You know, Aaron, I'm sick of you putting words into my mouth. I've never once said I thought you were full of crap. What I said is that you're a damn fool for giving anyone even the slightest reason to think that you're some kind of psychic wonder boy. What was the last thing Dad said to you?"

Aaron sucks in a breath and tightens his fist. I don't know why the question made him so angry, but judging from his narrowed eyes, things are about to get nasty.

I wonder if Aaron's spidey sense tingles when *he's* the one about to go medieval?

Sam sticks his two index fingers into his mouth and produces a shrill whistle. "Cut it. Both of you. Anna was talking."

I wait a few seconds, and when Aaron's face resumes something close to its original shade, I continue. "I was saying that the walls are usually to help me keep control of any hitchers I'm carrying around in my head. But this time, it helped me keep this Badea woman from learning about Molly. I'm doing my best to keep the barrier up, because I think she can do it from a distance. I had that same odd tingling sensation right before we left for the police station. In the car with Daniel, too."

Sam's head jerks back slightly and he stares at Daniel. "Go on."

"There's not much else to tell. She said she worked for someone who was interested in my talents, and I kept denying that I had any talents for them to be interested in. She was angry when she left. Frustrated. But"—I give Deo an apologetic smile—"if she got that information from Deo, then my blocking her out may not have done much good."

"Maybe, maybe not," Aaron says. "It really depends on whether her goal was to find out what you knew about Molly or to find out something Molly knew."

"Isn't that the same thing?" Daniel asks. "I mean, if she's in your head, then . . ."

"I can't access all of Molly's memories yet. She can tell me things, but I don't really have control until she moves on."

Aaron turns toward Daniel, and though there's still a bit of residual anger beneath the surface, he takes a breath and makes a visible effort to relax. "Have you searched online to see what you can find out about Badea? I mean, aside from what you learned at the station."

"No," Daniel says. "Haven't really had time."

Aaron slides his chair behind the desk. He seems much more at ease there than his grandfather was, so I'm guessing that's his usual workstation.

"Spelling?" he asks.

"B-a-d-e-a," Daniel says. "She called herself Dacia, but on the card, her full name was D-a-c-i-a-n-a."

And Molly goes completely batshit.

CHAPTER EIGHT

Before, Molly's protests felt like a hammer in my head. Now, they're more like a wrecking ball.

I lean back against the couch cushions and squeeze my eyes shut.

Molly, you heard what I said. I can't let you out yet. She might—

"Anna? You okay?"

Deo is tugging on my arm. I glance around and everyone else is watching me, too. I wish I could sink through the floor, but Molly's not letting up.

"It's Molly. She wants to tell me something, but that would mean I have to let the wall down. And I'm positive I felt something before we went to the police station, so this Badea woman must be able to—"

"No." Sam glances at Daniel again. "I don't know who this woman is exactly, but I find it hard to believe she can do anything like that from a distance. I've made a study of this kind of thing . . . given the family tendencies. Even with clairvoyants—like people who do remote viewings—most need to touch something in order to read it. Or at least be really damn close by." He fades off, then says to Daniel, "Why don't you take a walk around the building? See if anything looks suspicious."

Daniel and Sam exchange another one of their cryptic looks. I'm starting to wonder whether the two of *them* are trading psychic messages back and forth, because Sam tells him, "Just do what I asked. I'm not going to *say* anything. Aaron can go with you if you're a scaredy-cat."

"Yeah, right," Daniel scoffs, heading toward the door.

Aaron is still typing, and it looks like he's moved on to a different website now. I close my eyes and rub my temples, wishing I had something to drown out Molly's noise.

We're working on it, Molly. Could you just calm down please? What is your problem?

Even without hearing her, I know her response would include that she's stuck behind a wall inside someone else's head. But I can't really help that.

I hear Daniel in the hallway a few minutes later. His voice is angry. A woman's voice, also angry and also familiar, responds, and I tense up automatically.

But it's not the low tones of Dacia Badea. I place the voice right before the door opens and Daniel tugs his sister Taylor in after him.

". . . to go home."

"I did. And when Mom called, she said I could go back out as long as I'm home by midnight."

Aaron's eyes stay on the screen as he asks, "You told her where you were going?"

"Sort of. I said I was going to see Popsy." She gives her grandfather a big smile and crosses over to where he's sitting. Then she parks herself on the arm of his chair and plants a kiss on his cheek.

"Taylor, you know damn well you shouldn't be here." Sam's comment doesn't sound even remotely like a rebuke, however. Taylor very obviously has him wrapped around her well-manicured pinky.

"I haven't seen you in three entire days. And tomorrow's Saturday. No school, so I still have lots of time." She looks across the room at the couch where Deo and I are sitting. Her eyes linger for a minute on Deo, which is pretty much the norm for most females between the ages of ten and thirty and sometimes even older. Quite a few guys, too. Then she shifts her gaze toward me, and I see anger or maybe it's just hurt in her expression. Whatever it is, it feels unfair. I haven't done anything to her.

She looks back over at Aaron. "What did I miss? And don't any of you tell me this is none of my business. If it has to do with Molly, it's my business. If it has to do with Dad, it's also my business. And you know I'll find out either way. *I always do.*"

Aaron, Sam, and Daniel sigh. It's not quite in unison, but it's pretty close, and there's an almost identical expression of defeat on all three faces. Taylor flashes a little victory smile and then repeats, "So . . . what did I miss?"

"Well, apparently Molly has something to tell us," Sam says. "But Anna here had a little run-in with a woman at the police station who she thinks was trying to read her mind. Or Molly's mind. Did you finish looking around, Daniel?"

"I didn't see anyone out there besides Taylor," Daniel says. "The building appears to be empty, and it's only our cars in the lot. I can't guarantee she's not hanging out at the 7-Eleven, Popeyes, or whatever. But I really don't think she'd be able to read you unless she was close by. And you could always rebuild your mental wall if you feel anything, right?"

I'm not sure what it is about Daniel's expression that's bugging me. I don't think he's lying about the lot being empty, but something seems off.

Still, he's probably right. And since God only knows what the woman managed to find out from Deo, it may be a moot point anyway.

"I can't find any information on a Daciana Badea," Aaron says, pushing his chair back from the computer. "Or a Dacia Badea. Anywhere. The name itself appears to be Romanian. If she's employed by Senator Cregg, she doesn't show up on the official payroll. So, we're at a dead end for now without Molly's information . . ."

Everyone stares at me. Obviously, since I'm the one who has to make the decision, and since I'm where the show is about to happen, but I want them to look away. To give me some space. It feels weird to let control slip to Molly with all of them watching.

"It's okay," Deo says softly. "You really don't look as spaced as you think."

He's trying to be helpful. I know that. And in one sense, he is helpful. His comment makes it sound like I'm super vain however, and it's really not about how I look. It's more . . .

Okay, it's *partly* how I look. But it's also an issue of privacy. I hate being the center of attention even when I'm in full control of my brain.

My vanity and desire for privacy are trumped by the fact that we clearly don't have much choice, so I lean back and close my eyes. Then I visualize pulling a single brick from the top of the wall. It's not even all the way out before I hear Molly.

That's **not** Pa's number. Someone else placed that bulletin board notice.

She pushes a brief image of hands—her hands, I guess, back when all of her fingers were in place—dialing a number on an iPhone with a skin that looks like a colorful explosion of musical notes. I can't see all the digits, but the last four are 9949.

Maybe . . . he changed it? It's been nearly three years, Molly.

It's not even his area code! Aaron and Sam have his number. Get them to check.

Okay.

I wait, expecting her to keep talking.

Now! Get them to check *NOW.*

I'm tempted to press the point, since I think her info about Badea is more crucial, but Molly seems really frazzled. I don't think it's simply from being shut out. I've done that to her before, when I needed to focus and she was making me crazy. It's more like she's building up the courage to tell me the rest.

When I pull my eyes into focus, I'm not surprised to see that they're all *still* looking at me.

"She says the number on the post isn't Porter's. His ends in . . . 9949. Wrong area code, too."

Aaron digs both the printout and his phone out of his pocket, and after a moment, he nods. "She's right. Not his number. Might be his office number, though . . . or more likely a burner phone. That way he doesn't end up with a bunch of crank calls six months from now."

"I'll ask Jerome tomorrow," Sam says. "What did she say about the Badea woman?"

"Hold on."

Molly doesn't exactly rush to the front this time.

Come on, Molly. You were banging on the inside of my skull a few minutes ago, and now you go quiet?

There's a pause before she answers.

Daciana was one of the two girls at the house where Cregg was holding me. One of the Eastern European girls Lucas handed over to him. I thought everyone was saying Tasha, not Dacia. Otherwise, I might have pieced it together earlier. Her face looked familiar, but I assumed Cregg killed her after he killed me. She and I talked a bit when we were there . . . her English was really broken back then, but she said she was from this little place in Romania. Can't remember the name, but it was a port town on the Danube. I remember that because when she told me, I hummed the waltz—you know, "The Blue Danube"?

She pushes me a few seconds of piano music from her memory. *Ba bada bum bum, bum bum, bum bum.*

When I hummed the song, she smiled and nodded. And said that was home.

Something about this conversation with Molly feels wrong. I'm not sure what it is at first, and then it hits me. Usually, when Molly is talking, I get visuals and audio. Not like a video feed. More like flashes, like when she was telling me about calling Porter's number on her phone just now. Or I'll see a face. A room. Some little snippet from her memory.

But aside from that one bar of "The Blue Danube," there's no memory of sounds or smells. No visuals. All I'm seeing is the back of my eyelids. It's like Molly can't bring herself to remember the details. And that frightens the hell out of me, because these things that Molly can't bring herself to face right now, can't bring herself to tell me in words?

I'm going to get every bit of it in vivid color when I start unpacking her memories in my dreams.

I'm pretty sure Molly knows exactly what I'm thinking, but she ignores me and keeps talking about the girl.

> She said she left Romania looking for work. A company came around and posted flyers announcing jobs in the US. Good jobs. She took all of their tests and did well. They even showed her pictures of the children she'd be taking care of. But then there was some other sort of test. She just kept repeating the word "test," and saying, "no pass." I thought she meant like language tests, that her English wasn't good enough for the job. But she rolled up her sleeves and showed me bruises, needle marks. They injected her with something. And no, it wasn't tracks, it wasn't like she was shooting up. I've seen plenty of that.

I do get a brief visual then . . . of a pale, thin girl who looks to be in her late teens. She's beautiful, with wide blue eyes and long dark hair, but I'm not sure I'd have recognized her as the woman I met earlier tonight if Molly hadn't made the connection. The girl is holding up the sleeve of her blouse to reveal an upper arm with the mottled greenish-gold signs of fading bruises. There's a faint pink spot near the middle of the largest one.

And then as quickly as the image came, it's back to black again.

> *You said there was another girl, too. Was it the same with her? The tests, I mean.*

> I don't know. We didn't talk. She was the first one Cregg . . . finished. The same night Lucas killed my mom. The same night he handed me over.

Molly goes silent. I don't want to push, so I wait. When I hear her again, her words tumble out quickly.

> Just let me tell them, okay? Give me ten more minutes
> and let me get it over with. If I tell you everything, and
> then you have to relay it to them, that means I have
> to say it and then I have to hear it. I don't think I can
> do this twice. I know Kelsey isn't here. But Deo is. And
> Daniel's practically a cop. There has to be some sort of
> law against me stealing your body, right? I promise I
> won't fight you, and I won't ask to see Pa again. Please,
> Anna. Just let me get it over with.

And even though she doesn't mention it, I get a quick visual of Taylor's face from earlier tonight. When she was angry. Molly also wants to say good-bye. I don't entirely understand why, but she needs Taylor's forgiveness.

Fine.

Even as the word forms in my mind, I feel my muscles tightening. It's partly because giving her control makes me nervous, and partly because Deo's not going to like this. I hate to worry him. The icing on the crapcake, however, is that I know beyond doubt that Molly's story isn't one I want to hear. I'll have to relive all the details at some point, but there's a really big part of me that's perfectly okay with pushing that point as far into the future as I can.

"Deo," I say as I open my eyes. "I'm letting Molly move to the front for a bit."

I guess he can tell from my expression that my mind is made up, because he doesn't try to talk me out of it. He just gives me a worried shake of the head and says, "Bad. Idea."

"Maybe. You've got Kelsey on speed dial in case I get lost?"

It's intended as a joke, but he pulls out his phone.

All four members of the family Quinn are staring at me now.

"What do you mean . . . move to the front?" Taylor asks.

"It's Molly's story and she needs to tell it. Her words without me in the middle. I'm giving her ten minutes, and I'd appreciate it if you'd help Deo . . . enforce that?" It comes out as a question, because I don't really know whether I can count on any of them in that regard.

They exchange a look, and Aaron asks, "How? What should I do?"

"Just remind her we had an agreement. Molly's a good person, but she's scared, and . . ." I shrug, wondering now if Deo isn't right about this being a bad idea.

"You have my word," Sam says. The rest of them don't say anything, but they all nod, even Taylor.

I squeeze Deo's hand. "Back in ten."

"You'd better be."

Thanks, Anna.

Molly doesn't sound as eager about taking over as she did in Kelsey's office, but she slides forward and I feel the chicken and the biscuit I ate churn.

The room fades slightly around me. Molly glances at all four of the Quinns, saving Taylor for last.

"You been sayin' you were gonna cut your hair for what . . . five years? Can't believe your mama finally let you do it. It looks cute, Tay."

Taylor's lip quivers and her eyes become shiny, but she doesn't say anything.

Molly looks around at the others and shifts to a more formal tone. "First, thank you for everything you've been doing. Helping Pa try to find Lucas, I mean. And like I told Pa today, you *do* need to find him. While he's not the man who killed me, I'm pretty sure he killed Mama.

I don't think he really wanted to. I think maybe he really did love her in his way. But I overheard him talking about the girls they were bringing in. And . . . Mama may have had her issues with drugs and God knows she'd managed to ignore all the bad things about Lucas for years. But she was a *good* person. She just made the mistake of thinking Lucas was too, and when I explained what he was into, she confronted him. I told her not to. I told her we should leave, find Pa, let the police handle it . . . but she wanted to give Lucas a chance to do the right thing. Instead, I'm pretty sure he shot her. And then he handed me over to . . ."

Her voice shakes as she continues, "I heard his name as Craig, although Aaron seems to think it's really *Graham* Cregg."

Sam leans forward in his chair and reaches across to squeeze my hand. "Do you think you could identify him if Aaron finds a photograph, sweetie?"

Aaron slides his chair back to the computer and begins typing before Sam is even done with the question.

Molly nods. "Absolutely."

She pushes up from the couch and walks us over to the desk. Before she looks at the computer screen, she squeezes Aaron's shoulder. "I meant what I told Anna earlier. There's nothin' you could've done, Aaron."

His mouth tightens and he stares into my eyes. I don't know if he's trying to find Molly or trying to find absolution. Maybe both.

"Sure," he says, focusing back on the computer and not sounding sure at all.

Molly keeps her focus on Aaron, instead of the screen. I already suspected she had a crush on him, and maybe vice versa, but the wave of emotion that surges through me surprises me with its intensity.

"I mean it. And if you're thinking this really isn't me, *Airhead* . . . think again."

Molly smiles, because Aaron jumps slightly at the word.

"Mullet, Tater, and Airhead," Daniel says. "I'd almost forgotten about those nicknames. Glad I was old enough that I didn't get stuck with one."

Molly exchanges a look with Aaron, and I can feel my lips twitching like she's holding in a laugh.

But it's Taylor who speaks. "No, you had one. What was *his* name, Molly? You got that in your little file?" There's a definite challenge in Taylor's question, and the smile fades from my face.

Sam says, "Come on, Taylor. No need to be like that."

"It's okay, Sam." Molly jerks my chin up and holds Taylor's stare as she answers. "It was *Damn*-iel. And I picked it 'cause he was always yelling at us to keep out of his *damn* room. We just had to whisper it to keep from getting our butts kicked by the grown-ups. You satisfied now? I don't think anybody knew that aside from you, me, and Aaron. I could start listing the boys you used to crush on, or tell everyone about the spot where you stash stuff you don't want found, but Anna has me on a timer and I'd really like to use the next few minutes constructively."

She doesn't wait for Taylor's answer, just gives her a defiant look and turns back to Aaron's monitor, where a picture of a man in business attire is now center screen. His slight paunch and receding hairline suggest that he's in his midforties, as does the touch of gray near the sideburns of his closely cropped dark hair. Several other men are in the picture with him, but it's clear that he's the photographer's focal point. The caption reads *R. Graham Cregg Named to DSG Board.*

"Is this him, Molly?"

As Molly steps back away from the desk, it's like a massive weight has landed on my chest. The man's face flashes through my memory along with a strange buzzing noise in my ears.

No. It's not actually *in* my head. Molly's just remembering it, and the memory is so vivid that I can almost hear it. It's similar to what I detected at the police station and earlier at the townhouse, but not quite identical. Less of a tactile sensation and more audible.

For several seconds my eyes are glued to the computer, but gradually she pulls my gaze away. "Yeah. He's gained a little weight since I saw him, but that's definitely him."

My pulse is pounding so loudly as she walks us back over to the couch that I don't catch what Sam asks her. Molly does, however.

"I'm okay. But yeah, that would be nice."

Aaron gets up and heads to the kitchen.

"Eight minutes," Deo says, and Molly shoots him an annoyed look.

A few seconds later, Aaron presses a bottle of water into my hand. Molly tips it up, and despite the low-level panic I can still feel surging through my body after seeing the picture of Graham Cregg, I also detect a contradictory wave of pleasure. She drains the bottle without pausing, and breathes deeply.

Molly savors the faint spicy aroma that remains in the air.

Chicken smells good too. Wish you'd saved me some.

You can't be hungry.

No, but I haven't eaten in nearly three years. It's not the same when you're riding in the backseat, is it?

Now that she mentions it, no.

I felt the water slide down my throat, but it was kind of like feeling water on my skin in the shower. And I caught that stray thought running through my head so I *knew* why she was sniffing the air, but I can't actually smell the food.

Sam leans forward and looks into my eyes. "Listen, everyone in this room has seen the results of your . . . of your autopsy." He shoots a quick glance at Taylor. Her expression is guilty for a split second and then shifts to defiant, so I'm guessing the autopsy report is one of those things Taylor meant when she said earlier that they knew she'd find out anyway.

Strictly speaking, what Sam said isn't true. I haven't seen the autopsy report. Neither has Deo.

"So," Sam continues, "you don't have to rehash anything that makes you uncomfortable. We just need any information you have that might help us catch and convict the bastards. Where it happened, maybe? Exactly when? They found your body in the woods about an hour south of Philly. Do you think that's where you were killed? And we need to know anything you can tell us about your mom."

"Mama was killed at Lucas's apartment near Nationals Park. I was showing her the pictures he had of the girls in the extra bedroom he used as an office. The ads he was running. He'd told her he'd be in a meeting, wouldn't be back until around ten, but he came home early. Mama shoved me into the closet when she heard him turnin' the key in the lock, so I only heard the fight. Heard the gun. Didn't see it. I stayed as quiet as I could, but then he opened the closet to get a sheet, I guess to wrap her body in. He hit me with the butt of the gun, and the next thing I know, I'm in the back of the van."

"Do you know when?" Sam asks.

"About a week before Thanksgiving. I remember that because I was trying to convince Mama to go with me to see Pa and Mimmy for the holiday, and she said to give her a couple of days to think about it. And it was nighttime. I was tied up in the back of the van. The only window was in the back, so I didn't see much. I could see some of the interstate signs, though. Enough to tell we were on I-95, headed north."

"How long were you in the van?"

Molly thinks for a moment. "It was more than an hour. Closer to an hour and a half, I'd say. He had the radio on, and the second quarter of the Boston Celtics game had just started, right after we hit the road. The game ended just before we left the highway. We drove maybe ten minutes more before we stopped."

When she says the word *stopped*, she flinches and I get a flash of a man's shadow, framed by the open rear doors of a van. Lucas. This is the first time I've actually seen his face in her memory. He's a large man, bald, looks like he spends too much time at the gym or punching people. He wears one of those dinky little beards that I've never seen anyone pull off except for Johnny Depp. I'm pretty sure he was the guy driving the van that nearly hit me and Deo.

And then I know what she's holding back, what she's hiding. Lucas is on top of her, and she's trying to scream, but there's tape over her mouth.

Oh, God, Molly. No! You need to tell them.

She's angry that she let that bit slip and I feel her push—no, it's more like she shoves me back.

I'm sorry. But you weren't supposed to see that. I don't want them to know, and that's MY decision to make. Mine.

Even though I'm not happy about being pushed around in my own head, I feel too bad for her to argue about it.

Okay. I disagree, but . . . you're right, it's your call, not mine.

She starts talking again, faster now. "It was dark when Lucas pulled me out of the van. I saw a house off to the left, but we didn't go inside. He took me out back, to this smaller house, like a shed or a cabin. Cregg kept us in there."

"You mentioned a rear window. Do you remember seeing street signs, anything, before Lucas left the highway?"

My entire body goes rigid again. Thinking about leaving the highway means thinking about what happened shortly after, and she doesn't want to go there again. But she forces her mind back to the van. A few seconds later and something clicks into place. She's remembering one of those highway information signs that run across the top of the interstate.

"Yes! I-695. Twenty-two miles, twenty-two minutes. That's what the sign said—the one on the side of the highway headed south. I remember because it was the same number."

"That's perfect, Molly."

A few more minutes, and Aaron has narrowed it down to two exits on I-95—either Exit 89, to Havre de Grace, or Exit 93, Port Deposit. More likely the first, since Molly can't remember crossing a bridge just before the exit.

"I don't know any more about the roads after that," she says, and I'm pretty sure the steely tone she's using is aimed at me. "It was dark and I couldn't see anything. It was ten minutes before we reached the house. Fifteen, maybe. Then he locked me in the basement with the other girls. One of them was Daciana."

"And you're sure it's the same person?" Daniel asks.

"Yes. She looks different now, but I'm sure."

"You said 'girls,' right?" Sam asks. "How many others?"

"Just one. I don't remember much about her. She was only with us that first night. I think her name was Lily. Daciana and I were there for another six days. Maybe more. We kind of lost track. Cregg visited four times, always at night. We were in the cellar below the house when he was away. Dark the whole time, except for a little bit of light coming in through some of the floorboards. No windows. There was a toilet, a sink, and a shopping bag full of ancient granola bars. Pop-Tarts too, but they were moldy so they must have been down there forever."

"The other girl you mentioned," Daniel says. "Lily? Did she leave with him? Or did Cregg kill her, too?"

"Not . . . exactly." Molly hesitates, and then says, "Any other group of people and I'd worry about them believing what I've got to say next. But Pa's talked about Sam's hunches back when they were on the force. I knew to ask Taylor anytime I lost something, ever since we were little. Knew better than to play hide-and-seek with her, too. And I've suspected Aaron's little secret since he came running out of his classroom and across the playground back when Tay and I were in third grade. That Jeremy Villers kid was pissed off that Pa caught his uncle dealin' drugs, and I'm pretty sure his bat would've connected with my head if Aaron hadn't known what was about to happen."

She turns to face Daniel. "And you . . . well, you know everything I've just said is true. You've been in the middle of this craziness all your life. Plus, you're all sitting here talking to me in a body that I'm borrowing—"

"For a little under four more minutes," Deo says.

"In a body that I'm borrowing," Molly repeats, eyes narrowed at Deo's interruption, "because my own has been dead for nearly three years. When it was found, you all know I was missing a finger. I don't know if they could still tell by then, but there were . . . shallow cuts up and down my body."

The room feels cold now, and Molly has my arms crossed over my chest, hands clutching too tightly at my arms. When she starts speaking again, her voice is flat, and the words tumble out quickly.

"I could tell you Cregg did all of that damage. That he picked up the knife and sliced into me. That he picked up those garden shears and snipped off my finger. But if they'd gotten to my body sooner, I'm pretty sure the people at the morgue would have figured out from the angle that most of my wounds were self-inflicted."

Someone inhales sharply. I'm not sure who. Taylor and Sam are the only two I can see right now. Taylor has her hands over her mouth and little gray lines of tears mixed with mascara are streaming down her cheeks.

"They'd be right about that," Molly says, "except they wouldn't know that I didn't have a choice. Cregg can get in your head, and . . . like now, the way Anna's body is mostly in my control? It's like that, except I think Anna could push me away if she really wanted to. I couldn't push Cregg no matter how hard I tried. He made me cut Daciana, too. Made her cut me, cut herself. I'm guessing she has scars, and if you'd pulled off her gloves tonight, I bet she's missing the same finger I am.

"Cregg would sit there on the floor, cross-legged, like he was meditating or something. Then I'd hear this whistling noise, and next thing I know, he has control. That first night, he was controlling all three of us at the same time. Like it was a game, or like juggling maybe. Like he wanted to see how many balls he could keep in the air at the same time. He seemed really full of himself, so I think three was a personal best."

It feels like there's a giant lump in my throat. "Could you . . . is there more water? Or maybe a soda?"

Molly chugs most of the soda when Aaron hands it to her, so fast that I know I'm going to have a nasty case of heartburn. But after what she's been telling us, I can't really begrudge her the drink.

She looks at Deo. "Time?"

"You've got a little over ninety seconds," he says, but he doesn't sound quite as pushy about it now.

"I think Cregg trying to handle all three of us is why the other girl managed to kill herself. She'd been there for days before we arrived. There were cuts up and down her body, and I'm sure Cregg caused those, but she's the one who decided to cut her wrists, while he was focused on adding me to his game. I'm not saying he wouldn't have killed her eventually, because I think he would have. But he hadn't planned on doing it *yet*. He was angry when he realized she was bleeding out. He shoved me and Daciana back down into the cellar. We didn't see him for a long time after that. At least two days. And he brought us up one at a time that first day he was back. I think maybe he was worried that if one of us could get enough control to kill herself, one of us might get enough control to kill him."

She speeds up the next part. "That last night, Daciana seemed like she was sick. Or maybe it was just nightmares. She thrashed about in her sleep, yelling something in Romanian. Then she said he was here, in English. I thought maybe she was still dreaming. I hadn't heard anything from up above and I'd been awake. But sure enough, there was a door slam, and a few seconds later, the light hit my eyes. Then she grabbed his arm and started talking. The words were mumbled, but her English was almost perfect now. 'It's the black girl's turn to go first, maybe I should make her use the grill lighter for a change.' Cregg just stood there, staring at her. Then she started laughing, but it was like she couldn't help it, high-pitched and crazy sounding.

"And Daciana was right. The last time, Cregg had taken her upstairs first. So I was kind of surprised when he yanked her up and dragged her upstairs. I kept waiting for the screams, but they never came. After a while, I fell asleep." She pauses for a moment. "And then I heard someone coming down the stairs. Something heavy hit me. I tried to block the blow. I guess it broke my arm, because I couldn't move it to block the second blow or the one after that. Eventually, someone came to get my body. I stayed with it for a little while, but then . . . I had to let my body go."

I don't know if she's cold or it's just the memory, but she shivers and waits a moment before she continues. "After that, I just remember feeling . . . empty. *Needing.* I needed to find Mama. To find Pa and Mimmy. To find you, Tay." She wants to add Aaron's name but holds back. "I never made it, though. I'm not sure how I got back to the U Street shelter. Mama and I stayed there for a couple of weeks, right after I left Pa's house to join her. I almost had her talked into leaving Lucas—she was clean for twelve whole days, until . . . I don't know. She called him? He found her? So I think maybe I was looking for her at the shelter, but it's all fuzzy and confused. I don't know how long I was there or how long I'd have stayed there If Anna hadn't touched the piano keys. It was like I didn't have the energy to move. I just kept thinking that if I could play that song for Pa, he'd hear it somehow, wherever he was. That I wouldn't have to find him, because he'd find *me*."

Tears are running down my cheeks, but Molly doesn't make any effort to wipe them away.

I know I'm past the time limit, but I'm almost done, Anna. I promise.

Molly sighs and gives Aaron a fleeting look before her eyes come back to Taylor. "I am *so* sorry for not telling you where I was going, Tay. I was just . . ." She sighs and leans forward. "I was just tired of everyone thinking she was a lost cause. I knew if I could keep her away from Lucas long enough, keep her clean long enough, that she could get her life together. Everyone else had given up on her, even Pa, I think. And if I told you what I was planning, I knew you'd try to stop me. Maybe even tell Pa. You'd have been right to do that, too, because it was a stupid idea . . . but I had to try. If it was your mom, I think you'd have done the same. But I'm sorry for being stupid and for not trusting you and . . . for getting my stupid self killed. Okay?"

Taylor's eyes are glassy and she's biting her bottom lip so hard I'm afraid she's going to pierce through it.

"Just one question, Molly. Did you have your *L* purse with you? In that cabin?"

I have no idea what that means, and judging from the other faces in the room, neither does anyone else. Even Molly seems confused for a moment, but then she laughs. I get a brief image of a pink-sequined square. "Yeah. Back pocket, just like always."

Taylor nods, like she's filing that fact away.

I'd like to push one of them for an explanation, but Molly turns my eyes toward Sam. "Tell Pa I love him. I already told him, and he knew it anyway, but tell him again. And don't let him get too lonely, okay? Love you guys, too."

Molly doesn't wait for a response, simply slips backward with those last words. And it seems like she's farther away—*smaller, lighter*—than she's been at any time since I picked her up. Part of me would like to stay back there with her, where it's peaceful and quiet. Where no one is staring at me. Just curl up and sleep. But I'm being sucked back to the front, almost like an undertow. Except in reverse, because I'm being sucked upward, toward the surface.

I feel a little bad for putting the wall back up. It might not even be necessary the way Molly seems to be fading. But I do it anyway.

Sadness hangs in the silent room like a heavy fog. I was only the conduit, Molly's mouthpiece. Deo and I are intruders now, and I suspect the others in the room are wishing *they* had some privacy, that we weren't here to witness their newly reopened grief.

I don't know what to say, don't know how to deal with all of that raw emotion. So I steer things back to the practical.

"Daniel, could you take us back to Bart House now?"

Deo looks a little alarmed, but my distraction tactic worked. Daniel seems surprised at first, but he agrees with me.

"No," Aaron says. "Very, very, very bad idea. You've already said they don't have decent security, and I heard every thought going through that Badea woman's head when she was leaving. She was ready to rip you to shreds. The only thing that held her back was that she was in the middle of a police station, and she had somewhere to be. And I think maybe she didn't want the security goon with her to know she failed."

Sam and Taylor take Aaron's side. It's noisy, but at least I no longer get the sense that everyone in the room is going to shatter into pieces.

I let them squabble for a few minutes, then jump back into the fray.

"Listen, it's after eleven. I'm completely exhausted and my head is killing me. This . . . situation . . . isn't easy on me physically. I don't think anyone is going to come looking for me tonight, and Daniel's orders were to drop us at Bartholomew House. He may have quit the force, but—"

"What?" Sam's question is almost a roar, and the look Taylor and Aaron exchange make it clear that they weren't privy to Daniel's recent career shift either.

Daniel glares at me.

"I didn't know it was a secret," I say. Not that I owed him any favors in the first place.

"Whatever. Listen, Sam, I appreciate everything you did, with the references and so forth, but I need to cut my losses. I'm better off in the military."

"This is going to tear Mom to pieces," Aaron says.

"I told her before she left last week. She understands."

"No big difference," Taylor huffs. "Not like you've been around much the past few months anyway. How does your mystery girl feel about you being a soldier boy again?"

Then they're all talking at once, which seems to be a Quinn family trait.

I clear my throat. Then Deo pulls Sam's trick with the loud whistle. When they all stop and look at him, he makes a gracious little gesture, turning the floor over to me.

"Thank you, Deo. You clearly have family matters to discuss, and no offense, but I'm tired and I truly could not care less where Daniel works or where Daniel lives. I was simply suggesting that he might have less explaining to do if Deo and I actually show up at the place he told his former employer he was taking us. You can ask the police to keep an eye on Bartholomew House, right? Given what happened today?"

Daniel nods.

"And Aaron, we can set up a place and time to meet tomorrow. There's a lot of stuff you need to explain to me about all of this. But I *cannot* handle it tonight."

As I'm talking, I reach into my backpack and pull out the prescription bottle. I shake two pills into my hand and finish off the last of Molly's soda as they return to the debate over leaving us at Bart House.

Sam shifts his support to my side, and ten minutes later, over the fervent objections of Aaron and the more tepid objections of Taylor, Deo and I are again in the backseat of Daniel's car. I close my eyes, lean my head against Deo's shoulder, and pretend to sleep, but my fingers are tracing the outline of the two pills in my pocket.

The two pills I didn't take.

Everything I said about being tired and having a screeching headache is completely true, but I have absolutely no intention of sleeping. I won't be sleeping until Deo and I are on a bus out of Maryland, heading as far away from this insanity as the money we've saved can carry us.

CHAPTER NINE

"I know we'll stand out more in a smaller town. But there will also be fewer dead people hanging out to potentially complicate life." I keep my voice low, since we're past lights-out and I really should be back in my own room. It's not the first time I've been grateful that Libra sleeps like a rock. A snoring rock, but still . . . "I'm thinking middle-of-nowhere Ohio. Or Iowa. Someplace with more corn and cows than people."

Deo gives me a long look over the top of the computer screen, slowly arching one eyebrow. Even by the dim light of the computer screen I can tell the eyebrow is lined in dark blue, just like his eyes, and they make his point without the need for a single word. Deo and rural don't mix well. He lived at a group home in rural Maryland for six months. Six very bad months, between the fact that the place was horribly run and the fact that the kids at the local middle school had little tolerance for Deo's sense of style.

We've been over this several times already. He might be safe here, once I'm gone. But he's made it clear that he's coming. And the truth is, I'm not sure that leaving him behind is an option for me either, since all I can say is that he *might* be safe. Not knowing would make me crazy.

"Fine, Deo. Where do *you* suggest?"

"What about Asheville, North Carolina? I'd still prefer Chicago, but Asheville meets your criteria of moderate size and off the East Coast. And *Rolling Stone* called it the 'new Freak Capital' a few years back, so . . . I think we'd both fit in pretty well, don't you?"

"When does the next bus leave? And how much?"

"Not until Sunday. Tickets would be thirty bucks more than Chicago."

"Each?"

He nods and rolls his shoulders, the way he always does when he's stressed, before looking back down at the screen.

"We'd have enough left for dinner at Taco Bell when we arrived. Assuming we didn't eat anything on the bus trip. Also assuming that we stick to the dollar menu."

I fall back onto the ancient beanbag and unplug my phone, which clearly needs a new battery. The stupid thing seems to slide straight from fully charged to mostly dead since I got it back from Porter.

It's after midnight. Kelsey's probably already asleep. And even though I hate, hate, hate having to bring her into this, I don't see any other options.

But she answers on the first ring. Maybe she wasn't asleep after all.

"Anna! Where are you?"

"Back at Bart House." I give her a brief rundown of the past few hours, leaving out any names and any words that might put the conversation onto some sort of automatic alert with the NSA or whatever, then conclude with a simple plea. "She *knows*, Kelsey. Deo and I need to get out of here, which means I need a loan. I promise I'll pay you back, and we won't tell anyone that you helped."

"Anna." She was silent the entire time I was talking, not even stopping me to ask questions, and her voice has the same tone it always does when she's trying to calm me down. "I can't just let the two of you take off on your own like that. You may be close to eighteen, but technically speaking, you're still a minor. Deo's barely fifteen. I have an obligation to—"

"It's okay, Kelsey." I try to keep the disappointment out of my voice. "I understand."

"Don't you dare hang up. Let me finish."

I take my finger off the button. Kelsey's not psychic, but she knows me so well it's spooky.

"I was saying that I have an obligation to be sure you're safe. But that doesn't mean I think you should be at Bartholomew House right now. Maybe . . ." Her voice trails off for a moment. "Have you taken your sleeping medication yet?"

"No."

"That's good. Can you get out at this hour?"

"Think so. Not that either of us has actually done it, but . . ."

"Take whatever belongings you need and meet me here at the house. Do you remember the address?"

Deo, who's close enough to hear the question, shakes his head. "That's probably the first place they'll look."

"I know," Kelsey responds. "I said to *come* here. I didn't say you're *staying* here."

❖ ❖ ❖

Getting out of Bart House after hours isn't exactly easy. There's an alarm system on both the front and the back door, and also bars on the ground-floor and second-floor windows that give the house its cozy, welcoming appearance. But just because you can't get out through the usual methods, doesn't mean it *can't* be done. Libra has an on-again, off-again relationship with a guy named Lamar. He's maybe five years older than Libra, and even though she's cagey about it, I think he might have a record that would knock him off the list of people she's allowed to visit. The third time I noticed her sneaking out and back in without getting caught, I agreed to keep her secret, but only if she told me how she managed it.

Not that I had any intention of leaving Bart House at the time, but you never know. I learned long ago to keep my options open.

Ten minutes after my conversation with Kelsey, Deo and I are ready to put Libra's exit strategy to the test. After twelve thirty or so, there's never anyone in the living room, and Libra said that, most of the time, if you're really careful you can make it into the kitchen and to the door leading down to the basement without getting caught. There's no exit in the basement, but there's a narrow window about six feet off the ground. It's behind a row of shrubs, so maybe the security firm missed it. Anyway, Libra says that if you stand on the dryer and lean a bit to the left, you can lift yourself up and shimmy onto the back lawn. Then you just have to climb the back fence, work your way across a few neighboring yards, and you're two blocks off Georgia Avenue. In her case, Lamar is waiting there to pick her up, but since we don't have a Lamar and since the Y Line has stopped for the night, we'll have to hunt down a cab.

We make it to the kitchen without a hitch, which is a good thing. If Libra got caught in the living room or kitchen, all she'd have to do was pretend she came downstairs to get a drink or something and, worst-case scenario, call Lamar and cancel her plans for the evening. She'd only be in trouble if they caught her in the act of squeezing through the window. Deo and I, on the other hand, are already under scrutiny for missing curfew, even if it was—or maybe *because* it was—at the behest of the local authorities. And our backpacks are crammed with pretty much everything we own, including the pepper spray and sock full of coins that Daniel surprisingly turned back over to us without so much as a lecture when he dropped us off at Bart House. If anyone had seen us coming downstairs, we'd have been totally screwed.

The basement door squeaks when I push it open. To me, the noise is like a klaxon sounding.

"It's okay," Deo whispers. "Keep moving."

I do, and Deo follows, closing the door behind him. We're about five steps down when he says, "I feel like we've walked into a horror movie. Two teens sneak down to the basement, where the psycho killer lurks in the dark."

"If you're trying to lighten the mood, it's not working."

"Don't worry. The psycho killer always targets teens who are sneaking to the basement in order to make out. But I do wish we had a flashlight."

"I have a flashlight app on my phone, but I don't want to risk it. What if someone comes downstairs and sees the light under the basement door?"

By the time we reach the bottom, my eyes have started to adjust. I make out the washer and dryer below the window, which is the only source of light in the room, and nudge Deo toward it.

"Want me to boost you up?" he asks.

"No. You go ahead."

Deo hoists himself onto the dryer and inches the window open. It slides easily enough that I think Libra must have oiled it, even if she apparently didn't bother with the door at the top of the stairs. Once Deo shoves his backpack through the window, he pulls himself up and through the opening.

I climb onto the dryer and hand my backpack to him. That part is simple enough, but as I stand, I realize getting out the window is going to be a bit more difficult for me. I'm shorter than Deo—and shorter than Libra, now that I think of it.

"Should have let me give you that boost," Deo says, getting onto his stomach and reaching his hands down toward me. We lock arms. I kick off against the dryer, then use my sneakers to walk up the wall. I end up scraping my head against the window casing, but I make it.

Deo's still facing the window. He tenses, but before I can ask what's wrong, he says, "Run!"

I don't question him, just grab my pack and haul ass across the yard. When we reach the chain-link fence at the back, he doesn't ask if I want the boost. He simply grabs me around the waist and lifts me until I'm almost at the top. Our backpacks land in shrubs on the other side just as I grab the wire to flip myself across the fence. Deo and I hit the ground at almost the same instant and he tugs me down into the bushes.

"What was that about?"

He turns around so that he can peer through the leaves. "Light came on under the doorway at the top of the stairs. Someone must have heard us. And I doubt it was Pauline. She sleeps like the dead."

I look back at the house, relieved to see the basement light isn't on. "Maybe Marietta wanted a midnight snack. We should get moving, though. I wouldn't put it past her to do a bed check if she thinks she heard something."

Although I don't say it, we both know that if that's Marietta in the kitchen, she'll probably check *our* beds, even if she doesn't check house-wide. When Daniel brought us back, he told her a cruiser would be keeping an eye on Bart House and that he'd be picking us up tomorrow so we could answer some more questions. To his credit, he also told her that we'd done absolutely nothing wrong, but one look at her pinched face made it clear that she wasn't buying one little bit of it.

I call a local cab company to have a driver meet us outside an apartment complex just off Georgia Avenue. If Marietta discovers we're missing she'll alert the police. That makes hanging around on a street corner trying to flag down a cab a very bad idea.

The driver drops us about six blocks away from Kelsey's place, in a subdivision near Kensington, just to be on the safe side. Deo hasn't been here before, but I had secret sessions here twice a week for six of the seven months that the state had someone else assigned as my official therapist. I made stuff up to tell the other guy and saved my real problems to discuss with Kelsey as we sat in the white rockers on her front porch. Those rockers are still in the same spot, along with the spider plants in macramé hangers that Kelsey's daughter made when she was a teenager.

The only thing that's different is the car in the driveway. And Kelsey's behind the wheel.

"I thought you said she didn't drive?"

I shrug. "She doesn't. I didn't even know she owned a car."

Kelsey walks to the office, bikes to the grocery store. She takes the Metro or Uber if she needs to go anywhere more than a few miles away. Once, she admitted to me that she might have gotten past her fear of getting behind the wheel if she'd scheduled time with a therapist herself after her husband was killed. I said why not do it now, but she just laughed and said that walking the half mile to work was better for the environment, better for her health, and better for her nerves.

She gets out but doesn't close the car door. "I'd hoped we could do this tomorrow morning, after you'd gotten some rest, but I received a call about twenty minutes ago from . . . what's that dreadful woman's name?" She shakes her head, annoyed.

"That would be Marietta."

"Yes, thank you, Deo. I didn't answer, of course. But she left a message, asking me to call if I heard from either of you. She's probably alerted the police that you've run away again. Your best bet is to head out now."

"Whose car?" Deo asks.

"Mine, of course. I bought it two years ago so my granddaughter would have something to drive when she was taking classes at GWU, but she's living with that Jason boy now and they don't have parking spaces for both cars. I go out to the garage and crank it every few weeks, just to be sure it works. Are you sure you're not too tired to drive?"

"I'm not sleepy." It's not exactly a lie—I'm at the stage Deo calls *tired but wired*. "But in case you've forgotten, I don't have a license."

"True. But how many of your previous lodgers were licensed drivers? Five? Six?"

Seven, actually. Three of them even drove in the DC area. "But none of them have driven *recently*."

Deo rolls his eyes. "I'm not worried. You'll know how to drive the same way you knew how to fix that leaky pipe in Kelsey's office. The same way you know French, a lot of really boring history, and the capital of every country . . . or ice-skating. You remember last winter?"

I do. I wouldn't have gone at all if it hadn't been one of those mandatory group home outings. I was scared to death, not just of slipping my feet into shoes that might have been the last happy moment of some malcontented spirit, but also the more mundane fear of falling and breaking my neck on the ice.

But when I rifled through the memory banks, I discovered that Lydia, the sister who hung out on the porch swing for all those years waiting to tell her Vietnam vet brother good-bye, had spent every spare moment in the winter on the pond near her house. After my first tentative step onto the ice, that section of my brain kicked in, bypassing my fear and communicating directly with my body. I was doing figure eights and even managed a few pirouettes by the time we left the rink.

I was incredibly sore the next day, so sore I could barely walk after exercising muscles that I didn't even know I had. But once that wore off, I'd gladly have gone back to the rink. Ice-skating may be the most fun I've ever had, but that's the only chance I've had to do it. All of the outings since then have been bowling or movie nights, and there's no way I can fit an expensive hobby into my budget on what I make at Joe's.

Joe. Yikes.

I'm on the schedule for the next five days, and this will leave him short. I actually *like* my job at the deli, and I hate knowing that he'll need to hire someone to replace me.

"It's got all of those safety gadgets," Kelsey says, "like the autopilot lane control and sensors. Not that I've ever tried them, but Casey said they were useful. Oh, and I forgot to check the gas tank. Hopefully it will be enough to get you there, but if not, there should be plenty of stations along the way."

"Um . . . on the way to where?" I ask.

"My beach cottage. It's about an hour away. I don't go often, now that Barbara is gone. Mostly, I rent it out, but there's no one scheduled until Thanksgiving. If things aren't . . ." She stops for a moment, and a worried frown creases her brow. "If things aren't sorted out by then, we'll figure something else out. Just tell the GPS *Cottage* and it will navigate for you." She presses the keys and some money into my hand. "I'll e-mail you the QR code for the security system and the wi-fi. And this is all the cash I had on me, about a hundred and twenty dollars."

"Kelsey, I appreciate the loan. We'll get it back to you. But we should just take the bus or train. You could get into trouble."

"Anna, look at me. The worst that will happen if I'm implicated is that I retire a few months earlier than planned. So what? If your lives are in danger, crossing ethical boundaries is the least of my concerns."

As if to emphasize that point, she reaches out to pull both me and Deo into a hug.

Kelsey doesn't hug . . . or perhaps I should say she doesn't hug clients. She has made an exception exactly once, when I was seven and had just gotten rid of that creep Myron. On that occasion, she pulled me into her lap and held me while I cried. I remember it vividly—the feel of her sweater against my damp cheek, the way she smelled like vanilla, and the way she rocked me back and forth, whispering *shh* over and over as she smoothed my hair.

At my next appointment, she spent the first five minutes apologizing. She explained how her behavior at the previous session was a violation of the rules of her profession and a violation of my trust. And she promised she'd never cross that line again. I told her I understood, and I kind of did, even back then. But I still thought those rules were stupid. I'm pretty sure Kelsey thought they were stupid, too. I needed someone to hold me that day, and if not Kelsey, then who?

Her shoulders feel thinner now, more fragile. But she still smells like vanilla.

"Just *go*," she says, when she breaks away. "Don't worry about me. I haven't taken a personal day in three years, and I'm about to make up for that. A car will arrive in about an hour to take me to the airport, and I'll catch the five-fifteen flight to Indianapolis to spend some time with my daughter. I've already bought the ticket and canceled my appointments for the next few days, so don't argue with me."

I open my mouth to do exactly that, but we have so few options. And she seems to have everything arranged.

"Thank you." I slide behind the wheel and close my eyes for a few seconds to see what I can find in my collected memories of driving. I skip past Abner, the handyman with a DUI, and past a few more who probably never drove a modern vehicle with a GPS or power everything. Arlene Bennett, however, in addition to driving to work, and to her multitude of doctor's appointments, ran her kids to ballet, soccer, and everything else under the sun. The last time she drove was in early 2017, and that's about as close as I'm going to get to perfect.

Anna, this is a bad idea.

My puttering around in the files seems to have stirred Molly up. I'm pretty sure she doesn't mean driving is a bad idea. She means leaving DC, leaving her buddies who are trying to find Lucas and Cregg. And I do feel a tiny twinge of conscience. But I'm not safe here and I don't think Deo is safe here, either. Staying isn't an option.

Kelsey taps on the window. "Call my cell from the cottage phone when you arrive so I'll know you've made it. I'll either be in the cab or at the airport." She nods toward the backseat. "There are a few bags of food there, just some things I had in the house. Coffee is in the travel mug. Deo, I'm counting on you to keep up a steady chatter so that Anna stays awake."

"Yes, ma'am." He gives her a mock salute as I begin backing the car down the driveway.

And, just as Deo predicted, driving is a snap. A few minutes later, we're on the Beltway, and I shift lanes smoothly with the flow of the traffic. It's second nature, just like ice-skating.

Around one forty, I pull Kelsey's dark-red Volvo into a gas station on Chesapeake Beach Road. The indicator is nearly on empty with about twenty miles left to go, and I'm not sure how many more stations will be open this late. I add twenty dollars of gas to the tank while Deo runs inside to pay and grab drinks.

He's holding a bottle of water for me and one of those fruit-tea concoctions he likes when I meet him at the door.

"I'm going to hit the bathroom."

"Is the car unlocked?" he asks.

I push the little button on the key fob and the Volvo's lights flash. "Is now. Be right there."

I'm only inside a couple of minutes. The woman behind the counter nods and mumbles, "Haveagoodevenin'" as I push the door open to head back to the car. Her voice is tired, the words almost a snore.

The first thing I see is Deo's strawberry tea. The bottle is crushed, the pinkish liquid still oozing onto the concrete. I run to the Volvo, but he's not inside. His phone is there, however, stuck in one of the cup holders between the seats. His silver ear cuff is clipped to the top of the phone.

I turn around and scan the parking lot. "Deo! This isn't funny!"

But I know he'd never do anything like this. Especially not after the past few weeks.

I race back into the store. "My friend . . . the boy who paid for gas just now. He's gone. Did you see another car pull in?"

Her brow creases slightly. "Think maybe I heard a car turning around out there, but no. I didn't see anything."

> She's not going to be any help, Anna. The woman's eyes are barely open even now.

I'm relieved to hear Molly's voice. It sounds much calmer than my own and helps to stomp down the panic that's starting to build. Not much, but at least enough that I don't start screaming.

The door clangs behind me as I run back to Deo's abandoned drink bottle. Thick tire marks spread the liquid a few feet. I follow the tracks, but they don't go far enough for me to see whether the car turned left or right at the highway. Or maybe it turned down the other road?

No taillights are visible in any direction.

> Get back in the car! We're totally exposed out here.

Molly's right. I know she is. But I still stand, squinting in all directions, hoping against hope that I'll see a glint of red, a breadcrumb for me to chase after.

Aside from a few streetlights, and a pair of headlights from a truck that's now moving past me, all four directions are dark.

> Call Aaron.

"I don't know where I put his number. I think Deo has it."

Then my shoulders start shaking and tears stream down my face. *My fault. This is totally my fault. I should have never gotten involved. I should have told Molly no.*

Pull out your damned phone, Anna. Come on! Work with me! You're not doing Deo any good just standing here.

And then my hand is pulling out the phone, and my legs are running back to the car. Molly slides us behind the driver's seat and dials a number.

Taylor answers, annoyed.

"Where the hell are you, Anna? Aaron's been driving around for the last—"

"Tay? It's me. Could you get Aaron to the phone?"

"Like I just said, Molly. He's not here."

My voice, my phone. And somehow, despite that, Taylor picks up that it's Molly.

"Then call him! Tell him to call me back at this number. They've got Deo!"

The connection ends and it's less than a minute before the phone rings.

"Anna?"

"No," Molly says. "It's me. Anna's kind of freaking out right now."

"Why did she leave? I had the place staked out, like I said I would. Daniel had a cruiser circling by every hour. If anyone had—"

What if it had been Badea, flashing her badge or card or whatever? I'm pretty sure any creds that allowed her to question me in the middle of a police station would have been sufficient for her to haul me and Deo off in the middle of the night.

Molly ignores me and focuses instead on catching Aaron up to speed. I barely hear what she says because I'm mentally replaying the past hour, trying to figure out where I went wrong. We weren't followed after we left the city. Once we were out of Upper Marlboro, there were stretches where I didn't even see another car. So they got the info some other way. I didn't see anyone turn down the road behind the cab when it dropped us at Kelsey's place, although if Marietta put out an alert, the driver might have told the police where he dropped us. I don't think Kelsey would have told the police where we went, and I *know* she wouldn't have told anyone else. Not unless—

Molly! I have to call Kelsey.

But Molly is still ignoring me. She sets my phone aside, and dumps the contents of Deo's backpack onto the backseat. Her fingers run around the inside of the bag, and after a few seconds, she pulls something out.

Then she grabs the phone again. "Found it! At least, I can't think what else this would be."

"Okay," Aaron says. "Do the same thing to Anna's backpack. If you find another one, leave them both in a place we can locate them, outside the store."

She looks around. "There's a propane tank stand. I'll leave them behind the right rear leg."

"Good. Then get out of there. Pretty sure they're only planning on using Deo for information . . . or leverage . . . but—"

Anger surges inside me at the thought of them using Deo in any way. I can't be responsible for Kelsey, too. I push again, hard.

"Kelsey!" I yell, much louder than necessary, when I finally break through.

"What?"

"I have to call Kelsey, Aaron. If they know we're here, someone must have followed us to her place, or the cabdriver told them and—"

"No, no, no. Calm down, okay? Pretty sure it was the tracker. That thing Molly just pulled out of Deo's pack. Badea or her assistant must have slipped it inside at the station. You need to make sure it's the only one and get rid of it. Are you okay to drive?"

"Yes." Even though the panic is still there, and part of me is still screaming inside, knowing there's a chance that Kelsey is unhurt has pulled it down a notch. "I can drive."

"Good. First things first. See if there's a second tracker. I'll call Sam or Daniel and get one of them to pick the trackers up. Maybe they can find a truck stop near 95 and attach them to a semi heading out of the area. And they'll see if we can get any info from the clerk, maybe the surveillance feed."

"You might as well just destroy the trackers. If that woman can read anything in Deo's mind, she's never going to believe that I'd take off without him." I fight back the thought that they may well try to make *Deo* believe I've taken off without him, but they'd probably do that regardless of where the stupid trackers are.

I grab my pack and start to dump it in search of the tracking device.

Feel along the top before you dump everything out. It's probably in the same spot.

And she's right—it's at the very top of my bag. A thin, round disk, stuck to the lining.

I start to yank it, but my hands stop, almost of their own accord.

The tracker is how they found Deo. So it stands to reason that it's the easiest way for whoever has Deo to find me. And that's what has to happen. They have to find me, and let me know what I need to do to keep Deo safe.

My fingers brush over it one more time, but I leave it in place. I toss the tracker from Deo's bag in as well . . . might as well boost the damn signal.

Molly's confused at first, then angry.

What the hell are you doing? This isn't smart, Anna.

They don't want Deo, Molly. They're using him to get me to cooperate. I have to give them a way to find me.

She's still yelling at me. I can hear her, faintly, even after my wall is all the way up.

I pick up the phone. My thumb pauses over the end-call button, but Aaron sincerely thinks he's doing the right thing.

"Thanks for trying to help, Aaron. Molly was right . . . you're a nice guy."

"What? Anna—"

I end the call and turn off the ringer.

CHAPTER TEN

At 2:12, I pull into the driveway of a tall, narrow building that is light-years from my mental image of a cottage. It's a full-fledged house. There are two additional stories above the two-car garage, both with decks overlooking the rocky shoreline across the street. And there's another smaller level at the very top that's just a sundeck.

I get out and hold the QR code that Kelsey sent against the reader. I pull her car into the garage and retrieve my pack and the bags of groceries. Seeing Deo's stuff, still scattered over the backseat, is like a gut punch, but I shove it back into his bag.

Kelsey's sister had very different taste, or maybe there's a mandatory seashore décor if you live near the ocean. The entire place is painted in varying shades of blue and seafoam green. All of the lamps in the living room have seashells glued around the base, the windows look like portholes, and there's a fake-looking pointy-nosed fish over the mantel.

I call from the cottage phone, as I promised Kelsey I would. She answers on the second ring and I release the breath I was holding. She's safe.

"Anna! I'm glad you made it. I was beginning to worry. Did you have trouble with the car?"

"No," I tell her, trying to keep my voice light. "No problems. We stopped for gas, and I took it kind of slow on the road. Didn't want to get pulled over."

"You looked exhausted when you were here. I'm glad Deo managed to keep you awake on the drive."

I clench my fist, digging my nails into the palm of my hand. "Yeah. He was great."

"Well, get some sleep. We'll talk more in the morning."

"Yeah, I'm wiped out. Thanks again, Kelsey."

I grab a bottle of water, then drag myself up the stairs. Four bedrooms, each with a bath. I drop my backpack onto the bed in a room that overlooks the water and cross over to the sliding glass door that leads onto the deck. The road in front of the house is so narrow that you only see it if you look straight down from the railing. Otherwise, you can almost imagine that you're directly over the water. It's too cold to leave the door open, but I crack it to let some fresh air in.

When I put my phone on the nightstand—surprise, surprise— there are three calls from Aaron. Two texts from Taylor. Eventually they'll call Kelsey to get the address, and once they tell her about Deo, she'll either give it to them or come looking for me herself. But Kelsey will be on her flight to Indianapolis in about an hour, so I don't think they'll reach her before tomorrow morning at the earliest.

I set the alarm on my phone for 7:00 a.m., turn the ringer back on, and crawl under the covers. My mind is still racing. And each time it circles back around to Deo, it's like a knife twisting. As much as I want to take the two pills that are still in my pocket, I put them back in the bottle. If Dacia, Cregg, or whoever is holding him tries to contact me—

The phone buzzes and I bolt straight up, knocking the phone off the nightstand in my rush to grab it. The timing is almost like someone is reading my mind. Which, given the events of the past twenty-four hours, might actually be the case.

The text is just four words, two of them misspelled.

`Patients is a virtute.`

I type in that I'll do whatever they say, but before I can hit send, more words start popping up:

`Silents is golden.`

`Do not call police. Wait for instructiun.`

`Fiecare pasare, pe limba ei piere.`

I have no idea what the last one means, but I hit send on my response:

`Just let me know what you want. Please don't hurt him!`

Silence, which I find not at all golden, is what I get in return.

I run the last quote through Google Translate. The answer is an ominous "each bird perishes by her tongue," which seems to be Romanian for *be careful what you say.*

I send several more pleas, and get nothing in return. So I try calling the number that sent the texts.

A chipper woman's voice comes on immediately. "This number has been changed, disconnected, or is no longer in service. If you feel you have reached this recording in error, please check the number and try your call again."

❖ ❖ ❖

Sleep, when it finally takes me, is deep and dreamless, even without the pills. The only good thing about the events of last night is that they seem to have jolted Molly's consciousness a bit, and there were no memories to assimilate. In fact, it's Molly puttering around, rather than my alarm, that awakens me. I've yet to find a way to keep my wall up when I'm sleeping.

Nothing new on my phone, only the earlier unanswered voice and text messages from Aaron and Taylor.

You should call them, Anna. Do you really think you can handle this alone?

Didn't you read those messages? I'm supposed to WAIT and say nothing. I'm not going to put Deo at risk by doing anything else.

The sky is just beginning to show a hint of daybreak as I step into the shower. This place has four full baths, one for each bedroom, with a half bath on the main floor and another in the basement. There are only three bathrooms at Bart House, which means there's always a line and never enough hot water. I can't even remember the last time I was able to shower without someone banging on the door.

But I can't enjoy it. Even though the ring volume is at max, and I could probably hear it from downstairs, I keep glancing at my phone, perched on the sink next to a basket of shell-shaped soaps, hoping I'll get something more than the cryptic messages from last night.

I've been in the shower about three minutes when I do hear something—not the phone, but someone banging on a door. Okay, not really banging. It's more like tapping, and it's not the bathroom door, but farther away. I rinse the last of the conditioner out of my hair, then cut the water and open the door so I can listen.

The doorbell sounds this time, followed by more knocking. Rapid, staccato knocks that suggest the person knocking has been at it for some time.

I wrap a towel around myself and flick off the bathroom light, and also the bedside lamp, so that the room is dark. Then I walk over to the sliding glass door and peek through the vertical blinds. A black car is parked in the driveway. I recognize it even before I hear the voice from the porch below.

"Anna, come on. I know you're in there."

Aaron. There's a strange echo effect in my head as Molly thinks the same thing. *How the hell did he get here?*

I mutter a few curses under my breath, then slide the door open and step out so that I can whisper over the railing. "I'm coming. Shut up."

He steps away from the door and glances up at me. I realize a moment too late that he has a very interesting view right now, given that I'm in nothing but a towel and he's looking up from below. Ducking inside, I pull the door closed and rub the towel through my hair, now chilly from the breeze coming in over the bay. I take my time pulling on a sweater, jeans, and socks.

Aaron is leaning on the porch railing when I open the front door. He looks sad more than angry. "Can I come in?"

"No. You can get back in your car and leave. Molly told you everything she remembers."

Not true. I didn't know you were planning to—

And the wall goes UP.

"If you want this place to remain a safe house," Aaron says, "it would probably be a good idea not to draw too much attention."

"Maybe," I hiss through clenched teeth, "you should have thought of that before you started banging on the door at six a.m. And in case you haven't figured it out, I brought the trackers with me. I *want* them to find me."

"Yeah, I kind of pieced that together. But do you want the neighbors phoning the police?"

There's no movement except for a lone fisherman heading down the pier across the street. I'm not sure how many people are even around this time of year, but he's right. There's no sense in drawing further attention. I step aside and let him enter.

"Thank you." He rubs his hands together, blowing on them to warm up. "Sorry I interrupted your bath."

I try to fight back the blush, but it doesn't work. "Apology noted. How did you find me?"

Now it's his turn to blush. "Porter installed a tracking app on your phone when he had it."

He can clearly see what I think about that, because he says, "I'm sorry, okay? Wasn't me. But I called Ella and finally convinced her to ask Porter to give me the coordinates when the nurses woke him up to check his vitals this morning."

I start looking through my phone, trying to find this app that Molly's asshole grandfather installed.

"Give it here," he says. "I'll remove it."

I hand him my phone and watch as he uninstalls something called WhereUB.

"Probably why this thing has been a battery hog lately." I stash the phone back in my pocket. "Thank you. But you need to leave now. I've done my part. I delivered Molly's message. You know pretty much everything she knew. I hope you find that bastard Lucas, and I hope you find Graham Cregg, but I'm out. I'm not helping you."

"Even without the app, we'd have found you. Taylor had already narrowed it down to this street. I've been parked by the dock watching for any signs of movement for the past hour. The clerk at the gas station called the police after you left. They were debating issuing an AMBER Alert, but there's no evidence of force. They think it's more plausible that Deo left Bartholomew House with you and then decided to ditch you to head off with some other friends. Either way, though, they want to talk to you."

"No! No police. They said I can't tell anyone . . . that I have to wait. And that's what I'm going to do. I'm going to wait until they contact me again and do whatever the hell those people want me to do in order to get Deo back safe and sound. I need to get my stuff and—"

"Hold on. We thought that might be the case. Taylor and I are the only ones who know your actual location. Sam and Porter know that we know, but they don't want details. The security system at the gas station is crap . . . don't think they've updated it in a decade. The police couldn't read the tag on either car, but they do know that you're in a red Volvo, so . . ."

"Then I'll catch a bus—"

He grabs me by the shoulders. "You need to play this smart. This Badea woman works for Cregg. Do you really think that the man who killed all of those girls is going to just ask you for a little favor and then set you and Deo free?"

"They'll set him free before I do anything to help them."

"So that's your game? You're going to play martyr? You don't even know what they *want* from you!" His voice softens. "You heard what Molly said about Cregg. Could you really refuse to do what he wanted if he makes you watch while Deo carves himself up with a knife?"

My knees buckle and I collapse on the floor, wrapping my arms around my head. "Shut up, damn you! Shut up and go away."

"I'm sorry." Aaron drops to the floor next to me. His arms encircle me. "I'm so sorry, Anna. I know you didn't want to hear that, but it's the truth. And running from the truth isn't going to get Deo back alive."

I try to push him away, but he doesn't let go. He just pulls me in tighter.

"It's okay, Anna. You don't have to do this alone. We're on the same side. Let me help you."

The tears I've been fighting back for the past few minutes brim over. Aaron doesn't smell like vanilla—more like a forest, really, with a hint of the ocean spray he picked up waiting outside. But he makes the same soothing noises that Kelsey made when I was small, his lips pressed against my hair. I'm angry that Aaron has broken down my defenses, but there's also this very contrary part of me that doesn't want him to let go. That wants to be able to rely on his strength, just for a little while.

I give in to that weakness for a few minutes and cry into his shoulder. He smooths my still-damp hair and whispers, "It's okay . . . shh . . . it's okay."

When I pull myself together, I give him what I hope is a convincing smile. "I'm sorry for being difficult. I know you're right—this isn't something I should do alone."

And he probably *is* right.

But I also know that as soon as I hear from Dacia or any of Cregg's people, I'll be walking out that door without hesitation. And if they say come alone, I'll be coming alone. As long as they have Deo, they call the shots.

❖ ❖ ❖

For the next six hours, I alternate between the living room and my room upstairs, peeking out the windows and nervously checking my phone. I called Kelsey again and brought her up to speed. The fact that I hadn't told her about Deo last night made me feel bad, but I'm pretty sure she understood when I explained why.

I also called Joe. Told him I had to leave town. That family issues came up. He immediately asked if Deo was okay—I've worked there long enough for him to know Deo's the only "family" I have. And then I lied to Joe, too. Said Deo was fine, that I was sorry for leaving him shorthanded, and hung up before I started bawling like a baby again.

Aaron apparently got zero sleep last night between camping out in front of Bartholomew House waiting for his spidey sense to go off, and then trying to find me. He's crashed on the couch in the living room, his sock-clad feet hanging off the edge. I told him to take one of the rooms upstairs, but I think he's worried that he'll sleep too soundly. That I might grab my backpack and sneak out without him hearing if he lets himself get too comfortable.

Smart boy. I've considered it twice already, and talked myself out of it both times.

Sam called a little after nine a.m. and gave us more detail on the security footage from the gas station. Deo was walking back to the Volvo when a late-model BMW sedan, metallic blue or black, zipped in from Chesapeake Beach Road. It screeched to a halt directly in front of him. That's when he dropped his drink. Given the glare from the lights overhead and the tint of the windows, neither of the cameras got a clear shot of the passengers or the tags. But a second after the car appeared, the back door swung open. Deo hesitated briefly, then got in, glancing over his shoulder toward the entrance.

The local police think the fact that Deo didn't resist means that he was friends with someone in the car. But Sam said Deo looked frightened. He believes someone was pointing a gun at him. And he's right. Otherwise, there's no way in hell Deo would have gotten into that car.

They did discover that the car took a right at Old Solomons Island Road. So, aside from an approximate make and color on the car and which way they turned, the tape showed nothing I didn't know already.

I grab a bottle of water from the fridge and go back up to my room. The air is wet and salty, and I pull my sweatshirt around my body to ward off the chill as I step onto the deck to get a better view of the street. Nothing suspicious looking. Aside from a few passing cars and delivery trucks, the street has been empty all morning. It's a gray, rainy day, too late in the season for beachgoers. I doubt they'd be attracted to this particular shore anyway. There's no sand, just waves lapping against black and gray rocks. A few blocks down, there's a pier jutting out over the ocean. The handful of hardy souls who ventured onto the pier earlier this morning, dressed in rain ponchos and, in one case, holding an umbrella as he cast his line from the very end of the pier, have all given up now.

Right after her sister died, Kelsey mentioned how much Barbara had enjoyed fishing on that pier before she got sick, so I won't be going out there. If Kelsey's sister hasn't moved on to wherever, that's probably where she's hanging out. And while I'd be happy to help her pass on a final message, or catch that final fish, I can't take on any distractions until Deo is safe.

I'm about to go back inside when a car turns onto Atlantic Avenue. Not a blue or black BMW. Not a police cruiser. An unmistakable pale-purple Jeep.

The ghost of Emily MacAlister shudders at the string of words running through my head. What in God's name is Taylor doing here?

She pulls in behind Aaron's car, and a few moments later, the doorbell rings. Then the garage door goes up, and I watch through the blinds as they play musical parking spaces so that Taylor can get the Lavender Disaster into the garage next to Kelsey's car.

I'm in no mood for Taylor's angst. For the first couple of minutes, I stay in my room, but it's clear that's not going to work as soon as I hear them talking downstairs. I have to know what they're saying, on the off chance that Sam told Taylor some bit of info rather than phoning us again.

When I reach the bottom of the stairs, Taylor is sitting on the couch next to Aaron. Two sketch pads are on the coffee table in front of her. Her right hand is rummaging around in the front zip pocket of Deo's backpack.

"What do you think you're doing?"

She jumps, nearly dropping the bag, a guilty look on her face.

"It's okay," Aaron says. "I thought you were asleep or I'd have asked first. Taylor's searching for something she can use to track Deo."

"Exactly what do you mean by *track*?"

Taylor's nose wrinkles. "Yeah, Aaron. You make it sound like I'm a damn bloodhound. I'm looking for something that might give me a reading. Is there anything in here that Deo is especially attached to? Something he sleeps with? Or that he might have worn next to his body recently. Jewelry is better than fabric."

I try to rein in my skeptical look, but it's been an emotional day, and I probably fail miserably. Taylor rolls her eyes, then closes them, shaking her head wearily, as though praying for patience.

And yes, I realize I'm being unfair. I'd have realized it even without Molly muttering in the back of my head.

I told you already. Taylor finds stuff.

Taylor takes a deep breath, and with her patience wish apparently granted, opens her eyes. "I'm the only reason they found Molly's body, Anna. Officially, they got an anonymous tip from a hiker, but I sketched the woods where they took her. I drew a map of the winding dirt road that led back to the highway. It wasn't perfect, but it was close enough." Tears are building in her eyes. "It took me more than three months of doing nothing else but trying to match the map I'd drawn to satellite views, but I finally found the location. I hoped it would give her Pa and Mimmy some closure, but . . ." She's quiet for a moment, then shrugs, a defeated look on her face. "Maybe it would have been better for them to keep hoping. I don't know."

No, Tay. Not your fault.

"They needed to know," Aaron says. "Even if we couldn't find anything to pin it on Lucas, you finding Molly was a good thing." He gives her shoulder a squeeze, but she doesn't look convinced.

"Molly just said the same thing, Taylor. She doesn't want you blaming yourself."

I hold out my hand for Deo's bag, but I don't hold out much hope for this avenue of investigation. Even if Taylor succeeded in finding Molly, she admitted it took months. And she found a *body*. I shove that thought away so hard that I can feel the recoil. I can't even consider the possibility that all we'll find is his body.

"I think I put his phone back in here last night . . . ," I say, rummaging around.

"Um . . . not so sure about a phone," Taylor says. "Seems to work better if it's something they wore."

"Deo wore his phone more often than anything else. But . . ." I pull out the phone and unclamp the ear cuff from the top of the case. "I was actually looking for this. I gave it to him last Christmas. He was—"

"Wearing it at Sam's office," she says. "Yeah. I noticed."

I drop the cuff into her hand, and she scoops up her sketch pads and a pink sparkly bag lying next to her on the sofa, which I guess is a pencil bag. It looks familiar for some reason.

"I'm going to take over one of the rooms upstairs," she tells Aaron. "You didn't bring your headphones by any chance, did you? Forgot mine on the table back home."

He shakes his head.

I pull out Deo's purple-and-white earbuds from the pack, and my mind flashes back to him leaning against the brick wall at Carver's Deli with these in his ears, waiting for me to get back from my meeting with Porter.

"Here." I toss Taylor the earbuds. "No guarantees on the sound quality. I think Deo buys this brand as much for color coordination as anything else. And because they're cheap."

"They'll do. I just need something to help me block out any noise." Her eyebrows go up slightly. "Deo was carrying a blue set of these last night, wasn't he?"

I nod, even though I hadn't actually remembered that until she spoke.

Taylor turns to Aaron and hands him a folded note she's just pulled from the pocket of her sweater. "I found this next to the coffeepot this morning, which might explain why Daniel didn't answer his cell last night. I don't want to talk about it now, because it will piss me off and that interferes with my focus. But you might want to let Sam know."

She grabs the overnight bag next to the stairs and hurries up to the second floor.

Aaron curses and wads up the note.

"What is it?" I ask, as Aaron, who's apparently decided it was a bad idea to crumple it up, unwads and refolds the note.

"Daniel. Of course. Says he got a call last night and they want him to report early. So he's off again without bothering to tell Taylor or Mom a proper good-bye."

"Well . . . did he have a choice? I mean, one of my former tenants was in the Navy. When they say jump—"

"He had a choice about reenlisting. And this is just . . . typical. Sam would have been happy to take him into our business, happier than I'd have been actually, but Daniel was all worked up about how he could do more good as an actual police officer. They were excited to have him—Sam was ranting after you guys left last night about how Daniel was unappreciative and all the strings he pulled to get him bumped to the top of the list, but that's garbage. Five years of active duty, including investigative experience, meant the police training was a breeze—he was practically pretrained other than learning all of their administrative crap. But now he gets a bug up his ass four months out of training and he's off again, just as he gets to a place where he might actually be useful to us. Mom's always given him the benefit of every single doubt, so maybe he's right. Maybe she does understand, but Taylor sure as hell doesn't. And I'm pretty sure Mom thought she'd at least have a chance to say good-bye before he . . ."

He stops and gives me a rueful smile. "Sorry. I'm an idiot. You've been through enough in the past twenty-four hours without having to listen to me bitch about my inconsiderate jerk of a brother."

Aaron's smile is infectious, and despite everything I find myself returning it. "You couldn't say anything worse than what I was thinking yesterday when he dumped me on the sofa." I nod toward the stairs. "I don't suppose there's anything we can do to . . . help her?"

"Stay out of her way. Keep quiet. And have food around when she takes a break. Viewing makes her hungry."

"So . . . that's what this is? Remote viewing, like they talked about in the video I watched last night?"

"Pretty much, although remote viewers usually don't have an object to read. There are perfectly good blanket terms for what Taylor does—clairvoyance, psychometry. But the military didn't like the paranormal baggage attached to those. Taylor says she just sits there and meditates, more or less, until something comes to her. Then she picks up the pencil and starts sketching the image she sees in her head. Vague outlines at first, but then she goes back and concentrates until she can fill in the necessary detail."

"Did she have an object to . . . read . . . when looking for Molly?"

He nods. "One of those BFF necklaces, shaped like half a heart. Molly gave half to Taylor for her thirteenth birthday. *Partners in Crime* etched on the front if you pressed the two together." He gives a small chuckle. "Which described those two perfectly. And Molly was wearing the other half when they found the body."

"But it still took her months."

"Yeah, but she's got a quicker start this time. And Molly was in a ravine in the middle of the woods. In the middle of *nowhere*, the next state over. One stretch of woods looks a lot like another. Deo's probably in a building somewhere."

Unless . . .

I shove myself up from the chair and go into the kitchen, as though leaving the room will put distance between me and my thoughts.

It doesn't, of course.

Unless he's already dead.

Stop it. You need to stay positive. You can't sit here and work yourself into a panic. If they want something from you, they'll keep him alive.

"Then why haven't they *called?*" I slam my fists against the kitchen counter. And send a silent apology up to Taylor, hoping I didn't break her focus.

Aaron sits on one of the bar stools and looks at me across the blue tile counter. "They'll call, Anna. They're purposefully waiting, trying to worry you. Get you worked up enough that you'll be willing to do whatever they say."

"Yeah, well, if that's what they wanted, all they had to do was pull back around while I was standing there screaming in the parking lot. Deo doesn't deserve this. He's just a little . . . kid." I realize how dumb that sounds before I even finish the words. I expect Aaron to think it's stupid, but he doesn't react. He just watches me, with an expression very similar to the one Kelsey wears when she's trying to get me to calm down and think things through.

I open a bottle of orange soda that's in the pantry and pour it over a glass of ice before turning back to face Aaron. It's low on fizz, probably left behind by Kelsey's sister or some previous tenant, but I chug half of it anyway.

"I'm not delusional, Aaron. I know he's nearly six feet tall. Deo's not a little kid to anyone but me. But I held him when he cried. When he *was* a little kid. I promised him I'd keep the monsters away. That I wouldn't let anyone else hurt him. I *promised.* And now—" I stop and pull in several deep breaths. I don't want to lose it again like I did this morning. "It makes me so angry!"

"I can tell. And I'd feel the same way if someone had Taylor. But you're going to wear yourself out at the very time you need to be strong. Eat something. Sleep if you can. Turn on the TV. Read a book. Try to take your mind somewhere else. I know you can't, not really, but you need to try or you're going to make yourself crazy."

So . . . I try. When it becomes clear that the TV, even with its bazillion channels, isn't going to hold my attention, we resort to some of the board games stashed on the hallway bookshelves. Trivial Pursuit is a total joke—Aaron quickly discovers it's not the best game to play against someone with nine or more sets of random knowledge. We play one round of Aggravation, which lives up to its name but gives my mind way too much time to wander.

Aaron goes over to the window and pulls back the blinds a bit. He watches for a few seconds, looking concerned. I join him, but the street seems quiet. The only movement I see is someone on a bike at the far end of Atlantic Avenue.

"Is someone out there?"

"No. Just thinking." He lets go of the blind. "I'm going to make some coffee."

I hear him moving things around in the pantry as I go back to the game shelf, hoping to find a Scrabble board. With Emily's mad crossword skills at my disposal, I doubt it's any more fair to Aaron than Trivial Pursuit, but it would be much more likely to distract me. My search comes up empty, however . . . It seems to be the only family staple that no one bothered to stock.

"Instant okay?" he asks, leaning around the pantry door. He's holding up two tins of the powdery stuff that's at least as much sugar as coffee, and his expression suggests that it's really *not* okay with him.

I'd rather shoot caffeine directly into my bloodstream than drink that stuff, but I nod. "If that's the only option, then, sure."

"Suisse Mocha or French Vanilla?"

I opt for the chocolate version, and when he returns with the alleged coffee, I tell him, "This isn't working. I need to do something constructive. The other day—" I shake my head, realizing that it's been less than twenty-four hours. "*Yesterday*, at the townhouse. You said you think this program at Fort Meade is responsible for the things you and Taylor are able to do. And even if you didn't come out and say it, I'm guessing you think the program—or Cregg, or someone else involved with it—had something to do with your dad's death."

He nods once. "I'm positive about that last part. Whatever it may have looked like, Dad didn't commit suicide. And Molly's information about Cregg was the missing piece of that puzzle."

I feel incredibly stupid. That hadn't even occurred to me. "You think Graham Cregg *made* your dad step in front of that truck?"

"I do."

"But . . . why do you think Cregg wanted him dead?"

"They were trying to restart whatever they were doing before. Maybe Dad was going to blow the whistle."

"What else do you know about Cregg? And the company he runs—what's it called again?"

"He's on the board of directors for Decathlon Services Group. They're a government contractor." Aaron gives a humorless laugh. "And I've read pretty much everything there is to know about DSG that's in the public record over the past few years. It's an umbrella organization with lots of small companies involved in every aspect of military operations that can be contracted out—which, these days, means pretty much everything. Cregg generally doesn't get involved in the day-to-day operations of DSG. From what I can tell, he shows up at meetings and that's about it. But we believe he's much more hands-on when it comes to one of the subsidiary groups, Python Diagnostic. He's CEO of that one."

"Python. That's what Daniel said last night. When we were coming out of the police station."

"Yeah. We'd just gotten him up to speed after his time in the military. I thought he might actually be useful in piecing some of this together—" He stops and runs one hand through his hair. "I'm doing it again. Sorry."

"My fault. If I need to refer to him from now on, I'll just say He-Who-Shall-Not-Be-Named."

That earns me a full smile. He has a really nice smile.

"So . . . what exactly does this Python Diagnostic do?"

"Damn good question. The only information I've been able to get is that they handle human resources and staffing, but DSG has a second group that handles that, so I'd guess the description is a cover. Then there was an article in the *Guardian* a few years back. A woman claimed Python had something to do with the disappearance of her husband. I tried to follow up with her, because her husband was a celebrity psychic. Erik Bell. Had his own TV show for a while—"

"*Breaking the Veil* with Erik Bell?"

For some reason, the name carries the smell of antiseptic and a feeling of happiness, which is odd, because those two things definitely clash in my mind. I hate hospitals. They scare the hell out of me. But the hospital stay was a good memory for Bruno, Kelsey's homeless patient. To him, it was almost like a vacation, the first time in four years that he'd felt completely secure. He didn't like the needles, but the food was decent enough, the bed was warm and clean, and for part of the time, he had a TV remote all to himself. Kelsey even came to the hospital for his appointment, and she brought him a big tin of cookies. He was sad when they released him, even though the hospital stay had been enough to ensure him a guaranteed spot in a shelter until the worst of the winter weather passed. The shelter would be warm and he'd have food, but who knew when he'd get the TV remote again.

"Yeah," Aaron says. "That's it. You're familiar with the show?"

"Sort of. One of my hitchers. Bruno. He watched every episode. Are you saying Bell got his ability from this same program at Meade?"

"No . . . he was a touring psychic years before that. But in that *Guardian* article, Magda—that's Bell's wife—claimed that Python Diagnostic hired him to work with them around 2002. Promised to boost his natural abilities. She said she thought they actually *did* boost his psychic powers—that's about the time he started doing the *Breaking the Veil* show. But he had a nervous breakdown and quit in 2008. Only did theater performances, mostly in Great Britain, after that. He disappeared after a show in Edinburgh in 2017. His wife said someone contacted him, asking about his time with Python, the week before he vanished."

"And that's the only mention you could find of Python? Or anything that might be related?"

"I've searched government records, all the major news organizations. Every credible source out there."

I have the feeling I'm going to regret it, but I grab the laptop out of Deo's bag. "Then maybe we need to start rummaging around in some of the not-so-credible sources. If there was a government program operating for what—five years?—at Fort Meade and it had anything to do with psychic abilities, there's no way that would have escaped the notice of the conspiracy nuts. Bruno . . . he's the hitcher I mentioned? He spent a lot of time at the public library, combing through the conspiracy websites. And even though he was more into alien abductions, some of these sites have a little bit of everything."

"Okay . . ." He sounds dubious.

"Hey, I'm not saying we're going to find unassailable facts on these sites. But occasionally, there's a nugget of truth hidden inside the layers of crazy."

I don't add that those nuggets are really rare, and usually only tiny nuggets with so much crazy around them that it's hard to find the true bits. I'm tired of sitting here doing nothing, and it can't hurt to see what's out there.

I type in *allglobalconspiracies.com*. That was Bruno's one-stop shop for everything wack. I'm relieved to see that the site is still active. It actually looks almost identical to the memory I have.

Aaron sits next to me. "Well. Somebody likes bright colors."

"Yeah. Web design skills seem to be sorely lacking among conspiracy theorists. This particular site is sort of a hub. It's been around almost as long as there's been an internet. It doesn't have a search engine, but it is well organized . . . well, it was back when Bruno was using it."

"When did he . . ."

"Die? I was six, so . . . early 2008. Bruno was a nice guy, he just had some weird ideas."

And he liked to take stuff that didn't belong to him, but I decide Aaron doesn't really need to know that part. Bruno did his best to make amends—his entire reason for being in my head was to make sure that Kelsey and a few other people got their things back.

I scroll through the index. "Does psychological operations sound like the right category to you?"

He nods and I click the link. It takes us to a site called *EyeOnPsyops*. A big, garish eye stares out at me from the top of the page, and the article's title reads *Exclusive!!! U.S. General Admits Role in 9/11 Planning*. That headline alone is bad enough, but it's on a solid black background page, and *Exclusive!!!* is coded in bright red. The word actually blinks.

"This one's from 2014," Aaron says. "And it seems to be the most recent. Before that, new stuff was being added every couple of days. The site admin must have found a new obsession."

"Maybe." I'm doubtful, though. I think it's more likely the guy joined Bruno in the great beyond. Once they start down the conspiracy path, people don't tend to move on to video games, or knitting, or whatever. "There's a lot here. Why don't you grab your tablet and start at the bottom, while I start from the top?"

We spend the next twenty minutes skimming to see if there's anything of interest. Some of the links go to an outside site, and it's about fifty-fifty whether the link is dead. Luckily, a lot of the articles can be dismissed by the title alone, but about every third title is vague enough that I click to see if it's at all relevant.

And yes, I also click on a few that mention aliens. I know it's garbage, but I've got memories of almost every *X-Files* episode. Bruno had the first six seasons on VHS before he lost his job and his apartment.

Aaron nudges me with his elbow. "Hey, I may have something."

I quickly close an article on Area 52 at Dugway Proving Ground and go back to the main index.

"Scroll down to the section that says *Psychoactive Weapons*. There at the bottom. Two articles on something they call the Delphi Project. I haven't finished reading the first one, but it mentions Fort Meade, and also the Stargate Project. From the video I showed you, the one that was on *Frontline* back in 1995?"

"*Nightline*. Yeah, I remember."

The first link, dated 2008, reads: *22 Dead or MIA from Top-Secret Delphi Project.* Right below it is a link to another article, this one written in 2014: *Second Gen Delphi?*

"I'll skim through the second article while you finish the first."

It begins with a summary of the author's 2008 article, the one that Aaron is reading. Conspiracy Guy's source, an unnamed former subject he calls Smith, claims the Delphi Project was located near Aberdeen, Maryland, rather than at Fort Meade. The project emerged "phoenix-like from the ashes of the Stargate Project," pulling in around fifty individuals who ranked as slightly gifted on an entry test for psychic abilities. Most were from military backgrounds, including the anonymous source, but Mr. Smith claims several civilians, including Erik Bell, were attached to the program as well.

Delphi participants were treated with a drug designed to increase native psychic abilities. And according to Smith, it did—by several orders of magnitude. Unfortunately, the drug had unexpected side effects. Mental instability was the biggest problem. More than a dozen of the participants committed suicide between 1995 and 2002, when the program closed. Four of them took out at least one additional person when they went. This one guy appeared completely okay when he left work one evening in 2001. The next morning, he walked into a Denny's just north of Baltimore and opened fire, killing three customers and the guy behind the counter before turning the gun on himself.

But the key focus of this article is Smith's claim that the drug had epigenetic—that is, gene-altering—effects that were transmitted to offspring. Delphi participants were contractually prohibited from reproducing during their time in the program and for six months after it ended, due to a concern that the drug might be carried in the egg or sperm of the test subjects. But Smith says they didn't factor in the possibility of *transgenerational* epigenetic impacts—that possibility that the subject's genes might be altered in ways that would be inherited by *all* future offspring.

Hundreds of these children have been born during the past decade, not just to the official Delphi participants, but also to parents in the control group, those who didn't pass the Delphi entrance tests. Some of those offspring are perfectly normal. Others can at least pass for children with emotional or psychiatric problems. Many, however, are wholly unable to function in society. Those children are being rounded up by the corporation that ran Delphi, supposedly for the children's own welfare.

Smith has simply relayed the facts of the case. It is for others to consider the implications of what he has seen. What is this unnamed organization overseeing and possibly brainwashing these children who have the ability to read minds, predict the future, or even control the actions of others? Is it connected to the US government? Or perhaps to the UN? Are these children being protected or are they being trained by the New World Order as weapons to be used against an unsuspecting populace?

"Whoa, Aaron. You might want to take a look at this—"

I start to hand the laptop to him, but he's staring at his tablet, mouth open. "You need to see this." He looks at the laptop in my hands and his mouth twitches nervously. "Okay, yeah. Let's swap. You can skip the part in the middle where he goes off on a tangent about how the Delphi psychics contacted the Grand Duchess Anastasia while on these drugs. Pretty sure she'd have been dead by then—"

"Never stopped me."

He pauses for a moment. "That's . . . true. *Very* good point. Anyway, start here with the stuff that happened at Bragg."

He taps the screen and I read:

Smith claims that a test subject injected with the formula predicted that April 19, 1993, would be a day of fire. That over 120 people would die in three separate fires—one in Texas, one in South Dakota, and the last in South Korea. She said the fire in South Dakota would be from a plane crash, and she had the sense that it would be similar to Air Force One. Not actually Air Force One, but similar. The Texas fire would be at a church or a school, something involving children. And the one in South Korea might be at a prison. She drew images of shackles and burned bodies strapped to beds.

On April 19, three major incidents occurred that mirrored the woman's visions. A fiery plane crash in Iowa killed eight people, including South Dakota governor, George Mickelson. The siege at the Branch Davidian compound in Waco, Texas, resulted in seventy-six fatalities. And that very same day, a fire in a Seoul psychiatric hospital killed thirty-four patients, many of whom were tied to their beds.

There are about ten paragraphs after that, but I skim them because they're pretty much a rehash of the other article. He discusses the suicides but gives a little more detail. All of the deaths were in the Baltimore or DC areas, except for one—the murder of a middle-aged couple that took place near Fredericksburg in 1999.

"Oh my God . . . that sounds just like . . ."

"Yeah," Aaron says. "It sounds just like Daniel's dad."

CHAPTER ELEVEN

We don't find anything else of value at *EyeOnPsyops*. The rational side of me thinks that's because these really are the only truth nuggets in the vast sea of garbage on this site, but there's still a little bit of Bruno in there asking how I *know* the alien stuff isn't true. Maybe I just need something to put it into context so that I can *recognize* the truth.

That kind of thinking is the downside of spending too much time in my Bruno files.

Aaron and I have expanded our search to a few other sites when I glance up to see Taylor on the stairs. She's stripped down to a tank top and running shorts. Her hair is damp and her skin glistens with sweat, as though she's just finished an hour of exercise. The larger of the two sketch pads is tucked under one arm and a Scrabble game is tucked under the other.

"Do *not* tell me why you're huddled over those computers. It will just distract me. But here—this was in the attic bedroom." She hands me the game before she heads into the kitchen.

"There are chips in the pantry," Aaron says. "Some fruit. Cheese in the fridge."

Taylor tosses the sketch pad and pencil bag onto the counter and rips open a bag of Doritos. "Somebody has to deliver pizza around here, right?" she says, mouth half full. "It's the friggin' beach."

I glance down at the Scrabble game and then over at Aaron. "Did I say anything to you about a Scrabble game?"

Taylor shakes her head. "Didn't have to. I heard it floating around in the static when I was trying to focus. I knew what you were looking for was upstairs." She glances at the laptop on the coffee table. "So, there's internet?"

"Yeah. Want me to find a pizza place that delivers?" Aaron asks.

"Most definitely, but I could manage that on my phone. You're going to need the bigger screen to start searching for this." She flips the sketchbook open.

"You found something about Deo?" I'm off the couch so fast that the Scrabble box tumbles out of my lap.

"Oh . . . no. Not yet." Her shoulders sag. "I didn't mean to get your hopes up. I needed to fill in some details on the sketch of the house that I started after our meeting at Sam's last night. It's not that I prioritized this over finding Deo. It's more like . . . this was in my printer queue and I had to get it out before I could start on something new?"

Her voice rises at the end, like what she's just said isn't quite accurate, but pretty close. Or maybe because she doesn't think I'll believe her. "Molly's still around, right? Can she check it out and see if I'm on the right track?"

It's only then that I realize she means it's a sketch of the house where Molly was held.

"She's still here," I say, feeling Molly shrink as far back as possible as I reach for the sketch pad. The drawing is in pencil and it's not especially detailed. I can make out a large house off to the left, with a smaller house behind it. And I can tell from Molly's reaction that Taylor's pretty much nailed it.

I don't know about the area around it. I never saw any of that. It was night when I went in, night when they took me out, and I wasn't really thinking straight on the return trip. I . . . kind of freaked out about being dead.

Yeah, I can imagine.

I relay Molly's thoughts to Taylor and take a closer look at the rest of the drawing. The area around the house is heavily wooded, and beyond the first ring of trees, there's a section that's shaded in with the side of the pencil so that it looks smooth.

"What's that?"

"Water," Taylor says after chugging down the last of the flat orange soda. "I think the house has a swimming pool, too. That's the smaller square near the second building. This is farther away, though. Maybe a quarter mile. Much bigger, too. Might be a lake, but I think it's a river. Pretty sure that darker spot—kind of tear-shaped—is an island. And that thing?" She taps a section in the top left corner of the page. It's shaped like a long-necked squash or maybe a pear tipped on its side, outlined with concentric ridges. "Don't know what it is, but it's definitely within a mile or two of the house."

"And you're sure the bag is still there?" Aaron asks.

"No. But if we can find this place and you can get me in closer, I'll know for certain."

"What . . . bag?"

She pushes the pencil bag toward me. Now I remember where I've seen it. "Molly had something like this. I saw a flash of it last night when you asked her about a . . . some-letter-I-can't-remember purse. But it was square."

"Because she kept it folded in her jeans pocket. And it wasn't a letter . . . I asked if she was carrying her *Elle* purse. Like the character in *Legally Blonde*?"

That rings a distant bell. I'm guessing one of my tenants watched it at some point, and I'm pulling up blonde, chirpy, and pink all on my own, so I nod.

"Mom came in while we were watching this Disney Channel sequel a few weeks before Christmas when we were what? Nine? Ten, maybe? It was supposed to be about that *Legally Blonde* woman's cousins or something. They had pink everything. And . . . well, I guess Mom thought we were finally getting into girly stuff. We got these matching sparkly pink purses from her as gifts. We didn't want to hurt her feelings, so we both found a way to use them. Molly folded hers in half and used it as a wallet. I use mine to carry my pencils, even though I had to sharpen half an inch off each pencil to make the damn things fit. They didn't find the purse on Molly's body. So when she told me that she was carrying it that night, I thought I'd try to get a read on it."

Taylor rips a page out of the sketch pad and leaves it on the table. "And now I'm going to do the same thing with Deo's ear cuff. I can't promise anything. I knew Molly her entire life and I just met Deo. I've done readings with total strangers before, but it seems to work best with people I know, so even with something as recent as the jewelry . . ."

The bag of Doritos goes with her when she heads upstairs, and she pokes a finger at Aaron as she passes. "Find my pizzas, mister."

❖ ❖ ❖

Between Taylor's sketch and Molly's information about the highway exit, Aaron and I pinpoint the location of the house before the pizzas arrive. The pear-shaped thing is a quarry. The island is in the Susquehanna River. Finding the specific house was a little tougher, because it's at the end of a long private drive. We had to go with only the satellite images, rather than street view. But this one is in the right position in relation to the other things in Taylor's sketch, the landscaping is right, and it's the only one nearby with a smaller structure out back. No pool, though.

Another couple of minutes on the state property tax website, and we've learned the place is owned by HLMC Corp. Aaron runs some searches, but he can't find anything about an HLMC Corporation, or anything close to it, that's connected to the Creggs or to Decathlon Services Group.

I stack the last two pizza boxes on the counter. "You ordered enough to feed a football team."

"Maybe a chess team." He frowns at the slice I'm eating. "You took one with anchovies?"

I nod, tossing a few bits of sausage from my slice into the disposal. "Anchovies are good. I told you I was fine with anything. I just pick off the stuff I'd rather not eat . . . like sausage."

"When people say that, they usually don't mean anchovies. Go easy, okay? Taylor said *pizzas* . . . plural. Although to be fair, she picks half of the anchovies off herself. I think it's less that she likes them and more that she's marking that box so everyone will keep their paws off her slices."

"Do you really think she's going to eat two large pizzas? She's barely five feet."

"Most of the time she'd put away four slices tops. When she's viewing, though . . . Mom joked about taking out a second mortgage to pay the food bill during the months Taylor was trying to find Molly."

"And your mom is okay with her kids being in the middle of all of this?"

"Okay might be putting it too strongly. Mom's finally gotten to the point where she accepts that Taylor won't sit back and, as Molly's grandmother would have said, 'hide her light under a bushel.' At least not until she sees some justice done where Molly's concerned. And me? I guess I could hole up in some back room and crunch numbers or whatever, but Mom knows that would make me crazy. I need to do work where I can actually put this ability to use or my life doesn't make sense. Unfortunately, her one *normal* offspring can't seem to stay put—"

He makes a sound that's somewhere between a laugh and a sigh. "And I'm ranting about Daniel again. Sorry. This whole thing just has me wound up. I mean, it's nice seeing some sort of confirmation of what I've suspected, but an article on a conspiracy website wouldn't hold up in court any more than . . ."

"The testimony of Molly's ghost?"

"Exactly." He finishes his slice of pizza and turns back to the computer. "So we'll have to find out who Conspiracy Guy actually is, then track down his source. Must have been one of the people working at Meade with my dad."

"Except Conspiracy Guy claims it was near Aberdeen. That's only, what? Ten miles from the house where Molly was taken?"

"Yeah. Could be they moved the program at some point. Or maybe Meade was just where Dad *told* Sam and Mom he was working."

"So . . . here's what I don't understand. Porter goes around spreading my claim that I'm channeling Molly, and suddenly, I'm on Cregg's radar, even though no court in the land would accept my testimony as evidence. If your theory is correct, it's because one of my parents was with Delphi. But they *know* your dad was connected to Delphi. Apparently they believed he was enough of a problem that they killed him. So why haven't they scooped you and Taylor up for testing?"

"Well . . . on paper, we're *not* his kids. He adopted us when he married Mom. She listed someone else as the biological father for all three of us, because of the contract he signed that prohibited marriage and families. Although anyone who snooped carefully might question that. Taylor and I look more like Dad than we do Mom."

"Okay, then—why *Molly*? How did she get pulled into the mess with your dad?"

"Her mom was with Lucas on and off from the time Molly was a baby. He was bad news from the beginning, mostly low-level drug dealing, petty theft, that sort of stuff. Sam, Porter, my dad, all three of them arrested Lucas at some point. If Cregg was looking for someone to get information on my dad, someone with a beef against him, Lucas was a natural choice. And I guess Cregg found a few other jobs for him after that, from what Molly said."

A car passes by outside, the tires churning up the water on the street. Exactly like every other time that has happened today, I can't keep myself from going to the window to check. In case there's something unusual. This waiting, just waiting with no news of any sort, is killing me.

The view outside the window is a study in grays and blacks. The sky, the water, the rocks along the shore. Even Aaron's car in the drive is black. It's eerie. Almost as though you could step through the door and enter some ancient TV show like *The Twilight Zone*. When Aaron touches my shoulder, I jump, and the wooden slat slips through my fingers, setting the rest of the vertical blind in motion.

"Whoa," Aaron says. "I didn't mean to startle you. Relax, okay? I know that's easier said than done, but if there's anyone out there, I'll know before you see them."

"Only if they're planning something violent. You didn't sense anything when Dacia walked into the police station last night. Just when she left, right?"

"Yeah, but . . . that was a police station. It's one of those places where my head starts buzzing as soon as I step in the door from all of the low-level violent thoughts. Hard to pick out anything that's not a white-hot rage in places like that. Here, though . . ."

I give him a questioning look and he nods toward the street.

"It's mostly peaceful. Half the houses are empty, so it's not hard to pick up individual thoughts. Some guy drove by about five minutes ago with a pretty strong intent to slam his fist into his wife's face because she was hounding him about something. Money, I think. There's a girl at the end of the block who wanted to smash her sister over the head with the toaster just now, but her better nature or common sense took over and she settled for kicking her. The one that had me most worried was the kid on the bike—you remember? Before Taylor came down with the sketch? He was having some pretty serious thoughts about self-harm, and in my experience, those thoughts are a lot harder for our better natures and common sense to push away."

I sit down on the couch and rub my eyes. My three hours of sleep is starting to get to me. "I wasn't questioning whether you could pick out their thoughts. It's just . . . like you said last night, Dacia was mad when she left the police station, mad that I blocked her. Maybe mad that I embarrassed her in front of the guy who was with her. She could have cooled off by now, though. She told me her boss didn't want me harmed. And they might send a lackey . . . someone to grab me, someone who sees it as doing his job. Can you pick up on that?"

"Sometimes. People who work as hired muscle, who 'grab people' for a living, generally kind of like violence. That's even true of some cops I've known. Anyone driving by will see my car out there, so they'll probably assume you're not alone. Maybe even assume there are weapons, and they'll be thinking about contingency plans. Pretty sure that will be enough to trip my wires." He glances at the Scrabble box on the coffee table. "Maybe we should start a game? Taylor's going to be pissed if she hunted for it and we didn't even play."

I don't get the sense that Taylor did much hunting, but it's a diversion, so I agree. And Aaron turns out to be a good player. Not Emily MacAlister good, but he has a knack for strategy.

Taylor comes down when the board is nearly full. She's wearing Deo's earbuds and his turquoise cuff is attached to her left ear.

"We found the—" Aaron stops when he sees Taylor's raised hand. The gesture smacks of diva, but I keep quiet as well. She grabs one of the pizzas and a bottle of water, then heads back up to her cave.

I place the *o* and *s* tiles I'm holding at the end of Aaron's previous word, *path*. The last tile lands on the triple word score.

"Pathos." He curses softly and shakes his head. "I thought of *pathed*, but all of the *d* tiles were used, so I figured that was safe."

It's already dark and we're finishing up Scrabble Battle number two when Taylor comes back down. She's carrying the pizza box—empty, judging from the angle at which she's holding it—but no sketch pad. Deo's earbuds are around her neck now. Her clothes are drenched.

"Anything?" Aaron asks.

"I'm not finished, but I need a break. So show me what you found."

Aaron flicks on the computer and shows her the location, near Havre de Grace.

"I thought that was a type of cheese?" she says, as she pans around the map.

"Pretty sure that's *chèvre*," Aaron says. "And the people there pronounce it *haverty grays*, not the Frenchified way. You can't see much more on the map. There's no street view that far down the road. And judging from the satellite view, there's no pool."

Taylor sniffs. "No biggie. Could have been a kiddie pool, a big puddle, something like that. I just got the sense of water a few times when I was drawing. This is the place, I'm certain. What did Molly say?" She pushes the computer aside and snags two slices of pizza from one of the boxes in the fridge.

"Molly's been kind of quiet, actually."

And she has. It's been hours since I've felt her presence. The last time was when we looked at Taylor's sketch.

"She's still there, though, right?" Taylor's question comes between bites, and when I nod, she looks over at Aaron.

"Did you check the property records?"

"Dead end. Some sort of holding corporation."

"Maybe Sam—"

"Sam's at the hospital 'til nine," Aaron says. "Giving Ella a break for a few hours."

"I know. He told me earlier. But Porter's in his own room now. They can have phones in there. Let's FaceTime. Pa will want to know all of this, too."

Molly stirs, as I'm pretty sure Taylor expected she would, when she used Molly's name for Porter. I resist the temptation to give her a dirty look, because I'm not sure she's doing it intentionally. But either way, she's clearly wagging a conversation with Porter in front of Molly like a piece of cheese to lure a mouse out of its hole.

I glance around quickly, to be sure there's nothing that would give away our location. "Don't let them know where we are, okay? I'd rather they didn't have to lie in case the police ask them about my location."

Even though I don't say it, I'd also rather Sam and Porter just plain didn't know, in case one or both of them decides I've made the wrong decision about keeping the police out of this for now.

"And let's not say anything yet about Delphi," Aaron says. "I'll wait and talk to Sam first."

"What's Delphi?" Taylor asks.

"I'll fill you in after we hang up." Aaron finishes entering the digits, and a few seconds later, Sam's face appears.

"Yeah. What's up?" One of those over-the-bed tray tables is partially visible behind him, with a brown paper bag and two take-out cups.

Aaron laughs. "Busted, Sam. Does Ella know you brought *O'Malley's* to the hospital?"

"She does *not*." Porter says off screen. "And don't you be tellin' her, neither. A man gets shot, he deserves some real food. Sam was the only one with the decency to oblige."

"We won't snitch," Taylor says through a mouthful of pizza. "But you boys better be sure to take your cholesterol meds. Scooch over so we can see Pa, too."

Molly's listening—no surprise there. But she feels faint, wispy, as though most of her attention is somewhere else.

A chair screeches as both of them try to get in position. Taylor says he needs a selfie stick, and Sam mutters a curse in response.

"Why don't I just hand him the damn phone?"

Porter's propped up in bed. He somehow appears younger in the light-blue hospital gown. One arm is immobilized, but aside from that, he actually looks better than he did when I last saw him at Kelsey's office. Of course, he'd just received a pretty major shock yesterday.

He squints, then says, "Hey, Anna. Glad to see you're okay. I saw you open that door yesterday and heard another shot go off as I was going down. Is . . ."

I know the question he's hesitating over. It's the same one Taylor just asked me.

Need a tattoo on my forehead: Yes, Molly is still in the house.

Only if it's the temporary kind.

"She's still here," I tell him. "But . . . a lot farther back now."

His face twinges, but he nods. "You be careful, okay, girl? What Sam's been tellin' me sounds flat-out crazy, and I'm still not entirely sure I believe him. But I think it's clear these ain't people to mess with. Aaron and Sam will keep you safe and they'll help get your friend back. I'm sorry the two of you wound up in the middle of all this."

The words are such a change from yesterday's attitude of blaming me for everything that my eyes tear up a bit. I expect Molly to chime in with some variant of *I told you so*. But she doesn't.

"Thank you, Mr. Porter. I'll be careful."

Porter gives me a sad smile and hands the phone back to Sam.

"So . . . have you heard anything new?" Sam asks. "Or did you guys just call to check in?"

"Nothing else about Deo. But we . . . *found* . . . something."

"Ah," Sam sighs. "I wondered why Taylor was there. And why she was talking with her mouth full. Your mother—"

"Is in Barcelona today," Taylor says. "Two more cities and a half-dozen galleries left to go. And since the brother she left in charge packed up his bag and headed off to play soldier boy bright and early this morning, I did the only responsible thing and came to stay with my *other* big brother." She gives Sam a cheeky grin. "But yes, I've been working today. Aaron's company card is going to have a hefty charge from Domino's. Worth it, though. I found the house."

"Oh. Okay." Sam's eyes shift nervously. "On that *other* case. The one we talked about last night?"

I get the sense he's keeping things vague to avoid upsetting Porter, and that seems like a good idea. The man is still hooked up to drip bags, so any in-depth discussion of the house where his granddaughter was tortured and killed can probably wait.

"Um . . . yeah," Aaron says. "We just ran into a snag. It's owned by a corporation that I can't connect to any of Cregg's other businesses. I'll text you the info so you can run it through your databases. Maybe come up with something I missed."

"But you couldn't get anything on where they might be holding Deo?" Sam asks.

"I've got *something*," Taylor says. "Just not enough yet to start playing hide-and-seek. I need to clear my head and see if things come into better focus."

"Taylor?" Porter says, and Sam hands him the phone. "Sam told me you were the reason they found Molly's body. Said you drew the spot, that there never were any hikers—which sounds like somethin' off a damn TV show, but . . ." He looks down, shaking his head, then adds, "He also said you spent so much time on it you nearly had to repeat ninth grade. I know it hit you as hard as it did us, and you need to know that Mimmy was able to go with some peace in her heart because she finally *knew*, even though it wasn't the answer we hoped we'd get. So, thank you from both of us."

She shakes her head, angry. "I was too late—"

"Taylor Quinn." Porter's voice is stern. "I just said *thank you*. The only proper response to that is *you're welcome*. Although I guess

I'd also accept, *you're welcome and we're going to catch those sorry sons of bitches.*"

Her mouth quirks upward on one side. "We're going to catch those sorry sons of bitches."

Either Porter or Sam clears his throat. Probably Porter, because she grudgingly adds, "*And* you're welcome."

"Better."

Aaron ends the call. Taylor gives me an odd look. She must have been expecting Molly to say something. To ask me to tell Porter good-bye, that she loves him.

But Molly is in Zen mode at the back of my head.

"I wasn't blocking her, Taylor."

He has to let go. So do I.

I open my mouth to relay Molly's message, but I stop. Taylor needs to let go, too.

I check my phone again—nothing—and Taylor says, "What time is it?"

"Eight forty."

Taylor tosses the last bit of crust into her mouth. "A bit too early, but at least I can shower before we go."

"Go where?" Aaron asks.

She gives him a *duh* look and nods toward the computer. "To check out the house. The street should probably be quiet by eleven, wouldn't you think?"

"We're not going to check out that house."

Already halfway up the stairs, Taylor turns back and gives a shrug. "Thought Anna might need a distraction. She's pulled that phone out of her pocket to check for messages three times since I came downstairs, even though I imagine she's got the ringer turned up to full volume."

She's wrong. It's on vibrate. If a message comes in, I want to know what it says before I decide whether to share.

"But," she continues, "if you guys would rather stay here, I'll go myself."

"The hell you will!" Aaron says.

Her eyes narrow and she comes back down several steps so that she's just a smidge above eye level with her brother. "Like I told Sam, I have to clear my head. Each time I try to focus on Deo and the ear cuff, I get interference from that damned pink purse. So, yes. I *am* going to check this place out. If you want to come, great. If not, I'll take the Jeep."

CHAPTER TWELVE

We do not take the Jeep to Havre de Grace.

Taylor argued in favor of it at first, saying that its off-roading capabilities would come in handy if we needed to make a quick exit. I caught her little smirk as she said it, however, so I suspect she was picking on Aaron.

I'm pretty sure that Aaron would have continued trying to talk Taylor out of going, but Sam called around ten thirty with a bit of news. He couldn't find any connection between Cregg and the property in Havre de Grace, but the owners listed in the incorporation papers for HLMC CORP are Honoria Lucas and Miguel Cruz. Honoria Lucas has an older brother named Franco Lucas, who usually goes by his last name.

So that pretty much clinched it. They were going. I didn't see why that meant I needed to go, however. It would be beyond stupid to take the trackers with me when we'll be snooping around a location connected to Lucas. And it's been more than twenty hours now without any sort of contact concerning Deo. I'm more convinced than ever that they'll be coming in person. Being alone at the beach cottage when they show up is exactly what I want. And exactly what I dread.

Aaron's clearly aware of this. He refused to go unless I did, and since Taylor was clearly hell-bent on going with or without us, here we are. But I'm going to be on edge until we're back . . . although I guess I've been on edge all day.

Anyone watching us leave would probably think we're headed out for a late-night robbery or goth-fest. Taylor and Aaron are both in black—stuff Taylor grabbed from the closets at their house. I pulled my hair into a messy updo with a big barrette, and I'm in the darkest clothes I own, topped off with my gray-and-white Old Navy hoodie. Not exactly ninja mode, but the best I can do.

"You can sit up front," Aaron says as I go to open the car door. For some reason, that triggers Taylor's smirk again.

"That's okay. I'm fine back here."

That's not entirely true. I've been known to get queasy in the back, and normally I'd use that as leverage to ride shotgun. But if a message comes through on my phone when I'm riding up front, they'd both have a good view of it. Back here, I might have some privacy.

"How far is it?" I ask as I settle in.

"A little over eighty miles."

"Round-trip?"

"Um . . . no," he says. "Sorry."

As soon as he turns the key, a man with a heavy British accent starts talking about giants not being meant to live in groups.

"That's . . . Hagrid."

Order of the Phoenix," Aaron says. "I got the full set as a Christmas present from Mom and Tay, since I'm in the car so much. I've read the books, of course, but . . . nice to listen to them, too."

And so we listen for the next ninety minutes. Well, Aaron and I listen. Taylor is asleep ten minutes in.

I close my eyes and try to lose myself in the story. The entire trip, I only check my phone twice. That's the closest I've been to relaxed all day.

Harry is just wondering whether Cho cried because of Cedric Diggory or because he's a rotten kisser when Molly speaks up. It's almost a whisper.

Anna?

Yes?

I have to say good-bye. And thank you.

To Taylor and Aaron?

I already did that. To you.

None of my other tenants have said good-bye. A few said "thank you" after we completed whatever task was anchoring them here. Mostly, they just left behind their excess baggage and drifted away.

But . . . shouldn't you stay a little longer? So you can tell them whether this is the—

It's the place. I know it. Taylor knows it. And being there again will . . . pull me back . . . when I'm so close to letting go. I need to let go, Anna.

As much as I want to protest, I'm being selfish. Partly it's that I don't want her excess baggage when she goes, but I've also gotten used to her company. I'm going to miss her. Deo's gone, and now Molly—

I'm sorry for getting you into all of this, but I can see things more clearly now. This is your path. With or without me, you'd have found it eventually. And you will find Deo. I promise.

With those last words, my entire head . . . no, it's more like my entire being . . . is enveloped in music. Or maybe I dissolve *into* the music. It seems to be a variation on Arabesque, the song that was playing at the café the day I met with Porter, but this is beyond mere music. It's almost beyond comprehension.

I don't just hear the song. The music has a lock on all of my senses. I feel the notes against my skin, like a soft breeze, a warm blanket. It smells like the sharp, fresh scent of an orange when your nails first pierce the skin, like the woods after rain, like Deo's cheap cologne. It tastes like chocolate, like an almond cookie, like a cheddar-jalapeño bagel wrapped in a napkin. Love, and joy, and sorrow are embodied in each note.

When I open my eyes, the music swirls around me, a mélange of orange, gold, and purple. Everything I see and hear—the car, Aaron, Taylor's gentle snore, the street beyond—are transformed. Every element has its own distinct melody, and yet they are all connected. They all merge into one beautiful symphony—no, a polyphony, with so many melodies and colors that I cannot separate the threads of the tapestry. They are each whole and each part of the whole.

"You okay, Anna?"

I hear Aaron's words as part of the music. I can see his words, touch them, taste them.

"Anna?"

I vaguely realize that the car has stopped and he's leaning into the backseat. His eyes are concerned, bordering on alarmed.

I try to speak, but my brain and my body seem to exist on separate planes. Almost without realizing it, my hand reaches for Aaron's face, and I touch his cheek. The light stubble prickles against my palm and adds faint, staccato notes to the harmony, pulling in the scent and color of sage.

And then it all begins to fade . . .

. . . *perdendosi* . . .

My senses fall back into place slowly. I can now only see and feel my hand on Aaron's face, see and feel his hand covering my own. The surreal music and colors are gone.

I flush and pull my hand back, tucking it beneath me. "Sorry. I was . . . dreaming."

"I'm sorry I woke you. Your eyes were . . ." He smiles and shakes his head. "Miles away. Light-years away, maybe. Must have been some dream."

I look around. Since my surroundings are no longer painted with every shade in the rainbow, I recognize the neighborhood as the one Aaron and I saw on the map earlier. We're on a narrow residential street with small, older houses on both sides, parked cars crowding the road even further. I detect the glow of a TV in a few windows, and one porch light is on, but everything seems eerily quiet in the wake of Molly's strange parting gift.

"So, we're here?"

"Yeah." He nods to the road ahead. "The driveway is about a quarter mile beyond that last house, and then maybe another quarter mile to the house itself. Taylor?" He nudges her with his elbow and she groans, tugging her hoodie over her face. "Wake up."

Another extended groan, and Taylor flops onto her back. She finally sits up, chugs from a bottle of water, then splashes some into her hands and rubs her face. "Okay, let's do this."

Aaron pulls back onto the road. Shortly after the houses thin out, we see a paved driveway. He pauses at the entrance and closes his eyes for several seconds, breathing deeply. It almost looks like he's praying.

"I'm not picking up anything that's a problem . . . either here or along the street. Still, someone *could* be there. If so, we'll turn around and head out. It's a dead-end road. It's probably not the first time some-one turned around in this driveway in the middle of the night. But if the coast is clear and we go check out the cabin in the back, do not—"

"Touch anything," Taylor says, tugging on the boots she kicked off during the drive. "Even if most of my freakin' family weren't cops, I've seen enough *NCIS* to know that."

"Yeah, well, if that purse is there, the cops have to be the ones to find it. Not—"

My phone vibrates. It catches me off guard, and I jump so hard that both of them know I've gotten a message. So much for stealth.

"What's it say?" Aaron asks.

I scan the message quickly, ready to lie and say it's Kelsey if they're giving me instructions to meet them alone. But it's Dacia again. From a new number this time, but the same stupid game.

In your patience possess ye your souls.

Then:

By long patience is a prince persuaded

I text back:

Just tell me what you want me to DO!

The response:

Quietly endure, silently suffer and patiently wait

I am to WAIT, though waiting so be hell

And then it ends, just like last night. I try texting back. I try calling the number. Nothing but the out-of-service message.

I fling my phone down on the car seat. The sense of peace and wholeness Molly left behind has vanished. If I could find Dacia Badea, I'd rip her heart out with my bare hands.

"Do you think they know we're here?" Taylor looks around nervously. "Is that why they called *now*?"

Aaron shakes his head, but his expression is conflicted. "I think it's a coincidence. I usually don't *buy* coincidence, but I'm not sensing any problems nearby. Well, except . . ."

"Except what?" I ask.

"Except you." He glances down at my hands and gives me a wry grin. "It was muted because she's not around and you know you can't act on it, but the visual was very much like the human sacrifice in *Indiana Jones and the Temple of Doom*."

Taylor takes my phone, without so much as asking. "What's with the word games?"

"My fault. When Dacia told me her boss didn't like to be kept waiting, I made a smart-ass remark about patience being a virtue. Seems she's turning the tables on me, combing the internet for every quote on patience she can find."

She scrolls through the quotes. "Do you think they're random? Or is there some other meaning here?"

"I don't know. I'm not sure about the last one, but the third quote is definitely Martin Luther King and the first two are from the Bible."

"Whoa. Look at the walking *Wikipedia*," Taylor says.

I ignore the snarky tone of voice and hold out my hand for my phone. "I hosted a history teacher . . . who was also a preacher's daughter."

Aaron types something into his phone. "That last one is Shakespeare. Sonnet fifty-eight. I don't see any automatic connection between the quotes aside from the obvious . . . but are you sure it's still Dacia? There's not a single spelling error here, and the ones you showed me from last night were pretty sloppy. From what Molly said, Dacia wasn't well educated. I guess she could be cutting and pasting from *BrainyQuote* or whatever, but this looks more like communications are being handled by someone else now. Someone with an ego. I mean . . . *by long patience is a prince persuaded?*"

I get a sick feeling in my stomach as I remember Molly talking about Graham Cregg. *He seemed really full of himself.* "Can we go? Let's get this over with."

We turn into the driveway. A light is visible toward the end, but as we approach the house, I see that it's just an overhead streetlight. I get a flash of memory from Molly. There's no emotion attached to it. I never get a sense of their emotions once they leave. It's just a sterile memory of her arm being grabbed as Lucas yanked her outside, under this very same streetlight.

A *For Sale* sign flaps slightly in the wind, with a smaller sign attached to the bottom: *Pool and Patio!*

No cars are in the driveway, no lights are on inside the house. My first thought is that the place seems smaller, like it takes up less space on the lot than it did in the satellite images we browsed online. But as my eyes move toward the back of the property, I realize that's not the issue.

The lot looks larger because the guesthouse is gone.

Aaron notices it the instant I do. "Son of a bitch."

Taylor's door opens and she hurries toward the backyard.

"Damn it, Tay!" Aaron glances back at me. "You might as well wait here."

I survey the woods around the car, almost expecting to see Lucas's face pop up at my window. "No. I'm coming with you."

When we catch up to her, Taylor is crouched down on the brick patio, peering into the deep end of the empty swimming pool. "That's why the pool I was sensing didn't show up on the map. It's new."

Slowly, she works her way around the pool in a crab-walk, one hand brushing the inside edge.

"What are you doing?" Aaron asks.

Taylor doesn't answer, simply keeps moving around the edge until she reaches the middle. Then she swings her legs over the side and starts crawling toward the center of the pool.

"Come on, Taylor. They've leveled the place! You're not going to find any evidence now."

She ignores him and keeps crawling. When she's near the opposite side of the pool, she stops suddenly and sits down. Her eyes are closed and both palms are pressed flat against the concrete beneath her. "Here." She slides over an inch or two and pats the spot under her left hand. "It's right here."

"Under concrete," he reminds her. "Surrounded by a brick patio."

"Call Sam. See if—"

"It's nearly one a.m. On a Sunday. I'll talk to him tomorrow. And I don't know if he can even get anyone to issue a warrant based on another anonymous tip."

"If he can't get a warrant, I'll come back myself with a damned jackhammer. Because Molly's pink purse is right *here*."

❖   ❖   ❖

The lack of sleep hits me hard on the drive back. Aaron, too. He keeps rolling down the window so the cool air will jolt him awake. I offered to drive, but he could see that I wasn't in much better shape, and Taylor was out before we even reached the main highway.

I try to focus on the *Order of the Phoenix* again but catch myself nodding off a few times before we reach North Beach.

And I don't want to nod off tonight. I don't want to sleep, per-chance to dream. I definitely don't want to dream without the pills Kelsey prescribed. But if I sleep at all, it will have to be without the pills.

I won't risk taking them when there's the chance my phone could ring, even if it's only another round of texting *Notable Quotables.*

I unload the bags of supplies we picked up at a convenience store while Aaron drags Taylor out of the car. She stumbles up the stairs without speaking. He kicks off his shoes and stretches out on the sofa, as he did this morning.

"There are two other bedrooms, you know. Much more comfortable than the couch. Plus there's a security system. If anyone comes in, we'll have a warning."

He glances at the door and shrugs. "The couch is fine. I'll sleep better here."

"You are such a liar. I sat on that sofa today and felt the springs poking my ass."

Aaron doesn't argue, just pulls a pillow under his head and closes his eyes.

"Aaron, if I decide to leave, I'll drop down from the porch outside my room into the bushes below. Or I'll sneak out the back. If they contact me, and they tell me to come alone, I *will* be going alone. If the terms are me for Deo, that's what they'll get."

His eyes are still closed, but he says, "Why do you believe they'll let him go if you give yourself up?"

"Because Deo doesn't have anything they want. Dacia said her bosses are interested in what *I* can do."

"They've got a woman who can read minds. Cregg can apparently make people do whatever he wants. Why do they need someone who picks up ghosts?"

It's a good question. "I don't know. Doesn't matter, though. I'm the reason Deo is in this mess, but even if I wasn't, I'd still be following their instructions to the letter."

He doesn't budge from the couch. I stand there for a minute, debating whether to just let him suffer.

"Okay. I can't promise that I'm not going alone. But I *will* promise not to sneak out of the cottage without telling you. So would you please go upstairs and get some decent sleep?"

He agrees to the compromise, but he takes the room facing mine and leaves his door open. Trust but verify, I guess.

I close my door and splash my face with cold water. Then I turn on the TV, keeping the volume low. But there's nothing that seems likely to keep me awake, so I flick it off and look through the old books stacked in the closet, probably left behind by vacationers over the years. Mostly spy thrillers (no), murder mysteries (no), and horror (hell no). There are a few romances, and even though it's not my favorite genre, that seems like the best option for keeping me awake tonight. I pick the only hardback in the bunch, which looks ancient. Something called *The Middle Window*, from the 1930s.

It's clear as I thumb through the first couple of pages that the book is sappy and sentimental, but it's set in London. That's different enough that it shouldn't trigger any thoughts about my current circumstances.

I crank up the volume on my phone to max, in case I doze off, and settle in.

❖   ❖   ❖

It's dark and cold. A damp cold, almost like I'm in the snow. The person next to me on the tiny bed is shivering, her entire body shaking. "Are you sick?"

She doesn't respond.

I reach onto the floor and pull the thin blanket around us. The wound on my left hand throbs as I try to tuck the blanket in. It's pointless anyway—she's thrashing too much. Then she screams, "El vine acum! Ajută-ne! Ajută-ne!"

Daciana shrinks back against the wall, pulling the blanket with her. The words are in English now. "He is here."

I glance up at the ceiling, but there's no light coming through the floor-boards. "No! It's okay. You're dreaming."

"No. No dreaming."

And she's right. I hear a thud, and then pinpoints of light shine through the slats. I hear his boots as he crosses the floor. When he throws the cellar door open, the light that floods in is so bright that I have to turn away.

I expect Daciana to scream again when he comes closer, but instead, she grabs his arm. And then she begins to laugh, shrill and hysterical.

"It's the black girl's turn to go first." It's her voice, but it sounds more like him. "Maybe the grill lighter this time. That would be interesting."

Suddenly she grows sober, frightened, and backs away, cowering behind me. "What did you say?" He shines the lantern toward the bed and it's bright, wicked bright. It burns my eyes, and I duck my head into my arms.

His hand is in my hair, yanking me to my feet, then he's shaking me and saying—

"Anna! Anna, wake up!" Someone's hand pushes my hair aside and I tense up, holding back a scream.

I'm scared to open my eyes. "The light . . ."

A click, and he says, "There, it's off."

It takes me a moment to place his voice. "Aaron?"

"Yes. It's me. You're okay. You're okay now."

I slowly open my eyes, and the faint light coming in from the street doesn't burn like the light in my dream. The room isn't cold. It's Kelsey's beach house. I glance down at my hands and see that my fingers—not nine, but all ten—are knotted tightly in Aaron's T-shirt.

He wraps his hands over mine. "Breathe, Anna. You're safe. It was a dream. Just a dream."

There's a book in his lap. The one I was reading earlier. The one that apparently wasn't interesting enough to keep me awake.

A light flicks on in the hallway and I bury my face in his shoulder.

"Turn it off!" he says.

When I open my eyes again, Taylor's frame is silhouetted in the doorway. "What happened?"

"She had a nightmare. Go back to sleep, okay?"

Taylor doesn't move. "That sounded like . . . like Molly screaming."

"Yeah," he says. "I think it kind of was."

"Does she need some water or anything?"

I nod into Aaron's chest and he says, "Sure. Thanks, Tay. Just . . . don't turn on the light in the hallway, okay?"

"Sorry," I say, once my breathing returns to normal. "I'm sorry I woke you." I realize that my hands are still wrapped in his T-shirt. I relax them and scoot backward a bit so that my shoulders are against the headboard, but Aaron doesn't let go of my hands.

"You've got a pretty powerful set of lungs there. Waking Taylor after a reading is quite an accomplishment. Mom had to throw ice water in her face one morning."

Taylor hands me one of the bottles of water from the fridge and I take a few sips. She sits on the edge of the bed, tugging her threadbare nightshirt—*Team Volturi*—over bare knees. "Molly's gone, isn't she? That's why you're having those dreams."

"She left before we reached the house in Havre de Grace." I pause for a moment, trying to calm my breathing. "She was nearly gone anyway, and . . . she didn't want to relive everything. I don't blame her."

"So, is that the end of it?" she asks. "I mean, you just dream about it the one time and then . . ."

"Maybe." But it sounds like no, even to my own ears. I know better. And if they are in the same house with me the next time I happen to fall asleep, they'll know better, too.

She glances at Aaron's hand, still on mine. Then she leans over and gives him a hug. "Night, bro. I think you got this and I'm wiped out. Call me if you need me."

He pulls his hand back, looking self-conscious. "That's . . . ," he begins, but then shakes his head and waves her on. "Get some sleep, then."

"G'night, Anna."

When she leaves, Aaron picks up the book. "What's it about?"

I give a weak chuckle. "A *ghost*, as it turns out. Thought I'd made a safe pick, but . . ."

"The lamp was on when I came in. You were reading to stay awake, weren't you?" He looks at the bottle of pills on the nightstand. "Are those your pills? Can you take another one or—" A look of comprehension comes into his eyes. "Oh. You didn't take them. You're worried you won't hear the phone."

"Won't hear it. Won't be coherent enough to respond to it. Or I'll be so groggy I make a stupid mistake."

"Things are going to be as bad, if not worse, if you don't get some sleep."

"But if they call—"

"I'll wake you. It can't be any harder than waking Taylor." He picks up the bottle and removes the cap. "Two?"

I nearly tell him to just give me one, but I nod.

Once I swallow the pills, he takes my phone from the nightstand and sticks it in his back pocket. "Should I go?"

"Probably. The dream was *so* vivid. I'm not even sure that two pills will ward it off."

"That's not a reason for me to go. It sounds more like a reason I should stay. Unless you feel safer . . ."

I don't even have to think about it. I feel safer with him here. I *want* him here. And I'm too tired and too frightened to worry about how much of that is me and how much is coming from Molly.

"Stay."

He squeezes my hand and goes over to the rocker in the corner of the room. "If you decide you want the light on, it won't bother me."

I watch him for a moment as he tries to get comfortable in the small chair. I don't want him over there. I want him *here*.

"Everything I said about the couch downstairs goes double for that rocker." I slide against the wall. "I can't promise I won't bite or kick if the dream comes back. But if you're willing to take a risk, there's room here for two."

CHAPTER THIRTEEN

I'm lying in a forest. Tiny dots of greenish-yellow light dance on my skin. The scent of pine surrounds me like a warm blanket. It's safe here. A bird caws in the distance and my mind follows it, but I tug it back. I want to stay where it's warm. Safe. Don't want to wake . . . up . . .

Aaron's arm is under me. His skin is warm against my neck, and one jean-clad leg is flung over mine. My fingers are again tangled in his T-shirt. I'm not sure when that happened.

I close my eyes and try to recapture the feeling I had when I first woke up. *Safe. Warm.* But it dances away like the light coming through the trees.

The other dream came twice more. Each time I woke up well before Molly died. That's both good and bad. On the bad side, it means the dreams will stick around longer. I'll have to process the entire thing before they end. On the good side, however, this is one exit scene that I clearly need to take in small doses.

It was easier to pull myself out of the memory and back into this world with Aaron next to me. I was pretty sure that would be the case. Arlene Bennett, the soccer mom who overdosed, exited during one of the times that Deo and I were on the streets together. Deo would shake me and remind me to breathe, that I wasn't choking on anything. And he'd hold my hand until I could finally relax enough to believe that I wasn't going to die in my sleep if I nodded off again.

Waking up thinking you're drowning in your own vomit is miserable, but I'd take it a thousand times over the Molly dreams.

There's a long scratch on Aaron's neck. I don't remember doing that, but it's a close match for the scratches on my left arm. My nails are bitten almost to the quick. I'm very glad for that bad habit right now, otherwise the damage could've been much worse.

I don't see a clock in the room, and my phone is still in Aaron's pocket, but it's well past sunrise. And it looks like the sun is actually making an appearance today, unlike yesterday, when it never managed to break through the clouds.

Part of me wants to snuggle closer to Aaron, even though I doubt I can actually fall back asleep. It would be so nice to lie here for a bit longer and try to avoid worrying about Deo and this entire colossal mess. But the rational side of my brain that didn't fully kick into gear last night is working just fine now, and it's asking whether this desire to be close to Aaron is really coming from me. Or is it a remnant of Molly's feelings for him?

She's gone, so in one sense, it doesn't really matter. It's not like she'd come back and haunt me for taking her guy. In fact, I know I'd have her blessing.

But there's way too much going on right now to trust my emotions. More importantly, I don't want to mislead Aaron. And I don't want to misinterpret him. He was right last night when he told Taylor that it kind of *was* Molly screaming. Even if you can't really separate the two of us any longer, did he stay to comfort me or to comfort Molly?

I reluctantly pull my leg out from under Aaron's. He stirs long enough to roll over and sink his face into my pillow. My phone is wedged beneath him, and as much as I want it, I can't bring myself to wake him up to get it. I settle for leaving the door open. If it rings, I'll hear it.

I'm surprised to see that it's nearly eleven a.m. I grab a slice of cold pizza—one of only four that remain—and am just finishing my breakfast of champions when Taylor comes downstairs. She's still in the *Team Volturi* tee, over the black jeans she was wearing last night.

She grabs one of the other slices and leans against the counter. Her eyes flick to the scratches on my arm. "Did you get any sleep?"

"Some. It's always rough when my hitchers move on, but this one . . ." I shake my head, not really wanting to discuss the dreams. "It will pass eventually."

We're both silent for a moment, then she says, "Don't hurt him."

And I'm wishing that I'd *closed* the bedroom door. "It's not like that."

She takes another bite of the pizza and shrugs. "Maybe not for you. But I know my brother."

That could mean half a dozen things, and I'm tempted to ask her to clarify. Instead, I say, "You heard him last night. He was comforting Molly as much as anything else. Probably because he blames himself for not being around to warn her. And given everything that's going on right now, I really don't think—"

"I think you're a little naive when it comes to guys." She rips a paper towel off the roll and wipes the grease from her fingers. "That is, if you really can't tell he's attracted to you. Aaron's not exactly experienced in that regard either, so you're probably perfect for each other. I'm not saying hands off, or anything like that—although I probably would have to Molly. That would never have worked out. All I'm saying is *don't hurt him.*"

I can tell it's not worth arguing with her, so I focus on making coffee. The convenience store choices were limited, but Folgers is better than the syrupy stuff Aaron found in the pantry. Taylor gives the pot a dismissive sniff and grabs a soda from the fridge.

"I'm going back upstairs to finish the reading on Deo. I've got an outline, but it's going to take one more session. Maybe two. I wish I had more time, because I'm pretty sure they're going to call you either today or tonight with instructions."

"Where are you getting that from? Aaron said you could only do the remote viewing stuff."

"Right . . . but this isn't based on my sixth sense." She picks up Aaron's tablet and opens a browser. "It's just common sense, if we assume those texts last night were coming from Graham Cregg."

She waits a minute, then spins the tablet toward me. Across the top of the site is a picture of an older man in a dark suit shaking hands with a crowd of people. The banner behind him says, *Cregg For Our Future.*

"But . . . that's *Ron* Cregg," I say, still not following her logic.

"I know. He's running as an independent, so he's doing a ton of rallies, fund-raisers, and town hall meetings. Mostly on the weekends. And since Papa Bear can't hit every event on his own, he's had the entire family traveling, including his son. See . . . this one is from a few Saturdays back."

Sure enough, two of the images are of a speech by Graham Cregg at an event in Colorado. He looks thinner than he did in the photo we saw at Sam's office, but it could be the angle. A perky-looking woman with pale-blonde hair stands next to him at the podium, which is decked out in red, white, and blue.

"He's married?"

"That's not his wife. That's his stepmom. But yes, he's married. Two kids. An uber-rich senator's son, reasonably decent looking for his age? I'd be more surprised if he *wasn't* married. And the poor woman might not even *know* she's married to a psychopath. Lots of husbands have hobbies."

I laugh. Taylor's sense of humor is kind of dark, but I like it.

"There were a bunch of events listed on the schedule this weekend," she adds, "including a few in DC, Virginia, and Pennsylvania. Friday and Saturday night is prime time. They probably have events going late into the night. But they'll wrap things up earlier today, since it's Sunday and some of those people have jobs to be at tomorrow morning."

I'm about to click away when another picture catches my attention—a dark-haired woman shaking hands with an elderly man. Lurking in the background is a man who looks a lot like the bodyguard from the police station. I can't be certain, given the angle, but . . .

"That looks like Dacia Badea."

Taylor looks at the picture for a moment. "I'd imagine someone who can read minds is pretty handy on the campaign trail. Especially teamed up with a guy like Cregg who can make people whip out their checkbooks and contribute."

From Molly's memories, I get the sense that Cregg's gift isn't quite that flexible. I think he may have to focus really hard to get people to do his bidding, and it's not exactly stealth mode.

"But they'd know, wouldn't they? I mean maybe not in Dacia's case, since she's only snagging their thoughts. But Molly *knew* Cregg was inside her mind."

She shrugs. "Convincing someone to snip off a pinky is hard. But making some rich dude add an extra zero to a check he was already writing? Probably not so much. And Daniel said the card she flashed was from the senator's office, so I think it's safe to say they're putting her to good use."

"Isn't that . . ." I catch myself on the verge of saying *illegal*, but we're talking about someone who's been complicit in more than one murder. "Never mind. But you know, it actually does make sense, thinking back. Dacia was dressed up when she arrived at the police station. It was a suit, but more like something you'd wear to an event. And she made it clear that she had other places to be."

"They probably planned on waiting to deal with you until Monday . . . but then you and Deo took off and forced their hand. They're just pushing your buttons with these quotes."

"Maybe."

Most of the other photos on the site are of the candidate himself. One is a close-up of Ronald Cregg, a slightly overweight man in his sixties. He's down on one knee, smiling at two small children holding up one of his campaign signs.

"Do you think the senator knows his son is a killer?"

Taylor cocks her head to the side. "Meh. No way to tell. And from a practical standpoint, does it matter? He'd have to cover it up anyway. Ever heard of a president with a mass murderer for a son?"

When I look up, Aaron is at the foot of the stairs. His hair is standing up on one side and he appears a little worn out. "You made coffee."

And then he smiles . . . the same smile that made Molly all weak at the knees. It's having a very similar effect on me right now.

"It's almost finished brewing," I say, wishing I could control the blood rushing to my face.

There's a mischievous glint in Taylor's eye, as though she's thinking something snarky. But she decides to keep it to herself. "I e-mailed you what I have so far on Deo's location," she tells Aaron as she grabs a box of something out of the pantry. "I don't think you'll have any luck with it. I'm seeing a really old building . . . more like ruins, in fact. Near the water, but that could be almost anyplace around here. I need to get back to it . . . Anna can fill you in on the rest."

Then she's gone, leaving us alone. And alone feels very different today than it did yesterday. It's charged with a subtle energy when he passes me on the way to the coffeepot, probably because I can still remember the heat of his arm beneath me when I woke up.

Aaron pours two mugs of coffee and hands me one. "Fill me in on what?"

I show him the website with the picture of Cregg, with Dacia and the bodyguard guy in the background. Then I relay Taylor's theory on why they're keeping me on hold.

"If so, that's at least a *bit* of good news, right? I mean, the less time he's been with Deo . . ." He trails off, uncomfortable that he's pulled my mind to all of the things that could have been happening over the past thirty-six hours.

"Yes. Better than the alternative."

He opens the e-mail from Taylor and we examine her drawing. The building is intact, but there's a fire escape on one side that's barely attached. Four columns are sketched onto a small porch-like area in the front. It's four stories, with odd scalloped dormer windows that you might see on a castle or a fort, and rustic-looking stonework around the first floor.

"Beaux Arts," I say absently, pulling the reference from a file in my tenant archives.

"What?"

"The architectural style. Probably built around the turn of the last century. And since that was a really common style for large buildings back then, it's probably a useless bit of information."

"Well, it's more than I had. All I could say was that there's ivy growing on it . . . and I wouldn't even have recognized that if Taylor hadn't used a green pencil."

He takes the tablet back and his hand brushes against mine. I jump—and feel bad for jumping.

Relax, Anna! It's not Molly. It's me. But I'm thinking it in her voice and beginning to feel more than a little unhinged.

"Are you okay?"

Aaron touches my shoulder and I pull in a ragged breath. I need to get away for a few minutes. Get my head together.

"I'm fine. Do you have my phone?"

He hands it to me, and it's still warm from being in his pocket. "No messages. I meant what I said. I would have woken you up."

"I know." My eye lands on the red scratch that runs from just below his ear to the hollow at the base of his neck. "I'm sorry about that."

"It's nothing. You were rougher on yourself than you were on me. I tried holding your hands down to keep you from hurting yourself, but that only made you more frantic. You were dreaming about when he was . . . controlling Molly, weren't you?"

I nod. "Listen, I'm . . . I need to go upstairs. Check in with Kelsey. Get a shower."

"Sure." There's a note of uncertainty in his voice.

I hear Taylor's warning again—*don't hurt him*—and I can't get out of the room fast enough.

I'm combing the tangles out of my damp hair when my phone rings. I try not to get my hopes up. It's probably just Kelsey calling back. Beating me to the punch, actually, since I was about to call *her* back and apologize for hanging up on her. The entire conversation before I got into the shower was strained, to say the least. Kelsey is worried and feeling responsible since she loaned me the car. She kept saying she should have come with us, but I'm not sure what difference that would have made. They'd almost certainly still have Deo, and it's possible they'd have Kelsey, too.

By the end, she'd switched from supporting my decision not to bring in the police to saying that she can't allow me to simply trade myself for Deo. And I told her I'm old enough to make my own damn decisions, and if a trade is what it takes to get Deo back, then that's what will happen. We were both in tears, and I hung up before I said something I knew I'd regret.

My heart starts pounding when I pick up the phone. I don't recognize the number. But then caller ID kicks in and an image pops up. It's the logo for Quinn Investigative Services—*QIS* with the letter *I* replaced by a magnifying glass.

Must be Aaron. But why would he call rather than walking up the stairs?

"Hello?"

"Hi, Anna." Okay, *not* Aaron.

"Um . . . hi, Sam. What's up?"

His voice sounds a little hesitant. I sit on the edge of the bed, bracing myself for bad news. And I guess my voice sounds worried, because Sam quickly says, "Oh, no—there's no news. Sorry. I just need to talk to you for a minute without Aaron and Taylor around."

"Okay. I'm listening."

"I just got off the phone with your doctor." When he hears my exasperated sigh, he laughs softly. "I've heard that sound before, both as a father and a grandfather. Don't get all huffy. She's worried about you."

Even though I should probably be annoyed with Kelsey for calling Sam, I can't be. I hate worrying her, and I really hated fighting with her on the phone. And it's nice to know that she cares enough to try and stop me from doing something that even I know is stupid. Doesn't change my mind, since it's my only option. But it's still nice.

"I know she's worried, Sam. But what choice do I have? I'm responsible for Deo. Maybe not on paper, maybe not legally, but I am. And I'm the one who picked up Molly. I won't let Deo be hurt. Not if I can prevent it. Kelsey knows that."

"She does. And I'm not arguing that point. If the Creggs had the Metro PD jumping through hoops to give Badea access, I don't know how far their reach may be. And I think Dr. Kelsey understands that, too. Probably why she called me instead of the police. I reassured her as best I could. Told her we've got backup plans. Aaron will have advance warning if they come after you. If we can get one of them first, maybe we'll have some leverage."

I keep quiet, since I don't intend to let that happen. In my opinion, there's an even better chance that grabbing Badea or whoever they send to fetch me will be very bad news for Deo.

"And I told her that even if that falls through, we'll find you. We'll get you out of there."

"Hope so."

"Taylor knows what she's doing. She'll find Deo, and if worst comes to worst, she'll find you. If Taylor says Molly's purse is under the pool, it's under the pool. If I had any doubts about that, I wouldn't have just leveraged every bit of credibility I have in this state by getting the police up in Harford County to request a search warrant for that property in Havre de Grace on the basis of an anonymous tip."

"Wait . . . you called the police?"

"Sweetie, that's how it works. Private investigators can't get a warrant. I took every precaution I could, though. The cop I contacted is a friend. Harford's four counties north of the District, and we're keeping the whole thing quiet . . . well, as quiet as you can when it involves ripping up someone's swimming pool. My contact said I could be there when they rip it up—probably Tuesday or Wednesday—but he also said I might want to bring my checkbook just in case they *don't* find evidence." He laughs, although I get the feeling he's not actually joking.

"Like I told your doctor," he continues, "we'll get you out of there if all else fails. But it may take a little time. And I'm . . . concerned about what's going to happen if Badea starts digging around in your mind. I know you blocked her before, but I'm pretty sure the whole agreeing to cooperate thing is going to include the expectation that you don't *keep* blocking her. Won't matter whether there's a leak in the police department if you're giving up information voluntarily—not just on everything we've learned about Molly's case but also what Molly knew and what you now know about Aaron's and Taylor's abilities."

"I wouldn't . . ." I stop. No, I wouldn't do it on purpose. And I don't think I'd do it to save myself. But if the choice was between saving Deo and protecting Aaron and Taylor?

"I'm not saying you'd do it willingly. But the two of them have no idea how hard we've worked to keep them off Cregg's radar. And they haven't made things easy since Molly died. I know they want to help, but . . . I guess what I'm asking is whether it's all or nothing? I mean, is there any way you can—I don't know—compartmentalize, maybe? Give them some information, enough to make them think you're cooperating, without putting anyone else in danger?"

The wall marked *Myron* flashes into my mind. Kelsey and I built it to protect *me* from his memories—all of his memories—and I never pull it down. For a long time, some bits would sneak out when I was asleep, but they no longer have any real power, even when I dream. Could I do the same thing to protect some of my own memories from Badea's probe?

"Maybe," I tell him. "I've done something before that's similar. I can't say for certain that it will work, but I'll try my best. I don't want to jeopardize the investigation, and I definitely don't want to put Aaron or Taylor in danger."

After we hang up, I call Kelsey back. We both apologize, both wind up nearly in tears again, and she ends by simply telling me to be careful. And to call her as soon as I know anything else.

I erase all of the voice and text messages from Taylor and Aaron, just in case there's something that might "out" them. Then I close my eyes and focus on building a second wall, like the one I built when Dacia was burrowing her way into my head at the police station. Like the one that surrounds Myron. I'm glad I don't have to lock away everything that was Molly. That would feel . . . disrespectful, I guess. She was a good person. She didn't hurt people like Myron did.

Once the wall is up, I begin sorting through my mental files. The memories from Emily, Arlene, Bruno, Lydia, Abner, Josephine, and Didier all remain in front. Myron stays in his isolation chamber, but I move it back behind the second wall, since it would give away the fact that I can (hopefully) hide things from her probe.

Next, I let my mind drift through the assorted Molly memories that I've barely begun to process. It's usually a slow, gradual incorporation, but I don't have time to let things take their natural course. I leave most of her memories, including many of Taylor and Aaron, in front of the wall. The three of them playing on a Slip'N Slide. The fort they built in the woods behind the house. A trip to the beach with Porter, Molly's mom, and her grandmother. Other memories—the Christmas Molly and Taylor got the pink purses, Aaron rescuing Molly from that kid with the baseball bat, the search for a neighbor's lost cat that started with Taylor and a sketch pad—go behind the second wall.

Then I build a space for my own recent memories. I start with my conversation with Aaron right after Porter was shot. Our discussion at the townhouse. Taylor sketching the house at Havre de Grace. I slide those memories and others like them behind the second wall, along with everything I've learned about Delphi and Graham Cregg.

I've never done anything like this with my own memories. I don't like the feeling. It's similar to the frustration of having a word on the tip of your tongue, but not quite being able to reach it. I think there's a very real possibility that I could *lose* memories this way. That I could forget where I put them entirely and end up with gaping, Swiss-cheese holes in my mind.

I'm going to need a fully functional brain to get through this. But I want to be ready in case I have no other choice. So while Molly's dangerous memories stay behind the wall, I bundle my own memories of Aaron, Taylor, Cregg, and the whole Delphi insanity into a mental folder, and put it behind the wall. Then I pull it out again. And then I practice moving it back and forth, back and forth, until I can do it with relative ease.

A tentative knock pulls me out of my meditation. When I open the door, Aaron is standing in the hallway, hands in his jeans pockets. Looking worried. Awkward. A little sad.

"You've been up here a really long time. What did Taylor say to you?"

"Nothing!" I tell him. "Why do you think—"

"She's Taylor. Of course she said something." He glances down the hall toward the bedroom where she's working. "Can I come in? Or if you'd rather come down . . ."

"No . . . I mean, yes. Sure." I step back into the room and sit on the bed again.

Aaron seems to consider the spot next to me briefly but opts for the rocking chair. "So, *what did Taylor say?*"

I'm about to deny it again, but what's the point? Might as well clear the air now, rather than have this hanging over us.

"She said not to hurt you. And I told her she was jumping to the wrong conclusion."

He's quiet for a very long time, just staring at his feet. When he finally looks up, he says, "You've got so much on your mind right now and I don't want to add to that. I don't want things to be weird for you or for you to think that I'm pressuring you in any way. But I don't want to lie to you, either. I've only known you for, what? Two days? But I *like* being around you. It's nice to be open with somebody about . . ." He shrugs. "Who I *am*, I guess? I know these past two days have been some of the worst in your life and you probably wish you'd never laid eyes on me—"

"No. I don't wish that. But I do wish the circumstances were different. And I think we both need a bit of time to sort out Molly's role in all of this. She had such an enormous crush on you, and . . ."

I stop after seeing his face. He looks absolutely gobsmacked.

"You didn't know?"

"*Molly?* No. I mean, she was just a kid. She was like . . . *fourteen.*"

That makes me smile. "You don't think fourteen-year-old girls get crushes on seventeen-year-old guys? Or vice versa?"

"Well, yeah. They do. But . . . Molly was Taylor's alter ego. I never thought of her *that* way. Did you . . . or did she . . . think I was . . . I mean, did I *do* anything to make her think that I—"

"No. But it didn't stop her from going on about how gorgeous you are."

I instantly regret the way I phrased that. Now we're both uncomfortable. I could at least have said *were*.

I'm tempted to comb through my memory banks for something suave to say, something that won't make me sound like an idiot, something that maybe worked for somebody else as she tried to extract her foot from her mouth.

But I know better. It's like saving up that perfect comeback you read in a book or heard on TV—it always sounds good in your head, but it never quite fits in real life.

Fortunately, Aaron seems to be too preoccupied to notice that I'm at a loss for words. "Molly was like a second sister to me. At least, that's how I thought of her."

He looks miserable, and I realize he's probably thinking through the various things he said to Molly, especially near the end. Worried that he unintentionally led her on or said something that might have hurt her feelings. I feel bad for even mentioning it.

"Fourteen-year-olds are . . . really fickle, you know. If Molly had made it to fifteen, she'd probably have gone back to thinking of you as Taylor's jerky older brother. No, I guess Daniel had that title locked down . . . so, Taylor's not-so-jerky older brother. She'd have been crushing on someone from 5 Seconds of Summer or from her algebra class or whatever. You'd have been yesterday's news. She'd have looked back and said, *oh my God, what did I ever see in him?*"

Aaron laughs, which is exactly what I was hoping for. "You really think that, or are you just saying it to make me feel better?"

"Maybe a little of both?"

"I'll take that." He comes over and sits next to me on the bed. "What I was trying to say before you distracted me with that bit of news is . . . just let me know what you need from me. You need someone to be here if that bastard visits your dreams, then you've got it. You need space, then . . . you've got that, too. Okay?"

I nod. "Thanks. Molly was definitely right about one thing, you know."

A grin inches across his face. "That I'm gorgeous?"

Yes, I think.

"No," I say. "I *meant* that you're a really nice guy, but now it looks like you're developing this huge ego problem . . ." I swat at him playfully and he catches my hand.

"One more thing. When Deo is back safe and sound . . ." He stops and his shoulders slump.

"What?"

"Well . . . I was about to ask if you'd want to go to a movie or get dinner. But we'd probably have to worry about you picking up a ghost or me realizing the guy at the next table is about to punch his waiter. Maybe we could just watch Netflix and . . ." He stops again and closes his eyes. "I truly suck at this. I was not going to say *chill,* I swear to God. I was going to say watch Netflix and order takeout."

I lean forward and kiss him. It's a quick kiss, just a featherlight brush of my lips against his.

He looks surprised. I probably do too, because that wasn't at all planned. It just seemed right.

"I'd like that, Aaron. When all of this is over, I think I'd like that a lot."

❖　❖　❖

We spend the rest of the day waiting.

Taylor emerges to eat and drink pretty much everything left in the house (other than the coffee) and spends maybe twenty minutes on the deck to get some fresh air. Then back into her cave.

We play Scrabble and rummy. We search online for more info about the Creggs. We search for Beaux Arts buildings in the area and find far too many to wade through, but spend an hour doing just that anyway.

We even watch some Netflix.

And we wait.

Just before nine, Taylor comes down with her sketch pad. And she's smiling.

"You've got something?"

"Yeah," she tells me. "I'm not done, but it's definitely something." She tosses the pad on the coffee table in front of us and heads straight for the kitchen.

The drawing shows a tiny version of the Beaux-Arts ruin she showed us earlier, surrounded by green. Trees, grass . . . and sidewalks or paths of some sort running throughout the area. It's near a river, which she's shaded the way she did in the drawing last night. But there are other rectangular patches scattered about, shaded a lighter gray, and a vehicle of some sort.

"What are the rectangles?" I ask. "And is that a . . . tractor?"

She looks around the pantry door. "Maybe . . . maybe a bulldozer? And I don't know what the rectangles are. They're man-made, though. Parking lot? And I get a strong sense of people nearby. A lot of them, but . . . it's like something is dampening the signal. Or some*one*. Deo's there, and he might be in the building I drew earlier, the one near the top. But check out the bottom-right corner. Look familiar?"

It does. It's the same pear-shaped location from last night.

"The quarry. Which means that's the Susquehanna River." Aaron grabs his tablet and starts to pull up the map, but Taylor takes it away.

"This needs to wait. Food supplies are down to mustard, ketchup, and an expired can of green beans, and my blood sugar is so low I'm seeing spots."

Aaron calls for Chinese takeout. The place doesn't deliver. Apparently there are no delivery options other than pizza, at least not during the off-season. And since Aaron won't leave the house unless Taylor and I go too, we all head into Chesapeake Beach.

We're on the return trip, about two blocks from the beach house. Aaron reaches into the container for another egg roll, then suddenly slams on the brakes. I catch his expression in the mirror and I know, even before I see the car parked across from the beach house.

He reverses and takes a left at the intersection we've just passed.

"We're going around the back way. Taylor, as soon as we're out of the car, slide into the driver's seat and head straight to Sam's. I'll call you when I can. Anna, follow my lead, okay?"

"Sure." I grab the file folder of Aaron and Taylor memories and shove them behind my second wall. Before Aaron can accelerate again, I fling open the door and take off. It's not a graceful exit, and I twist my ankle in the process, but I don't think I'll need to run on it for long.

"Anna!"

His car squeals to a halt behind me. But I don't have time to look back.

The BMW meets me at the corner and someone flings open a rear door. I dive inside, and the other passenger reaches across me to slam the car door shut. Through the window, I see Aaron running after me. I wish he could read the thought I'm sending—*I'm sorry, I'm so, so, sorry*—but the only one who gets that message is Dacia Badea.

She laughs and tosses me a sealed plastic bag. There's a mask of some sort inside. "If you are ready to cooperate this time, take that out and put it on."

One last glance through the rear window. Aaron is standing in the middle of the street, growing smaller as we drive away. Then we turn the corner and I can't see him at all.

I'm sorry.

My eyes shift to the front seat, and I catch a glimpse of the driver's face in the rearview mirror. Bald, with a dinky half beard. The last time I saw that face clearly was in Molly's memory. And even though

Molly's emotions are no longer part of the equation, I remember her fear vividly.

But I need to focus. I pull my eyes away from Lucas and rip the plastic bag open with my teeth. Once the mask is out and the loops of elastic are over my ears, I turn to Dacia and say, "Now what?"

She places the palm of her hand against the outside of the mask and pushes forward with a bit more force than seems necessary. The plastic edge of the mask digs into my chin and I suck in a mouthful of air. That seems to cause the mask to clutch my face even tighter.

I don't know if it's the gas that's released or the mask itself, but I catch a faint whiff of vanilla. Which makes me think of Kelsey.

A memory I'd almost forgotten flutters through my mind—sitting on the banks of Rock Creek with an eight-year-old Deo, sharing a small box of vanilla wafers when we were on the run that first time.

And then I'm thinking of someone else, who doesn't smell of vanilla, but who smells warm and safe. But my mind can't grab his name because it's drifting away on a vanilla cloud and because I have that memory behind . . .

CHAPTER FOURTEEN

The wall.

It's my very first thought, before my eyes open. Before I'm even aware of the queasy feeling in my stomach or of the bed beneath me.

Although "bed" might be a bit too generous. It's more like one of those narrow examination tables in a doctor's office, with bars on the sides and a slightly elevated head. Except there are sheets instead of the crinkly paper strip down the middle.

I'm in the hospital again. Why?

I close my eyes and remain still and silent for several minutes, trying to get my bearings. Trying to remember why my first thought was the wall, even as I'm checking for gaps, for signs that anyone has been tinkering while I was unconscious.

Kelsey. I need to ask for Kelsey before I talk to any other doctors.

As my eyes adjust, I realize it's not actually a hospital room. Aside from this bed, which appears to have been rolled into the room, the place looks more like a hotel suite or a tiny apartment. A small kitchen with no table, just a single stool at the raised counter. A desk. A second bed that actually looks like a bed instead of the gurney I'm on. A large monitor mounted on the wall across from the bed. No windows. Three doors, with only the one to the bathroom open. The only light coming from a fixture above the bathroom sink.

I prop myself up, but that only makes the nausea worse, so I lean back into the pillow. Sitting upright will have to wait.

When I pull my hand up to brush the hair out of my eyes a few minutes later, I see the scratches on my arm. That brings the past few days flooding back.

Deo was taken. Hopefully Deo was taken *here*, wherever here is. Kelsey's in Indianapolis. Molly is gone. Aaron and . . .

The wall.

Forcing myself to sit up, I look around the room more carefully. I don't see Dacia, and more to the point, I don't *feel* her mental probe tap, tap, tapping at my brain. But I'm sure she'll be back.

As I lower my feet to the floor, my right ankle throbs. Not too bad, though. I test it and it easily supports me. Just hope I don't need to run a marathon any time soon.

I'm surprised to feel the familiar weight of my phone in my back pocket. Someone turned it off, so I'm guessing they've already collected any information they found interesting. And, when I check, I see that I have zero bars, which means we're either someplace remote, someplace underground, or (most likely) they're blocking the signal.

Once I check the time—12:22 a.m.—I power it down. Not a good idea to waste the battery, on the off chance, even if it's probably a very, very off chance, that my lack of signal is temporary.

I'm still a bit on the woozy side, and my head pounds each time I move. I initially thought maybe whatever Dacia doped me with was nitrous oxide. Arlene had bad teeth, along with her myriad other health problems. Somewhat ironically for a hypochondriac, she hated needles, so she always opted for dentists who offered laughing gas. The dentist she liked best had scented masks—orange, spearmint, and vanilla. But whatever Dacia used, I don't think it was nitrous. That wears off within a matter of minutes, and you're fine afterward. Arlene was able to drive herself home after dental appointments. My head, on the other hand, still feels very fuzzy.

Dehydration, maybe? I go to the kitchen in search of a glass, which I find after opening several of the cabinets. I find Tylenol as well, along with a standard first-aid kit and an unlabeled medicine bottle. When I open the bottle, I see dozens of the familiar pentagon-shaped sleeping pills that Kelsey prescribed for me.

Finding my pills here gives me the feeling I'm being watched, although I probably should have assumed that already. I visually scan the room for cameras but stop after a few seconds. The tracking devices they hid in our backpacks were minuscule. There could be dozens of cameras in here and I'd never find them. Better to *assume* I'm being watched and act accordingly.

I open the fridge in search of bottled water, and find a case of Dasani, along with string cheese, baby carrots, milk, apples. Butter pecan ice cream in the freezer.

An icy finger that has nothing to do with the still-open freezer runs down my spine. The kitchen is stocked with my favorites. Oreos in the pantry. Deo once joked that I could eat my weight in Oreos. Walkers Shortbread, which I love but rarely buy because it's so expensive. Jalapeño pretzels. Ritz Crackers. Peanut butter—extra crunchy, because otherwise, why bother? Cheetos. Honey Bunches of Oats. Dunkin' Donuts Pumpkin Spice coffee, Sleepytime tea. Honey. Kit Kat Dark. Reese's Cups, Hershey's Kisses.

I take two Tylenol and carry the bottle of water back into the main room. The clothes in the dresser and the closet aren't *my* clothes—these appear to be new. But they're about the right size and they're the stuff I usually wear. Jeans, sweaters, T-shirts.

Everything in this room makes me feel violated, like they've stolen things that make me *me*. But I know without a doubt that it's Deo's mind they raided for this information, not mine. He knows what I like almost as well as I do, but Hershey's Kisses are way too sweet. Yes, I buy them occasionally, but only because Deo likes them.

The door, which has a security panel on the left, is locked from the outside. I knew that would be the case, but, hey, gotta try. Not that I'd even think of leaving without finding Deo. But I'd like more information about where I am. Whether he's even here.

No phone. There's a very basic-looking computer tablet on the desk, however. As I expected, there's no internet, but there appears to be an intranet of sorts for entertainment. Books, games, music.

The TV doesn't connect to the outside, either. It only plays what's on the intranet.

Unlike the room, where everything seems tailored to my individual taste, the entertainment options are varied. There are even foreign-language books and movies. Not just a few languages, either—it's a pretty large assortment. I scan for French, simply out of habit. My French isn't the textbook variety and, like the hitcher who left it behind, it has a heavy African accent. I can understand the language pretty well, though—well enough that I've watched a few French movies online.

But the only French movie I see is *Amélie*, dubbed not into English but Russian. Very few Spanish or German films either, which seems a bit odd to me. Mostly Eastern European.

A tap on the door, and an almost imperceptible pause before it opens.

"Oh, good. You're awake. May I come in?" The woman sticking her head around the door looks to be in her mid- to late twenties. Blonde, short, a little on the plump side.

I nod, mostly because I'm sure she's coming in either way and at least she bothered to be polite about it. She's wearing blue scrubs, has a stethoscope around her neck, and is lugging a navy-blue bag with a white caduceus on the front.

"It's Anna, right?"

I nod again.

"I'm Ashley-your-nurse," she says, stringing the phrase together like it's a single word. "Checking in to see how you're doing. Any nausea or confusion?"

"The nausea passed. Still confused. Perhaps you could tell me where I am and how I got here?"

I have a pretty good idea on the latter question, but I ask anyway, just to see what her response will be.

"I'm sorry," Ashley-my-nurse says. "You'll go through the full orientation process tomorrow, and I'm sure those questions will be answered. I'm here to make sure you've recovered from the anesthesia. And to get a blood sample."

We go through the usual battery of physical checks—pulse, blood pressure, temperature—then she pulls out a needle and vial. "Just a little pinch."

I look away as the needle goes in. My needle phobia is secondhand from Arlene, but I still don't like watching when it breaks the skin.

Once she has two rather large vials of my blood, she pops a piece of gauze and a bandage over the puncture in my arm.

"If you're still feeling queasy," she says as she puts her equipment away, "I'd suggest a light snack of crackers, dry cereal, or something like that before bed. And you really *should* try to get to sleep soon. I would imagine they'll be in to get you no later than nine, although given that it's nearly one, I'm going to recommend they give you a bit longer. If you need medical attention, hit the button near the door and someone will contact me."

When Ashley stands to leave, I put a hand on her arm. "A boy was brought in several days ago. Taddeo Ramos, he's—"

"I'm sorry. I can't give you any information about other—"

"Just tell me if he's okay. *Please*."

"I'm sorry." Her voice is firm, but not unkind. "I really can't."

Her eyes move toward the ceiling, very briefly, but it's enough for me to be certain of what I assumed already. I'm being watched. *She's* being watched.

Ashley waves the band on her wrist in front of the security panel to open the door. As she wheels the empty gurney out, I get a brief glimpse of the empty, dimly lit hallway.

"Try to get some sleep, Anna." She gives me a fleeting look of sympathy. "You'll need your rest."

Her emphasis on the last sentence is clear, and it only ratchets up my anxiety. I'd love to break something right now, just to hear it shatter. I settle for hurling my empty water bottle at the wall. It connects with a very unsatisfying thwack and falls to the carpet.

I take two of my pills and eat a few of the Ritz Crackers, since dinner was the single egg roll I grabbed on the way back from the Chinese restaurant. When I'm finished, I crawl under the covers and change into one of the nightgowns from the dresser, tossing my clothes into a pile next to the bed. The idea of undressing in this place creeps me out. Are there cameras in the bathroom too, or only in here?

Once the lights are out, I meditate and focus on my mental walls. Whenever a stray thought about Aaron, Taylor, or their relationship with Molly wanders into view, I push it into the folder near the back wall so that I can quickly shove them away from Dacia's prying eyes. I visualize that inner wall as an impenetrable fortress, surrounded by a force field, encased in a Cone of Silence, and covered by a Cloak of Invisibility.

The Aaron and Taylor memories are recent. I don't think they'll be that hard to hide. But the Molly memories are still unpacking, and I don't know how to manage that process or speed it up. I usually spend weeks working with Kelsey after one of my tenants moves on, sorting through their memories and trying to get my head in order. It's not something I control. The Molly memories keep piling up when I'm distracted. They're disorganized, and way too many of them involve the Quinns.

Half an hour later, I've done my best to sort through my incoming memory mail. But I'm still too wound up to sleep. So I browse through the audiobooks on the intranet, hoping I'll find the one I'm looking for.

It's there. *Order of the Phoenix.* I skip to Chapter Twenty-One and forward to a section near the end. Hermione is accusing Ron of having the "emotional range of a teaspoon."

I wonder if Aaron is in the car now, listening to the same thing.

And then I shove *that* thought into the folder with the others.

❖ ❖ ❖

I dream of garden shears and X-Acto knives. Cold, pitch-dark basements. A girl with ice-blue eyes. Light that feels like it's burning straight through my retinas. And then the light turns into a snake, and I turn into a snake, although I'm pretty sure those last two are due more to my choice of bedtime reading than to Molly's memories.

Twice, I wake up huddled in a ball, whimpering. But the pills give me just enough control that I don't cry out. Just enough control that I can—eventually—fall back asleep. That part was so much easier when Aar—

No.

Back into the fortress with you.

Raise shields.

Lower the Cone of Silence.

Sleep.

❖ ❖ ❖

". . . get her to wake the hell up."

When I open my eyes, the television is on, even though I'm positive I didn't turn it on. A guy of maybe twenty-five is staring at something on a computer screen. A newscaster, maybe? He seems a bit too average looking, though, and his khaki-colored shirt is more like a uniform. There's a name tag, but I can only read the first four letters—*Timm.*

"Finally," he says, when he glances toward the camera. "I was about to send someone to knock on your door. Was beginning to wonder if you understand English."

It takes me a second to realize that he's talking to me. I sit straight up, yanking the covers around me.

"You *do* understand English, don't you?" Timm-Whatever's tone is snide, almost combative.

"Y-yes."

"Good. That's what my chart says, but I've been calling your name for the past ten minutes."

"The volume was low," I tell him. "And I had a rough night."

"Yeah, well, that's why they let you sleep two extra hours. Anyway, you've got twenty minutes to get showered and grab breakfast."

The screen goes dark again.

After I shovel down some cereal, I force myself to shower. I lock the bathroom door and try to forget that the ceiling might have eyes. I'll think of it as the school locker room. People might be watching, but so what?

The water is blessedly hot and steam hangs in the air, fogging up the glass shower door and mirror. I feel a little more alive by the time I'm finished. I wrap the towel around me and then open the cabinet above the sink to search for a toothbrush.

When I close the cabinet, a word has appeared near the center of the mirror, drawn in the condensation as if by someone's finger:

PEEKABO

I step back quickly, nearly slipping on the damp tile. The door behind me is still locked, although I'm sure they have keys.

Is the word misspelled? Or did I just catch the steam graffiti artist before he or she could finish?

As I watch, a second letter *o* forms—*PEEKABO* becomes *PEEKABOO*. Then on the next line, the letters pop up one at a time as I watch: *WELCOME TO THE WARREN!*

The word triggers an Emily memory of a book about rabbits. *Watership Down.* The rabbits lived in tunnels called warrens.

A heart appears at the end of the welcome, then the entire thing vanishes, as though an invisible hand has wiped the slate clean. All that remains is a damp smear in the middle of the mirror.

I dress under the blankets again. Maybe hallucinations are an aftereffect of whatever drug Dacia made me inhale last night?

My heartbeat has almost returned to normal when the door opens—they don't even bother with the pretense of knocking this time. It's a different woman. Her name tag reads *Bellamy*, and she's wearing a khaki shirt like the guy I saw on the TV. An odd-looking gun is holstered on the hip of her dark-brown pants. She doesn't look friendly. She doesn't even make eye contact.

"Come with me."

I grab my phone and start to stick it in the back pocket of my jeans.

"Leave it. No personal items."

I drop the phone on the bed and follow her into the hallway. Her hair is pulled back in a tight knot, and there's a distinct military influence in her stride. She grabs my arm right above the elbow. I fight the urge to yank it away, since I'm guessing that would be seen as uncooperative, and fall into step beside her. Everything about her says *no chitchat*, so I don't bother asking about Deo or where we're headed. I just walk quietly and try to observe as much as I can about our surroundings.

Plain gray walls, with no paintings or other decoration. No windows. The floors are a slightly darker shade of gray. We pass a half-dozen doors numbered in the eighties, then turn right. Maybe twenty yards later, I see Timm-Whatever, my cheerful personal alarm clock. He's in a cubicle off to the side, typing something into the computer, and doesn't look up when we walk by.

Still no windows or exit doors. No exit *signs*, even.

As we pass Room 81, I hear a loud thud and the door vibrates slightly, like it was hit by a shoe or something. Then someone starts yelling. I can't make out the words, but the voice is high-pitched, angry. Frightened.

"That's . . . that's a kid." I pause and turn back for a moment.

"No," she says, but I can't tell if she's disagreeing or saying it's none of my business.

I glance at the door one more time. *Thump. Thumpthumpthumpthumpthumpthump.* The door is vibrating again, but as I look more closely, it's not a normal vibration. Only the center third of the door seems affected. It seems to bulge into the hallway a fraction of an inch and then returns to normal.

Or maybe I just didn't get enough sleep . . .

Bellamy yanks my arm. "Follow me *now.*"

We eventually reach a second computer station. Behind it is a woman, her eyes glued to a large wall-mounted monitor divided into four numbered squares. The images on the screen are identical—a room with two chairs facing each other across a table. The only difference is that the chairs in the rooms numbered 1 and 4 are occupied.

The woman looks up when we approach, avoiding eye contact with me as she hands Bellamy a clipboard. "We've got you in Testing Room 3," she says.

"Standard entry tests, right?"

"Yeah. Just cover the checklist for now. They'll either start differentiation after lunch or first thing tomorrow, since you're getting a late start. Don't rush it. This one is a 2A, so take whatever time and precautions you need." The woman's gaze passes over my face as she says the last part. Then she looks away quickly, as though she's frightened or maybe disgusted.

I follow Bellamy. When we're a few steps away, she stops and turns back. "Oh, get someone to check in on 81."

"Again?"

The woman gives Bellamy a look I can't interpret, but Bellamy doesn't respond to the question.

The doors in this corridor aren't numbered, but Bellamy opens the second one on the left. She nods toward one of the chairs, and I search for the camera as I sit. It's mounted in the rear of the room, pointing directly at the table. I'm tempted to wave at the woman from the hallway, since I'm certain her monitor now shows Bellamy and me in square number 3. But that would probably be construed as smart-ass, so I keep my hands folded in my lap.

Bellamy extracts a small deck of plain gray cards from a drawer beneath the table and places them next to her. Then she picks up the clipboard and pen.

"Subject is Anna Elizabeth Morgan, age seventeen-point-nine-two. Race?" She waits a moment and then repeats the question. "Your race?"

"Oh. Caucasian."

"Hispanic?"

Might as well get this over with. I set my mouth in a firm line and say, "I'm not answering any more questions until someone proves to me that Taddeo Ramos is safe."

Bellamy sighs and places the clipboard on the table. "I have no information. My assignment is to conduct your entry tests. Once those are complete, you'll be assigned a handler and you can ask her or him whatever questions you like. You have two options. Answer my questions or I will handcuff you and escort you back to your room—and if you resist, I will tase you first. Then we'll start this process again tomorrow morning, at which point you'll face the *same two choices*. Rinse and repeat until you decide to cooperate. The quickest way for you to get the information you want is to let me do my job."

Her voice isn't unkind or angry. It's just bored, and very matter-of-fact. Monotone, even.

"So, I'll repeat. Are you Hispanic?"

"To the best of my knowledge, no."

She reels off a few more demographic questions, several of which aren't relevant for me, since I have no idea what level of education my parents achieved. Then Bellamy puts the clipboard aside, peels off the first card in the deck, and slides it toward me. There are five colored circles on a gray background—red, blue, yellow, white, and black.

"In this test," she says, "you will be asked to predict the color of the card before I draw it. Please respond with one of the colors in front of you. Do you have any questions?"

"I'm supposed to guess?"

"Focus on the card and make a prediction. What is the first card in the deck?"

"Blue."

She draws the top card, looks at it, and puts it facedown in the open drawer next to her. I have no idea whether I've guessed right or wrong. Then she taps the deck and I make my next prediction. "Green."

Bellamy huffs and taps the card in front of me. "Not one of the options. Please focus and try again."

"Oh, sorry. Yellow?"

She puts that card facedown on top of the first one, and we move on. Occasionally she puts a card in a second stack, but most of the cards follow the first two.

When we complete the deck, Bellamy counts the shorter stack—which I suspect are my correct guesses—and jots something down on her clipboard. Then we do the whole thing again.

After that round is finished, she shuffles and slides the deck to me. "Now, I want you to draw a card and focus on the color. After I make a prediction, place the card faceup on the table."

I comply. If she gets one correct—about one-third of the time, which seems a bit unusual—she pulls the card toward her. At the end, she writes something on the sheet and then pulls out another deck of cards. Shapes, this time.

"Couldn't they just automate this?" I ask. "Seems like it would be pretty easy to have a computer program . . ."

"They could automate some of them. But several experts think that the machinery blocks . . ." She stops, apparently realizing that she's been conversing with me as though I'm a human being. "It works better this way."

Personally, I think these so-called experts have been reading too many Dresden Files books, but I keep that opinion to myself.

She taps the card on top of the deck.

"Star."

And so it goes for the next hour and a half. Shapes, then numbers, then words. Then we move on to something that sounds a lot like remote viewing. I'm supposed to let my mind go blank and think of a location, then draw what I see.

I take the sheet of paper and pencil. "Just so you know, I can't draw. Even my stick figures are unrecognizable."

"Do your best. I'll be back in fifteen minutes."

But even as I'm telling her that my drawing abilities are crap, I have the sense that it's not necessarily true. It *used* to be true. But I have this new memory of Molly and Taylor, sitting in someone's kitchen, sketching a bowl of fruit. Molly's good. Maybe even better than Taylor.

Another memory to shove inside the invisible fortress. At this rate, I'm going to need to add a few rooms. So many of Molly's memories seem to be of things she did at the Quinn house.

As I stare at this blank sheet of paper, the only locations that come to mind are the house in Havre de Grace and the ruined building that was in the last sketch Taylor showed us, the one with the columns. I'm definitely not in that building, but the lack of windows or exits has me wondering whether I might not be *below* it. And who knows—Deo could be somewhere else entirely.

I'm tempted to draw that building, if only to shake things up a bit. But that might build expectations I'd never be able to match a second time.

So, with two minutes to go on the timer, I do a crude sketch of the outside of Bartholomew House. Home sweet home. It's definitely not the location I'm seeing in my head, but they won't know that unless they've found a way to read my mind without the Pop Rocks sensation I had before.

And they could be doing precisely that. Just because I had a warning with Dacia Badea doesn't mean—

Bellamy comes back in. "Finished?"

I nod and push the sketch toward her. She adds it to her clipboard, her face completely blank, as usual. I'm tempted to ask her if that's part of her job description. The ideal candidate will have a monotone voice and a face incapable of displaying human emotion.

"You have a little over an hour before someone picks you up for the second set of tests. We'll stop by the cafeteria and you can grab some lunch to take back to your room."

After Bellamy hands off the clipboard to the woman at the monitors, we turn down a different hallway. It's quiet, just like last time, until we reach the end, where I start picking up sounds off to the right. They get louder when we turn, but it's not a boisterous noise. It sounds a bit like a classroom doing group work . . . the low-level hum of many voices that are supposed to be keeping the volume down.

The many-quiet-voices theory is proven correct when Bellamy opens the door. A guard stands right inside the door, and the room is fairly crowded. Two guys who look a bit younger than I am go into a smaller room with sofas and what looks like a pool table in the back. A half dozen or so people are clustered around it.

What surprises me is the age of the people in both the cafeteria and the room beyond. I'd say twenty of the forty or fifty people eating at the tables are between five and twelve. The kids are seated in groups of four or five, monitored by an adult in a uniform like Bellamy's. Another dozen or so look like they're in their teens or early twenties, but the vast majority are female. The younger group seems pretty evenly split between boys and girls. The remaining people in the cafeteria are older, and most of them seem to be employees.

I take my time picking out food, surreptitiously scanning the faces on this side of the room. And I get the sense that a number of them are checking me out, too. Not the employees, but the others. They don't all turn and stare, nothing obvious like that, but their eyes dart away quickly when I look in their direction. Twice I feel a mental tap, similar to the feeling when Dacia scanned me, and I struggle to keep my walls in place.

But I don't see Deo.

He's not here.

I jump and turn to Bellamy. "Did you say something?"

Even before she shakes her head, even as I'm asking the question, I already know better. That voice was inside my head. Not a voice I know, either—it's a young girl.

And my walls are *up*.

Try Room 67. Tell him Pavla says he has nice *zadek*. So do you.

That's followed by laughter and another girl saying, "Oh, you are so bad, Maria!" But that voice is fainter and not in my head. I spin around and see two girls in their early teens. When one of them realizes that I'm watching the two of them, she collapses into giggles again. The third girl at the table seems to be off in her own world.

I put a yogurt on my tray and go over to the salad bar, watching the nearby tables out of the corner of my eye as I pile toppings onto my lettuce at random. One of the few adults not in a uniform is sitting by himself at a table next to me. At first, I think he's really old, because his hair is long, gray, and matted. A thick layer of salt . . . or maybe it's sugar? . . . is scattered before him on the table.

As I step closer, he whips his head up and I realize he's not as old as I'd thought. Maybe midforties? His pale eyes briefly lock onto mine. Then he looks back down at the table and uses his finger to write something in the pile of white granules in front of him.

NOT DEO

I take a step toward him, to ask what he knows about Deo, but he erases the two words and writes

HURRY UP BITCH

"Hurry up," Bellamy says. She doesn't actually say the word *bitch*, but it's definitely implied by her tone. "I'd like to have time for lunch, too."

The man stares at someone sitting one table over for a second, then runs his hands through the pile of white and begins writing something about tomatoes.

He doesn't know anything about Deo. He's simply pulling stray thoughts from people's minds. From *my* mind, too, which has me worried about the structural integrity of my walls. It also makes me wonder briefly if he's the phantom graffiti artist from my bathroom mirror, but I can't imagine him drawing a curvy little heart at the end of a word.

"I'm nearly done," I say to Bellamy. "Just let me grab a sandwich." I've got more food on the tray already than I'll ever eat, but the case that holds the wrapped sandwiches will get me closer to the three tables on the other side of the room, and one of them includes a group of teens.

I grab a sandwich without even looking, my eyes fixed on that table. There's one guy with dark hair, but he's too heavy to be Deo.

One of the men at the next table over catches my eye, however. His back is to me, but something about him is familiar. He's tall, muscular, with light hair, and dressed in the same khaki-and-brown uniform as Bellamy.

"I said it's time to go." Bellamy is behind me now.

I'd really like to stay and get a closer look, but Bellamy's moving her hand to the holstered taser. Damn, she must be really hungry, if she's willing to tase me for cutting a few extra seconds into her lunch hour.

"I'm coming, okay?" As I say the words, the guy turns slightly toward me. I can still only see part of his face, but it's enough that the resemblance clicks into place.

He looks like Daniel.

❖   ❖   ❖

I have a different escort for the afternoon round of testing, although there isn't a dime's worth of difference between her and Bellamy. Same uniform, same attitude, and pretty much the same response when I ask for information about Deo before the testing begins. The only notice-able change is that several of the afternoon tests are on computers. I guess the experts who thought technology and psychic abilities don't mix lost a few battles along the way.

As before, I have no clue whether I pass the tests or fail them. In a few cases, I can't even tell what the test is trying to measure. All I know is that each time they ask me for an answer, I pull it out of thin air. I don't see a blue card or a red card or any card in my mind, no matter how hard I focus. It's pure guesswork every time.

Later in the day, they tape thin wires to my scalp and ask me to move various objects with my mind. I play along, but it's all I can do to take them seriously. I don't exactly doubt that some people can do these things. In fact, given my own abilities and what I've learned over the past few days, I'd say it's entirely possible.

But even if some people are telekinetic, why would they assume that I'd voluntarily use that power during a stupid test? If I suddenly discover I can move objects with my thoughts, the first time they'll have any indication will be after I find Deo, when I fling every object in the building into their path to block them as we run for the exit.

Assuming I ever locate an exit. We passed what looked like an elevator earlier, just down from the rooms where I was tested this morning, but I didn't get a close look. This is the only large building I've ever been in that didn't have at least a few signs pointing you toward the exits in case of emergency.

The afternoon session wraps up around six thirty. I follow my escort toward the cafeteria, confirming along the way that it was indeed an elevator I saw earlier. There's a security panel next to it however, so I doubt it would work without one of those bracelets.

I'm not the slightest bit hungry given how much I piled onto my tray at lunch, and even if I was, there are leftovers back in my room. But I got more information about this place from five minutes in the cafeteria than I've gotten all day. And I'm really hoping I'll get a closer look at Daniel's doppelgänger. Although the more I think about it, the more I'm wondering if it isn't Daniel himself. I keep remembering that weird exchange between him and Dacia at the beginning of the meeting at the police station. He lied about his eye color, and I don't know which I find more puzzling—the fact that he lied about it, or the fact that she believed his lie. The lighting was less than perfect in the interrogation room, but she was only a few feet away from him.

I hear the faint noise of the cafeteria at the end of the corridor, but we stop before we reach it. "I thought we were going to the cafeteria."

The woman doesn't respond. She just gives me a *guess-that's-what-you-get-for-thinking* look and waves her wrist in front of the security panel.

After the various tests today, I'd have sworn that the only psychic ability I have is my unfortunate knack for sweeping up psychic residue and hoarding it for future use. But there must be a tiny bit of intuition, some hint of precognitive awareness in the mix somewhere, because I quickly shift my thoughts about what I saw today in the cafeteria into my *Recent Memories* folder, then shove everything behind my second wall and raise every shield I can muster.

Dacia is curled up on a well-padded sofa, thumbing through something on her phone. Compared to the spartan testing rooms I've been in all day, the décor here is much more comfortable and welcoming.

Her smile when she sees me is far from welcoming, however. It's closer to predatory. She's discarded the power suit from our last encounter in favor of jeans and a sweater, similar to the one I'm wearing, although she fills it out much more dramatically.

That same little voice that told me she was here is whispering that I need to distract her—keep her off guard, maybe a little angry. Tell her more than she wants to know so that she has less reason to look closely at things I don't want her to notice.

Dacia takes my arm from the guard whose name I've already forgotten. Bellamy II, I guess. The buzzing sensation starts instantly. "This will be quick. Ten minutes."

Once the guard is gone, Dacia releases my arm and nods toward the sofa. "Don't want to keep you too long. Because you are hungry . . ." Her voice rises, making it almost a question, like she's unsure of that point. "Disappointed not to go to the cafeteria. Is the food really so extraordinary here?"

"No, the food actually kind of sucks. Still, beats hanging out with you."

I sit down and she grabs my wrist. The buzzing . . . I'm not sure if it starts again or simply increases when she touches me. I pull my hand back but she tightens her grip.

"What happened to you saying 'I'll cooperate. I'll do whatever you say, just don't hurt him'?"

Her voice takes on a mocking tone. If I had any choice in the matter, I'd be slamming my fist into her face rather than cooperating.

"But you *don't* have choice, do you?" She's quiet for a second, and I feel her in my head, checking out the terrain.

Her brows crease with suspicion. "You have done . . . *rearranying.*" I don't recognize the word as *rearranging* until she taps the side of her head. Her hand is still encased in a black leather glove. The effect of her pale skin against the single black glove is like Michael Jackson in reverse.

Dacia definitely picked that thought up. I get the sense it's not the first time someone has made that comparison, and she doesn't like it.

"Molly left," I tell her. "Those memories are still being unpacked. You remember Molly, don't you?"

She flinches the tiniest bit and I keep going. "That's what you want to know, right? What I remember about Molly? I remember that she was trying to comfort you that very same night you woke up screaming, and now here you are, working with the man who beat her to death." That catches her attention, and she cocks her head slightly to the side.

"Or do you want to know what I remember about you? That you're from Romania, a little town on the Danube. That they came through your hometown, promised you a good job, working with a family. Watching their children. But you did well enough on their little card tests or whatever that they injected you with something. It didn't take at first, and you wound up with Graham Cregg. But lucky for you, the magic potion eventually kicked in and now you're out of that basement, out of the nightmare. Only Molly didn't get out. Do you want to know about the other people I've hosted? How they died? Thank God they were all luckier than Molly. No one murdered *them.*"

"Shut up!" Dacia digs her nails into my skin. "You do not do the talking. I do not need you to tell me about your other phantom . . ." She waves her hands, like she can't find the word. "The dead-in-your-head people."

The phrase catches me off guard and I laugh. She can read my thoughts enough to know that I'm not making fun of her frustration— I actually think the description has a certain ring to it—but my tiny smidgen of approval seems to anger her even more. She's combing through the files marked *Abner* now. The sensation is sort of like someone running their fingernail very lightly across your skin . . . it almost tickles and I want to brush it away. Except it's *inside* my head.

I'm not even sure why she'd bother with Abner except to prove that she can do whatever the hell she wants. She races through the farm chores and swimming holes and other images from his childhood in 1940s Indiana. Next are the plumbing tips, how to wire an electrical outlet, and other odds and ends from his work, some of which he learned in the Navy, and the majority of which he couldn't even use by the time he retired because he didn't have a special license in those areas.

Mostly, however, Dacia is getting information about his dogs. Abner never married. Never had a family. His dogs were his life. The last one was a beagle mix named Bumper. She's the reason Abner couldn't move on. He had to be sure someone took care of Bumper. Only Abner had been dead for fifteen years when I picked him up on the park bench. I finally found an elderly neighbor who remembered him. Remembered that a family two blocks over had adopted Bumper after the police found Abner's body in his backyard garden. She saw the kids taking her for walks for a few years, but then the dog either died or they moved away. The woman couldn't remember which.

And that was the last time I heard Abner's voice. His memories, the ones that Dacia is tearing through now, gradually accrued and I filed them away, but he was able to let go once he knew that Bumper hadn't starved to death after his stroke. That someone had taken her in and cared for her.

Dacia's probe shifts to Emily, but she's only in that folder for a few minutes. Apparently she's not a history buff. She glances at the others, but skips them and goes to Molly's file, which is disordered and definitely not chronologically arranged like Abner's memories.

A woman—Molly's mother—laughing as she helps a younger Molly build a snowman.

Molly crying as Cregg forces her to cut her own leg in the main room of the cabin.

"Holes," Dacia says. "There are holes here. Molly's is not like the others."

"Her memories are still unpacking. It's . . . um . . . think of it as a zip file. The memories are there, but they aren't extracted yet. There's no . . . file structure."

It's not a bad analogy for what's going on. But it doesn't seem to satisfy Dacia.

She mumbles something. The only words I pick up are "what is this zip files," then she starts rummaging again.

Playing a song from the Harry Potter movies on the piano at Porter's house.

Molly falling off the swing and breaking her wrist.

Holding up her arm to ward off the blow as Cregg swings the base of the metal pipe toward her.

No . . . as Dacia *swings it toward her.*

"You?" I yank my arm away. Dacia's nails carve shallow grooves into the underside of my wrist. The mental probe leaves my head so quickly that I can almost hear a pop. "But she tried to protect you!"

I can't remember. Did Molly ever *say* that it was Cregg who killed her? And does it even matter if Cregg was the one forcing Dacia?

Was he the one forcing Dacia?

I lean forward and put my head between my knees, fighting against the queasy, dizzy feeling that came in the wake of our sudden disconnection. My arms are clutched tightly to my sides. Does she need skin-to-skin contact in order to read me? Or does that just boost the signal? Either way, I don't want her to touch me again.

But when I raise my head, I can tell that Dacia's exhausted. She's leaning back against the couch cushions, eyes closed.

When she finally opens them, they brim with loathing. "If Graham did not want you unharmed, I would find something heavy to hit *you* with." The words are harsh, but her voice is flat. Tired. "And then you'd see that I made it quick for Molly. Quicker than he would have."

Dacia is slightly unsteady as she stands, the way she was at the police station. She stares back at me when she reaches the door, and for an instant, her eyes seem . . . wounded, I guess. Did she actually believe that killing Molly was an act of mercy?

"*Much* quicker than I would for you."

And with that parting shot, she leaves me alone to wait for Bellamy II.

The cafeteria is empty by the time we arrive, except for two uniformed employees talking at a back table and a few cafeteria workers cleaning up. The air smells like there might have been hot food earlier—chili, maybe?—but the only options available now are packaged sandwiches, bagels, cookies, yogurt, and such.

As we get closer, I see that one of the two uniformed employees is the guard who was with Dacia at the police station. His head jerks up when he sees me, and he exits quickly. There's no sign, however, of the guy that I'm more and more certain is actually Daniel.

Back in my room, I unwrap the bagel I selected. One bite is enough to make me realize I should have grabbed another sandwich instead. It's not that the bagel is awful, although the round shape is pretty much the only thing it has in common with the ones Joe makes at Carver's Deli. It's more that the bagel triggers a wave of homesickness. Joe wasn't simply a boss. He was a friend. If there were extra hours up for grabs, I got first dibs because he knew I needed the money. If I helped him close up, he'd drop me at home rather than letting me walk at night.

Simply put, he was kind. I don't get the sense that there's much of that in this place. I miss Kelsey, I miss Molly, I miss Aaron, and most of all, I miss Deo. I've been here almost an entire day and I don't seem any closer to finding him and securing his release than I was when I woke up on that gurney last night. Bellamy II refused to answer any questions when she locked me in. Her only comment was that someone would let me know when my next tests were scheduled.

My conversations with Sam and Kelsey echo in my head, and I know they were right. It was naive to think that I could waltz in and negotiate for Deo's release, and it seems even less likely to happen now.

Before, I thought I was dealing with Dacia, Cregg, Lucas, and maybe a few other goons. Now, it looks like I'm dealing with an entire organization. How many of the kids I saw in the cafeteria are missing children? Were they snatched off the streets at random for testing? Or worse, as guinea pigs for the drug used in the Delphi Project?

And now I'm not even certain of things I thought I knew. Did Molly hide that it was Dacia swinging the pipe? Or did I simply jump to the conclusion that it was Cregg all on my own?

Does it matter? If Dacia wants to sit me down tomorrow for a second round of hide-and-seek, I'll play her game, no matter what it costs me. Like I told Aaron, as long as they have Deo, they call the shots.

I toss the rest of the bagel into the trash.

❖   ❖   ❖

"AN . . . NA."

I'm stretched out on the bed, eyes closed, listening to another chapter in my book. Even though *I* don't recognize the voice, every hair on my body is at attention before my eyes open.

Because Molly knows it all too well.

I spring upright and breathe a sigh of relief when I see that Lucas is *not* in the room with me. His voice is coming from the TV. Someone apparently cranked the volume way, way up when they came in to make the bed and empty the trash while I was at testing.

Actually, I must have dozed off. The clock in the lower right corner of the TV screen says 11:27 p.m.

The downside of Lucas being on the TV is that his face is larger than life, and that makes it hard to keep my expression that of someone startled awake, instead of someone who's freaked out at seeing the man who killed my mom and raped me. Because even though I know Molly isn't me, the dreams are so vivid and real that it's sometimes hard to make that distinction.

He appears to be at the same desk as the Timm guy who woke me up this morning, but Lucas isn't wearing a uniform—just a gray North Face jacket, unzipped partially to show a black dress shirt.

I turn down the volume, fighting a very strong urge to turn off the television entirely.

He gives me what he probably thinks is an amiable smile. "What you listenin' to?"

"A book." I grab the tablet and press the stop button.

"Well, duh," Lucas says, still smiling. "Kind of figured that much, seeing that the Brit guy was saying *he said* and *she said* and what have you. You know who I am, right?"

"You're Dacia Badea's driver. I saw you in her car."

Lucas's eyes are a light-gray color that looks slightly exotic against his caramel skin.

That's why he almost always wears gray. Someone told him it brings out his eyes. A Molly memory.

Those eyes are narrowed slightly now. "Just because you see someone driving a car doesn't make him somebody's *driver*. I don't work for Daciana. Didn't anyone ever teach you why it's a bad idea to make assumptions?"

He raises his eyebrows, waiting for an answer.

Oh, dear God. Does he really think that joke is original or witty?

"It makes an ass out of you and me."

"I see you're both smart *and* pretty." He laughs and settles into another smile.

That's the one he thinks is sexy. The smile he practices in the mirror.

I get a flash of a cartoon shark, and another Molly memory comes roaring in. This one is from when she was seven or eight, before she was frightened of Lucas. Back when he bought her Webkinz and Beanie Babies whenever she visited her mom. Before she started connecting the number and shape of the perpetual bruises on her mom's arms with Lucas's fingers.

On that particular day, when Lucas smiled at Molly's mom, Molly thought for the first time that the smile made him look a little scary. A bit like Bruce, the shark in *Finding Nemo*. And not fish-friendly Bruce, but Bruce when instinct kicks in and he's about to munch on Nemo's dad and Dory.

I keep my face blank and file that memory away with the others.

"Listen." Lucas leans toward the camera, moistening his lips with a quick flick of his tongue. "You've got an appointment later tonight. I just got here early because I was thinkin' maybe you might be interested in a little trade for some info about your friend. But that's probably somethin' better discussed in person."

He winks, and the screen goes black.

CHAPTER FIFTEEN

I'm frozen in place for several seconds after Lucas's face disappears. As soon as I'm able to pull in a breath, I run for the door, hitting the button that the nurse, Ashley, mentioned last night. I'm not sure what to expect—will someone speak to me through the security device?

"Yes, Anna?" The TV screen is on again. Lucas is sitting there, grinning. "If you're looking for Timmons, we're buddies. I told him to go for a smoke break, maybe Skype with his girlfriend. That I'd keep a very close eye on you 'til he got back. So it's just you and me, sweetheart."

"I was . . . looking for the nurse. A question about my medication."

His expression makes it clear that he's not buying it. "I'll be sure to leave her a note." He gives me the shark smile once more, and the screen is back to black.

I tear into the kitchen, looking for something, anything, that might be useful as a weapon. But everything is plastic, lightweight. No glass. Nothing heavier than the small tub of peanut butter. The most lethal tool in the entire place is a damned spork.

What I wouldn't give for my pepper spray or my sock full of pennies right now. But I've spent nearly fifteen years in group homes. You learn to make do with what you have.

I drop the spork with the business end facedown on the floor and use a bottle of water from the fridge, cap down, to crack parts of the plastic away from the handle. It's a half-assed shiv, but it's a whole lot better than nothing. I shove it into the back pocket of my jeans and pull out the bag of apples and a few bottles of water—anything I can throw at Lucas that might slow him down long enough for me to get away.

Except . . . I'll need his identification to open the door.

Fine, then. Anything that might slow him down long enough for me to jab this shard of plastic into his throat—something that would give me great personal pleasure—and take his ID.

Except . . . leaving aside how unlikely that is to work, would attacking Lucas improve Deo's chances of getting out of here alive?

No. I really don't think it would.

Closing my eyes, I reach into the file marked *Molly*. It's nowhere near full yet, but I'm hoping I'll find something, anything, about Lucas that might be a weakness.

If she's got anything of that nature, I don't find it. Lucas is strong and he's mean. He's not even all *that* stupid, just not half as smart as he thinks he is. Or half as good-looking.

Why, out of the ten people I've hosted, couldn't at least one of them have been into martial arts or some sort of self-defense?

Haven't checked Myron's file . . .

I stomp that thought down and grind it under my heel. Nothing like panic to get you thinking of all possible ways to make a bad situation worse.

Okay. Deep breaths. Since I can't overpower him, I'll have to outwit him. He's vain. If I flatter him, he'll believe I'm interested. He thinks *every* woman is interested.

I'm well aware that anything Lucas tells me will probably be a lie, and there's no way I'm bartering any favors for information. But . . . playing along, stalling for a bit, getting him off guard, might not be a bad idea.

Assuming I can do it. Assuming I don't just start shrieking the minute he shows up.

When I hear the footsteps in the hall, the hand on the doorknob, I sit down—on the stool near the kitchen. Because there's no way in hell I'm going to be sitting on that bed when he walks in.

Relax. You don't have to smile, but you can't act like a scared little girl. This is a business negotiation.

I try to get a look at the hallway when the door opens. It's dimly lit, like it was last night when the nurse left. Lucas closes the door behind him and stands near the closet for a minute, surveying the room.

"What's with all the apples? You plannin' to bake me a pie?"

"No oven, no microwave." I pick up one of the larger apples. Abner played baseball in high school and spent many hours playing fetch with his dogs. I can picture cocking my arm and letting it fly, but I can't picture what happens next. I somehow doubt that an apple upside the head would do much more than make Lucas angry.

So I toss it to him instead.

He catches it, then parks on the edge of the bed as he takes a large bite. "So, tell me, Anna. How you liking your stay so far?"

"I've seen better," I say with a shrug. "And you know my name. If we're going to . . . make any sort of deal . . . maybe you should start by returning the favor?"

"Most people just call me Lucas." He gives me a sly smile. "Molly used to call me daddy sometimes, since her old man bailed before she could even walk."

That's a lie—not the part about Molly's dad bailing, but the daddy bit, since she never called him anything other than Lucas. He's clearly trying to rile me up, to see how much I know about Molly. How much I know about what he did. But I'm not taking the bait.

"Only things I know about Molly are what I read in her diary and what she told me in the few days we were at the same shelter. And that was years ago. She didn't mention a dad or anyone named Lucas. Just

Pa and Mimmy. And her Pa was a cheap bastard, wouldn't even cough up a few hundred bucks for the info I gave him. If I hadn't apologized to him, I'd have ended up back in juvie. Deo too, most likely."

I make myself look at him as I speak. I don't think he's believing any of it. If he's on more than chauffeur terms with Dacia, he probably knows everything I've said is a lie anyway. But it's hard to tell if he's even listening. His eyes keep breaking away from my face and traveling south.

"You said you had information about Deo."

He nods. "I do. But I need a better idea of what you're offering up for trade. Maybe you could come over here and let me take that sweater off."

I give him a tiny smile, like I'm considering his proposal. Force my eyes to take a leisurely sightseeing tour of his body, the way he keeps doing with mine. I linger on his wrist—no bracelet, so he must have used a badge or something to open the door. He wasn't holding it when he walked in, but I don't see it. Back pocket?

"Maybe we could . . . compromise?" I pull my sweater slowly over my head and toss it on the ground. I'm still in a camisole and jeans, but I've never felt less clothed in my life.

He gives me an appreciative nod. "A step in the right direction."

I smile again. "So . . . is Deo here? In this same building?"

The question seems to piss him off. "What makes you think our . . . *transaction* . . . is going to be tit for tat? If you'll pardon the joke. Your little boyfriend might get turned on by strip poker, but I ain't got time for games."

He gives a humorless laugh and rises to his feet. "And since the rest of our party's due to arrive in about half an hour, and you're gonna want a little time to . . . clean up . . . you need to decide if we're gonna do this the fun way or if you'd rather make things difficult."

By the time Lucas says that last word, he's directly in front of me. There's a faint hint of something on his breath. Whiskey? Rum?

My entire body tenses as his hand slides beneath my camisole. "Wondering if maybe you should yell? Go ahead. Like I told you, Timmons took a break. No other guards in this wing this time of night. So the only ones who'll hear you are locked up in these rooms just . . . like . . . you." He must be able to hear my heart pounding because he says, "Nothin' to be afraid of. I can play nice and gentle, Anna. You want us to play gentle, don't you?"

All I can see is this same face in my dream, holding me down. *You're the reason your mama is dead, you ungrateful little bitch. You think I wanted to kill her?*

I somehow manage to nod, and I place my hand on his neck. At the same time, I reach around with my other hand to grab the mangled spork in my back pocket. This will probably get me killed. It will probably mean I can't help Deo, that he'll be stuck here, but I can't do this. The memories from Molly are too strong and I just *can't*.

Lucas isn't fooled even for a second. He realizes what I'm doing, or at least that I'm planning something. As soon as I make my move, his hand tightens around my forearm.

He twists and I scream, kicking out. It's no use—he grabs my leg and lifts me, by one leg and one arm, and tosses me onto the bed. I land hard, my shoulder connecting with the wooden headboard.

"Looks like you don't want gen . . . tle." Lucas pauses. Someone's tapping on the door.

He curses softly and takes a few steps back from the bed as the door opens.

It's the nurse from last night. Ashley. Except now she's carrying a taser like the other employees.

"What's . . . going on here?"

Lucas doesn't miss a beat. "Came to fetch her for some additional testing down at the main lab. But she decided to put up a fight."

Ashley flashes him a teasing grin as she taps the taser on her hip. "And that's why even you big, burly types should be carrying one of these." When her gaze shifts to me, the smile vanishes. "Miss Anna here is a handful, isn't she? She seemed fairly calm last night, but I guess the drugs hadn't worn off. Fought me like a damned wildcat when I came in during lunch."

She puts her bag on the counter and pulls out a blood pressure cuff. "A bit late to be taking them for testing, isn't it?"

Lucas shrugs. "I don't schedule them. I just fetch when they say fetch."

"Tell me about it. They hauled me out of bed at midnight last night when they brought her in. That's why I'm back now. Standard protocol after anesthesia for someone with her medical history. Have to check her vitals every twelve hours for the first two days."

She approaches the bed, holding out the cuff. "You're not going to fight me again, are you, Anna? Otherwise, I'll have to tase you like I did earlier and that wasn't pleasant at all, was it?"

I don't have any idea what she's talking about. In fact, I think it's almost as likely that she's crazy as it is that she's here to help. But I'd rather be tased by a crazy nurse than have Lucas touch me again.

"No, ma'am. I won't fight."

"Yeah, well I won't be turning my back on you again, that's for sure." She puts one hand against the side of my neck "Son of a bitch. You had to go and get all pissy with him, didn't you? Now your heart is racing like a rabbit in a snare."

She glances over her shoulder at Lucas. "Go tell them I'm gonna need fifteen minutes, maybe twenty. I have to wait until her pulse slows down a bit or my supervisor will want to give the brat a full workup, maybe even postpone the tests for a few days. Which lab? I'll have someone drop her off as soon as we're done."

"Lab 1." He starts to go, then seems to change his mind. "But leave her here. I'll come back in twenty."

Lucas gives me one last look and backs into the hallway. I let out a shaky breath as the door clicks shut behind him.

"Relax, okay?" Ashley says in a softer voice.

"How did you—"

"*Stop talking.*" Ashley's eyes flash a quiet warning and flicker almost imperceptibly toward the TV. "Sit here quietly for a few minutes. Take some deep breaths."

I nod. As much as I'd love to know how she knew to burst in at that exact moment, I'll have to accept that she did and be grateful. Maybe the medical personnel also have spying privileges?

Either way, I suspect that she's put herself way out on a limb by lying about me attacking her earlier. That has to be really easy to check, if someone decides to investigate.

"Thank you."

Ashley pats my knee and goes into the kitchen. "You can thank me by doing what you're told for a change." She opens the refrigerator. "Where is your medication?"

"Um . . . in the cabinet?"

She gives her head an exasperated shake and takes the bottle out of the cabinet. "It's *supposed* to be kept in the *fridge*. It should be okay just this once. But when you take your pills tonight, put the bottle back in here."

I'm leaning back toward the Ashley-is-crazy hypothesis. I've been taking those pills for five years now. They're basic tablets. No refrigeration necessary.

But I nod. "Okay. Will do."

We sit there . . . quietly . . . for the next five minutes. Then she quickly takes my blood pressure, temp, and draws blood again. I think that's overdoing it, personally, since this is probably just a dog and pony show, but whatever.

"There. All finished." She smiles and pulls a cell phone from her pocket. Or, at least, it looks like a phone. It's in this odd case with an antenna on one side. "This is Swinton. I'm over in Highside. Could I get an escort to the main lab for a 2Alpha? Room 94."

The person on the other end gives her an affirmative and she stashes the phone back in her pocket.

"Lucas is going to be angry that you didn't—"

"He told me to have someone take you to Lab 1 in twenty minutes. Get yourself something to drink. Maybe some of that apple juice I saw. Oh . . . and *don't take the medicine out of the fridge.*"

"Sure." I nod to show that I follow what she's saying. I guess that's true, even if the only thing I've followed is that she's trying to convey a message that has something to do with the fridge.

She picks up my sweater from the floor and tosses it to me. "Might want to put that back on."

"Definitely. Thank you." I emphasize the last two words.

Her pale cheeks flush slightly, and she nods briskly. Then she waves her bracelet in front of the panel. "Be careful. And get something to drink and a snack, like I said. Night testing can be . . . strenuous."

As soon as she leaves, I go to the fridge. There's a small note, handwritten in ink on one of the cafeteria napkins, right next to my medicine.

Ashley's emphasis on the refrigerator now makes perfect sense. They may have cameras in the kitchen, in the main room, even in the bathroom for all I know. But they don't have a camera in the fridge.

Standing inside the partially closed refrigerator door, I open the apple juice and drink while I read the message. It doesn't take long.

> *Deo is safe. Working on getting both of you out. Hang tight. FLUSH THIS.*

I cap the juice and scoop the paper into my palm before closing the door. Time for a bathroom break.

The note isn't signed. Is it from Ashley, or is she simply a courier? I would have guessed the latter, but she's a pretty good actor. I almost believed the story she was telling Lucas, even though I knew she was lying.

Maybe a minute later, there's a knock on the door. I tense up instantly, thinking it's Lucas, but I doubt he'd knock even if he believed Ashley was still in here.

I've gotten used to the door opening right after the knock, but when I don't say anything, there's a second knock.

"Come in?"

"I'm here to escort you to the lab."

It's the guy I saw at lunch, and this time, I get a clear look at his face. His eyes. His very *brown* eyes that are giving me a warning right now to keep quiet and play along. The name tag reads *Corben*, but I have no doubt that this is Daniel Quinn. And I'm pretty sure that answers my question about who wrote the message.

"Ready to go?"

I'm not sure if he's asking if I'm ready to go to the lab, or if I'm ready to go, as in get the hell out of here.

The answer to the first is *no*, and the answer to the second is *only if Deo's already free*. But I can't ask him any questions to clarify, and I don't really have much choice either way. "Yeah. Sure."

"Do I need to cuff you? Your record says you had to be subdued this afternoon . . ."

"Taser's not nearly as much fun as I thought it would be. I'll behave."

His mouth twitches upward slightly. "After you."

I grab my phone off the counter, half expecting him to tell me to put it back, but he doesn't seem to notice. He takes my arm right above the elbow, the same as any other time I've been escorted in this building, but gives it a brief squeeze as we start walking. His arm is rigid next to me, and he's walking a bit faster than usual. Not a run, or even a jog. Just a brisk pace that requires me to double step in order to keep up with his longer stride.

We turn the corner and approach Room 81. It's quiet. No hint of a child crying. But as we move closer to the door, the *thumpthump* begins again. I stop and look back. *Thumpthumpthump.* Softer now, but definitely there, and the door—I can't fully describe it. It kind of shimmers, almost like that section of door is a picture that's being smudged outward so that it enters the space a few inches in front of it.

And then someone laughs.

Daniel tugs my arm. "Let's go."

"Did you hear that? *See* that?"

"No, Anna. *And neither did you.* Let's go."

I feel the slight sensation of pressure at my temples, and I instinctively whip my head around to look for Dacia. But the hallway is empty, except for the two of us and that door, which I did see do something freaky, no matter what Daniel says. And now that I think about it, this is not exactly the same as the buzzing that I felt with Dacia, more like the feeling when I was at the townhouse—

My mouth falls open. "It was *you* at the townhouse."

"Anna!" His voice is low but needle sharp. "We've got less than five minutes to get you out of this building. After that, the cameras will be working again. So unless you—"

"Deo," I hiss. "Where is he?"

"Someone is working on it! Will you just shut up and keep walking?"

I shut up and keep walking.

As we pass the room where I was tested by Bellamy, I hear a mechanical noise up ahead. It's coming from the hallway where I saw the elevator earlier. Daniel sucks air through his teeth and pivots us around to the closest door. He scans one of the panels with his access badge, but the light blips red.

Daniel mutters a curse below his breath and pulls me closer to him. *"Hang tight."* His voice is barely audible—I feel the words against my ear more than actually hear them. "I'll try again tomorrow."

"Get Deo out first," I hiss.

Daniel doesn't respond, simply whips us back in the other direction to face two men coming toward us. The first, moving at a rapid clip, is Lucas. The second is Graham Cregg, who lags behind, in no apparent rush. He's pale, with thinning hair, and his expression is relaxed.

Cregg seems small, but then I realize he's just dwarfed by Lucas's bulk. He's nearly as tall as Daniel. As he comes closer, the outside of my left hand begins to throb. I remember the weight of the garden shears in my right hand, fighting hard against the compulsion to pull the handles together. Wanting to throw them at Cregg, who's sitting cross-legged in the middle of the room, bare from the waist up—a grotesque parody of a yoga instructor, hands raised slightly above his thighs as he focuses all of his energy on me, on controlling me.

No. Not me. *Molly.* I'm shoving the new memory behind the wall, patching the bricks, raising the shields, when Lucas yanks my arm away from Daniel. His fingers dig into my flesh.

"Glad you finally showed up," Daniel says. "I was about to call for clarification since Room 1 is empty."

"Who the hell told you to bring her *here?*"

Daniel shrugs. "Someone from the Med Unit said the 2A in 94 needed to be escorted to Testing Room 1."

"*Lab* 1, dipshit." Lucas says. "And I didn't say for anyone to es . . . cort . . ." But then he frowns, rubbing his forehead. He looks confused, like he's thinking now that maybe he *did* tell Ashley to send me to Testing Room 1.

Daniel's eyes are still locked on Lucas. It's a neat little Jedi mind trick: *This isn't the patient you're looking for. Move along.*

Cregg steps forward, taking control of the situation. He doesn't even glance at me, just flashes his ID at Daniel.

"No need to get overworked, Lucas. There's no harm done. We're headed to the lab now, so we'll take it from here. You may return to your post."

Cregg's voice is smooth. It has a soothing quality, kind of like the auditory equivalent of a cough drop.

"Yes, sir." Daniel shoots me a fleeting look of apology, then heads down the corridor.

We turn the opposite way, back toward my room. Lucas's hand, which is already like a vise around my arm, squeezes tighter as we change course. I refuse to give him the satisfaction of crying out, but it catches Cregg's attention anyway.

"You're disgusting, Lucas." There's no emotion in Cregg's voice, just a straight-up statement of fact. "Let go of her arm. I overlooked your . . . liberties . . . with the others, but that doesn't mean I would do so with a girl who could be of"—*thumpthumpthump*—"actual value."

Room 81 is ahead on the left. The noise is louder than before. Cregg steps slightly to the right as we approach, moving away from the door that seems to bubble out into the hallway.

"So rein it in," he continues. "She'll follow without you manhandling her, as long as we have something she wants."

Lucas releases my arm. I rub the bruised area.

Ouch!

It's a child's voice, and it echoes in my head at the exact moment we pass.

BOOM . . . BOOM . . . BOOM . . . NO!

That last sound is almost a scream. Cregg does an odd stutter step, nearly tripping over the carpet, so I'm positive that he heard the voice, too. Lucas, on the other hand, is oblivious.

The racket—*thumpthumpthumpthumpthumpthumpthumpthumpthumpthump*—follows us down the hall, gradually fading as we pass the monitoring station. Timmons is there. Lucas breaks out of his sulk long enough to give him a wassup, then we keep going, passing my room on the right.

We eventually reach a door marked *AUTHORIZED PERSONNEL ONLY*. There's another sign below that reads *NOT AN EXIT*. Cregg pulls up a token of some sort on his phone and waves it in front of the security panel.

Ahead is an even darker hallway. It narrows and dips downward as we go, almost like a tunnel. Lights are farther apart than before and we cast long shadows as we walk. It's colder too, and there's no sound aside from our footsteps on the concrete floor.

Under normal circumstances, this place would probably feel creepy, but I seriously doubt anything worse than these two will spring out of the darkness.

About a hundred yards later, the hall widens and we begin the slight ascent to a well-lit area ahead. I hear a faint hum. Maybe a heating unit? It's definitely warmer here.

Another monitoring station, identical to the one at the testing rooms, sits unattended at the intersection of two hallways. Beyond it are two large rooms encased in cement block at the bottom and a clear material at the top. It distorts the view slightly, so I think it's plexiglass or something other than plain glass. The unit on the right is dark, except for a small overhead light at the back of the room. I see machinery of some sort in one corner and what appears to be a smaller, clear unit in the very back of the room.

The lights are on in the room on the left. But black curtains block most of my view, letting only a few narrow ribbons of light shine through.

We turn into the left corridor, which ends at a door a few yards down. Cregg waves his arm at the security panel and we enter a second hallway. The glass or plexiglass reaches from ceiling to floor on the right-hand side, but again, a black curtain hides whatever is in the room. I'm guessing they pull the curtain at some point, however, because two rows of chairs are lined up on the other side of the hallway, sort of like a home theater setup. Just beyond the chairs is another doorway, leading into what looks like an office break room, with a sofa and fridge.

I stay on alert for the popping sensation of Dacia's probe, and also for the humming sound that Molly remembers before Cregg took control of her body. Could I block him the way I did with Dacia? I don't know.

For now, I sense nothing out of the ordinary. Even so, every bit of intuition tells me to stay out of that room.

When Lucas opens the door, however, I immediately change my mind.

Deo's in there, sitting in the middle of the room with two other people—a girl about my age and a man. There may be someone else, but Lucas's shoulders are blocking my view. I recognize the man instantly. He's the older guy from the cafeteria, the one with the gray dreads who was writing mental graffiti on the table. The girl also looks vaguely familiar. She was probably at one of the other tables. It's hard to be certain because her head is tipped back, almost like she's napping.

I move to follow Lucas into the room, but Cregg puts his arm out to restrain me.

"Perhaps you should wait here with me. Lucas has something to attend to. It will only take a few moments . . . but you would probably find it unpleasant to watch."

I push away from him, but the door clicks shut before I can reach it.

"What are you doing? I said that I would cooperate and I will. Just—"

The sound is muted, making me even more certain that this wall is something other than glass. But there's no mistaking the fact that the booming noise was a gunshot. Followed by a second boom. And a third.

CHAPTER SIXTEEN

"No!" My knees give way and hit the concrete floor so hard that I bite my tongue.

Cregg's jaw tightens. "I was under the impression that Lucas's gun was equipped with a silencer, but apparently not. You've jumped to the wrong conclusion, Anna. Deo is fine."

It takes several seconds for the words to reach my brain. When they do, a flood of relief washes over me, followed immediately by white-hot rage at the way we're being manipulated. But I swallow the words I want to shout at him. Assuming Cregg isn't lying and Deo is actually okay, I can't afford to lose my temper.

If Cregg can tell I'm angry, he doesn't react. He simply steps forward and pushes a button on the security panel.

"Place a cover over the bodies before you open the door, Lucas. I'd like to avoid anything *else* that might undermine the testing."

I fight down a gag, either from the taste of blood in my mouth or Cregg's words or both. And I was out here. Deo was in there when Lucas began firing, right next to those people who are now just bodies. Probably thinking he was next.

Cregg reaches a hand down to pull me to my feet, but I ignore the offer and make my way to one of the chairs on my own. As much as I want to avoid angering him, I can't make myself touch him.

If he's offended by my refusal to accept his help, he doesn't show it.

"That's also why Daciana isn't here this evening, in case you're wondering. She would have been disruptive. Daciana was very angry that you managed to block her, and I need you to be able to focus on the task at hand rather than trying to keep her out. As useful as it would be to know for certain whether you're being truthful with me, I decided to rely on my own knowledge of human nature. Because even if I told her to behave, I'm not certain Daciana could resist diddling with your brain."

The phrasing is odd enough by itself. But in Cregg's soft-spoken voice and usually formal phrasing it sounds almost obscene.

He seems to be referring only to our encounter at the police station. Nothing about my chat with Dacia earlier this evening. Does he even *know* about that?

Lucas's voice comes over the speaker again. "What do you want me to cover them with?"

"You have an entire medical lab at your disposal, Lucas. I'm sure you can find something if you actually look." When Cregg turns back to me, he adds, "Have a seat. Unless there's something in there marked *Use This to Cover the Dead Bodies* in large red letters, this could take a while."

He pauses expectantly. I think he's expecting a laugh or at least a smile.

"*Why?*" I ask him. "The girl in there . . . she was just a child!"

"No, Anna." He looks insulted. "The young woman you saw in there was twenty years old. It may surprise you to know that she's been in our care for quite some time. We've prevented her from committing suicide on eleven different occasions. There is a school of thought that would argue Lucas just engaged in a mercy killing."

"Was Molly Porter's death a mercy killing, too?" I regret the words instantly. He must know I have Molly's memories, but I don't want to do anything to further endanger Deo. I'm sure Lucas has a few more bullets he'd be happy to fire.

Cregg smiles, a patronizing expression that goes nowhere near his eyes. "Of course not. Molly's death was unfortunate yet unavoidable. At the time, I believed Lucas's lax security was a single mistake, but I'm beginning to detect a pattern where he's concerned." He tosses a brief scowl in the direction of the door, then says, "As I suspect you're aware, *I* did not kill Molly. But, as with these three, I did approve it. I couldn't let the girl jeopardize national security and the lives of everyone in this operation."

The scary thing is, he seems to believe what he's saying. He's actually trying to justify cold-blooded murder. I'm tempted to ask how he excuses forcing someone to mutilate herself. Cregg may not have delivered the deathblow. He may not even have been the one holding the garden shears when they snipped off her pinky. But he was the driving force behind all of it.

And national security, my ass. That's what all of his kind claim when the bodies start piling up.

I sit silently until Lucas opens the door. As we enter the room, I avoid the three plastic-draped figures and focus on Deo. He's clearly shaken and far from his usual stylish self, dressed in mismatched sweats and looking like he hasn't seen a shower or a comb in days. I take a few steps into the room and then stop.

This is the first time I've been in a room with the newly dead. The "freshest" hitcher I ever picked up was Bruno, who'd only been dead a few months. A jogger found him in the park the morning after he died, staring up at the sky. The weather had been decent the night before and the sky was clear enough that he could pick out a few stars. Aliens were the last topic Bruno thought about—no surprise there. A lot of his thoughts were about aliens. But he wasn't thinking of the scary kind that night. Just the Grays. He fell asleep wondering if E.T. was a baby Zeta Reticulan and if so, did all of the Grays' fingers glow orange like his did?

The trio I'm trying not to look at are a different matter altogether. I can *feel* their presence in the room. If I let down my walls, I'm pretty sure I would suck them up like a vacuum.

Cregg seems to think I've stopped because I'm waiting for his approval. "Oh, by all means, Anna. Go speak with your friend. I assure you he has not been harmed in any way."

At a bare minimum, Deo has been abducted, forced to watch as three individuals were murdered, and probably led to believe he was next. All of those things fall well within my personal definition of *harm*, but I don't argue with Cregg, and he moves on to berate Lucas for failing to use a silencer.

I give the corpses a wide berth and crouch down next to Deo. My hug is an awkward gesture that includes the chair, since his arms are secured behind it with duct tape.

"Are you okay?"

The question is stupid, given all that has happened, but he nods. "Why's your mouth bleeding?"

Even though I usually don't give Deo the partial-truth treatment, I can't bring myself to add that it's because I thought he was dead. He's had to deal with enough without feeling guilty about that, too. "Bit my tongue."

He raises one skeptical now-barely-blue eyebrow. "Really?"

Maybe it's shock, but that strikes both of us as funny, and for a moment we half laugh, half cry as I hold him close.

Cregg is apparently done reprimanding Lucas. I feel his eyes on my back. Apparently Deo notices too, because he whispers, "I heard him say *Lucas*. Is the other guy Cregg?"

I nod.

"What do you think he wants with you?"

"He said it's a test."

I glance at the bodies, which I now realize are covered from the waist up with trash bags. Duct tape around their calves secures them to the chair legs. Blood drips onto the floor, flowing in rivulets that converge about a foot behind them, pooling up in a small, recessed drain in the floor like one we have in the kitchen area at the deli.

The apple juice I drank earlier rises into my throat, and I have to pull my eyes away before I lose it.

Cregg claps his hands once to get my attention. "Anna, you'll have more time to speak with Deo later, assuming all goes well. We need to get started."

"Deo, I promise. I *will* get you out of here." I give him one last hug before I go.

"You should have a fairly good idea what the test will entail," Cregg says as I approach, "given the setting. But—"

"I wish you would have talked to me before. Because it doesn't work that way. I can't just decide to pick up someone's . . . psychic remains. I don't have control over when it happens. Not everyone sticks around. And I don't pick them up *where* they died."

"Are you finished?" Cregg asks. His voice remains level, but his eyebrows move downward.

When I don't respond, he continues. "Clearly you *do* know why you're here. You aren't the first person I've encountered with this ability, Anna, so I probably have a better understanding of how it works than you do, since you have only your own limited experience as a guide. These three individuals experienced a traumatic death. Which is unfortunate but necessary, since in my experience, that means they have not yet entirely—in the words of the great bard—shuffled off this mortal coil. In order to pass this test, you will need to convince us that you have, as you put it, *picked up* at least two of them."

"You should have done one at a time. I don't . . . I don't think I can pick up more than one, especially when I'm still processing Molly."

It's only partly a lie. I've never had more than two hanging out at once, and since I've gotten better at keeping my shields up most of the time, I've been able to hold it to just one. There were even a few glorious months at a time where my head was all my own.

The problem is more that I can feel them hovering in the room. I can almost taste the panic, the confusion. I'm not sure I can handle even one in that state, and I'm not sure how I'll hold the others off.

"I hope you're wrong about that," Cregg says. "Because if you can't pick up at least two, then you will have failed an important facet of this test."

"And we'll know if you lie," Lucas says. "We know everything about those three." He looks like he's about to say more, but stops when he sees Cregg's expression. I don't think Lucas likes having to curb his tongue. His jaw is twitching like it did in my room when Ashley walked in.

I ignore Lucas's comment and focus on Cregg. "And if I pass you'll let us go?"

His mouth turns down in a look of exaggerated sympathy. "You know that can't happen." Cregg's voice stays smooth. It reminds me of the snake in that *Jungle Book* movie. It could almost lull you to sleep. "If you fail the test, Anna, you'll be in the same sad situation Molly found herself. You know too much about me and this facility for me to simply let you go, yet you won't be of any value to me. On the other hand, if you pass the test, you become a valuable commodity I can't afford to lose. Given the trouble we've gone through to get you here, I don't think any incentive would convince you to work with me if I allowed you to come and go at will. The reward for passing is that Deo will be allowed to come with us."

"No deal. If I pass your test, I'll stay, but you have to let him go." Deo is protesting, but I keep my eyes on Cregg. "As long as I can check in with him regularly and be certain he's okay, I'll do whatever you want. And he'll keep quiet about everything he's seen for the very same reason—you'll have me as a hostage."

Deo's shaking his head vehemently. "No way, Anna."

"Aww. Looks like lover boy wants to stay."

Since I really couldn't care less what Franco Lucas thinks, I don't bother to correct him, but Cregg makes an exasperated sound. "This is what I was talking about, Lucas. You are an incredibly poor student of human emotion. Have you never been in a relationship that didn't involve sex? If you'd observed Anna's face when she looked at the boy, you'd have seen that hers is not a romantic attachment. She feels . . . parental. Responsible for his well-being. And I'm sensing a great deal of guilt for putting him in danger in the first place."

It annoys me when Kelsey slips into this sort of psychobabble, but coming from Cregg it's almost laughable. I'm tempted to ask how many years he spent in analysis. Clearly not enough. I doubt he would appreciate the snark however, so I focus instead on clarifying the rules and regs of this ungodly test he's cooked up.

"How long?"

Cregg looks surprised.

"How *long* do I have to finish the test?"

"I hadn't really considered that," he says. "I guess the best way to put it is that this isn't exactly a *timed* test. Our schedule has a bit of . . . flexibility. But at some point, if there is no result, I think we might have to conclude that you're not really trying. And that would be . . . unfortunate."

His eyes move very deliberately toward Deo.

"So, that's the stick side of the equation. The carrot, per your request, is that we'll release him. If he cares as much about your well-being as you do about his, I think we can trust that he'll keep quiet about our little arrangement. So . . . are we agreed?"

I'm not sure I believe him. I have a feeling that Cregg's lying face is indistinguishable from his regular face. But it comes back to the same question I asked myself earlier: What choice do I have?

"Agreed."

"Then I shall leave you to it. I can never focus with people watching over my shoulder, and I doubt you can, either."

I try to keep my expression neutral, but it's hard, because suddenly I'm seeing Cregg again in the cabin. Half dressed, half lotus, eyes half closed as he struggles to make Molly dig a small knife into Dacia's upper arm.

"Should we take the boy with us?" Cregg asks.

"No. I'll be able to focus better with him here." That's completely true, because I won't be distracted wondering whether Cregg is practicing his skills on Deo. "In fact, could you untie his hands, please?"

Lucas snorts and says no instantly, but Cregg asks me why.

Deo beats me to it. "Because those three people just took bullets to the brain. If she manages to pick one of them up, it's not going to be pleasant. It might even be dangerous. She may need someone to pull her back, to remind her that she's Anna, that she's still alive."

Cregg considers this and nods. "I guess that's reasonable. Go ahead and release him, Lucas. The door will be locked and we'll be right outside. They're not going anywhere."

As Lucas frees Deo's hands and feet, Cregg nods toward a cabinet at the back of the room. "There's water in there should you need it. Hit the call button once you have a result. Or if you need food. Many of us have a high caloric burn rate when we're active. I've noticed that's especially true of the second-generation adepts like yourself."

"I'm fine."

The idea of eating anything in a room with three still-bleeding corpses nearly pushes me over the edge. I just want Cregg and Lucas to go.

And even though they leave the curtains drawn when they do go, I'm under no illusions. We've been monitored every second since we entered this place, and as soon as they get to the computers, they'll be monitoring us again.

I take advantage of the few seconds of possible privacy to hug Deo again. "Did they hurt you?"

"No. Threatened me, that's all. Said they'd made you an offer . . . if you'd come in, they'd let me go, but you refused. Which I knew was a lie. The worst part was Dacia. She grabbed my arm and asked me all kinds of bullshit questions. Stuff about Molly. Stuff about everyone in your spook menagerie. I knew what she was doing this time, with her head-buzz routine, but it didn't make it any easier to stop her." He shrugs, looking embarrassed. "I don't think we have any secrets left."

"Hey, I had a session with her, too. It's not your fault."

"Maybe. But it *is* my fault we're in this mess, so stop pretending it's not. You'd never have been at the U Street shelter if I hadn't called you. If I'd just gone back with Carla, you'd never have picked Molly up."

Carla is Deo's mother. Every few years, she decides to enter Deo's life again. That decision usually coincides with leaving her abusive husband, Deo's stepfather, whose approach to family relationships begins and ends with his fists. Her bravado usually lasts a few weeks, then Carla convinces herself that Patrick has really changed this time. That he'll be good to her and good to Deo, too. He just needs to scrub that eyeliner off his face and act like a real boy. Then maybe Patrick wouldn't get so angry at him and they could be a family again.

It's exactly like Molly's mom crawling back to Lucas each time. Minus the drugs—but there are different kinds of addictions.

Different types of blindness too, I guess. I've been so caught up in my own guilt that this stupid curse of mine picked up Molly. I never even noticed that Deo was feeling guilty about pulling *me* into this situation.

"I . . . think it might have happened anyway, D." The dramatic roll of his eyes suggests that he gives that idea a big fat zero on the old plausibility meter, but I can't really elaborate on why I think I'd have ended up on the Delphi radar at some point. Not here, not with Cregg listening. And we've got other issues to worry about aside from our collective guilt burden.

Looking back at Lucas's three victims, the first thing that strikes me is the garbage bags. I don't want to see their bodies, but I know Cregg is right about their spirits being here. I felt the change when we walked in. Whatever fragments of their consciousness that exist are hovering in this room. I remember Molly saying that she stuck with her body for a long time. And it just feels *wrong* for these people to see their remains being treated like garbage.

"Did you look at them?" I ask Deo. "I mean, did you see the bodies . . . afterward?"

"Yeah. My eyes . . . well, they were shut when he fired the third bullet, because I was pretty sure number four had my name on it. But then, when I realized he wasn't firing again, I looked."

"How bad is it?"

He gives me a WTF face. "They're *dead*, Anna."

"I know that. I just mean, is it . . . graphic? As much as I don't want to see them, the garbage bags . . . well, they feel disrespectful? And I may need some visual backup if they don't believe they're dead."

"I've seen worse," he says. "I mean, not in person, but . . ."

That doesn't exactly make me feel better. Deo has been known to watch some pretty gruesome stuff.

"Are we talking *CSI* or Tarantino?"

"In between. But a little closer to *CSI*."

"Let's do it, then." I step toward the body closest to me. I didn't see this person before he was shot, but the body is large enough that I'm pretty sure it's a man.

Deo grabs my arm. "No, just stay back. I got this. I've already seen it once, and . . . I don't want you close to all three of them at once. I'm going to . . ." He pulls in a shaky breath. "I'm going to move the chairs a bit farther apart before I uncover them. And you need to work on diverting power to shields, if you know what I mean."

I do. I take a few deep breaths, close my eyes, and focus all of my energy on my walls—both front and back—as I listen to the scraping of metal chair legs when he moves the bodies across the floor.

Then comes the rustle of plastic, and a few muttered curses from Deo.

"Okay," he says. "Just . . . you might want to stay in front. The back is a little . . ." He doesn't finish, but he doesn't need to. I get it.

It's not as bad as I'd feared. There's blood—a lot of it—but the shots are relatively clean, all three to the right temple. Mostly I feel sad. And furious that anyone would even consider the murder of three innocent people in order to test me. Both the girl and the third person at the end, the guy I didn't see when Lucas opened the door earlier, appear almost peaceful. The guy with the dreads, who is the oldest of the bunch by about a decade, is in the worst shape. I think he may have struggled.

I move toward the girl first, but Deo stops me.

"The guy at the end. Jaden Park. Or maybe Parks. He said for you to grab him first."

"*What?*" I ask, in a low voice, even though I'm pretty sure Cregg has equipment that could hear a pin drop in here.

Deo matches my whisper. "He *knew* what was about to happen. Everything. When we were here alone, before Lucas came back, he told us everything. Said Lucas would shoot the three of them, but not me."

The guy appears to be in his early twenties. Average height, slightly above-average weight. Mixed race, I think. Maybe Asian and African heritage. And from what Deo's just said, he also had a little something extra that you'd never guess from looking at him. You'd think the ability to see into the future would be a useful talent, certainly a much more useful talent than my own. Yet Cregg ordered him killed—ordered him killed almost certainly knowing that he would see it coming. But how would this guy know about me? Could he foresee what was coming even after his death?

"I didn't exactly believe him until I saw the gun," Deo said. "And I still thought Lucas was going to shoot me. The older guy—Jaden called him Will—he started freaking out as soon as they brought him in, but he never spoke, just kept trying to yank his arms free. I'm thinking maybe he was mute. The girl, though . . . I think he called her Roxana. It was so weird. She *smiled* when that Jaden guy told us. At first, I thought maybe she didn't believe him either, but looking back . . . yeah, she did. Then at the end, right before Lucas walked in, Jaden looked straight at me and said to tell Anna to pick him up *first*."

Okay, then, Jaden. I guess you're first.

I crouch next to him, placing one hand on his knee, and visualize pulling one small brick from my front wall.

The force of his psyche coming through that tiny space is so strong that it hits me physically. I think I'd have fallen backward if Deo hadn't been there to catch me. Picking Jaden Park up is easy. The tough part is getting that brick back into my wall. It's like closing the door against a windstorm, because there are others out there.

And not just the two whose bodies are next to us.

There are *dozens*.

CHAPTER SEVENTEEN

Jaden Park's thoughts fill my entire head. At first, they aren't coherent. Mostly confused, random sensations. But then they start to take on form.

Cold.

Head hurts.

Then he laughs. Not a full laugh, just a short ironic chuckle.

My head most definitely should hurt. So . . . I guess you're Anna?

Yes.

This is the first time I've been staring at someone's body while I heard their voice. The first time I've ever actually seen the body of someone I picked up, aside from those ghostlike glimpses I catch sometimes in the mirror. I'm not really sure what to say to him. Sorry you were shot? That somehow doesn't seem adequate when I'm pretty sure he realizes I'm the *reason* he was shot.

He picks up the stray thought.

Sorry works for me. But you didn't shoot us. From what Will told me, you and your friend could be next, so you don't need to be apologizin' to any of us.

So . . . he's not mute then? Will, the guy with the dreads?

No, he's mute . . . or was mute, I guess.

He seems sad to see the other man's body, so I look down at the floor again.

But he could write. And if it was only you and Will, and you kept your thoughts kinda quiet, he'd write what he was thinkin' too, not just stuff he pulled out of your head. Especially if he'd known you a while, like he had me. We'd been roommates for three years. He's learned to filter me out.

Deo's hand presses my shoulder. "You got something?" he asks, as he helps me to my feet.

"Not yet. I'm just a little . . . dizzy. Maybe if I sit down for a few minutes. Close my eyes and see if I can clear my mind, open up some space. Could you get me some water?"

"Sure." He walks with me to the chair he sat in earlier. "Be right back."

Deo probably knows I'm talking nonsense. But I need some time to see what Jaden knows before I let Cregg in on the fact that I've managed to download the first half of his test. If I sit there like a zombie while we're chatting, Cregg will probably put the pieces together.

I close my eyes and lean my head back.

> *How did you know this was going to happen? And why didn't you try to stop it?*

As soon as the thought forms, I realize how harsh it sounds.

> *Way to go, Anna. Blame the dead guy for letting himself get killed. That's . . . really not how I meant it.*

It's okay. Fair question.

And when Jaden answers, it's not like it was with Molly and the others, where things trickled in gradually. I didn't even realize Molly was murdered for the first week or so. All that came through was that she needed to find Pa. Eventually, all of my hitchers seemed to figure out what was going on, that I could help them get out of the perpetual loop they were in. But at the beginning, most of them were kind of clueless.

Jaden, on the other hand, knows exactly what I am and why he's here. His story doesn't come to me in dribs and drabs. More like it's under pressure, whooshing out like whipped cream from the can.

For as long as he can remember, Jaden has seen flashes from the future. When he was a kid growing up near Boston, they were short flashes of something that would happen within the next few hours or a day at the most. Kind of like déjà vu, but he'd remember things in full detail. Once he hit his teens, the flashes started to get longer and usually further into the future. Sometimes one a week. Sometimes one a month. It might have been an asset if he could schedule the flashes—who hasn't wondered what would be on a biology quiz?—but they were random.

You couldn't change anything?

Nope. Believe me, I tried.

Everything anyone said or did in those visions, that's what happened when the time rolled around. Including his own actions. He simply couldn't do anything *else*. Occasionally, he'd predict something that would make his parents kind of wonder if his claim wasn't true, but mostly he saw stuff like eating lunch in the school cafeteria, watching a video, or tae kwon do practice. When the flashes hit, he'd go into an almost catatonic state. His parents put him in a psychiatric center close enough for them to visit. And they probably think he ran off, because a few months later, he woke up in The Warren with all of the other Fivers and hasn't been able to contact anyone.

Fiver? That's from Watership Down, right? The rabbit who had visions?

Yeah. The name's a good fit—we live in tunnels underground and they don't let us out. Run tests on us like we're rabbits. And most of the rabbits down here get visions like Fiver did. Not sure who named it, but everybody's called the place The Warren as long as I've been here. Just not in front of the Fudds.

For a second, I think he said *fuzz*, and that it's some weird 1970s throwback name for the police. But then I get an image of Elmer Fudd, holding a taser instead of a shotgun, dressed in the khaki uniforms all of the employees wear.

Yep. And we're the wabbits.

Jaden kept getting flashes after he arrived at The Warren, but at least now he wasn't alone. Everyone else here had some kind of weird ability, so except for not being able to let his parents know he was alive, he was happier than he'd been in years. Until people started disappearing. "Transferred to another facility" was what the Fudds would say if you asked, but there are no secrets in this warren. It's like a small town—everyone knows everything, and not just the stuff you tell them or the stuff they observe. What you're thinking is fair game too, for wabbits like Will, and most of them aren't mute. So all it took was a few of the Fudds knowing what was happening or even having suspicions. The info zipped through The Warren faster than a forest fire.

Then two months back, Jaden got his final forward flash. Well, not exactly his *final* flash . . . because this one, unlike the others, kept repeating. He was in a room with Will, Oksana, and some kid he didn't know—Deo, as it turned out. Then Lucas comes in with a gun. He skips the kid, but shoots Will and Oksana. And the last thing Jaden sees each time is the gun pointing at him.

I got as far as him pointin' that gun at my face. After that, same damn vision every time. I've had maybe two hundred of these in my life. But never the same vision twice. I had this one nine times. And I knew . . . if the visions were repeating, then I don't go beyond that time. Couldn't change it, so I decided to make my peace with it and hopefully make it count for something.

But, if that's the last thing you saw, how did you know about me? You told Deo that I should pick you up first.

Girl, you been in The Warren—what? Two days now? Any secrets you had are long, long gone.

My thoughts rush to my second wall.

> Yeah. Will's circle said you had some stuff hidden. Not
> easy to hide anything from that crowd, so I'm impressed.
> They do know you got some allies on the outside, but
> they didn't get that from you. Came from one of the
> Fudds. And that blonde nurse, Ashley. She has a sister
> here—at least, I think it's a sister.

Deo puts a bottle of water into my hand, startling my eyes open when the cool plastic hits my skin.

"What took you so long?" I ask.

I can tell from his expression that I'm talking crazy talk. That look, along with a tiny, almost imperceptible headshake, reminds me that my chat with Jaden isn't exactly happening in real time.

"Sorry," I tell him. "Still a little disoriented. Give me a minute."

"Take your time. I'm not going anywhere." He grins and sits on the floor a few feet away. That's one of the things I love most about him. Even if hell is breaking loose all around us, Deo can still manage to smile.

My eyes briefly land on the door, and I remember that I can't take my time. That they could come in at any moment and wipe that grin off Deo's face, unless they think I'm putting forth a solid effort, and there's not much I could do to stop them.

> *You mentioned tae kwon do, Jaden. Were you any good?*

He seems a little surprised at the question.

> I didn't suck. So . . . when I'm . . . gone, do you keep my
> skills? My memories?

Your memories, yes. Things you know. Physical skills might take a little longer, if I haven't developed the right muscles.

What about the psychic skills? Because I'm pretty sure that's what this test is really about.

Of course it is. I feel like whacking myself upside the head for missing it. Why would Cregg go to these lengths to set up a test and require me to pick up not just one, but two dead people? Why, as Aaron wondered, would Cregg be interested in me when he already had someone who could read minds? When he himself could change them?

He wants a combo. Someone who can read minds, see the future, pull a Jedi mind trick, and who knows what else. The abilities you need, when you need them, all in one package.

I've never carried a hitcher who was psychic, so I have no idea if those skills transfer. But if they don't, I'm pretty sure Cregg will decide that I'm superfluous. Deo and I will be dead weight he should ditch. Like Molly. Like the three bodies in this room.

Why did you want me to pick you up first?

So I could tell you that you've gotta stop whatever's been going on in this room. Twelve people have disappeared. None of the little ones . . . They seem to give them a lot of latitude, even the ones who are all kinds of trouble. But for the past few months, anyone over eighteen who's . . . difficult to manage? They're gone. Mostly the immigrant girls, but a few of the military brats, too.

Military brats?

Maybe three-quarters of the people in The Warren have parents who were in the military at some point. Almost all Army, too. Some were actually in the military themselves, but I think Will's the last of that bunch. Anyway, Will and the others who can pick up thoughts from the guards say they keep thinkin' about movin' day. And lately, they've been thinkin' about it a lot. Only . . . we're split on what it actually means. Some think it really does mean movin' to a different facility. But others think somethin' else is going on. That movin' is a . . . what do you call it?

A euphemism?

Yeah. That they're plannin' to kill everybody and be done with it. Maybe not the ones who make them money, but most of us. And the three of us here in this room? I doubt they'd consider us worth transporting.

But . . . you said Will could read minds?

Bits and pieces. Mostly out of context. And Will . . . he had a temper. He's been in solitary more than once for hitting a Fudd.

What about the girl?

Oksana? I think she burned out. She's one of the immigrant girls who came in right after I arrived. The Peepers—sorry, that's what they call the ones who can get inside your head. They can't read Oksana at all. It's like she shut down part of her brain. Or maybe she could block them like you do. The only time Oksana showed any sign of life was once when she attacked that Lucas guy in the cafeteria.

What happened?

I wasn't there. Some say she threw a chair at him, but . . . others say she yelled at him. Something in Russian. And then the chair flew at him all by itself.

My *you-go-girl* thought must be pretty clear, because Jaden laughs, then sobers a bit when he picks up on exactly why I like the image of a chair connecting with Lucas's head.

Hey, you ain't the only one. He's not around too often, but I've known girls to stay holed up in their room when they get news he's prowlin' about the halls. None of 'em want to catch that *gaesaeki*'s eye. Bad enough that he might touch you, but that black-haired girl—

Dacia?

Don't know her name. Blue eyes. Pretty. Got a Michael Jackson thing going on with . . .

The glove. Yeah, that's her.

Well, she's a nutjob with a jealous streak. All the girls know that if you catch Lucas's eye, you end up on her list. She'll start picking your brain, and then odds are you get quote-unquote relocated. Although I don't think any of them have been relocated any further than this room, or maybe the one across the hall.

Dacia and Lucas? I wouldn't have connected them as a couple. And while I didn't think the ick factor could go any higher for either of them, this definitely ratchets it up a notch.

I glance up at Deo. "How long have I been . . . resting?"

"Two minutes. Maybe three."

"Okay." I finish the water. "Guess we should get back to it."

I can tell that Deo really, really wants to ask what's going on, what I've found out, but he just nods.

Faking it feels weird. I don't know what I look like when I pick up a hitcher. That part hasn't happened often enough for me to ask Deo to capture it on video, so I'm flying blind here. While I doubt my observers have seen it enough times to call me on the fake, I lean forward so my hair shields my face from prying eyes.

After about a minute, I stand up. "Got something. His name is Jaden Park. Can you hit the call button by the door?"

I'm guessing the call button is totally unnecessary. But I might as well follow all the steps in their stupid protocol.

Lucas comes in first. "Why'd you uncover the bodies? It was a pain in the ass gettin' them into those bags."

"They're not garbage. And they're very angry at you for treating their remains with such disrespect."

I haven't gotten a sense that they care one way or the other about the bags, and I suspect they're much more pissed off about things he did when they were still alive. Killing them is probably pretty high up on that list. But it gives me a sense of satisfaction to see Lucas glance nervously at the bodies.

Cregg is dabbing at his mouth with a napkin when he walks in, so I must have interrupted a midnight snack. There's a clipboard in his other hand, with a pen through the clip.

"That was quick, Anna! I'm impressed. But now we need to find out what you know. I'm going to ask you a series of questions and I'd like for Mr. Park to answer them."

"Sure."

"In what room do you live?"

"He's in Room 17," I answer, as soon as Jaden relays the information.

Cregg looks displeased. "No. I'd like Jaden to answer these questions."

I exchange a look with Deo, whose expression pretty much mirrors what I'm feeling.

"Okay," I tell Cregg. "But I need to sit down. And someone might want to find a garbage can and bring it over. I already feel a little like I might hurl and . . . letting him take control will make that worse."

It's an exaggeration, but only a slight one. When neither Cregg nor Lucas responds, Deo says, "I think there's one at the back. I'll get it."

Cregg tosses his napkin inside the can Deo brings back. The napkin is smeared with something red—spaghetti or pizza sauce, probably—but all I can think of is the blood still flowing into the drain behind us, and I nearly lose it.

Jaden's clearly picking up on my trepidation about letting him take over. He seems nice enough, but we just met. It's not like with Molly, where I had a chance to get to know her before handing over the steering wheel. I'm suddenly getting Myron flashbacks. I shove those thoughts back behind the damned wall, but not before Jaden gets a glimpse.

Hey, no! Not gonna claim this is the end I'd have picked, and I wasn't lookin' to make an early exit like Oksana was. But I ain't got no agenda, aside from hopin' you

find a way to bust the lid off what they're doin' here.
I'll back off when you say, soon as I've answered his
questions.

I think he's telling the truth.

Hopefully I can do that.

There's also an unspoken wish in the mix. He'd like for his parents
to know he didn't run away if I make it out.

I can do that, too.

I start moving toward the backseat, but he has a question.

So . . . when I leave? Do I just . . . disappear? Or is there
someplace . . . after?

*No clue. All I know is that most of my hitchers seem relieved.
Happy, almost.*

Except . . . that one guy, right? The one you just shoved
into a safe or somethin'.

*Except him, yeah. But he was crazy. And mean. Also . . . that
area is a secret. Don't tell Cregg, even if he—*

Won't tell him anything more than I have to.

Good. Then let's get this over with.

I slide back. The tummy-tossing sensation seems to hit a little harder than usual. My nails bite into my palms as Jaden imagines punching Cregg in the face. Then he glances at Lucas, who's leaning against the plexiglass wall, and thinks how much fun it would be to sink a side kick into his gut.

Bad idea, Jaden. You want to die twice in one night?

Chill. I'm not really gonna do it. Just thinkin' it would feel damn good.

I can't argue with that point.

He stares straight into Cregg's blue eyes. "You got questions for me, dude? Go ahead and ask, then. Ain't got all day."

Cregg's eyebrows go up slightly. "Am I speaking with Jaden Park, then?"

"You got him. Who the hell are you? I've seen you around, not as much as your attack dog over there, but no one ever seems to mention your name."

"I'm the person asking the questions. What psychiatric center were you in prior to being transferred to Delphi?"

It's the first time I've heard anyone here use the word *Delphi*. There haven't been any signs or logos on the paperwork. Nothing to identify the place in any way. It's nice to have it confirmed, but also seems ominous. Would he be tossing out information like that in front of Deo if he planned to actually honor our agreement? I don't think so.

"I was at Greenbriar Psychiatric in Waltham. But I don't think I was transferred. I was a minor, and my parents never signed any papers."

"Oh, you'd be surprised. Insurance covers so little these days. Most parents are more than happy to sign away rights to their crazy offspring simply to be rid of the responsibility."

"I notice you didn't say *my* parents. Just most. And I'm guessin' what that really means is a few. The rest of the time, you don't even bother with the formalities."

Cregg doesn't respond, simply moves on to the next question. "When was your last clairvoyant episode?"

"Little over a day ago. Usually running a day or so apart, unless somethin' has me really on edge, then they come more often. I logged it with Marnie as usual, but didn't mention the details. She stopped askin' for specifics about a month back, so I'm thinkin' you been plannin' this little tea party for a while now."

"What was the last thing you foresaw?"

"Same thing as the last few times. The Rock over there playin' executioner. Did he drug Oksana before bringin' her in? Sure looked like it."

"What happened after that?"

Jaden snorts. "My head exploded."

Cregg is silent for a moment. "After that, please."

"I wasn't in my body anymore. I could see my body, sort of. But I wasn't in it. It was cold. Kind of . . ." He's thinking *crowded* but decides not to share that. "Loud. Maybe the heating system. I don't know. I saw him bundlin' us up like garbage. Next thing I know, somebody pulls off the trash bag and this hand"—he lifts my hand and waggles my fingers at Cregg—"is touchin' my leg. And then I'm seein' my dead body through these eyes."

"Could you continue to control the body if you wanted?"

That gets Deo's attention, as well as mine, but Jaden says, "Don't know. Don't think so. Wouldn't want to test it, either way. Seems like that would be . . . bad karma. In fact, if that's all you want to know, I'm gonna clear out. Let the lady have her body back."

He doesn't wait for Cregg's permission. And the physical sensation of zooming back to the front, combined with the smell of blood that hits my nose as soon as I'm in control again, is the last straw for my stomach.

When I lean back from the trash can, Cregg is looking the other way, his nostrils pinched.

Sorry about that, Anna. Didn't know—

Not your fault.

Deo is holding a wet paper towel and another bottle of water. He nods toward the trash can. "Still need that?"

I shake my head. "I'm okay now."

"It's after three a.m.," Cregg says. "I have one other thing I'd like to know concerning Park, but I suspect it may take a while. Perhaps you should rest before attempting to acquire the next one. I'll have someone bring in two cots and some food."

There's a part of me that wants to tell him no. That I want to get this over with. But Daniel's comment that he would try again tomorrow echoes in my head. While I doubt he can do anything with us in here, I'm also pretty sure that Daniel is our only hope for getting Deo out of here alive. Anything that buys us more time is a plus.

"Thank you," I say. "I only got a few hours of sleep last night and this kind of thing is always exhausting."

I really want to ask for my pills. The odds of me getting much sleep without them are basically nil, no matter how tired I am. But I'm worried that Daniel may have left another note in my room, so I stay quiet.

Cregg nods toward the bodies. "I'm afraid you'll have our friends here as company. But you're used to hanging out with the dead, I guess."

"True." I glance at Lucas, then back at Cregg. "Sometimes, they're better company than the living."

❖ ❖ ❖

The guard named Timmons brings in two roll-away beds and a bag of food about twenty minutes later. He doesn't go near the bodies, but he doesn't seem surprised to see them, either. I'm guessing this isn't the first time he's seen Lucas's handiwork. Or maybe Lucas isn't the only one who's willing to get blood on his hands to please the boss.

We push the beds to the very back of the lab, as far from the bodies as possible. The area around the bodies feels . . . crowded, I guess, and the smell isn't exactly pleasant. Jaden seems more at peace when we move away, too. I don't blame him. Can't exactly be comforting staring at your own dead body.

This side of the room is almost blindingly white . . . the walls, the cots, the floor. The only splash of color is a fire extinguisher mounted on the wall, but that brings to mind the red of the blood on the white tile beneath the chairs.

I hunt for a switch to dim the lights. Once we have everything set up for the night, Deo tosses me a sandwich, a bag of chips, and a familiar-looking brown prescription bottle.

"Oh. Good."

He gives me a questioning look, probably because I sound less than enthusiastic. He knows as well as I do what kind of hell tonight would most likely be without the meds. But I can't explain why it worries me that they were in the bag. And maybe it's a different bottle of pills. Or maybe there were no new messages inside the fridge when Timmons or whichever Fudd they sent retrieved them. Maybe.

We eat in silence for a few minutes. I debate whether to take the pills, since I have no idea how long it will be before Cregg or Lucas pops in again. But I'm already exhausted. If I don't get sleep, I'll be worthless.

I go to the small fridge along the back wall and grab a bottle of water to wash down the pills, taking a moment to snoop. In addition to the water, there's a container of black cherry yogurt with the name *Megan* written in black marker on the side. It expired six months ago.

Near the back is a small white plastic case with maybe twenty smaller sections. About half contain tiny glass vials, like the ones nurses use for immunizations. Acting on instinct, I snatch one and slip it into my bra. It will be less conspicuous there than in my pocket.

The vial is icy against my skin. What made me grab it? It's probably a flu vaccine, or someone's insulin. I'd blame the theft on remnants of Bruno's kleptomania or Arlene's hypochondria—she was a world-class hoarder of pharmaceuticals and wasn't above "borrowing" a few pills from the medicine cabinets of friends and family without asking permission. But even Arlene would have shied away from something that required a needle. And there's a part of me that's hoping maybe whatever's in this vial is something more.

"That Jaden guy's still in there, right?"

"Yeah. Cregg said he's not done with him."

"I know. That seemed weird to me. I mean, it was pretty obvious he believed you'd picked up the guy's ghost. What's he going to do? Run those . . . what do they call them? Those brain scans?"

"EEGs? No—at least I'm pretty sure that's not it. He wants to see if I'll start having the kind of visions that Jaden did."

He curses and wads up his sandwich wrapper. "That's the last thing you need. You're still processing Molly, right?"

"Yeah, but I think I'm through the worst of it. A few more nights, maybe."

That's probably wishful thinking. I keep stopping before Molly dies, sometimes going back a bit, even as far as to what happened in the van. There's no need to worry Deo with that, however. Hopefully, the pills will do their job and I won't even wake him.

That starts me thinking about Aaron and the night at the beach house. I'm glad beyond belief to have Deo here and safe, at least for the moment. And I'm glad he'll be here tonight, in case I do wake up, to help talk me out of the dream and into reality. As comforting as Deo's presence may be, though, it's not the same sense of safety that I felt waking up with Aaron's arms around me. It was only a few minutes, but it was really nice while it lasted.

I push thoughts of Aaron aside and scoot my cot closer to Deo's. "I'll get you out of this, D. I promise. You'll be back—"

He rolls up his sleeve and I see a round Band-Aid on his bicep.

"What's that?" I have to ask, even though my stomach is sinking and I have no doubt at all what it is. Maybe that's what made me grab the vial from the fridge. Some inchoate sixth sense telling me that we might need a sample?

"They didn't give me an information pamphlet when they stuck the needle in. But I seriously doubt it was a tetanus shot. It's probably whatever they gave Dacia and the other girls."

I can tell from Deo's expression that he suspects this isn't a good thing. And that's without knowing everything that Aaron and I read about the Delphi Project. Without knowing the side effects that hit so many of the test subjects.

"But you heard Cregg. He said if I do what they ask, he'll let you go."

"*He's not going to let me go, Anna.* I don't know if they injected me so that they'd have more leverage over you, or if I'm part of a control group. But . . . when Cregg comes back in, tell him you've changed your mind. That you want me to stay here with you. Because no matter what he promises, the only other option is that I end up like those three."

He nods toward the bodies on the other side of the room.

It's the same thought that I had earlier. And as much as I don't want to admit it, I'm pretty sure he's right.

"No, D. I don't think—"

"Anna." Deo leans forward and looks me directly in the eye, keeping his voice low. "Stop, okay? I'm not a kid. Don't get me wrong. You've been there every time I've needed you. You're the *only* one who's ever really been there for me, and I love you. But I don't need you to lie to me."

"I'm sorry. I know you're not a kid, D. In some ways you never were, and I guess that's—" I shake my head. "That's what I wanted for you. I wanted you to know that someone else was taking care of the difficult stuff, so you'd have a *chance* to be a kid."

He rolls his eyes. "Oh, yeah. Right. You mean the same chance you had?"

"No, but that's the whole point. I wanted it for you *because* I never got that chance. I thought maybe if you had someone to watch out for you . . ."

I don't even bother to finish. He knows what I mean.

"Tell you what," he says as he stretches out on his cot. "We get out of this, we'll go be kids together. Save up our extra cash and go to Disney World. Ride in those teacup things. Take pictures with Mickey Mouse, Buzz Lightyear, Scooby-Doo. All of 'em."

He's trying to lighten the mood. Trying to take my mind off the fact that the little round bandage on his arm completely wiped my hopes of keeping him out of this insanity.

The distraction didn't work, but I don't guess there's any harm in letting him think it did. Maybe he'll sleep better if I play along.

I snort. "Riiight. Then we'll zip over to Hawaii for a week or two. And . . . you do know that Scooby-Doo isn't Disney, right?"

He reaches over and squeezes my hand. "Don't bother me with details, *amica*. I've got a vacation to plan. G'night."

Deo's asleep almost as soon as the words leave his mouth. I look at his profile and realize how much he's changed in the past couple of years. His feet hang off the edge of the cot. The ghost of a moustache runs across his upper lip.

Definitely not a kid. Hasn't been for a while. And present circumstances aside, does he really need me to watch out for him anymore?

That question and its implications fill me with a sense of loneliness that's almost ironic, here in this room with its multitude of inhabitants.

CHAPTER EIGHTEEN

I'm staring at a blue horse. The horse is wearing a pink hat, and a blanket hangs over its back. On the side of the blanket is the number 713.

The image is on a computer, with a clock that reads 12:41 near the top of the screen. When the time flips to 12:42, the image changes as well. Now I'm looking at a neon purple-and-yellow zebra, wearing a blue jacket with the number 282 printed on the side.

Deo says, "Do you think this is someone's job? I mean, does someone actually get paid to come up with these?"

"Probably. But shh for a minute . . . I'm trying to remember something."

I keep staring at the screen. Just before it flips to 12:43, I say, "Next one is a green dog. A dachshund. Orange sweater. Number is 83 . . . 7? I think."

A brief pause and the image shifts. The number is 831. And the sweater is closer to red, I guess.

"Whoa," Deo says. "That's . . ."

I turn toward Deo and—

I've been fading in and out of sleep for a while. I rub my eyes and lie still for a few minutes. Stupid, surreal dreams are better than the Molly dream, which I had three times tonight. The second time around, I woke up as Dacia brought the metal bar—which, upon closer inspection, I think may actually have been a metal bat—down on my forearm. Then I bounced back to Lucas and the van, so I don't get the sense this is going to be a linear progression.

Jaden stirs uneasily in my head. He's a quieter guest than most, definitely quieter than Molly was.

> Yeah, well, I've had people messin' in my head before. It's not fun. Will. That Maria girl who likes to make a damn game out of it.

The name is familiar and I'm about to ask him about her, but he's not done.

> And that woman with the black hair.

Dacia?

> Yeah. She checked my head out a few weeks back, wondering how much Will had shared with me. I think she put the last nail in my coffin, so to speak. But . . . anyway . . . I'm not sure that thing with the green wiener dog was a dream. It felt a little more like one of my visions. I don't know if that's good news to you or bad, but . . . thought I should let you know.

The crazy dream—or whatever it was—had almost faded away, but now I can visualize the dog again. Stubby legs. Orange sweater. A number on it. 831, I think. Or maybe 837.

When I roll onto my back, I feel the outline of my phone in my pocket. We're clearly on Delphi Standard Time here, and testing will resume whenever Graham Cregg decides. But I remember seeing a clock on the computer—12:41?—so I check to see what time it is now.

A little before noon. I turn the phone off again and stash it back in my pocket, then lie back and stare at the ceiling. My brain is still too groggy to sort through the implications of being host not only to Jaden but also to his visions.

"You sleep okay?"

I hadn't realized Deo was awake so the question startles me.

"Well, I *slept*. Some Molly dreams. Some just plain weird."

"What kind of weird?"

"Neon-colored zebras and green dachshunds weird." I decide not to mention Jaden's suspicion that it's more than a dream.

"Yep, that's weird even for you," he says as he digs around in the paper bag on the counter. He pulls out the rest of my sandwich from last night. "You gonna eat this?"

I tell him to go ahead, and as he's popping the last bite into his mouth, the door opens. It's Timmons again, which makes me wonder when the Fudds sleep.

Twelve hours on, twelve off. Four-day weeks. Three months of that, then a one-month furlough. Pay is good, especially for asshats like Timmons who are in the loop about what happens on this side of The Warren. And see, what did I tell you?

Timmons is holding a laptop computer that looks exactly like the one I saw in the dream. Or vision, I guess. He ignores us, and goes over to a table in the front left corner of the room, averting his eyes from the three bodies in the center. He may know what goes on in here, but apparently it still makes him a little squeamish. Might be a human being in there after all.

Nah. He's just got a weak stomach. Maria said he tossed his cookies when they brought the last bunch through here.

Maria?

Yeah. She's a real . . .

He can't seem to find the right word, and I get an image of a teenager, about Deo's age, maybe younger. I think she's one of the girls from the cafeteria.

A practical joker, I guess? Maria don't mean no harm. She's just got this neat toy in her head and nobody ever taught her right from wrong, I guess. Will and a few of the others tried to tell her to use some restraint, but she and that other girl she hangs out with, Pavla, they like to play games.

Yeah. I think I met her in the bathroom. A little message scribbled on the mirror when I got out of the shower yesterday.

Sounds like Maria. The writing is the other girl. But Maria is a world-class peeping Tomasina.

Deo nudges my arm. When I open my eyes, Timmons is in front of me. I can tell from his expression that I've been zoned out, and I can also tell that frightens him. More than a little disgust in the mix, as well.

"Get up. You've got work to do at the computer."

Is it the sneer on his face or his tone of voice? Maybe both. For whatever reason, I can't resist needling him. "Oh? Are we going to look at brightly colored animals with numbers on their sides?"

Timmons visibly startles at my words. I manage to hold back my laugh, but Deo doesn't. And that's all it takes for Timmons to whip out his taser.

The wires shoot out of the weapon before I can react, and Deo goes completely rigid. I yell at Timmons to stop. Either he does or the weapon has a set time, because Deo slumps forward. I catch him, but he's heavier than me. We both go down, but at least I manage to break his fall so that he doesn't crack his head on the cement tiles.

Timmons is already reloading and has the gun aimed at me this time. That's a good call on his part, because right now, I would gladly hand control over to Jaden and let him demonstrate his tae kwon do skills.

> Whoa. Hold up. I said I didn't suck. I didn't say I was Jackie Chan. I'm a blue belt. That's only halfway through the rainbow.

I have no idea what that means, but Timmons is in my face so I can't ask.

"Don't try anything, freak." He motions with the taser, but his hand is shaking. "I'll use it on you, too. Just leave him where he is and do as you're told."

I ignore Timmons and look down at Deo, whose breathing is starting to return to normal. "Are you okay, D?"

He nods but doesn't speak.

Timmons motions with the gun once more. *"Move it."*

"Go," Deo says, his voice small and weak. "I'm okay."

I must hesitate a moment too long, because Timmons yells in my ear, "You want me to hit him again?"

He's smarter than I gave him credit for. Threatening Deo gets me to my feet a lot faster than threatening to use the damn thing on me. It also buys my silence, although if any of the resident psychics are snooping right now, they've gotten a very graphic picture of what I'll do to Timmons if I ever get my hands on his taser.

Pretty sure they can't read anything in here. Will thinks they've shielded the rooms somehow. Did you notice that hum when you walked in the door?

No. But Cregg was talking. And I was kind of preoccupied once I saw Deo and . . . the three of you.

Timmons has a chair set up in front of the computer. He shoves me onto it with a lot more force than seems necessary, but I keep quiet.

The screen shows a teal-colored dolphin bouncing a red ball. The number 124 is on the ball and the clock at the top of the screen says 12:04.

"This computer will remain on until Mr. Lucas tells me the test is over. They didn't give me any instructions other than to turn it on, so don't ask."

"I don't need instructions. You can leave now."

Timmons's face is conflicted. I'm guessing he was told to leave since I'm pretty sure he wasn't standing there when the vision began. But he's not at all happy about being dismissed by the "freak."

"Was already planning on it," he says, but taps the taser one more time. "Don't get sassy with me."

"No, sir." I fight to keep my expression blank, which is probably a good thing, since he's scanning it to see if I'm being a smart-ass.

He straightens the laptop screen and pushes my chair even closer. Once he's satisfied that he can leave without losing credibility, he casts one last glare at Deo, and—still giving the bodies a wide berth—finally leaves.

"Are you sure you're okay?" I ask Deo, although I really have no idea what difference it will make if he answers yes or no, aside from making me feel better or worse.

"I'm fine." He gets up and walks over to where I'm sitting, as if to prove the point. "But all things considered, I'd rather not do that again. What are we watching?"

"*Sesame Street.* Brought to you today by the color blue and the number 124."

As I speak, the time changes to 12:05 and the picture flips from a red elephant holding a pink umbrella to an orange lizard on roller skates.

"Why do they want you to watch this?"

"Another test," I say absently, trying to remember exactly what I saw in the dream. At 12:41 it was a blue horse. Something similar at 12:42. A zebra, I think . . . but I'm drawing a blank on the colors. And looking at the screen as a new image flips in front of me isn't going to make it easier to remember.

I stare down at my shoes and whisper, "Talk to me. Tell me about . . . I don't know. Clothes you saw online you wish you could buy. That Disney dream vacation you were planning last night. I need to focus on something other than that screen for the next thirty minutes, so assume you have unlimited funds."

"Ohhh-kay."

Deo's more used to having people tell him to stop chattering than asking him for more. Not me so much as his teachers. He never even makes it to Disney World, because he spends a good five minutes on this one jacket he saw that he thinks he could replicate, which I suspect is actually more appealing to him than the possibility of buying it. Or maybe it's just that the idea of unlimited funds is too far out there to imagine.

I glance up at the screen occasionally, to keep an eye on the time. At 12:41, the blue horse appears.

"Okay. Blue horse, pink hat, 713." I still can't come up with anything more than zebra for the next one, so I don't say anything else.

As the clock flips to 12:42, a purple-and-yellow zebra in a blue coat appears. God, no wonder I couldn't remember the color.

"Do you think this is someone's job?" Deo asks. "I mean, does someone actually get paid to come up with these?"

Major déjà vu. I try to remember what I said next, but again, I can't.

"Probably," I say. "But shh for a minute . . . I'm trying to remember something."

Green . . . dog. Green Chihuahua?

> Nah. It's a wiener dog, ummm . . . whatchamacal-
> lem . . . . a . . . dachshund. Yeah.

I wait a few more seconds and then say, "Next one is a green dog. A dachshund. Orange sweater. Number is 83 . . . 7? I think."

When the image comes up, it is indeed a green dachshund. The sweater is reddish-orange and the number is 831.

"Whoa," Deo says. "That's . . ."

I turn toward Deo and nod. "Freaky. Yeah."

"So what's the next one?"

"I have no idea. That's when it ended. I thought it was a dream, at first. I just . . ." I look around the room, searching for recording devices, and say in a louder voice. "I just hope someone was *watching*. Because I have no idea if or when that will happen again."

There's no response. Deo and I just sit there, watching as the rainbow zoo parades in front of us.

"Do you think this is some sort of psychological torture?" he asks after a few minutes. "Like making us watch that singing purple dinosaur?"

I shudder. "You really shouldn't give them ideas."

At 2:27 (red-and-blue giraffe, pink scarf, number 584) Timmons enters. Now that we're closer to the doorway, I hear the hum that Jaden mentioned. It's faint but definitely electrical. It reminds me of the buzzing noise from the faulty ballast in the light fixture at the police station.

"Move back to the cots." He tosses Deo another paper bag. I get a whiff of tuna when he catches it. I think Deo does too, because his nose wrinkles. He's not a fan.

We do as we're told and Timmons goes over to the computer, keeping an eye on us and a hand on his taser. He stops the animal show and brings up the intranet.

"Boss says you can watch something 'til he gets back. Could be a while. But if you get any other sneak previews, you're to speak up, you hear?"

So . . . we watch Marvel movies. Deo has seen them all. He'd forgo clothes and possibly even food in order to be in the theater on the day of release. The last one I saw was the second Ant-Man, which means I'm three or four movies behind, but Deo is more than happy to see them a second—or in several cases, third—time.

Unfortunately, I'll need to watch them again at some point, because my mind keeps straying back to reality. I envy Deo's ability to lose himself in fantasy for a while. That type of break seems almost as useful as sleep for keeping stress at bay, and I've never really mastered it.

We're on movie number four when Lucas comes in. He snaps the computer shut, cutting off this villain named Thanos who's going on and on about some stone he wants.

"So . . . no more *visions*?" Lucas's tone is sarcastic. I'm not sure why. He's clearly had solid proof that all of this is real. But I guess it's part of his nature to act like a jerk.

"No. Just the one."

Lucas tucks the computer under his arm. "Move on to the second body then. Let me know when . . . if . . . you're done."

No explanation as to why we've been just sitting here for nearly eight hours. He simply heads for the door.

I wait until he's gone, then turn toward the bodies. I've avoided looking at that side of the room since last night, although they've definitely loomed large in the lab, like the proverbial eight-hundred-pound gorilla.

As I get closer, I see that the blood has now dried or congealed. Somehow, that makes it worse. The coppery tang hits my nose more strongly and I fight back a gag.

Which one, Jaden? You knew them both. Which one should I go for?

He hesitates a long time. That makes me pretty sure that what he really wants to say is *neither*. But he finally answers.

> It depends. Oksana won't stick around, but . . . I'm not really sure the full extent of her talent or even what it is. She might have picked up that chair the normal way when she hurled it at Lucas's head . . . I heard two different versions of that event. The only thing I know for certain is that she's not the most stable isotope in the lab . . . and here in The Warren, that's sayin' a lot. Something definitely rattled a few of Oksana's screws loose.

That's considerably less than comforting, and I step toward Will. But Jaden isn't finished.

> Thing is . . . Will was a little flaky, too. But the biggest downside there is he's got a huge chip on his shoulder about this whole Delphi thing. He might not be so eager to leave. Personally, I'd pick Will, because crazy kind of scares me, but . . . your head, your call.

Crazy kind of scares me, too.

"So, which one?" Deo asks.

"Jaden thinks he's our best bet." I can't bring myself to look at him directly, but I nod toward Will.

Crouching down, I place one hand on his knee. Yesterday, when I did this with Jaden, the body was still warm. Will's leg is cold and hard beneath my palm.

"Okay," I say. "Let's do this."

I visualize pulling one of the mental bricks from my wall very slowly, a fraction of an inch at a time.

Picking up Will is no more difficult than picking up Jaden was. But this time, the others are ready.

My walls come crashing down.

CHAPTER NINETEEN

When I open my eyes, I'm on one of the cots, with Deo standing over me. Worried. I think he's saying my name, asking me something, but I can't quite hear him. I start to ask him what happened, where we are, when it all comes rushing back.

Unfortunately, the memory of what happened isn't all that comes rushing in. My return to consciousness stirs the pot and the inside of my head goes from silence to the busy roar of Glenmont station at rush hour. A swarm of voices in different languages.

My name is Legion, for we are many.

One section of the curtains has been pulled back, exposing the hallway and the rows of chairs where Lucas now sits, talking on his cell phone. It's in one of those weird cases with the tiny antenna like Ashley had.

When I look at him, the roar in my brain becomes even more frenzied. But I don't think the anger is directed at me. I'm pretty sure it's aimed at Lucas.

One at a time. I need to take them one at a time and push them behind the back wall. I'll have to deal with them all eventually, and I don't think even the wall will shut out all of them entirely. But it will at least get the bedlam down to something manageable, something that might allow me to think without this whirl of distraction.

I close my eyes again and try to find some coherent thread to follow. Finally, I sort Jaden's voice out of the roar, answering the question before I can ask.

Will, Oksana, and two other women. Only four.

ONLY four?

I draw a few calming breaths as I try very, very hard not to freak out. Molly isn't even fully assimilated yet, and counting Jaden, I now have five additional voices in my head. At once. And I can't exactly call Kelsey to schedule an emergency appointment.

But in another sense, Jaden is right. I sensed way more than four others when the walls crumbled.

Yeah. Oksana and the other two were chosen as . . . representatives, I guess? The rest held back.

Why?

They were thinkin' too many voices might . . . be counterproductive. And they want to help, not make it harder.

Help . . . with what?

With getting you out of here.

Really? That's it?

> Well, umm . . . no, actually. They might also be plannin'
> a bit of payback.

I open my eyes and look back at Lucas, who's still on the phone, staring through the window at me as he talks. It only takes that brief glance to get a reaction out of my new hitchers, who seem pretty keen on sitting Lucas down in here and adding a fourth corpse to the room.

If I *have* to kill Lucas in order for me and Deo to escape, I won't shed any tears. Given what he did to my hitchers, what he did to Molly, and what he would have done to me if Ashley hadn't showed up, I seriously doubt I'd lose even a single karma point. I might actually gain a few.

What they're envisioning would be an execution, however—murder, plain and simple. If I could, by some miracle, force Lucas to sit down so that I could duct-tape him to a chair, I'd grab his security badge and focus on getting us the hell out of here. My new hitchers don't seem to care much whether I approve of their plans, however. That means we're going to need to have a little group chat.

But first, I need to get my head together enough to speak to Deo, to let him know that I'm okay. I can't hear him, but he's clearly saying my name. Tapping my cheek gently.

I try to put up another wall, to drown out the noise, to close the new hitchers off in some corner of my head. But it's no use. I'm too scattered, too *divided*, to function. My head feels like it's on the brink of exploding. As a group, they are stronger than I am, and that terrifies me.

QUIET!!

I don't have much confidence that mental bellowing will work, but it's all I can do. I'm not even sure how well some of them understand English, given the cacophony of different languages I'm hearing.

Jaden echoes my plea for quiet, and the furor dies down a bit.

Anna can't function if we're too close . . . to the front.
Everyone needs to pull back. Give her some room!

Two voices I don't recognize join him. One is male, which must be
Will. That kind of surprises me . . . I guess I'd expected him to be mute.
The female voice is halting, and I think she may not be accustomed
to thinking in English. Both echo what Jaden said. *Back off. Give her
room. Chill.*

Gradually, the crowded room that is my brain grows silent enough
that I gain control.

"I'm okay, D."

He lets out a sigh of relief. "You passed out."

"How long was I out?"

"I don't know. Ten minutes, maybe longer. Long enough for him to
notice and start making phone calls. And then your eyes were open, but
you weren't answering. It was like you could see me, but you couldn't—"

"How did I get back over here?"

"I carried you. Do me a favor and lay off the Doritos, okay?"

"Funny. Ha-ha. Maybe *you* need to hit the gym." I give him a play-
ful punch in the arm. "But really, thanks."

His face darkens. "Wasn't going to let that bastard touch you."

"Did I . . . say anything while I was coming to?"

"Not a word. Why? Did you manage to pick up that Will guy?"

"Uhhh, *yeah.*" I look up to where Lucas was sitting. He's no longer
there, but I still can't really say much more when they could have every
inch of this place wired. "This could be very interesting. He's . . . strong.
That could be a prob—"

*I'm outside and I'm running. Deo is a few feet in front of me. It's cold,
but he's not wearing a shirt. Only sweatpants.*

Usually, I can keep up with Deo. In fact, most of the time, he's the one running a little behind. But my ankle is throbbing, a slow dull ache that keeps me from putting my full weight on it.

We're in a clearing, with just a few scattered trees, running slightly downhill toward a more densely forested strip of land. Even though the sky is dark, I can make out the shape of a building off to the right and another one, at a distance, to the left. A muffled noise, like a car alarm, sounds several blocks away.

As we run, the alarm noise either stops or grows too faint to hear. I look back over my shoulder again at one of the buildings. The one we came from. The structure looks as though it's damaged, but it's not the ruined building from Taylor's drawing.

A light from above sweeps over the ground behind us. Once, twice. There's a rapid thwop-thwop *noise overhead, but it fades quickly. A plane. No, a helicopter. It sounds familiar, like one that Abner rode in during Vietnam.*

I turn to see if I can spot where it's going, and that's when I see someone behind us, closing in fast. A man. He wasn't there the last time I looked back. He's not big enough to be Lucas. Thinner. More like—

"Faster, Deo! I think it's Cregg!"

The man is shouting my name. We push into the trees, and the ground begins to drop off. The tree cover is dense, but I see a road ahead. A flash of lights from a car. Power lines above us. And in that split second that I'm looking upward at the utility lines, I trip over something. A rock, or maybe a tree root. My ankle howls in protest.

A hand grabs my arm as I start to fall. I open my mouth to tell Deo to keep running, certain that it's Cregg, but all that comes out is a scream.

And then I realize it's Daniel.

He says, "You're going—"

". . . wrong with her? She was awake a minute ago."

Deo's arm is around me and I'm leaning against his chest when Lucas's hand connects with my face. It's not a gentle tap like when Deo was trying to wake me up earlier. This is a full-bore slap, and it's all I can do to keep control away from the three Furies roaring inside my brain. My fingers clench into claws, ready to rake the eyes out of Lucas's head.

Most of their thoughts aren't in English, but the few that are make their intent pretty clear.

Stop his heart.

Throw him through the glass wall.

The ideas keep on coming, each a little more gruesome than the last.

STOP! I can't think!

". . . happens sometimes. Most of the time, actually. Her brain had trouble . . . allocating space . . . for the new guy. She had to . . . shut down for a while."

I doubt Lucas can tell that Deo is lying. He also might not realize that Deo's having a very hard time controlling his own temper, something that's clear to me not only from the sound of Deo's voice, but also from the way his arm is shaking.

"And you hitting her sure as hell isn't helping, so just—"

"I'm okay." I open my eyes before Deo can finish his sentence. Lucas might do more than tase him.

When I speak, Lucas takes a step back. There's a touch of fear in his eyes that I haven't seen before.

I *like* it. And so do my resident Furies.

His hand slides inside the jacket he's wearing as he moves away, making me think that Lucas might have a little sixth sense of his own. He doesn't actually draw the gun. But he keeps his hand there, at the same spot where Aaron wore the holster he showed me that night at the townhouse.

"Did you pick him up? The deaf-and-dumb guy?"

"Will? Yeah. Not deaf. Just mute."

Lucas gives me a *who-cares* look. "So . . . you know what I'm thinkin' now?"

"You're thinking you'd like to shoot both of us and be done with it. But I didn't need Will's gift to figure that out."

Deo's arm is still around me, and it's hard to catch a breath. "It's okay, D. You can relax."

"I *am* relaxed." His arm loosens, but he doesn't step away from me. And given that he's watched me keel over twice in the past half hour, that's probably not a bad idea.

Then I get a flash. It's visual, like a written note:

DON'T LIKE THIS.

THEY NEED TO HURRY.

I'm confused momentarily, until I realize Will must be feeding me Lucas's thoughts, the way he jotted down thoughts he swiped from people in the cafeteria. It's nothing I couldn't have guessed—Lucas glanced toward the door a few seconds ago. I suspect most of Lucas's thoughts are pretty obvious. He's about as deep as a puddle in the middle of a drought. But I can definitely see where this ability could come in handy.

Wait. Will said THEY. Cregg and Timmons? Cregg and Dacia? Someone else?

There's a pause, and the answer comes from Jaden, not Will.

Not sure. He sees it as words not . . . full thoughts.

That's okay. Just . . . let me know if you get anything else from—

I stop midthought, startled by a loud sneeze. It's Lucas. A second sneeze, even stronger, follows, then a third. Both hands instinctively fly to his face.

The very instant they do, I discover that I'm no more in control of the three Furies in my head than Lucas is of his body right now.

Deo steps away from me, back toward the wall.

Lucas stumbles forward as two more gargantuan sneezes hit him.

It still feels like I'm at the front, like I'm in control mentally, but I'm physically unable to pull my eyes away from Lucas. And I hear laughter, even though I don't think I'm actually laughing. It's just echoing in my head.

Either way, it scares me. Because whatever is going on with Lucas right now, they're doing it. *I'm* doing it.

Lucas's hand gropes for his holster, but before he can grab the gun another sneeze hits, this one so violent that it drives him to his knees. A thin line of blood runs from one nostril.

I hear the plink of metal against metal behind me, then a thick spray of white dust hits Lucas square in the face. He keeps sneezing. I can't tell if the Furies are doing it or if it's from the fire extinguisher. My guess would be the Furies, because I still can't move, still can't look away from his face.

"Get his badge!" Deo screams. He pushes me forward as the spray begins to sputter out.

A burst of anger surges through me, directed not at Lucas, but at Deo for pushing me. I turn back and snatch the red canister from his hands.

"Ne chipayte mene!" The words fly out of my mouth before I can mentally translate. *Don't touch me.*

Deo raises his arms and steps back. "Anna?"

My hands are brandishing the canister like a weapon. The other voices are talking now, and whoever the hell has control of my hands is distracted just long enough for me to shove her backward and spin around to face Lucas.

Who is still coughing, still trying to catch his breath, and very clearly reaching for his gun.

I swing the metal canister with every bit of force I can muster straight toward Lucas's temple. His head snaps to one side. Before he can slump to the floor, I swing back, in the opposite direction. This time, the bottom of the canister connects directly with his forehead and the skin splits.

Deo rushes toward Lucas and kicks him over. One of the security bracelets is in his back pocket.

I stand there, frozen, with the canister lifted over my head, remembering how frightened I was back in my room. Imagining how it would feel to bash Lucas again. And again. The scariest thing is that I'm pretty sure this time, it's all me.

"Anna?" Deo's voice is hesitant. He looks at me, a question in his eyes. "Are you okay? Because we need to *go*."

I toss the canister onto a cot and follow Deo to the door. He waves the bracelet at the panel, but the door opens before Deo's hand even touches the knob.

Cregg stares past me to where Lucas lies on the floor. A look of disgust passes over his face as he reaches inside his jacket. He drops the cell phone he was holding into his breast pocket, then reaches toward what I'm positive is a holster.

Damn it! Why didn't you grab Lucas's gun?

It's not one of the hitchers this time. Just me, yelling at me. And yes, I was distracted by way too many voices in my head, but it didn't even occur to me to grab the gun. I totally suck at this.

When I look at Deo however, I discover that he does *not* suck at this. He's holding Lucas's badge in one hand and Lucas's gun in the other.

"Hands where I can see them!" Definitely not a kid anymore, although his voice does crack the tiniest bit when he yells, "Drop your ID onto the floor and kick it toward Anna."

Cregg does as he's told. "The lab is being monitored. There are dozens of employees in this building. You've got about thirty seconds before—"

"Shut up!" Deo says.

I scoop up the bracelet. "He's got a gun, D."

"I know. Down on the floor," Deo tells Cregg. "Slowly."

As Cregg drops to his knees, Jaden speaks up.

He's lying about the monitors. Yes, there are dozens of employees in The Warren, but only ten who work the Highside, the side where you were staying. That's where they place the newbies and the . . . problem children. And only six of the workers know what goes on in this lab. Those six include Lucas and Dacia. All of the others believe we were transferred, except for—

Daniel and Ashley. Yeah, I know.

Deo waves the gun at Cregg. "Now lie on your stomach and put your hands behind your head. If you move at all, I *will* shoot you. Anna, take his gun."

Cregg complies with Deo's order, taking a deep breath as he stretches out on the tile. Once he's down, I put a foot on the small of his back and tug at Cregg's jacket to expose the gun. I take it, but as I stand back up, I catch a glimpse of his face, eyes closed, his expression almost serene.

Déjà vu hits me, but it's not one of Jaden's flashes. It's a Molly memory of Cregg sitting in the cabin, legs crossed, as she snipped off her own finger.

"Deo, watch out!"

When I look up, Deo has the muzzle of the gun flush against his right temple. His hand is shaking, and his mouth simply opens and closes for a few seconds, like he can't get any sound out. Then he croaks, "Move away. Or I'll do it. I really will."

The words may be coming from Deo's mouth, but I have no doubt that they are Cregg's. I do as he says.

"Now, slide the gun toward me."

I don't even consider taking the command literally and sliding the gun toward Deo. I know exactly what he means.

Cregg lies there, hands behind his head, not moving. His eyes are mostly closed, just tiny slits, so I don't know if he can see me. If I pointed the gun and pulled the trigger, would it buy Deo enough time to move the gun from his head? Or would there be an instant chain reaction? *Boom-boom.* Two guns, two bullets, two bodies.

There's a very good chance of the latter, I think. And I won't risk it.

I bend down to slide the gun across the floor, but a rumble of protest is building inside me. This time it's not only the Furies. Will's voice is in the mix as well.

SHOOT THE SON OF A BITCH. YOU'LL SAVE WAY MORE THAN ONE LIFE.

Will is moving forward now, trying to take control. I shove the gun toward Cregg so hard that it bounces into his shoulder. For a moment, I'm terrified that I've startled him, that the gun Deo has pressed against his head will go off.

STUPID MOVE. HE'LL MAKE THE KID PULL THE TRIGGER ANYWAY. YOU WATCH.

The sick feeling in my stomach says that Will is probably right. Cregg told Lucas not to harm me because I could be of value. I think that probably still holds true. I've passed his tests after all. But Deo? It's a pretty safe bet that Cregg considers him completely and totally expendable.

Will isn't the only one who's angry. I don't recognize many of the words the Furies are using, although *idiot* seems to be the same in several languages. And even though I'm still at the front, my eyes are now locked on Cregg the same way they were locked on Lucas a few minutes ago.

Not on his head. On his chest.

The popping sound of the explosion is almost drowned out by Cregg's scream, a high-pitched shriek. His suit jacket catches fire almost instantly. As he rolls onto his back to escape the flame, a gun goes off.

My head whips around to Deo, who's still standing, his face pale. He's holding the gun, but it's pointed toward the glass wall now. Definitely not regular glass, because it didn't shatter at all, despite the brand-new hole about five feet from the floor.

Deo's shock breaks suddenly. He lets out an anguished noise, then points his gun at Cregg, who's on his back, still screaming. Deo fires, then turns and fires at Lucas, who is still right where we left him.

I don't know if Deo hits either target. Cregg is writhing on the floor, his shirt in flames. He makes a whimpering, almost mewling sound as he claws at the black cell phone case adhered to his chest. His pants are on fire too, but I guess the *roll* part of *stop, drop, and roll* is hard to implement when you've got a flaming cell phone stuck to your chest.

"Let's go!" I yell, over the protest of most of my hitchers. I'm pretty sure Jaden will back me, but the rest of them want me to snatch the gun from Deo and finish both Cregg and Lucas. But that wouldn't be self-defense, and it wouldn't be defending someone else. It would be murder. Probably *justifiable* murder, but regardless, I don't want that on my conscience. I don't want it on Deo's conscience, either.

We need to run. Most importantly, *I* need to run. If I'm moving, it will be easier to stay in control, to keep my head to myself.

I take off through the open lab door. Deo seems torn, but he follows, slamming the door behind him. I wave Cregg's ID at the access panel in the corridor, and the door opens to reveal the empty monitoring station across the hall.

Dacia Badea stands a few steps in front of us, a shocked expression on her face. When Deo raises the gun, she doesn't even seem to notice. Her focus is on the window, through which she can see Lucas, collapsed on the floor. She shoves me aside with her elbow and swipes her arm at the entrance to the lab.

SHOOT HER!

The Furies are screaming too, and it's all I can do to maintain control. I reach out and grab the back of her shirt as she opens the door.

"Give me your ID or Deo will shoot."

From the expression in Dacia's eyes, I think this is the first time that Deo's gun even registers. She calls me something I can't translate, strips the security bracelet from her wrist, and hurls it toward my face as she yanks out of my grasp. Cregg calls out to her, but she doesn't spare him a glance in her rush to get to Lucas.

Before I can close the door, my hands freeze. I feel a whoosh as Oksana and the other two women leave. There's the briefest hesitation, then Will follows.

It's different from all of the other times that hitchers left. Not like they're moving on, but more like they're simply moving the hell *out*. Like they'd rather stay here than stay with me.

And I'm perfectly okay with that.

"What's wrong?" Deo asks.

"Nothing." I slam the door and lean against it for a second to get my bearings. "Let's go."

Even though we run at full speed, the dark, cold corridor seems longer heading back than it did when I was walking this way with Cregg and Lucas last night. Maybe it's because every muscle is tense, waiting for an alarm to go off, or for us to encounter one of the guards. We have all three bracelets, so I doubt Cregg and the others can get out on their own, but that won't stop them from sounding an alarm. For that matter, if someone didn't find a way to put Cregg out, his flaming body might trigger a fire alarm all by itself.

The tunnel starts to tilt upward now, and the lights are getting brighter. I reach the door before Deo does and wave Cregg's bracelet again, and then we're in the hallway, just a few doors down from my room.

As we pass, I hear a door open behind us. It's Ashley.

"Oh, thank God! How did you . . . ?" A quick shake of her head as she pulls her phone out. "Never mind. I have to tell Daniel and the others to abort." She looks down at Cregg's ID in my hand. "That should work on the elevators. Do you know where they are?"

Daniel and the others? But there's no time to ask. "Yes, I do."

"Then go. Get out of here!"

I'm terrified that Timmons will be in his cubicle when we reach the monitoring station. But it's as empty as the rest of the Highside.

Well, except for Room 81. The noise starts when we're a few yards from the door.

thumpthumpthumpthumpthumpthump

RUN RUN RUN, ANNA

I hurry past, but then stop and look back at the door. Deo halts too when he realizes I'm not next to him.

"What?"

"You don't hear that?"

"Hear what?

"It's a little kid, Deo. A little boy, I think. And Jaden says—"

Whoa! Hold up. No, no, no, no! Absolutely not.

But you said they might not actually be moving the other patients. That they might—

No. They won't hurt the little ones. And, Anna, you cannot handle that kid. You cannot hide that kid. Believe me.

He could be right. I remember Cregg's face when he spoke about the kids here. His righteous indignation, like they were doing a service for these children.

The door starts doing that weird thing again, almost like it's pulsing into the hallway. Almost like a heartbeat.

"A kid?" Deo says. "Are you sure? I don't hear—"

"You don't *see* that? The door?"

"No. Anna, we need to get the hell out of here."

Jaden echoes the sentiment, but it's not his urging or Deo's that gets my feet back into gear.

RUNNNNNNN, ANNA! HURRY. BWEE-OM, BWEE-OM. GOGOGOGOGO.

The door throbs in time with each syllable.

Jaden is right. How do you hide a kid who can do *that*?

So I run.

All of the rooms are dark, and the monitoring station is empty as we turn into the hallway between the testing center and the cafeteria. I grab Deo's arm and pull him into the corridor with the elevators.

"Up, right?"

I nod, really hoping Jaden's comments about this being a rabbit warren are correct and we're not headed for an even higher floor in some windowless building. The elevator door slides open instantly. We hit the up button again and the car begins to ascend.

Deo leans against the side of the elevator, catching his breath. "Whew. I thought someone would have sounded the alarm by . . ." He falls silent as we both hear the alarm blaring below us. "Guess I jinxed it."

All I can think is that the alarm sounds exactly like the noise—*bwee-om, bwee-om*—that the kid in Room 81 was making.

The light in the elevator goes out a few seconds later. I stifle a scream, expecting us to halt or drop suddenly. But we keep going up.

When the door opens, I look out into a room that's as dark as the elevator. I can just barely make out a door directly in front of us with another security panel.

I step out into the hallway. Deo doesn't follow immediately. He's standing in the elevator doorway, stripping off his sweatshirt.

"What are you doing? It's freezing in here."

He wads the shirt into a ball and shoves it into the gap so that the elevator can't close. "Maybe this will slow them down a little."

"When did you get so smart?"

"Born this way. You're just getting more observant in your old age." He tugs my arm and we go through the door.

"You got that flashlight thing on your phone?" Deo whispers.

"Yeah." I pull it out of my pocket. As my eyes adjust, I detect a very faint hint of moonlight off to the right.

"Does that way look brighter to you?"

"A little," he says. "Come on."

I turn on the flashlight app and we head toward the light.

But the moonlight isn't coming in through windows or doors. Well, that's not entirely true. Some light is shining in through the windows, which are big gaping holes in the wall across from us. Most, though, is coming from the utter lack of a roof on this side of the building. Moonlight pours down, illuminating a large room filled with piles of debris.

Deo curses as he surveys the room. "Looks like the place was bombed."

"No. More like a fire that started on an upper floor." I nod toward the back where the plaster has burned away, exposing the brick behind it.

A lot of the junk seems to have come from the collapsed level above us, but there's an empty bottle of peach schnapps and some cigarette butts that suggest teenagers may have been exploring. The room smells slightly of mold and smoke, but overall, the air is fresh. Trees, a hint of water, like maybe it's rained recently. It's a nice change after two days of breathing recycled air.

There's a noise in front of us, like something shifting in the pile of junk. Deo whips Lucas's gun up and points it toward the sound. Until now, I hadn't even realized that he was still carrying it.

After a few seconds, he lowers the pistol. "Probably just an animal."

I tap the phone to launch the flashlight again, then shine it in front of us. Nothing moves, and if there are any eyes staring back at us, they're well hidden by the rubble.

Shining the light around, I search for a path through the junk. I can't get closer to the windows, but from here, I'd guess that the ground drops off sharply on this side of the building. It looks like we're fairly high up. There's a road or maybe a bridge off in the distance, and every few seconds another car drives by.

I don't see any way out except for the way we came in.

As I turn in that direction, a light shines back at us. Deo and I both gasp, though my gasp is very nearly a scream. It's only a dim reflection, though, and as we get closer, I realize my light's bouncing off a blackboard.

Turn back!

BEWARE

Right beneath the chalkboard, there's another empty bottle, along with an open square foil wrapper.

"Hmph," Deo says, shaking his head. "Looks like someone had a little ghost-hunting party in here. Because nothing gets your sexy on like a crumbling building."

We turn back into the hallway and work our way past the still-open elevator, me holding out the phone flashlight, and Deo holding out the gun. The alarm grows louder as we approach. At the other end of the hallway, looking left and right, we again have pitch-black in one direction competing with a faint glow in the other.

"Could be another caved-in roof . . . ," Deo says, but we head that way regardless. It's still the more logical alternative to going farther into the building, and the continued blaring of the alarm tells me we don't have much time.

Once again, we end up in a section that's too cluttered to navigate. Here, the ceiling hasn't collapsed entirely. You can still see a partial floor above, and some sections of roof above that. But the place must have been abandoned years ago. A branch from one of the tall trees outside has grown into the room. It looks like a skeletal arm, reaching toward what's left of the wall.

The idea of going back toward the elevator yet again, with the alarm still sounding, sets off a panicked flutter in my chest. But then I see Deo, his bare back in front of me in the moonlight. That triggers a memory. Trees, sky . . . running.

I'd completely forgotten about the vision.

"It's okay," I say, as much to myself as to Deo. "We're going to get out of here. I saw it in one of Jaden's flashes."

There's something else at the very edge of my memory that seems a little less encouraging, but I can't grasp it. And we don't have all day for me to stand here trying.

We go back toward the darker end of the second hallway. It opens into a foyer, and if not for the flashlight, I think there's a good chance we'd have missed the staircase.

"Well, that explains a lot. We're on the second floor." I shine the light at our feet, and we hurry down the curved stairway toward the door below. The stairs are covered with chunks of rock and other hazards. There's a metal railing, but it seems to be rusted out in a few spots and I'm not sure I trust it. These stairs would be perilous enough in daylight, moving at a normal pace.

"What kind of idiot builds an elevator that only opens on the *second* floor of the building?" Deo grumbles, when we pause about midway to navigate around a large pile of debris.

"I don't know. Maybe someone once had an office up there? And maybe not everyone who worked in the building knew there was a facility belowground?"

"Wonder how long ago it was torched?"

"No clue. But I think I can make a pretty good guess as to how it happened, after the fire we just saw in the lab."

"Um . . . Anna? *I* saw what happened in the lab. You, on the other hand, weren't simply watching. You were doing it. How the hell . . ."

"Didn't only pick up Will. Oksana. Two other women, as well. Wouldn't be at all surprised to learn that one of them did all of this when she was alive."

He kicks one of the larger rocks out of our path and turns back to me, clearly worried. "And you think you can control her? Or them? Because you didn't really look like you were in control."

"I couldn't back there. But I don't have to. They stayed behind in the lab. So did Will. It's just Jaden now."

Deo lets out an audible sigh of relief, followed by a bitter chuckle. "You were trying to control five people in your head. I couldn't even handle one."

"It's not the same thing, D. Not the same thing at all. My invaders were actually on our side. Cregg on the other hand—"

"Whatever. Let's just get out of here."

The windows on the lower level are barricaded. Only tiny ribbons of light shine through. When we reach the main level, I work my way to the door and twist the knob. The door opens a fraction of an inch, then stops. No security panels here, just plain, old-fashioned boards and nails.

Deo backs up a few steps and rams it with his shoulder. The door creaks, but that's about it.

He takes another try, with pretty much the same result.

Then I hear Jaden.

I got this. Probably. I mean . . . I'm used to a bigger body, but the principle's the same.

I'm reluctant to give Jaden control. He didn't seem nearly as angry about my refusal to shoot as the others were, but I'm pretty sure Jaden also wanted me to pull that trigger.

Yeah. I think I'd have killed them, but, hey . . . you know what you can live with and what you can't. And even if that wasn't the case, I ain't stupid enough to go back up there.

Okay, then. But hurry.

I grab Deo's bare arm as he's backing up to charge the door again. "Hold up, D. Let me take a stab at it."

He raises an eyebrow, and gives me a look that I'd definitely find insulting if I had time to stop and think about it. But he steps aside.

Jaden takes a deep breath once he's in control and moves me forward a few steps. I feel my knee lifting up, high enough that it should throw me off balance. But it doesn't. He twists slightly and thrusts my foot toward the door.

I hear nails popping, but the door remains in place.

We back away, and he kicks once more. Harder. This time, the door swings open, but I also feel a sharp twinge in my ankle . . . the same one I twisted jumping out of Aaron's car.

But we're out. That's all that matters. And Jaden slides back gradually this time, rather than the quick exit that left me bent over a trash can.

Deo's expression is a little less dubious now. "Whoa. Short Stuff got some new moves."

"Yeah. New moves, but same body, unfortunately."

"You okay?"

I nod and test my weight on the ankle as we move outside. It's tender, but not too bad. I'll be able to run, although I doubt I'll make top speed.

Illegible graffiti is scrawled on the four columns in front of us. The fire that blazed through the building couldn't take out the sections made of stone. Like the columns, the steps are still standing, although some sections seem to have been chipped away.

"Which way?" Deo asks.

I scan the area, trying to find something that seems familiar from the vision. Off to the right, I see water in the distance. To the left is the clearing, with buildings on both sides and a line of trees beyond.

"That way."

As we run, I discover why these visions landed Jaden in a psychiatric center. It's like being trapped in a dream.

I hear the noise of the helicopter—I'd forgotten that part entirely. But some part of my brain still goes through the motions of thinking it's an airplane before recognizing the sound of the rotor.

When I turn back and see the man running toward me, part of my mind knows it's not Cregg.

I know it's Daniel.

But the section of my brain that controls my mouth doesn't seem to have gotten the memo. "Faster, Deo! I think it's Cregg."

I hear the man yelling my name, and that other part of my brain, the part that isn't in control, recognizes Daniel's voice. But that doesn't stop me from running in a blind panic, terrified that Cregg is going to catch us.

I know I'm going to trip as we begin to run downhill. I can even see the street ahead, and the lights of the car driving past, just beyond a layer of brush and briars. But I can't slow down. Can't stop myself from looking up at the power lines. Can't stop myself from stumbling, and can't tell whether it's a damned root or a rock that trips me.

I know it's Daniel behind me, but I still feel the fear rush through me when his hand closes around my elbow. I still try to scream for Deo to keep running, but all that comes out is Deo's name.

"You're going the wrong—"

The gun is loud. Not as loud in the open as it was when Deo fired it in the lab, and it's also competing with the screech of brakes from the car on the road, maybe twenty feet below us.

But it still echoes.

And then Deo is yelling an anguished "No!" as Daniel and I slide the rest of the way down the hill.

CHAPTER TWENTY

My shoulder crashes into the chain-link fence at the bottom of the hill. A split second later, Daniel collides with me, and I'm shoved into the fence a second time.

The path downhill was rock and brambles, some of which we carried with us. One long vine of briars is wrapped around my shoe.

Deo comes scrambling down the steep incline after us.

"I'm sorry!" Deo says. "Oh my God, I'm so sorry, man. I thought . . ."

That's when I notice the blood. Daniel is clutching his chest a few inches below his neck.

He reaches out his free hand and grabs Deo's arm. "Thought I was Cregg. I know. Where's the gun?"

"I . . ." Deo looks back uphill. "I dropped it. I didn't want to touch the damn thing after . . ."

"Get it . . ." Daniel's eyes close and his head collapses back against my shoulder.

"Go!" I tell Deo. "Hurry!"

Now that my pulse isn't pounding in my ears quite as loudly anymore, I can pick up the faint *bwee-om, bwee-om* in the distance.

Daniel's shirt is turning red alarmingly fast. I yank off my sweater, which I notice is now ripped down the back from the briars or maybe the rocks, and press it against the wound.

A familiar flash of purple catches my eye. It's the car whose brakes I heard squealing a few moments ago.

A Jeep, actually.

Two doors slam, almost in unison.

"Anna!"

"Aaron! Call 911!"

"The ambulance is . . . coming. Oh, God. No." Aaron curls his fingers through the fence, and shakes his head, unbelieving. "I knew . . . someone. I just didn't . . . *Daniel?* What the hell is he . . . ?" He stares up at me, his fingers brushing the side of my face. "Are you okay? Where's Deo?"

Taylor shoves something at Aaron. It looks like . . . bolt cutters? Then she drops to her knees on the grass and reaches through the fence toward Daniel.

"What happened?" Her eyes are frantic. "Why is he even *here?*"

Daniel's eyes flutter, and he pulls one hand up to hers. "M'okay, Taylor. I'll be fine."

Sounds like me talking to Deo. Making promises that may be beyond his power to keep.

"Hold still." The bolt cutters make quick work of the fence. Aaron stops about halfway up and then starts cutting parallel to the line of barbed wire strung across the top. By the time Deo comes down the hill, Aaron has nearly cut away a section large enough to get Daniel through.

I reach up and take the gun from Deo, who's holding it away from his body like it could go off at any second.

"I'm so sorry. I thought . . . I thought it was Cregg. I couldn't let him . . . not again."

"It was an *accident*, D. They've already called the ambulance. And it was my fault. I'm the one who said I thought it was Cregg."

Even when I knew it wasn't.

Why couldn't I have told Deo that before, when we were trying to get out of the building?

> Stop kickin' yourself. Like I told you, nothin' changes. Nothin'. If you'd tried to tell him earlier, you couldn't have. I couldn't stop my cousin from getting killed in a car wreck. Knew he was gonna die when he was getting into the car, but my stupid mouth just keeps sayin' I'll see him on Friday.

I know Jaden is right. I felt it happen. But it doesn't stop me from wanting to change it.

Daniel opens his eyes for a moment. "Wipe the gun clean. Throw it back. Don't want the kid caught up in this."

Deo stands there shivering in the cold, the round bandage pale against his tanned arms. How much of his jumpiness is the aftereffects of whatever they shot into him? Of course, it could also be the aftereffects of being kidnapped, having someone rake through your brain, watching three people get killed, and having a crazy man take over your body and make you point a gun at your head. I'm pretty sure Deo is completely caught up in this no matter what we do, but yeah, he doesn't need legal trouble on top of everything else.

I start to wipe the gun off with my camisole, but Taylor takes it from me.

"I've got it." She flips a switch on the side—the safety, I guess—then starts wiping it down with her sweatshirt.

"Deo, Anna, help me get him into the car." Aaron bends back the section of the fence he snipped. "The ambulance will come up Route 222—it's the only main road through here. We need to intercept it."

I press my sweater against the wound as we carry Daniel toward the Jeep. "Where are we?"

"That's the Tome School. It was part of a naval training center back in the forties, but it's been abandoned for decades. The quarry Taylor drew is across the river and down three, maybe four, miles."

"Okay. I ditched the gun." Taylor crawls into the Jeep and shoves aside two backpacks, which I recognize as the bags I left at the beach house. Then we slide Daniel, who has now passed out, into the cargo area. A towel replaces my nearly soaked sweater, which wasn't very absorbent in the first place.

"You and Deo will have to double up in the passenger seat," Aaron says as he heads for the driver's side.

"No problem. Come on, D."

Deo is staring mutely into the back of the Jeep, misery scrawled in giant letters across his face.

"Not your fault. You *know* that. I'm the one who said it was Cregg." He doesn't answer, just climbs in next to me.

"Damn it," Aaron says as he slides behind the wheel. "No built-in phone. Why does Mom keep this hunk of junk?" He pulls out his cell and tosses it onto the console. "Call Sam."

Aaron does a quick three-point turn in the middle of the road.

"Got them both," he says, when Sam answers. "They're okay, but Daniel's been shot."

"What? How the hell?"

"I don't know, Sam."

"How bad is it?"

"Looks bad. I already phoned it in, maybe five minutes ago, as soon as I knew something was going down. Can you call Mom? Then contact emergency services and tell them we'll intercept in the Jeep."

When Sam hangs up, Aaron says, "I hope the ambulance gets through, before . . ." He nods toward the school. "Things are about to get crazy around here. Soon, I think. Had a fire started when you left?"

"Yes. Cregg was on fire."

Aaron's eyes shift to meet mine briefly. "Guessing you guys didn't stop to put him out?"

"We did *not*."

He takes my hand and runs his thumb gently across my palm. My pulse races. I feel a tiny rush of a very different sort of fire as his thumb moves back and forth, and it isn't entirely doused by the flush of guilt that follows for feeling this way under the current circumstances.

"But . . . that fire was contained to a lab," I tell him. "I don't think it could have spread. And they could call for help, even though the fire extinguisher had been put to a very different use thanks to Deo's quick thinking."

Deo huffs. He's not taking compliments right now. His forehead is pressed against the window as he stares at the trees rushing past.

"The fire spread," Aaron says. "Or, more likely, another one was set. What I felt . . . it was definitely intentional. I'm just not positive about the timing. Did you see that copter? Big one."

"Yeah." I comb through my Abner memories. He's standing on an aircraft carrier looking up as a gray-green chopper approaches. Dozens of troops come pouring out when it lands. That sound is similar to the one I heard. Although I don't really know how different one copter sounds from the next. "Pretty sure it's a military transport. A . . . Chinook, maybe. Sounded like it was landing. Did you see where?"

"I didn't get a good look. But if I had to guess, it's headed for a flat paved spot we saw on the maps." He nods ahead as we take a sharp curve. "This whole area—over a thousand acres—was built up during World War II. It's been lying here undeveloped since they closed it down in the 1990s . . . First there was some sort of environmental cleanup, and then it's been tied up in court or something. And now I've got a pretty good idea why. What in God's name was Daniel doing there?"

"Undercover. There are . . ." I stop and ask Jaden.

How many people do you think? Total?

Now? Maybe sixty. Ninety, if you're countin' Fudds. Usually a new kid every few weeks.

"There are around ninety people in there," I say. "At least half kids, some of them really young. All of them . . . gifted . . . in some fashion."

Aaron is watching my face from the corner of his eye. "I thought Molly was gone?"

"She is. But I picked up new hitchers."

He's silent for a moment, and then his grip on my hand tightens. "Hitchers? Plural? You're sure you're okay?"

"I'm fine. All but one are gone now. And you need both hands."

I put Aaron's hand back on the steering wheel and place my hand next to his leg on the car seat. He's driving much too fast for the narrow road, but he doesn't have much choice given Daniel's condition.

"Aaron's been on a hair trigger every time we got close to this place." Taylor is holding Daniel's head in her lap, one hand pressing the towel and the other against the pulse point on his neck. "We've been here for the past day on and off. Looking for a way to get in or something we could use to get the authorities involved. But then tonight, he started getting a flash on something big. Bigger than just a few people. The place is underground, right?"

I nod.

"That's why it was muted. That's why I kept seeing paths that weren't there. Why I kept seeing you in places you couldn't be . . . in the middle of that open area. They found it, by the way."

I give her a blank look.

"Molly's purse. Sam was there when they dug up the swimming pool this morning. They've put out a warrant for Lucas."

"He was in the lab with Cregg tonight. So was Dacia. She wasn't hurt, but . . . Lucas might be dead. I don't know."

I spend the next few minutes giving them a very abbreviated version of the past few days. Deo's shoulders tighten next to me a few times, but he doesn't add anything to what I say. I don't mention that they injected him. I don't want to bring that up right now, not when he's already so stressed.

But I do reach into my bra and retrieve the vial I snagged from the fridge. "We need to find someone to analyze this. It may turn out to be nothing, but—"

I stop as we round a curve and I see red lights in the distance. "Is that the ambulance?"

Aaron starts flashing his headlights and pulls the Jeep onto a gravel parking lot.

Then we stand out of the way, helpless, as the paramedics move Daniel into the ambulance.

"Are you okay to follow in the Jeep?" Aaron asks. "I really hate to ask, given the hell you must have been through, but . . . Taylor. I don't want her to be alone . . . just in case Daniel . . ."

"I'll be fine," I tell him, even though I'm far from certain on that point. "Go. Be with Taylor."

"Okay." He glances over at Deo, who's leaning against the Jeep, trying not to look at the ambulance, and says in a lower voice, "I think maybe Deo needs some time with you anyway."

Aaron's hand lingers on mine when I take the keys, and he reaches up to touch my face. "Don't run off with my mom's Jeep, okay? I wouldn't miss the Jeep, but I'd have to come looking for you again. And I *would* come looking."

He starts toward the ambulance. I can see the paramedics inside hooking Daniel up to a machine of some type. "UM Harford. And be careful!"

We get into the Jeep and wait for the ambulance to pull out.

"Deo, you can't blame yourself for this. I'm the one who said it was—"

"Anna, stop. I can't talk right now, okay?" He bites his lip and looks out the window again. His dark eyes are glassy and I know how very much he hates to cry.

"Sure." I bite back the urge to tell him I love him, because even that might push him over and maybe now isn't the best time. I toss him my phone. "Can you navigate to UM Harford? In case I can't keep up with the ambulance."

And I can't keep up. I'm not willing to put my secondhand driving skills to the test at eighty miles an hour. It doesn't matter anyway. My phone rings a few minutes later and Aaron tells us there's been a change of plans. They've decided to transport Daniel to the shock-and-trauma center in Baltimore via air ambulance.

Deo enters the new address into the GPS and we turn around to catch the interstate on-ramp.

After a few miles, I push play and the audiobook starts. It might be nice to ride through the night, believing in magic for a while, magic of either the Hogwarts variety or the Muggle sort that will keep Daniel alive.

But Aaron and Taylor must have been in the car a lot over the last few days, because they're way past the point where we left off. And I'd forgotten how dark this one is at the end. They're past the Ministry of Magic and back at Hogwarts now, where Dumbledore and Harry are arguing about Voldemort. About Voldemort crawling inside Harry's head and trying to control him.

Way too close to what happened in the lab for comfort.

Deo and I both reach to turn it off at the same time.

❖   ❖   ❖

We pull over at a rest stop north of Baltimore to change into clothes that aren't soaked with blood. Even at three a.m. there are people around. I pull a clean sweatshirt over my camisole, which is more red than white now, grab the backpack with my clothes, and keep my head low.

There's no shower, no paper towels. Just the sink, cold water, and hand soap.

Girl, you look like a poster for that *Carrie* movie.

He has a point. There's blood on my arms and neck, even in my hair. Nothing to do but start scrubbing, hopefully before someone walks in with sleepy kids in need of a bathroom break. I'd probably give them nightmares for a week.

When I've done as much as I can, I shove the dirty clothes into my bag and start cleaning up the sink—

Ashley closes the door behind her, and just as she did back at The Warren, jumps when she sees me. This is a different hallway, though. Beige and green. It's a hospital. The room is 219.

"My God, Anna!" Ashley clutches the clipboard she's holding to her chest. She's in scrubs again, but they're different from the ones she was wearing before. Pink now, with STC *on the pocket, like the orderlies here. "You have to stop sneaking up on me. I've had enough excitement for one night."*

"I'm sorry. I was looking for Aaron. We need to leave and—"

She looks over my shoulder. "He's not in there. I think he and his sister went back down to talk to their mom. I've—I've got to go. Tell them I said good-bye. I'll be back in the morning."

Ashley hurries off toward the elevators. I tap on the door and then—

". . . should get a doctor? Your head is bleeding."

I catch a whiff of jelly donut before I open my eyes. The woman's face is directly above me, and there's a bit of powdered sugar on her dark lipstick.

"You okay, sweetie? Looks like maybe you passed out. Your head—"

Damn. I press my palm against my forehead. Only a tiny bit of blood compared to what I've seen tonight, but this time it's my own. I must have clipped my head on the sink. Or maybe when I hit the floor.

"Um . . . she's with me."

Deo steps hesitantly into the door of the women's restroom. He's changed clothes, too. I'm still disoriented, and my first thought is that it's weird to see him in two different colors—black jeans and a blue shirt. They don't clash exactly, but I haven't seen Deo in anything that wasn't color coordinated for at least two years.

"My sister has . . . epilepsy. Must have forgotten her meds. If the coast is clear in there, I'll come get her."

"Sure," the woman says. "It's just me and her, come on in. You sure you don't need me to have someone call an ambulance?" She's looking at me suspiciously, like she thinks it's more likely drugs that I *took*, rather than drugs that I forgot, that landed me on the floor.

"No, ma'am. She'll be fine. Usually only lasts a few minutes."

He gives her a weak version of his best smile, and as usual, wins her over.

"Well, okay, then. But don't let her drive for God's sake."

She has a point. I didn't even think about the visions when I told Aaron I could follow in the Jeep. If that had happened while I was driving . . .

Sorry. I didn't think of it either. But you should be okay. They don't come back to back. You got a coupla hours at the very least. Usually much more.

I'm fine by the time we reach the exit, but Deo holds on to my arm. "Another vision? Anything helpful this time?"

He's not being snide. He doesn't even know exactly what I saw, how much I remembered from the vision. At some point, I'll tell him. But right now, we've got enough drama without me trying to explain how these stupid things work.

"I don't think so. All I saw was Ashley . . . the nurse we met in the hall on our way out. She was at the hospital seeing Daniel. I think maybe she works there, too? Or maybe only visiting. I don't know. I'm glad she's safe, though."

"The woman in the bathroom was right about you not driving," Deo says, but I can tell from his voice that he knows we don't have a choice.

"Jaden seems to think it's okay. I should have a few hours. And the sooner we get back on the road and get to the hospital, the better off we'll be. Unless you want to try your hand at the wheel?"

He casts a dubious glance at the highway. I-95 is always busy, even in the wee hours of the morning. "I'm not sure this is the best spot for me to have my very first driving lesson."

"Okay. But keep an eye on me. Just in case you need to grab the wheel."

❖ ❖ ❖

It's a little before four a.m. on Wednesday morning when we reach the waiting room at the trauma center. My eyes go first to Aaron, who looks exhausted, but his face brightens when he sees us coming down the hallway.

"Glad you found your bags," he says. "I forgot to mention we picked them up."

I'm surprised to see Kelsey there, talking to Sam. Taylor is there too, asleep, her head against Sam's shoulder. She's wearing a pink cotton shirt someone here at the hospital must have loaned her to replace her blood-soaked sweater. It brings Ashley-my-nurse to mind, although the shirts at The Warren were blue.

"When did you get here?" I ask as Kelsey comes over.

"Flew back yesterday," Kelsey says. "I called the landline at the cottage Sunday night when I couldn't reach your cell. Aaron's sister answered and told me what happened. I asked them to let me know as soon as . . ." She stops and gives me a look that's equal parts exasperation and relief. "Are the two of you okay?"

I nod and return her hug. The longer, more complicated version can wait for later.

"How's Daniel?" Deo asks.

"He's alive," Sam says. "That's the good news."

"It was touch and go on the way here," Aaron says. "They nearly lost him. My mom is on her way back from Europe. Turns out she's the only one who knew where Daniel was, so . . . well, let's just say I have a whole lot of questions."

Sam shakes his head, and I get the feeling they've already had this discussion once or twice. "Come on, Aaron. It's not fair to blame it all on Michele. She and Daniel didn't share everything with me, but I knew he'd been doing something with Python for the past few months when he was with the MPD. I just didn't realize he'd been undercover with them since he got out of training. Like Taylor, I actually bought the story that he'd finally found a girl willing to put up with his grumpy ass and *that's* why he wasn't at home most of the time. So your mom and Daniel weren't the only ones keeping secrets."

"That's okay. I can be pissed at you and Mom at the same time. Daniel, too."

I notice he doesn't say the last bit with quite his usual level of venom. Hard to be too pissed at a guy when he's in the ICU.

"You up for a walk?" Aaron asks. "The nurse said there's an Au Bon Pain past the chapel. I need fuel."

"Sure." I'm about to ask if he minds if Deo joins us, but then I realize Kelsey has Deo off to the side. That's good. I think he probably needs a session with her right now more than he ever has.

Aaron tells Sam to call his cell if they hear anything. He waits until we're out of sight, then takes my hand. "How's Deo?"

"Not talking about it. At least not to me. Hopefully Kelsey's having better luck. I should have taken the gun. He kind of lost it in the lab when he got control back from Cregg. Fired at Cregg and at Lucas . . . Don't blame him, but it was more like an automatic response. I don't even know if he hit them. I should have taken the gun from him and made sure they were both dead. Then this would never have—"

Nope. You already had the vision, Anna. Wouldn't have changed a damn thing.

Aaron echoes Jaden's point without even knowing it. "Stop it. This isn't your fault, and it isn't Deo's fault. It's Cregg's fault. You heard Daniel. He understood that perfectly. But . . . I'm pretty sure the police will be here soon to talk with both of you. We've been going with the story that Lucas grabbed you guys because he believed you knew something about Molly's death. That we tracked him down."

I give a bitter laugh. "Ah, Selective Truth. We meet again."

"Huh?"

"It's a joke Deo and I have. We've had many occasions where we had to avoid telling the whole truth, and nothing but. I'm a little worried that Deo may be a problem, though. He feels so incredibly guilty—"

"That's one thing Kelsey is talking to him about now."

I sigh, finding it hard to believe that we're now in a reality where Kelsey is coaching Deo on why he needs to lie to the police.

"Don't suppose we've considered the possibility of bringing the police in on this? I mean, there's an entire underground facility an hour up the road that backs up our story."

"Well, they definitely know there's a facility of some sort there, since most of the firefighters in northeastern Maryland are currently battling a fire there."

Good . . . assuming they got the kids out. But . . .

Shh. I'm trying to have a conversation here.

Jaden has been pretty good about keeping quiet and keeping out of my head since we left The Warren, but then again, most of that time I was focused on driving. I'm not sure I have the energy for extra wall building right now, and I don't want Aaron to think I'm tuning him out.

". . . not going to find much evidence to connect it to Graham Cregg. The story you need to give them is that you were kept in separate rooms, but you think you were next to each other. You thought you heard Deo's voice. The only person you saw was Lucas. Daniel broke the two of you out once the fire started. You don't know who shot him. We'll deal with all of the other questions . . . like why we decided to attempt a rescue without contacting the authorities."

We enter an atrium that looks more like a shopping mall. Or maybe a hotel lobby. Several of the shops are closed, but Au Bon Pain is thriving, with four or five tables occupied, despite the ungodly hour.

"Okay. I'll keep it simple. I just . . . I can't see how the fire in that lab could have spread throughout the facility. It was separated from the main rooms by a really long tunnel."

"Fire can zip through a tunnel pretty fast," Aaron says, lowering his voice a bit now that there are others around. "But from what I was picking up outside the facility, it was torched on purpose. To cover their exit, I guess, and maybe get rid of evidence. Pretty sure they were planning to get rid of some people, too. Even leaving my hunch out of it, I don't think the appearance of a transport helicopter was just a coincidence."

"So . . . does a military copter mean the military is giving Cregg support?" That idea sends a shiver through me. It's bad enough to think that his father might know what's going on. A conspiracy that includes the military however, goes a lot deeper.

"Not necessarily. If it was an older model, they could have purchased the chopper at auction. But . . . I'm not sure we can rule it out."

He grabs three sandwiches, a few bags of chips, and some pastries, then tells me to get whatever I think Deo and Kelsey will want. I'm filling a coffee for Kelsey when Aaron lifts my hair back from my face.

"Ouch. When did that happen? I didn't notice it before."

"Didn't have it before. Another one of Jaden's visions hit me when we stopped to clean up on our way here. It's a little more . . . disruptive . . . than having extra people in your head. I must have banged into the sink—"

"Okay, that's . . . scary. You don't get any warning with these visions?"

"Nope. And don't worry. I won't be driving anymore until . . ."

"Until? They'll go away, won't they? When he leaves?"

"Maybe." I shrug. "No way to tell. None of my previous boarders have had dubious superpowers."

Once we pay the bill, Aaron pulls me toward one of the tables.

"Do you mind eating here? I've been sitting in the waiting room for the better part of an hour. I need a change of scenery."

"Works for me. This looks less like a hospital. I really, really hate hospitals."

"I don't think they're anyone's favorite place."

For a second, I'm reminded of Bruno, happy to have a warm bed, the tin of cookies from Kelsey, and a TV remote all to himself. But I simply nod.

"I kind of need a break," he says. "I don't want to be rough on Sam right now. We've got enough to worry about with Daniel. But he's not just my granddad, he's my partner, and now I find out that he's been working with Mom and Daniel, hiding things from me—"

"Okay, I'm not exactly following that part."

He tears open a sugar packet with a little more force than necessary. About half of it ends up on the table rather than in his cup, and he has to try again. Once he's finished, he takes a sip, then says, "You know how Mom's been on this business trip to Europe?"

"Yeah . . . I think someone said it was a buying trip, although I don't know exactly what that means."

"She's an interior designer. Junior partner in a firm in DC. It's not the first time she's had to travel, so I didn't think much of it. But . . . this wasn't a work trip like she said. Daniel set it up. She was in London to meet with Magda Bell."

"Magda . . ." I shake my head. "It rings a bell, but—"

Aaron laughs and I face-palm.

"Sorry. Bad pun. I need sleep."

"You and me both. Magda is Erik Bell's wife. Remember how I mentioned that I tried to follow up with her after I read the *Guardian* article? I thought she never got back to me, but it seems Mom took the call and didn't bother relaying the message. She didn't want me drawing attention to myself by digging into the case, and I guess that's partly my fault because I told her I wouldn't, but . . . The Bells have two daughters—twins—*and* . . ." He gives me a *you-fill-in-the-blank* look and takes a bite of his sandwich.

"They're gifted."

"Intensely. To the point they can barely function. Anyway, they've been corresponding for the past two years—mostly Magda and Daniel."

"So, if they've been in touch for a couple of years, why did your mom travel over there *now*?"

"Daniel was supposed to go, then he got the undercover position at Delphi. So Mom took his place. Sam says Bell wants to bankroll a search for other gifteds, or *adepts*, as they're calling them. She wants to find them before Cregg does."

"Cregg used that word," I tell him. "He said something about a lot of second-generation adepts having high caloric burn rates or something. Which made me think of Taylor and the pizzas."

An uncomfortable expression crosses Aaron's face. "That's the other thing that I was a little ticked at Sam about. You and Deo were actually there, in danger, and I'm—"

He stops and reaches across the table to take my hand. "Okay, I'll just admit I was going crazy, Anna. From the moment you jumped out of the car until I saw you on the other side of that fence, I was worried out of my freakin' mind. I know why you did it, but you scared the holy hell out of me."

"I'm sorry." And I am, especially now, looking into his eyes. I wonder if he's even slept. "But like I said before—"

"I know. And I'm not trying to give you grief about it." He pulls my hand forward to press a kiss against my knuckles. "That's not the point I was trying make. I kind of got sidetracked because I'm really, really glad to have you back safe. What I was going to say is that every time I talked to Sam the past few days, he started going off about how hard Mom and Daniel have worked to keep me and Taylor safe all these years, and how he hopes you didn't spill about our abilities. Like that's the most important consideration right now. I was *this* close to punching him. Taylor was even getting annoyed, and she's crazy about the old goat."

"You're his grandkids, Aaron. Family first. I understand that. And I don't think Dacia got anything from me about the two of you. I just can't guarantee that the others didn't."

"Others?"

"Yeah. That place—I didn't go into detail when we were in the Jeep, but being in that place was . . . weird. Jaden talked about this group he called The Peepers. I'm pretty sure Dacia has to touch you to get information, or at least to get much information. But there are kids in The Warren who make her skills look like a parlor trick."

I tell him about the message on the mirror and the kid in Room 81.

"I tried to keep my walls up as much as I could, but . . . assuming that they actually managed to evacuate the place, there could be half a dozen psychic kids who know everything I've ever said, done, or thought. And that might include information about you and Taylor."

Aaron's phone starts to buzz as I'm talking.

"Yeah, Sam. We're on our way."

I grab the bag of food. "Is it news about Daniel?"

"Yes, he's out of surgery. I don't think he's out of the woods yet, but Sam says they've upgraded his condition to serious."

"That's an upgrade?"

"Apparently. But the main reason he called is that the police are here, and as we expected, they've got questions."

"Great." I wad up the wrapper from my mostly eaten Danish. "My head hurts and I'm exhausted. All I want is to curl up somewhere and sleep. I'd even risk the Molly dreams at this point."

He tips my chin up so that our eyes meet. "You'll be fine. Just . . ." His serious expression morphs into a smile. "Did anyone ever tell you that you have the most amazing eyes?"

I blush and look away.

"No fair! I say you have gorgeous eyes and you take them away from me."

"You're trying to distract me," I say. But I look back up.

"Yes, I am. Doesn't mean it's not true." He traces the edge of my lip with his thumb. "And you started it. What I was saying before you distracted me is that you'll be fine. Just stick to the plan. We'll get through this."

CHAPTER TWENTY-ONE

For the next half hour, I sit in the far corner of the waiting room and answer questions from a Maryland State Police officer. I give her our prearranged nuggets of truth. I try not to elaborate or throw in any extra details that might trip me up or contradict the story that Deo is telling a second officer on the other side of the waiting area.

But I'm really tired. So tired that I almost wish it was Dacia sitting here and I could just stick out my arm and say go ahead. Grab it. Find the answers your own damn self.

I suspect the officer can tell I'm not being entirely honest, but we go through several grueling repetitions of the same basic drill. She has a lot of questions about other people at the facility, which she keeps referring to as a *cell*. I think at first that she means a single room, like a *jail cell*, but then it becomes clear that she means it in the other sense—like a *terrorist cell*. What languages did I hear? Did I see any of their faces? Could I identify any of them?

Somewhere in the middle of the second iteration a small blonde woman rushes in. All of the Quinns get up to greet her. Must be Aaron's mom. Porter follows behind her, his arm in a sling. He looks around the room and gives me a worried smile.

". . . head? Anna?" The officer snaps her fingers in front of my face. "Are you still with me?"

"Oh, sorry. I think I need more coffee. Could you repeat the question?"

Finally, the officer hands me her card, saying I should call her if anything else comes to mind. And then she adds that someone from Bartholomew House will retrieve me and Deo within the next few hours.

I manage to smile and tell her that's good. That it will be nice to get home. But all I can think is, *here we go again.* The exit sign over the door—nice to be back in a building that actually *has* exit signs—is practically shouting my name, and my mind starts whirring as I try to map out the details. I still have the keys to the Grapemobile in my back pocket. There's no way I would keep it, but it will get us to Kelsey's beach house. I still have the code to get in. I'm guessing Kelsey's car is still there, but maybe we should take the bus.

In fact, maybe I should start back at square one, since driving is now on my verboten-list.

The other officer seems to have finished with Deo. Kelsey demanded to sit with him while they talked, claiming in loco parentis status. Which they accepted, probably because she actually is a formal member of his "team," but I'm guessing the fact that they didn't want to wait on a Bart House employee to arrive also played a pretty big role in their decision-making.

The police move on to Aaron and Taylor. Deo sits there for a moment, leaning forward, head in his hands. Then he shakes it off and heads down the hall, away from the waiting room.

I start after him, but Kelsey holds me back.

"Give him some space, Anna."

She's right. And this is a public place, police coming in and out on a regular basis. No one is likely to snatch him away in a busy hospital.

But it's going to be a while before I'm comfortable letting him out of my sight.

I grab a drink from the Au Bon Pain bag. Then I drop down into one of the sage-green chairs next to Kelsey. The entire building, or at least what I've seen of it, is decorated in muted natural tones—beige, pale greens, wood floors. While calm colors are probably a good call for a shock-and-trauma waiting room, they're also the decorating equivalent of Ambien for the sleep deprived. And personally, I don't find them calming. The colors are a constant reminder that I saw this place in my mind an hour before I walked in the door.

"Deo stuck to the script, if that's what you're wondering. But anyone could see something's bothering him. I pointed out that he was held captive for several days and recently witnessed a shooting. That he's in shock. And I think that's true."

"Did he tell you they injected him?"

"Yes, but he made light of it. Said he only mentioned it because it was worrying you. Do you think it's the same compound they were using on the girls who were trafficked?"

"I don't know. I hope not. But Molly said Dacia was injected numerous times, so . . . even if it is, maybe one dose won't be a problem. Hopefully Sam will know someone who can analyze the vial I took from the lab. Or maybe take a blood sample from Deo to see if there are any markers or whatever. Not sure what we can do about it, but it would be nice to know."

"Okay. Enough about Deo. How are *you*?"

I'm not sure where to start. We could spend weeks unpacking the past few days, and I'd still have more to say. So I settle for a very general overview.

"And that's why Cregg was after you? Because you can absorb their gifts, too?"

"Yeah. I'm just glad the other three left. I . . . I don't think I was in control. Although . . ."

I flash back to the lab, when I was standing with a fire extinguisher cocked like a bat, hurling words I didn't understand at Deo. The Furies would have bashed Deo's head in without thinking twice, but I managed to shove them back. To redirect their anger at Lucas, which is really what they wanted anyway.

And did they do anything to Cregg and Lucas that I wouldn't have done if I'd known I had the ability? I don't think so.

"Maybe I wasn't *entirely* out of control, but it was close. The remaining hitcher, Jaden, isn't so bad, although his visions aren't exactly convenient."

"And the dreams from Molly?"

"I'm handling them."

Kelsey's arched eyebrow suggests she's not entirely buying it, but she drops the subject. "Aaron seems nice. Are you having sex?"

I nearly choke on my orange juice. "For a psychoanalyst, you have an appalling lack of subtlety. Where did you even get that idea?"

"Something Aaron's sister said earlier. He turned fifty shades of red and told her to mind her own business. And your eyes strayed in his direction when I mentioned the dream. Plus, it's obvious you're attracted to him."

I've talked to Kelsey about sex before, but that was in her office. I mean, when you're six and you pick up the memories of an adult, some general discussion of sex is going to come up. But there's no way I'm discussing my feelings for Aaron when he's right across the room.

"I'm attracted to him. But . . . so was Molly. We have a lot of things to sort out." Kelsey seems like she's about to say something else, so I quickly switch topics. "Porter looks much better."

"Yes, thank heaven." She sighs. "Two shootings in less than a week. I hope Daniel is as lucky."

"Me, too." I try to keep the doubt out of my voice, but I remember the blood soaking through my sweater from Daniel's wound. How much I rinsed off in the sink at the rest area.

Kelsey squeezes my hand. "Daniel is about forty years younger than Porter. And this hospital is one of the best in the nation. He'll pull through."

"I hope so." I stare down at the floor, screwing up my courage. "The thing is, I *knew*, Kelsey."

She frowns. "Knew what?"

"I saw us running in one of Jaden's visions. At the very end, I realized it was Daniel, not Cregg. But I couldn't warn Deo. I couldn't keep myself from yelling for him to go faster. From saying I thought it was Cregg behind us, even though part of my brain knew it was Daniel. Jaden says that's just how the visions work. Whatever you saw happen, that's what happens. I forgot about Deo having the gun. It wasn't in the vision. And once I reached that part of the vision in real life, the words just wouldn't form in time. If they had, Deo would never have shot Daniel. That's why I was going after Deo. He's kicking himself for something that's not really his fault."

"Well, I'm not surprised." Kelsey's mouth does this *thing*, where it kind of squinches up on one side. I've seen it dozens of times, and it means she's about to hit me with some insight that's almost certainly right but isn't what I want to hear. "You've given him an excellent role model."

"What?"

"You're doing it right now. Blaming yourself for something over which you have no control. Trying to shoulder all of the responsibility. He's not a child anymore—"

"I know."

"Then let him take some responsibility for his actions."

"But it wasn't—"

"If you only see what happens, if you can't *change* it, then the vision is irrelevant. The mistake *you* made was thinking the man chasing after you was Cregg. The mistake Deo made was firing the gun based on that information. He was terrified that Cregg might get into his head again. Make him turn the gun on himself or even on you. And he made a very understandable mistake, as you did. If you want to help Deo get through this, let him *own* his mistake."

"And if Daniel dies? That's a big mistake for a fifteen-year-old kid to own."

"So you should take on both halves? With everything else you have on your . . ." She stops, probably because my attention is now elsewhere.

Ashley's here. She stands in the middle of the corridor, eyes darting nervously.

"Ashley?"

"Anna." She doesn't seem surprised that we made it out. "I'm looking for Daniel. Is he okay?"

"His condition was just upgraded to serious. You'd know what that means better than I do. All I know is that he lost a lot of blood."

"What happened?" Her eyes are red and swollen, and her hands work nervously at the strap of the purse on her shoulder. She seems on the verge of even more tears. That makes me wonder if Taylor's assessment that Daniel was seeing someone wasn't correct after all. Ashley looks way too upset to simply be checking up on a coworker, even if they were also coconspirators. "Is he conscious? Can I see him?"

Her volume rises with each question. Several other people in the waiting room give her an annoyed glare before going back to their books, naps, or iPads.

"I'm so sorry." Kelsey is using her soft voice, the one she seems to slip into naturally when someone is in emotional distress. "It's only immediate family right now, but when they get back, they might be able to put in a special request for you to see him. Why don't you sit down over here? Anna, could you get . . . ?" She pauses, waiting for me to fill in the name.

"Ashley," I say. "Ashley Swinton."

Ashley physically startles. I have no clue why my remembering her last name sets her off, but it obviously does.

"Could you get Ashley something to drink, Anna?"

"Sure. I'll be right back."

Whoa, she's freakin' out. I did not know she and Daniel
had a thing.

Why would you?

Jaden laughs.

The morning after you arrived, Maria took great pleasure
in telling all the guys in the place that the new blonde
on the Highside wasn't going to be impressed with their
sorry asses 'cause she had a thing for someone on the
outside. But . . . Ashley might just be upset about her
sister. Maybe she was one of the wabbits they decided
not to transport. I think I'd believe that before I'd believe
Maria missed a hookup between two Fudds.

Aaron shoots a questioning look over the officer's shoulder. I
don't know if it's because I'm standing here, spaced and blushing,
or because he's wondering about Ashley. Either way, I can't really
answer him.

Ashley mumbles a thank-you when I give her the water, but her
eyes keep shooting over to the police talking to Aaron and Taylor.

"I'm glad you escaped before the fire got out of control. I never got
a chance to really thank you for helping me when Lucas—"

"You thanked me already." Her tone makes it clear that she really,
really doesn't want to discuss it, and I'm actually okay with that.

"Do you know what happened? Was the place on fire when you left?"

"No," Ashley says, still watching the police. "I mean, *yes.* But it was
still small. I heard on the radio . . ."

I wait for her to say something else, but she's staring ahead. At first, I think it's just a blank stare, but then a woman holding a baby gets up, and her eyes follow them.

"Were they able to evacuate the kids? I heard a helicopter—it sounded like a big one—as we were leaving. But I don't know how it could hold everyone."

"They have buses, too. The chopper was for the ones who need to be . . . contained."

"How did you get away?"

"I *drove*." And then she fixes me with a look that very clearly translates as *shut the hell up*.

So I do. We sit there for the next few minutes, mostly in silence. Kelsey speaks to Ashley a few times, and gets short but generally civil answers. Ashley seems to relax a bit when the police leave, but she tenses right back up when she realizes that means Taylor and Aaron are about to join us.

"I need to find a bathroom," she says, quickly capping the water bottle and tossing it onto the seat next to her.

"Down the hall to the . . . right." Kelsey concludes with a little huff because Ashley is already well out of earshot.

"Who was that?" Taylor asks.

"A friend of Daniel's. Ashley. She worked at The Warren. At Delphi, that is."

Ashley's long gone now, but Taylor tilts her head in that direction anyway. "Seems very upset to be just a friend."

Aaron is only half paying attention. He's looking up something on his phone. I move to sit next to him. Since Kelsey and Taylor have deemed us a couple, I might as well take advantage of it.

"What are you looking for?"

"Just . . . picked up on a few things when he was taking my statement. Nothing concrete, but . . . checking to see if CNN or one of the local stations—hold on. Holy . . ."

He clicks the link. A reporter is in the foreground. Off in the distance is the building Deo and I were in. Fire blazes from every opening. Two of the other buildings in the courtyard are also in flames, and smoke pours from the windows of a third.

"Firefighters from five neighboring counties struggle to contain a baffling fire in the sleepy river town of Port Deposit, Maryland. For the second time in five years, fire has swept through Memorial Hall, the one-hundred-and-seventeen-year-old building directly behind me. Once part of a prestigious private campus, the Tome School buildings were purchased by the federal government during the mobilization for World War II, as part of the Bainbridge Naval Training Center. The historic buildings you see here are pretty much all that remain. Local authorities attributed the 2014 fire to teenage arsonists, but some are questioning that conclusion today with the discovery that these fires actually *began* underground. Gunshots were also reported earlier this evening, and at least one person captured video of a military-style helicopter touching down nearby sometime after midnight.

"The Department of Homeland Security is on the scene, and an unofficial source has confirmed that a terrorist organization was operating out of this abandoned, underground government facility. Authorities have been following reports that Franco Lucas, a suspect in the murders of several local women over the past few years, was operating a human trafficking ring in neighboring Harford County. The speculation now is that he may have been using that ring and other illegal activities to fund the group. The source had no comment on whether they have Lucas in custody. There was also no comment on whether the fire was set by the terrorist group itself, or by the government in an effort to . . . well, smoke them out."

The image goes back to the news desk, with an inset screen of the reporter at the scene on his right.

"Thank you, Vince. Do we have any word yet on the nature of the terrorist group? Is this a foreign threat or domestic?"

"No word yet, John, but rest assured that there will be updates on this breaking story throughout the day."

The fire disappears and is replaced by a woman in a red suit who looks appallingly chipper for 5:15 in the morning.

"News of a potentially massive terror cell less than seventy miles from the nation's capital . . . less than a year from the presidential election? Let's check in with our political correspondent, Cindy Barr."

"Well, as you can imagine, John, Twitter is heating up fast. It's still well over an hour before sunrise, but candidates from both parties have already jumped into the fray. The most interesting so far, however, may be a message that appears to come from independent candidate Ron Cregg himself, known to be an early riser.

"As you can see in the screenshot the tweet from @RonCregg reads: @Whitehouse incapable of managing threats in our backyard. Info on this cell provided to DHS by source close to Cregg campaign back in JULY."

Aaron turns the phone off and shakes his head. "He's good. Take the whole fiasco and find a way to make political capital out of it."

When I look up from the screen, I see that Deo has been watching over my shoulder. I didn't even realize he'd come back into the waiting room.

"They didn't mention anything about the shooting, did they?"

"Just that there were reports of gunfire," Taylor says. "But then they moved on to the helicopter. Don't worry. No one saw you running from the scene."

Deo pulls in a sharp breath. Taylor looks the tiniest bit guilty, probably because Aaron is shooting daggers at her with his eyes.

"I didn't mean it that way," she mumbles. "Sorry."

But I kind of think she *did* mean it that way.

"It's okay," Deo says. "Did you know that nurse is here? The one from The Warren? I passed her in the hallway."

I nod. "She's here to visit Daniel. Said she needed the bathroom."

"If she got out," Aaron says. "I'm guessing she's not the only one. When you say Cregg was on fire when you left the lab, do you mean a five-alarm blaze or . . . ?"

"His clothes. And the cell phone case was kind of . . . melted to him."

"Then we have to assume he made it out alive. Possibly Lucas and Dacia as well. And that means we need to get the two of you *out* of here before your house parent or whatever shows up. You can't go back there. It's the first place they'll look."

"I tried to explain that to the police," Kelsey says. "But they seem convinced that you wound up with Lucas *because* you left the safety of Bartholomew House. He said they'd have additional security, and that we shouldn't worry. I think they just want you where they can keep an eye on you in case they have additional questions."

"So . . . options?" Aaron glances around at the four of us.

"Kelsey's beach house is no good anymore. That's where they found me last time, so it's probably the second place they'd look."

"Same goes for my house," Kelsey says. "The State of Maryland is already questioning my ability to be objective where the two of you are concerned." She gives me a stern look. "And that's not a problem for me. I wasn't planning to take on any new patients after this year anyway. A gradual retirement suits me just fine."

"Before all this happened, Deo and I were planning to catch a bus out of town. We had a location all picked out. As much as I hate to admit it, that may still be our best option. Driving is kind of out for me as long as I'm having these visions, and—"

Aaron shakes his head. "Bad idea anyway."

Taylor barks out a laugh. "Now how did I know you were going to say that?"

"I'm serious, Tay. The two of them off on their own, with no backup if Cregg's people *do* happen to track them down? That's a *bad* idea."

I'm not surprised in the slightest that Kelsey agrees, but I am a little surprised to hear Deo taking that side. "Aaron's right, Anna. Think about how close we came to not making it out of there. Safety in numbers."

"Maybe you're right," I admit. "And . . . to be honest, I'm not certain we're the only ones at risk. Something that Jaden said earlier has me worried. I think at least a few of the kids in The Warren got enough of a glimpse into my head that they know about Aaron." I feel my face growing hot, so I add, "Taylor, too. Whether they also picked up that you're gifted, I can't say. I'm sorry. I could block Dacia, but . . . it's not possible to keep the walls up 24/7, and some of those kids . . . you would not believe."

Taylor shrugs. "Had to happen eventually. Maybe it's for the best." Her voice rises intentionally as she looks behind me. "Maybe Mom and Sam and Daniel will stop treating us like teeny-tiny babies in the cradle now."

"Hi, Mom. Hi, Sam." Aaron doesn't even look around to confirm it, but I do. Michele Quinn and Sam are a few yards behind us. Porter, too.

"Hello, Aaron." She gives her daughter an exasperated half smile. "Taylor, your claims of maturity would be a lot more credible if you acted like an adult when making them."

Taylor sticks her tongue out. "I have no idea what you mean."

Her mother responds in kind, and even though their coloring is different, I think pretty much anyone would tag them as mother and daughter right now.

Mrs. Quinn turns to me and Deo. "Kelsey, I've already met, but . . ."

"I'm Anna Morgan. And this is Deo Ramos." Deo nods, but he doesn't seem able to meet her eyes. "We are so, so sorry about Daniel, Mrs. Quinn."

"It's Michele. And the fault lies with Graham Cregg. Daniel said it was an accident, that there was no way you could have—"

"He's awake?" Aaron says.

Taylor is already on her feet. "Can we see him?"

"Yes," Sam says. "He's awake, but very weak. You'll need to go in one at a time, but he wants to see you both. It's on the second floor—Room 219."

Aaron gives my arm a quick squeeze before he goes. I don't know if anyone else catches it, but Taylor must get her sharp eyes from her mother. Michele's face isn't nearly as expressive however, and I can't tell if she approves or disapproves.

My inner-Emily says it's neither, that she's withholding judgment for the time being.

Porter sits down in one of the chairs across from me. "Hey, Anna." He gives Deo a little nod. "I'm glad the two of you made it home safe."

"That's actually what we were discussing," Kelsey says. "I'm not sure that their current home *is* safe, but that seems to be where they're expected to return."

Michele and Porter exchange a look, and then she says, "We may have a solution, but before we get into that, how much *do* you think Delphi knows about Aaron and Taylor?"

"I don't know." I repeat what I just finished telling the others. "I did my best, but . . ."

"From what you've told us," Michele says, "they could just as easily have gotten information from Daniel. Taking the Delphi position was a risk. I wasn't entirely behind his decision, but Magda wanted more data, more names, before we began. Daniel has put together a pretty solid file over the past two months. I was worried the data might have been lost in the fire, but he slipped this to me when we were in the room." She opens her hand to reveal a flash drive about the size of a Starburst. "So she definitely wants to move forward."

"Move forward with what?" Deo asks.

Kelsey nods. "And who is Magda? I'm kind of lost here."

"She's a very rich lady who has the same grievance toward Cregg and the Delphi Project that I do. That hundreds of parents both here and in Europe do. She wants to establish an alternative treatment facility for the psychically gifted offspring of Delphi subjects. And eventually, she hopes to find a cure. But first, we have to *find* the kids."

"She's also the new owner of my barely used long-bed pickup truck and fifth wheel," Porter says. "For which I still think she overpaid, especially since I'd have donated it to the cause."

Sam snorts and says, "Hush, Jerome. The woman had Michele flown home in her personal jet. She probably has shoes that cost more than she paid for your camper."

Michele laughs. "Those would be some expensive shoes, Sam. But yeah, she can afford it."

"Camper?" Deo asks, beating me to the punch.

"A damn fine camper," Porter says. "Sleeps eight. Full kitchen, satellite dish. Made two trips in it before Molly's grandma died. Didn't have the heart to use it after that. Or the heart to sell it."

"The original plan," Michele says, "was for Daniel to fly out and investigate each of the cases. But he called me the other night, before he went back to The Warren, and mentioned the camper as an alternative. He was still hoping at that point that Aaron and Taylor would be okay at home, but he thought Anna might be helpful in assessing the cases. Something about your ability to block the Badea woman."

For the next ten minutes or so we discuss the details. It's not a perfect plan, but it's a plan. It's just a matter of looping Aaron and Taylor in to finalize things. And I'm starting to get a little antsy about finalizing things quickly, since I have no clue when our ride back to Bart House might arrive.

Kelsey tugs on my sleeve. "Do you think we should go look for Ashley? I'm a little worried, given how upset she was."

"I'll go," I tell her. "I need a bathroom break anyway."

"Who's Ashley?" Michele asks.

I let Kelsey explain and head down the hallway, realizing that I already know where she is, or at least where she'll be by the time I get up to the second floor. She'll be coming out of Room 219.

And that's exactly where she is. Once again, I startle her and she jumps. She's wearing pink scrubs, with STC on the pocket, and there's a red lanyard around her neck. The clipboard is hiding her badge, and she's sticking her phone in her pocket.

"My God, Anna! You have to stop sneaking up on me. I've had enough excitement for one night."

"I'm sorry. I was looking for Aaron. We need to leave and—"

Ashley looks down the hallway behind me. Her eyes, still pink around the edges from crying, remind me of a frightened animal. "Aaron's not in there. I think he and his sister went back down to talk to their mom. I've—I've got to go. Tell them I said good-bye. I'll be back in the morning."

Ashley hurries off toward the elevators. I tap on the door, then inch it open. "Daniel?"

When he doesn't respond, I nearly close the door, in case he's sleeping. But something feels off.

Yeah. Open it. Something's definitely off.

"Daniel?"

I open the door and breathe a sigh of relief. He *is* sleeping. He's propped up in bed. There's some sort of tube in his throat.

Except . . .

I don't think he's breathing.

And that line on the monitor . . . I'm pretty sure it's not supposed to be flat.

CHAPTER TWENTY-TWO

I find the nurse call button. I hit it twice and yell, "We need help in here!"

I grab Daniel's hand and start tapping it, though I have absolutely no idea what that might accomplish. "Daniel! Daniel! Wake up."

Two medics arrive within seconds.

"What happened?"

"There was a woman in the room when I got here," I said. "She had on scrubs like yours. But I don't think she actually works here. I've seen her before. I think she . . . did something."

"Okay, miss. You need to move aside and let us get to your brother."

I start to move toward the door, but my sweater catches on the railing of the bed. As I'm untangling it, my hand brushes against Daniel's arm, and I feel that strange slipping sensation as he comes on board.

"No!" I scream.

"Miss, you need to get out of here." One of the medics grabs me around the waist and pulls me from the room.

"I'm sorry," I tell him. "I was trying to leave, I just . . ."

"It's okay. Can you tell me what this woman looked like?"

"Blonde, curvy. About my height. Wearing what you're wearing."

"And you're sure she's not an employee?"

"Yes!"

"Okay. Stay out here. I'm going to see if we can get security."

He glances back over his shoulder as he walks away, and I can read his expression as clearly as one of Will's salt messages.

He thinks I'm lying. He thinks I'm crazy. And he thinks I did it.

Anna?

It's Daniel's voice, and I don't want it to be in my head.

Anna, come on. He's just realized you're not the sister he saw in here earlier. We need to get the hell out of here before security shows up.

It's the *we* that gets my feet moving. I run back toward the elevators. The doors have closed and I'm pushing the button when I hear the medic yell for me to wait.

When the door opens again, I bolt for the waiting room. Everyone else is there.

Don't tell my family you've picked me up. They don't need to know that right now.

Okay. But Deo needs to know.

That one's your call.

Deo sees me coming and knows instantly that something is very wrong. Aaron is only a few steps behind.

I grab Deo's arm. "We have to go now!"

"What happened?" Aaron says.

"You need to stay with your mom. We'll meet up with you later. Ashley, she was in Daniel's room . . ." I shake my head. I can't say it. "They called security and I don't think they're going to believe it wasn't me."

"Oh, God. No." Aaron glances over to Taylor and his mom, then takes a shaky breath. "Go! You need to get out of here. Do you have your phone?"

"Yes."

He looks nervously back at his family, and I know he's dreading breaking the news to them.

"I'm so sorry, Aaron—"

"It's okay. Just go back to the Jeep and wait. We'll call you."

❖　❖　❖

"Turn it back on for a minute."

I crank the engine again until the Jeep warms up a bit. It's been about twenty minutes, but it feels like an hour.

"Why do you think she did it?" Deo asks.

They threatened to leave her sister behind. To let her burn. She had Cregg on the phone, watching the monitor as I flatlined for a full minute. That was the deal. Me for her sister. She didn't have a choice.

She had a choice.

What if it was Deo? If the deal was me for Deo. Are you telling me you wouldn't have done the same thing?

I'd have found another way.

But my inner voice doesn't sound convincing, even to me.

361

"They had her sister," I tell Deo. "Which means Cregg made it out of there."

Deo sighs. "Then she didn't have a choice."

"She *had* a choice."

He doesn't argue with me. "I just don't get why they wanted Daniel dead. Was it to punish us for getting away?"

"Maybe."

Because I have their data. The list of the kids they have. The ones they're watching. The results of their tests over the past year. I'd hoped I could get more, but there wasn't time.

But your mom has that data now. She showed me the flash drive.

She showed you the *encrypted* flash drive. Ashley knew it was encrypted. She . . . helped me collect the data.

Something about the pause makes me think they were doing more than collecting the data. And I'm apparently not the only one, because Jaden's voice chimes in.

Well, damn. So it *was* both. How'd you manage to keep a Fudd hookup from Maria?

I don't hear the answer to that question because the phone rings. It's Porter.

"Where are you?"

"Level 4, Penn Street Garage."

"Daniel's alive."

"What?"

WHAT?

"Yeah," Porter says. "They were pretty happy to pull him back. But . . . there's not much brain activity. It's probably only a matter of time. But we can hope, right? Be there in a few."

When I hang up the phone, Deo says, "How did that happen?"

"I don't know. He was flatlining when I touched him. Maybe . . . if we go back in and I touch him again . . ."

Maybe.

You don't sound very excited.

Because I'm pretty damn sure I'm dead. Or brain-dead. Either way, nothing to get excited about. And any tests you may have in mind will need to wait until things cool down a bit.

"But you can't try it now," Deo says. "Security will be looking for you."

"Yeah. I know."

Porter shows up maybe five minutes later. He's driving an oversized white Ford pickup. We toss our bags into the back and climb into the cab. Deo takes the backseat, stretches out as best he can, and immediately closes his eyes.

"I don't know who's cursing your name the loudest right now," Porter says as he follows the signs toward the garage exit. "Hospital security, that house parent who came to fetch you and wound up getting an earful from your doctor, or Taylor and Michele."

"But . . ."

"Oh, Taylor and Michele are just for show. Complaining at security for letting you get away is a distraction, gives us a little smoke screen."

"Where are we going?"

"Walmart outside Laurel." He catches my expression. "Not to buy anything. That's where I parked the camper. Sam's gonna meet us there with Aaron and Taylor in an hour or so. We'll get the truck hitched up. Then Sam can take me home and head back up to be with Michele."

"You're not coming with us?"

"Not yet. I'm actually not supposed to be driving yet, but I've never been one to listen to doctors. I'm thinkin' I may quit the job in DC and see if Sam needs my help, with Aaron gone and . . . well, we don't know what's gonna happen with Daniel."

He navigates us onto the street. Even though he doesn't tell me to slump down, I do. I've been in trouble with the police before, but always for running away. Oh, and once for swiping bread and peanut butter from a convenience store when Deo and I hadn't eaten in two days. But this is different. The look in that medic's eyes terrified me, so I'm happy to stay down until we're well away from the hospital.

Porter and I both relax a little once we're on the interstate. I glance into the back and see that Deo is already asleep. I'm pretty close to nodding off myself when Porter says, "She's gone, isn't she?"

"Yeah. A few nights back."

"Did she know they had the evidence to nail Lucas?"

"Yes. Well . . . actually, no. But she trusted Taylor's gift enough to know the evidence was there. That they would find it. She didn't want to go back to that place . . . and she said it was time. I'll be the first to admit that Molly drove me crazy sometimes, but I miss her now that she's gone."

"Did she say anything about . . ." He looks a little embarrassed. "Seein' any angels? That kind of stuff?"

"No. But she was happy. Peaceful. There was music, and colors, and I can't really explain it, but . . . it was . . . beautiful, and I was grateful for that tiny glimpse of what Molly's heaven would be like."

He sniffs and looks out at the highway for a few minutes. "How about you? You handlin' things okay?"

I shrug. "I've barely slept in the past few days. The dreams are bad when they come, but everything else we've been through recently has kind of put bad dreams into perspective. You wake up and after a minute or two, you realize the dream is over. This?" I wave my hand. "Real life? It just keeps piling on more. You get out of a crazy man's underground bunker, and a few hours later, you're on the run because it looks like you might have killed the guy whose life you were actually trying to save. And that's leaving out what Daniel called the *psycho mumbo jumbo*."

I'm pretty sure I said *psychic* mumbo jumbo.

You said psycho.

"Been a rough week, huh?"

"Been a rough *day*."

"But you got your . . ." Porter nods toward the backseat. "What exactly is he to you?"

"Yes. Deo's back. That's the upside. And, let's just say brother."

"Well, on the one hand, that's a relief. I don't think Aaron's ever even looked at a girl before, and I hated thinkin' he finally took an interest and it might be one-sided. On the other hand, now I'm wonderin' if you might need a chaperone after all."

"Taylor will be chaperoning."

"So will Deo." That one comes from the backseat. Okay, not asleep after all.

And Daniel.

Jaden's voice chimes in next.

> Hey, definitely not me. I don't care what the two of you
> do. I might even . . . well, maybe not, given that he's a
> guy, and I'm really not into guys. Never mind on that.

"Aaron's an adult. I will be too, in a little over a month. After that, it's nobody's business."

Porter chuckles. "So it's definitely *not* one-sided then."

"I plead the fifth."

"Well, I think this is going to work out as long as you guys are careful. Aaron's pretty good about keeping in the background. Just listen to his hunches."

It takes me a few seconds to realize that he's shifted away from talking about my personal life and is now on to work. And I decide not to point out that he wouldn't be wearing that sling if he'd listened to Aaron's hunches.

"Maybe you can help some of those kids. Michele was telling me about those two girls in London, and . . . well, somebody needs to do somethin'. And this way, you and Deo aren't off on your own without any support."

My phone vibrates in my back pocket, and I fish it out. Probably Aaron or Kelsey.

But it's a text. And I don't recognize the number.

```
I'll never pause again, never stand
still,

Till either death hath closed these eyes
of mine
```

`Or fortune given me measure of revenge.`

Shakespeare again. Which leaves me absolutely no doubt who sent it.

"D? I need your phone."

"Whyyy?"

"Just give it, okay?"

He hands it to me, and I push the button to open the window. Then I hurl both phones out, watching in the side mirror as they clatter down the road behind us. I feel ten pounds lighter, knowing that Cregg doesn't have any way to contact me now.

"Was that *really* necessary?" Deo asks.

"Mmhmm. We'll get you another one." A huge yawn hits me in the middle of the sentence.

"You two go on and sleep if you can," Porter says. "I'll put on the radio to keep me company. Classical okay? Or we can do R&B."

"You choose."

When I close my eyes, Porter is playing finger piano on the edges of the steering wheel to something by Rachmaninoff. Molly would know it, I'm sure, but I'm too tired to dig through her files . . .

❖ ❖ ❖

. . . and the moonlight on the water reminds me of the glimpse of the river from Memorial Hall that night, right before everything went up in flames. But mostly, it's just quiet. And peaceful. And as close to private as we're likely to get, at least until my head is entirely my own again.

I lean back against Aaron's chest. "It's nice. Are you sure this is still Ohio?"

He laughs and pulls me closer. "Hey, it's not all corn and cows. But to be honest, I think that bit"—he points off in the distance—"that might be West Virginia."

And then he kisses me, and I don't give a damn what state we're in, because this is where I'm supposed to . . .

. . . always to-mah-ah-row

I jolt awake suddenly. Porter has swapped out the classical station for R&B, and abandoned the steering wheel piano. Now he's singing "Lean on Me," in a mostly on-key duet with Bill Withers.

The moon is gone. Aaron's gone. But it's so warm and it would be so easy to slip back to sleep. There's a blanket—no, a jacket—around my shoulders. It's not mine or Deo's, so I guess it must be Porter's.

Was that thing with Aaron just now a dream or a vision?

Don't ask me.

I wasn't asking you, Daniel. I was asking Jaden.

Um . . . I don't know. It's hard to tell when you're half asleep. But the visions aren't all bad. Sometimes, they let you experience the good things twice. And even if it was a dream, doesn't mean it won't happen, right? In this case, it's win-win. Just pick one.

Hmm. But which to pick? A vision of something good that you know is going to happen? Or a dream that would be really nice to work toward?

I snuggle back under the jacket and close my eyes, still trying to decide which is better as I drift off to sleep.

ACKNOWLEDGMENTS

The idea for this book popped into my head in early 2013, and I wrote the first five chapters in less than a week. Shortly after that, my first novel, *Timebound*, won the Amazon Breakthrough Novel Award, and *Delphi* was shelved as I focused on completing The CHRONOS Files. So first and foremost, I want to thank Anna, Deo, and the rest of the crew for having the patience and perseverance to stick with me, and for remaining clear and vivid in my mind even as it was being mauled and twisted by time travel. Shifting gears took a little longer than I'd planned, but coming back to Anna's story was like crawling into a warm sweater hung at the back of the closet when the first autumn chill arrives.

There's not as much history in this book as in The CHRONOS Files, but I want to continue my tradition of highlighting the bits of fact that hang out in my fiction.

- While the Delphi Project is my own creation, predecessor programs like Stargate and Project MK-ULTRA are very real, and the military's remote viewing program is well documented.

- All three fires predicted by the fictional Delphi psychic actually did occur on the same day—April 19, 1993.
- The remains of the Tome School still exist in Port Deposit, Maryland. It was part of the Bainbridge Naval Training Center, which the government abandoned long ago. To the best of my knowledge, there is no underground bunker that houses children with psychic powers below the school, but attempts to develop the property have been delayed for decades. So I could be wrong . . .

This book is dedicated to Gareth, my oldest son and the intrepid photographer who helped me map out the Tome School for the final scenes of the book. He also made me aware of my parental inconsistency, since he was forbidden to go exploring a supposedly haunted house in high school and then <mumble, mumble> years later, I asked him to explore a supposedly haunted school for this book. The pictures turned out incredibly well, and if you're curious, you can view them at rysa.com/tome.

I have an incredible support team at Skyscape, and I can never find enough words to thank them. Courtney Miller had faith in my work from the very beginning, and without her unflagging confidence, I'd almost certainly still be working my day job. Amara Holstein lent her considerable talents to the developmental edit, and this book is infinitely better for her suggestions. Thanks also to Britt Rogers, Kim Cowser, Adrienne Procaccini, Michelle Hope Anderson, Nicole Burns-Ascue, Christina Troup, Rebecca Jaynes, and the rest of the behind-the-scenes crew who do so much to get my books into the hands of readers. Mike Corley—thanks for creating a gorgeous cover!

When I'm not in the Writing Cave, my writer and reader friends on social media keep me entertained and informed. Some of those friends are also beta readers, and their input helped to make this book a better read. I am deeply indebted for their feedback. This is a partial list, but there are many more: Alexandria Ang, Ariana Ascherl, Mary Anna Ascherl, Blair Babylon, Annie Bellet, Karen Benson, Bill Brooks, E. B. Brown, Shell Bryce, Allison Clowers, Kristi and Marshall Clowers, James Cobalt, Lorca Damon, Susan Allison Dean, Fred Douglis, Elizabeth Evans, Patrice Fitzgerald, Rebekkah Ford, Joe Frazier, Mary Freeman and Maddy Freeman-McFarland, Jen Gonzales, Dori Gray, Donna Harrison Green, Meg Griffin, Al and Bonnie Harrison, Mike and Lana Harrison, Susan Helliesen, Matthew Izen, Stephanie Johns-Bragg, Cody Jones, Joy Joo, Autumn Kalquist, Theresa Kay, Dana Kolbfleisch, Jeff Kolbfleisch, Richard Lawrence, Mary Frances Lebamoff, Oleg Lysyj, Jenny MacRunnel, Cale Madewell, Nooce Miller, Tasha Patton-Smith, Trisha Davis Perry, Susan Kaye Quinn, Sara Reine, Lesa Ruckman, Simon Rudd, John Scafidi, Sarah Short, Lydia Smith, Gareth Sparks, Karen Stansbury, Teri Suzuki, Janet B. Taylor, Hailey Mulconrey Theile, Billy Thomas, Antigone Trowbridge, Ian Walniuk, Ryan Walniuk, Meg A. Watt, Jen Foehner Wells, Libby Wells-Pritchett, Jen Wesner, Dan Wilson, Jessica Wolfsohn, and my multitude of nieces and nephews. Special kudos to Chris Fried for noticing several gaffes in my depiction of group home security.

A special shout-out to the person or persons I've forgotten . . . you know who you are and what you did and, hopefully, why I'm grateful. And if you don't, please remind me to tell you.

An extra-big thank-you to the readers, book bloggers, and reviewers who have been so supportive of my work. You are the reason I write—well, you and the fact that I'd probably end up crazy if I didn't. But seriously, your love of and appreciation for our books is what keeps writers like myself energized and creative.

A furry person—our golden retriever Lucy—has been my companion in the Writing Cave for the past five years. She was a rescue dog, nearly six years old when we adopted her, and many of her personality traits found their way into Katherine's dog, Daphne, in the CHRONOS Files. We added a second golden earlier this year, and much of this book was written while Griffin and Lucy played nearby. Sadly, we're down to one golden again. We'll miss you, Lucy. If you're still wondering who's the good girl, there's no question—it was you, from the very beginning and always.

Finally, many thanks to my family for everything you do and just for being who you are. Plus, I'll toss in some extra kudos for your patience when I freak out over deadlines. I'd promise you that it won't happen with the next book, but you're way too smart to believe me. Love you guys!

ABOUT THE AUTHOR

Photo © 2014 Jeff Kolbfleisch

Rysa Walker is the author of the bestselling CHRONOS Files series. *Timebound*, the first book in the series, was the Young Adult and Grand Prize winner of the 2013 Amazon Breakthrough Novel Award.

Rysa grew up on a cattle ranch in the South, where she was a voracious reader. On the rare occasions when she gained control of the television, she watched *Star Trek* and imagined living in the future, on distant planets, or at least in a town big enough to have a stoplight.

She currently lives in North Carolina, where she is working on the next installment in The Delphi Trilogy. If you see her on social media, please tell her to get back to her Writing Cave.